© David Ignaszewski/Koboy

ROXANA ROBINSON is the author of five novels, including *Cost*; three collections of short stories; and the biography *Georgia O'Keeffe: A Life*. Her work has appeared in *The New Yorker, The Atlantic, Harper's* magazine, *The New York Times, The Washington Post, The Wall Street Journal, More,* and *Vogue,* among other publications. She is a finalist for the NBCC Nona Balakian Citation and has received fellowships from the NEA and the Guggenheim Foundation. She lives in New York City.

ALSO BY ROXANA ROBINSON

Cost

A Perfect Stranger and Other Stories

Sweetwater

This Is My Daughter

Asking for Love and Other Stories

A Glimpse of Scarlet and Other Stories

Georgia O'Keeffe: A Life

Summer Light

Additional Praise for *Sparta*

A BBC Best Book of the Year

"An assiduously researched tale of war and disillusionment." —*Vogue*

"Utterly believable . . . [Robinson's] artistic manipulations with language [make] the everyday world seem suddenly strange—and scary."
—*O, The Oprah Magazine*

"*Sparta* beautifully weaves the tragic irony of modern warfare fought in the 'cradle of civilization.' . . . The author's compassion and meticulous research render this returned veteran's experience—as well as the premises of war itself—searchingly." —*The Christian Science Monitor*

"Intricately observed . . . Without a whisper of sensationalism or melodrama, *Sparta* views a warrior's homecoming through Conrad's increasingly traumatized consciousness. . . . What happens to Conrad and to thousands of veterans like him is an urgent national concern, and responsibility, and we ignore it at our own peril." —*The Seattle Times*

"Conrad suffers and commits violence that for most Americans is simply unimaginable. . . . Compelling." —*More*

"*Sparta* gives us an unflinching portrayal of the costs of war, costs that go far beyond what the tallies of killed and wounded can tell us. There are plenty of losses that can be measured only in the language of the spirit, and it's books such as this one, *necessary* books, that guide us to a fuller appreciation of war's costs." —Ben Fountain, author of *Billy Lynn's Long Halftime Walk*

"Roxana Robinson's *Sparta* is a feat of the imagination. Vividly and with unflinching wisdom, Robinson has given voice, substance, and profound reality to her protagonist, Conrad Farrell of the Marine Corps—and in so doing, to thousands of veterans like him."
—Claire Messud, author of *The Woman Upstairs* and *The Emperor's Children*

"Roxana Robinson's *Sparta* delicately explores the fissures between the military experience and civilian life. . . . This book is not simply about war, but about the horror and enforced isolation of trauma, the inevitable merging of the personal and the political, and the possibilities and trials found within the bonds of familial and romantic love."

—Phil Klay, author of *Redeployment*

"Extraordinary . . . Roxana Robinson has written a tour de force."

—*Los Angeles Review of Books*

SPARTA

Roxana Robinson

PICADOR

A Sarah Crichton Book
Farrar, Straus and Giroux
New York

This is a work of fiction. All of the characters, organizations, and events portrayed in this novel are either products of the author's imagination or are used fictitiously.

Printed in the United States of America. For information, address Picador, 175 Fifth Avenue, New York, N.Y. 10010.

www.picadorusa.com
www.twitter.com/picadorusa • www.facebook.com/picadorusa
picadorbookroom.tumblr.com

For book club information, please visit www.facebook.com/picadorbookclub or e-mail marketing@picadorusa.com.

Designed by Abby Kagan

The Library of Congress has cataloged the Farrar, Straus and Giroux hardcover edition as follows:

Robinson, Roxana.
Sparta / Roxana Robinson.—1st ed.
p. cm.
ISBN 978-0-374-26770-4 (hardcover)
ISBN 978-0-374-70957-0 (e-book)
1. Iraq War, 2003–2011—Veterans—Fiction. 2. Westchester County (N.Y)—Fiction. I. Title.
PS3568.O3152 S63 2013
813'.54—dc23

2012034611

Picador Paperback ISBN 978-1-250-05017-5

Picador books may be purchased for educational, business, or promotional use. For information on bulk purchases, please contact Macmillan Corporate and Premium Sales Department at 1-800-221-7945, extension 5442, or write specialmarkets@macmillan.com.

First published in the United States by Sarah Crichton Books, an imprint of Farrar, Straus and Giroux

First Picador Edition: June 2014

10 9 8 7 6 5 4 3

To those young men

The man who does not wear the armour of the lie cannot experience force without being touched by it to the very soul.

—SIMONE WEIL, *The* Iliad, *or, The Poem of Force*

SPARTA

1

There was a change in the engine pitch. The droning roar turned lower and more purposeful: the plane was changing angle. They were leaving the level flight path, nosing downward. Conrad felt an uneasy drop inside. After a moment he realized he was bracing himself against the seat, feet pressing hard against the floor as though against brakes. He made himself relax.

He leaned toward the window, looking out: until now, there'd been nothing to see. They'd left Frankfurt at night and had crossed all of Europe in darkness. The whole continent had lain below them, dark as the night sky itself, revealed only by constellations of city lights. By daybreak they'd been high over the gray emptiness of the Atlantic, far above the miniature waves and the distant, frozen whitecaps. Now they were over land again. Nova Scotia? Newfoundland? Anyway, North America. *Home ground.* Again Conrad felt the uneasy drop.

Below him lay dense green forest, broken only by the drifting silver shapes of lakes. From here the lakes seemed to be in motion, languidly swirling and eddying, as though the edge of a swamp had been stirred with a stick. All around them were woods.

Conrad imagined walking through the trees below: the leafy, springy duff, soft underfoot. The clean, aromatic tang of balsam, flecks of sunlight scattered across the dim trunks. The soil beneath these trees was always in shade. The air was always cool. *Always cool.* The notion gave him a kind of vertigo, and he closed his eyes.

What came into his mind was the place he had left, which was still there. He was here, descending over this place, cool, verdant, silent.

The place he had left, which was still there, was arid, brown, deafening. Suffocatingly hot, heat pressed over it like a mattress. At this moment, while he was here, that place was there. But he could not hold both places in his mind at once. Trying to do so felt risky.

Conrad turned away from the window and looked at the man beside him, who was asleep, out cold.

Corporal Paul Anderson, Conrad's second-squad leader, was slumped in his seat, his big head flopped sideways, wide chin sunk in his neck. His white-blond eyebrows were bright against the charred red of his sunburned face. His hair was blond, like his eyebrows, but it was barely there, buzz-cut, shaved down to a pale mist over his skull. Anderson's lips were slightly parted, and saliva glistened faintly at one corner. He was a nice kid from Minnesota, quiet and reliable. Ordinarily, Conrad would have been sitting next to another officer, but there was an odd number of them on the flight. Conrad had taken his seat and beckoned to Anderson, who was also odd man out, without a seatmate. Anderson had barely moved since Germany; none of them had. The plane was full of sprawling, loose-lipped Marines, lost, gone, dead to the world.

Conrad liked seeing them like this: sleep was like salary, his men were owed. They were infantry grunts, and they'd been seven months on duty without a single day off. They deserved to sleep for months, years, decades. They deserved this long, roaring limbo, this deep absence from the world, from themselves. This plane ride was the floating bridge between where they'd been and where they were going—deployment and the rest of their lives. They deserved these hours of unconsciousness, this gorgeous black free fall.

There was something else they deserved, something he couldn't define. They were all, himself as well, part of something large and interlocking, in which movements were slow and tectonic. Deep, shifting currents would carry them on to some form of deliverance. He trusted in this. He couldn't define it or identify it, the movement or the destination, only sense it. His brain felt blurred, as though the plane were flying too fast for his thoughts.

Everything in his mind felt provisional, in fact. Lack of sleep: it was hard to think. His thoughts felt loose and shifting, temporarily in place. The way everything in-country had been provisional, nothing certain.

Life had been improvised, moment by moment, for seven months. Tension was the steel skeleton on which everything else hung. He woke up early to it each day, white heat beating into the roof, urgency already flooding through his system. Fear. You didn't call it fear, but that's what it was. All that was over now, but the habit was hard to break. Was it a habit or a way of life? He wondered how long it would take to become a different person, how you'd know when it happened.

The flight attendant appeared in the aisle. She was blond but old, with waves of dry, ashy hair. Her face was small and foxy, she had a pointy nose and a thin, tidy mouth. She was wearing a sort of uniform, navy vest and skirt, long-sleeved white blouse. Smiling, she leaned into the little private space made by the high seatbacks. Her face drew nearer to Conrad.

"May I take that glass, sir?"

Her chapped lips were outlined in neon: her pale orange lipstick had worn off in the middle. On her vest was pinned a small winged gold emblem. Conrad glanced at it, automatically checking for rank, but of course she had no rank. It was an airline pin, she was a civilian. For some reason this irritated him, his glance, his realization. Irritability was also a result of sleep deprivation.

Conrad held out his glass, and she reached for it across the sleeping Anderson. She glanced down at him, then back at Conrad, pursing her mouth in a conspiratorial smile.

"Anything else I can get you, sir?"

She was half whispering, and her manner was both patronizing and intimate, suggesting that she and Conrad were partners, sharing a kind of parental responsibility for the sleeping Anderson. As though Anderson—who was a lion in combat and had once saved Conrad's life—were a small child. A tiny black point of anger flared in Conrad's chest. He looked at her without smiling.

"No, thanks," he said.

She still hovered, but Conrad said nothing more. She leaned in farther toward him, and a small gold cross on a chain swung out from her neck. She was too close, and he could smell her perfume, sweet and fruity.

She spoke confidingly. "You know, I just want to say thank you." Her voice was husky. "For what you've done for our country. All you boys. Helping to make us safe back home."

"Thank you," Conrad said, nodding; the black point was sharp inside his chest.

"Really." Beneath her eyes were dark smudges of mascara, defining the wrinkles.

Conrad said nothing, gazing back. She waited, too close. They were alone in the space between the seats. Conrad breathed through his mouth so he wouldn't smell the perfume.

"Thank you," he said again, to make her leave.

She looked at him, her small blue eyes bright and liquid. She waited, but Conrad only stared, and her smile faded. She drew back, and the little cross swung back inside her blouse. She was still smiling, but now the smile was impersonal. She put the glass onto her stack and moved to the next row.

Conrad wondered if she'd say the same thing to the next officers. What was it that she thought they'd done to make her so much safer? He thought of the woman with the basket, Olivera whispering. The dog. The brown streets of Ramadi, the blowing trash.

He looked out the window again. They were now descending rapidly. Along the coastline was a filigree of miniature bays and islands edged with bright foam. At the shore the water was turquoise and transparent, but as it deepened, it darkened to cobalt, becoming opaque.

Conrad felt his chest constricting, the point of anger widening. He thought of her fruity perfume and the little gold cross swinging out from her collar.

His breath began to feel trapped. He looked down at the forest stretching inland, a dense green scumble going on forever. He scanned without thinking for roads, rooftops, the gleam of cars, metal, weapons, but there were only trees. There were no people in this landscape. No weapons.

He took a long, deliberate breath. At the bottom of his breath, deep inside his lungs, he felt a gritty scraping: sand. Trapped in his chest, rising and settling in sluggish swirls, clogging the airways. Sand was mineral, stone dust, it would never decompose, it could never be absorbed by his body. *Iraq, inside him, forever.* He wondered, panicked, if that was true. Everyone there had a cough. They called it the haji hack.

He breathed more shallowly. In seven months he'd breathed buckets of sand, everyone had, you couldn't help it. The sand was fine as talcum powder, like a dry mist. It was in the air all the time. During a sandstorm there was nothing else to breathe, sand instead of air, sand instead of sky. During a storm the desert left the ground, lofting upward, whirling, weightless.

The first storm he'd ever been in was at the camp in Kuwait, near the Iraq border, after he'd first arrived. It was early morning. He'd been out jogging the perimeter when the wind came up. He'd heard about *shamals,* but he'd never been in one.

In a few steps the world closed around him and he was blind and alone. Around him the sand roared and seethed, swirling into his eyes, his nostrils, his ears. He could barely open his eyes, though there was no need, there was nothing to see. It was a strange kind of isolation. He began to grope his way through the frenzy, inching along step-by-step. He had no idea where he was, no idea where he was going. He breathed sand. His eyes stung; his face was scoured by airborne grit. His mouth and nose were full of it. His eyes narrowed to slits. He inched along, and finally his foot knocked against something: the tire of a Humvee. Miraculously, he'd been shuffling toward the camp, but it was just chance. He might have been headed toward a ravine, the enemy, anything.

After that he'd learned not to move and to hunker down until it was over. He bought a kaffiyeh, a long, fine-woven scarf, the kind the Iraqis wore. He coiled it around his neck, over his blouse, and in a storm he pulled it over his face to breathe through. It was against regulations to wear civilian clothes with your uniform, but he told his men they could wear the scarves. Anything that made them more effective was a weapon.

Before he'd gone there, Conrad had imagined the desert as like a beach without the ocean. He pictured pale, glittering sand, radiant and sunny, like a Caribbean shoreline. But the sand in Iraq was dull and dun-colored, and powder-fine. It was dust, not sand. Beneath your feet it felt packed, solid as concrete, but actually it was fine and weightless, the top layer always afloat. A brown film coated everything—boots, pillow, toothbrush, tongue. It was in your ears, in the tents, the mess hall, the latrines. After a storm you coughed it up for days. Your snot was dirty brown, your lungs full of grit. You were never free of it.

Conrad looked away from the window, across the aisle. Those Marines were slumped in their seats, too, dead to the world like Anderson.

The thing was that Conrad didn't want to see them, didn't want to think about the sandstorms or the other Marines or anything else from over there—the rattle of machine guns, the stink of the shitters, the hot, smoky air, the closed faces of the people on the streets; he wanted none of those thoughts in his head, but what else was there to think about?

The thing was that he was tired of himself, tired of his thoughts, tired of the anxiety that permeated his brain like a bad smell. Being inside his head, just thinking at all, just being conscious, was like walking across a minefield. At any minute something might detonate, hurling him into someplace where he didn't want to be. He was sick of it. There was nowhere to go.

He pulled the paperback out of the seat pocket again. It was a thriller he'd bought at the airport in Frankfurt. On the cover was a picture of a running man, silhouetted against a red hammer and sickle: the book was set during the Cold War, in Eastern Europe, the fifties. Spies meeting in cafés, getting on and off trains, shooting each other in dark alleys. It was like paintball; it wasn't war. It was bullshit. He'd tried several times to read it, to get his mind off everything else; now he found his place and tried again.

> Harding sat down at an empty table by the window. From here he could see all the way down the block, nearly to the Bergenstrasse. The waiter came over to him, a thin older man with a gray mustache and a peremptory manner. Harding ordered coffee. He put his newspaper on the table, folded back to show its name. He lit a cigarette and sat, waiting.
>
> It was Viktor who came first. Harding watched him making his way down the street toward the café. He wore sunglasses and a black leather coat, and he carried his own folded copy of *Der Sturm*. He pushed open the door, looking around before he stepped inside, but Harding could see from his movements that he knew already where Harding was sitting. It was the waiter, then.
>
> Viktor came over and sat down.
>
> "Welcome," he said, taking off his sunglasses. His eyes were cold and blue.

All this was meaningless. It had nothing to do with walking patrol down a brown street, heart hammering, blood roaring in your ears, watching the point man ahead of you who was walking gingerly, all of you walking goddamned gingerly, watching the faces of the men in the doorways and waiting for the sound of gunfire, for the big orange bloom of an explosion. Lying awake at night and listening for incoming. Not knowing if you were actually hearing it, the first sound of it, or if your brain was making it up, over and over.

Conrad looked up from the book. His heart had begun racing. He looked around the plane: nothing, there was nothing to alarm him. In a way, that was worse; he was helpless. Anderson was still slumped beside him. Across the aisle were two sleeping Marines, legs askew, heads tipped sideways. Conrad was not on the streets of Haditha but on a commercial airline bound for Bangor, Maine. The airplane droned steadily, hanging in the air at thirty thousand feet, following the complicated hologram of international flight patterns. He was not in control here. There was nothing for him to check, no reason for alarm, and so what was it? He felt a high, choking presence inside his chest. His heart still pounding, he wondered if this was evident, if other people could see his racing pulse, the anxiety flooding through him, the way alarm was rising up through his body to take over.

He couldn't imagine what lay ahead: civilian life seemed unthinkable. He couldn't remember what it was like. The last time he'd been in the civilian world he'd been in college, but that was years ago, and everything was different now. He'd no longer be in college, no longer in the Marines. He couldn't think how to move on; it seemed like a cliff that he was approaching. Beyond was a dark drop.

He didn't want to remember what lay behind him in Iraq. He couldn't bear the images that rose up as soon as he closed his eyes. Olivera's whispering. The dog, its ears flattened, tail curved between its legs. Again he felt the uneasy plummeting. The woman, holding up the basket, walking toward them. The girl on the bed. The pattern on the wall.

The thing was to get away from all this, get the thoughts out of his head. That was the thing.

He put the book back in the seat pocket and rubbed his hands on his thighs.

He should think about his parents and Claire. He should prepare himself to see them. Though the thing was that he couldn't prepare himself, because he wasn't the person they were expecting to meet. He felt an obligation to be the person they'd known, the one they were expecting, but he didn't know how to change himself back. They wouldn't want this new person, the one he now was, but he couldn't remember what that other person was like. Even if he could remember, he couldn't become him again.

Another problem: he couldn't exactly remember what everyone looked like, his parents and his girlfriend. If Claire was his girlfriend. He wondered if this was part of what had happened in Iraq, and did it mean that he had post-traumatic stress disorder? Was losing your memory, or part of your mind, some kind of PTSD symptom? He didn't want to ask. Could you lose a part of your mind? That was all in the bleak, broken wilderness beyond the cliff drop, ravines and rocks—what was wrong with his mind.

He could remember only parts of their faces. He could call up his mother's mournful dark eyes, the glossy sheen of Claire's red-brown hair, his father's closemouthed smile, but he couldn't seem to produce a whole face. Was this going to be permanent? Was this what it would be like? Would he keep discovering things he couldn't fix? He felt the uneasy drop.

He couldn't imagine talking to any of them. What would they say? At least Claire wasn't coming out to Pendleton. He'd see her when he flew back east; he could dread that later. His brother and sister weren't coming out to meet him, either. He thought of the thicket of braces crowding Ollie's mouth, Jenny's look of frowning intensity. He remembered a time, years before, when they were little kids. One summer morning they were out on the lawn in their pajamas, playing leapfrog and singing at the top of their voices. He couldn't remember the song. That was all; nothing had happened. Why did he remember that, and not the way his brother and sister looked now? Frustrating.

Anyway, they wouldn't be there; it would be only his parents. Conrad had another whole flight, from Bangor to San Diego, to summon his parents' faces and to think of things he could say. He'd try to talk as if he were the person he'd been four years ago.

The plane was dropping fast now, through intermittent clouds. The window went suddenly dark, then bright again, the light flickering. The strobing flashes made Conrad uneasy, and his chest felt tight again. He thought of the woman in the car, the sudden bloom of flames against the windshield, and the noise blotting out the world, that silent echo that seemed to go through your body, though these were exactly the things he was trying not to think about. It was like having to watch a movie: the movie was inside his head, and he couldn't stop it by closing his eyes. He had strategies, but he was never sure they'd work or how long they'd last.

The plane slid suddenly into a dense layer of cloud, and the sound of the engine turned loud and urgent. The windows were closely sealed with gray. Conrad's chest tightened further and he began to count backward from ten. He could feel his heart—big, pounding beats. He focused on the numbers, *nine*, breath, *eight*, breath, *seven*, spacing them evenly. With each one he drew a deep, slow breath. By the time he reached six, the plane had passed through the cloud layer and the windows were no longer sealed. Conrad stared out at the drifting wisps of mist, the view below. More green forest, now closer, the texture of the trees becoming sharper and clearer. Everything seemed more dangerous the closer they drew to the ground. The plane's racing descent seemed full of risk. He listened for gunfire: they shouldn't be coming down like this, so obviously, so slowly, in broad daylight, with no defensive maneuvers. He drew long, measured breaths, counting slowly until the air was entirely clear of clouds. His heart was still pounding.

They were approaching the airport, making a long loop over Bangor. The landscape now was semi-urban: roofs, buildings, a grid of roads and highways. Tiny cars moved steadily along like markers in a game.

When the plane banked hard, heading for final approach, the roar of the engines became deafening. Conrad felt his heart respond, his pulse rising.

Anderson opened his eyes, closed his mouth, sat up.

"We landing, sir?"

Conrad nodded. He didn't want to risk speaking, didn't want to let Anderson know what was happening to him.

Anderson rubbed at his face, his eyes, his pale rabbit's lashes. Everyone around them was waking up; Marines were starting to talk and laugh, excited. Conrad's heart thundered.

The airport runways and buildings stretched out below them, straight axial lines, like a mechanical drawing. The plane dropped rapidly, and the long flat buildings, the dark tarmac, rose up alarmingly to meet it. The engines became louder, the pitch ascending toward some unbearable climax. The plane fell sickeningly toward the earth. There was a pounding inside his skull.

He could feel it coming: the moment in which you heard the sound. It was before anything had hit, when the air was full of ozone, the moment in which you understood that something was happening but not yet what. It was the moment that you knew in your body before you knew it in your mind, the moment when you felt the sound, like a great silence taking you over, the shock wave rolling through your body, your heart and lungs, time stopping around you. Everything flying apart into fragments. That limitless radiant moment, glittering behind your eyelids, before you knew.

He was frozen and still, his muscles clenched. His palms were sweating. Inside, he was huge and cavernous, and his heart was doing something monstrous and unnatural. Tears, horribly, brimmed at his eyelids. Some avalanche was poised, ready to break loose. He couldn't stop it. Something was running riot through him, some cloudburst of panic and confusion, noise and smoke and terror. He was consumed by fear. It was sweeping through him as though he'd been overtaken by fire, as though he were now rippling and radiant with flames. Somewhere he was screaming. Terror was blowing him apart.

He was counting and breathing, making his chest rise and fall, rise and fall, in, out, silently saying the numbers. *Nine,* he told himself desperately, breath, *eight,* spacing them evenly, breathing in, out, and then they were no longer over the runway but on it. The plane came down hard and fast, thundering roughly onto the tarmac, making the miraculous transfer from element to element, from air to earth at a hundred miles an hour. Undecided, the plane bounced twice, up into the air, then settled on earth, transforming itself from something free-floating and weightless into something massive and ponderous, lumbering, ungainly.

As the plane settled onto the tarmac, the cabin exploded with cheers. Relief flooded through Conrad, a wild wave of gratitude loosened him inside. Tears still threatened, but they were now from relief. It shamed him, but he was helpless before these towering gusts of feeling.

The plane raced down the runway, roaring and rattling. As they neared the end of the pavement, the engine scream rose further, revving to a wild, unthinkable pitch. The plane braked hard, flinging everyone forward. An empty can ricocheted down the aisle. The plane slowed abruptly, a weird, unnatural deceleration, and came to a sudden rolling stop. Conrad was sweating, his body damp and hot inside his uniform.

The pilot's voice came over the intercom. It sounded like God, deep and annunciatory. "Gentlemen, welcome home."

The cabin erupted again into shouts and whistles.

"Oo-rah! Back in the USA!" The Marines stamped and hooted, clapping. Conrad heard them from a great distance, through the louder pounding in his ears. He was actually on fire—was that it? He felt stunned. He turned to Anderson. He was trying to breathe normally and wondered how his face looked. He wondered if this showed.

"We made it," Conrad said. He hoped he was grinning.

Anderson looked at him, his gaze sober. "You okay, sir?"

Conrad nodded.

He was shaking. He didn't dare lift his hand or speak. What he wanted was to lean back against the seat, close his eyes, and let this thing, whatever it was, roll through him, take him over, and close him down.

2

Near the barracks, a low temporary grandstand had been set up. The seats were mostly empty, but kids were running up and down the empty risers, chasing one another. The bleachers overlooked the parade deck, a big square field of scuffed dirt, now partly filled with waiting families. When the buses appeared from beyond the barracks, people began gathering. The buses were unmarked, but everyone knew who was in them. People turned to face them, holding balloons, waving tiny American flags. Homemade signs were raised: WELCOME HOME BOBBY. WE LOVE YOU JESUS. Behind the families, towering over the crowd, were inflated balloon figures: a purple castle, rigid pennants fluttering from its turrets; a huge red and yellow smiling bear. They swelled against the sky, weirdly smooth, like giant babies.

Conrad's parents were both tall; they stood out among the others. Marshall was lanky and spare, with wide shoulders and a concave chest. He wore an old narrow-striped polo shirt and khaki pants. He stood with his hands jammed into his pockets, his head thrust forward, his fine, colorless hair falling across his forehead. He was oddly awkward, his elbows and wrists always prominent, always at the wrong angle.

Lydia was nearly his height, also lean and long-boned. She wore dark pants, a loose light jacket. Her hair was short and thick, deep brown, but graying slightly. Her eyes were dark and deep-set, with a mournful slope. She stood next to Marshall, her arms folded against her chest, her dark eyes searching for her son.

Next to the Farrells stood a young blond mother with two small children, and behind her an older man. They all held pale blue balloons inscribed WELCOME TOMMY. White ribbons hung from the balloons. The mother wore a short-sleeved pink sweater, and a balloon was tied to each of her wrists. She held a small boy against her chest. She kept rising onto her toes, craning to see, then sinking back onto her heels, unbalanced by her son. The balloons followed her movements languidly. The little girl clasped her mother's thighs, staring resentfully upward. A balloon was tied to the center of her plastic headband. Behind them stood a grizzled, stocky man wearing aviator sunglasses, legs spread, arms tightly folded, a balloon tethered to one buried hand.

The bus doors hissed open. The families held back, anticipatory. When the first Marine stepped down, everyone began to cheer. As the line of them appeared, there were claps and calls, names were shouted out. "Hey, Durell!" "Yo, *Jimmy*!" Mothers waved and called; children screamed joyfully, whether or not they saw Daddy; wives began weeping; fathers beamed and whistled.

The blond mother suddenly set down her son. "Tommy!" she called. She raised her hands, clapping, the balloons bobbing around her face. She gave a high-pitched laugh, then started to cry. She called again, "Tommy!" Her voice broke.

"Mom," the little girl said accusingly, unable to see.

The grizzled man cupped his mouth and called, "Hey, Tom!" The balloon floated jerkily over his head.

The Farrells watched silently, scanning the faces of the men stepping down from the bus. Marshall pushed his hair off his forehead, but at once it fell back.

It was the end of the day, and the California sky was darkening to a transparent violet. To the west, the palm trees were turning a deep red-black against the liquid glow. Over the crest of the hill, to the east, the sky was still blue, but it was becoming deeper and dimmer. Once everyone was off the bus, the staff sergeant gave the order and the men began to march, three abreast. There were two platoons of infantry grunts, all in clean desert camouflage uniforms, blurred brown and tan. They marched in unison, heads high, arms swinging. His platoon was Dingo Three; Conrad marched alongside. As an officer, he did what his men did, but apart. In the mess hall, officers always ate last. You put your men first.

The ceremony would be small, there were only two infantry platoons returning, about ninety men. If it had been a whole company coming back, two hundred or more, there'd have been a big ceremony, food and bands. But this would be brief. The big blow-up toys were about all there was, and they were aimed at kids. Most of Conrad's Marines didn't have kids, they were too young. Most of them were not even twenty-one—though they were no longer kids.

As the platoons marched along, children ran daringly out in front of them, then raced back to their families. Wives waved, babies began to cry, fathers called through cupped hands. The Marines kept their eyes front. When you marched, you separated yourself from everything else. You didn't make eye contact with the crowd, even if it was made up of your own families. You were part of your unit, not part of the people watching. This was how they'd been trained.

The walls of the purple castle were made of netting. Inside, kids bounced relentlessly on the trampoline floor. The compressors, inflating the castle, made an industrial roar. Beside the castle stood the bear, with staring eyes and manic grin. It seemed to be female, its bottom half a huge brown skirt with a white apron as the doorway. A little boy in desert cammies stood outside it, a miniature Marine. He was holding his hands over his ears, his mouth open. A little girl, her face painted in cat whiskers, came out the door and stood beside him. She saw the marching Marines and lifted her hand in a wave. Over the loudspeaker a brassy march struggled against the thundering bass of the compressors, which were winning.

The platoons reached the edge of the parade deck and drew up before a balding and stern-faced colonel. He stood frowning and erect, chin high, shoulders back. Beyond him, the long packed clouds of evening were drawing across the lower edge of the sky.

The Marines stood before him at attention, heads high, eyes straight ahead, arms stiff at their sides. The blue dome of the sky was darkening, becoming deep and endless as the stain of night spread smoothly down its sides. Suddenly the arc lights went on, illuminating the field with a dry white glare. The sky overhead became dark, and all at once it was night. The Marines were irradiated, surrounded by darkness. In the sudden illumination they became mysterious—their mottled uniforms, their smooth, close-cropped heads, their fixed stare. They carried something of the place they'd come from, the life they'd lived there, something of those who had not returned. The field, and the waiting men, illuminated by the lights, seemed clouded by that invisible awareness. Darkness lay beyond them, and the vast nighttime sky lay overhead, the landscape turning shadowy across the continent as the sun dropped away from their side of the earth.

Lydia leaned toward Marshall and whispered, "Have we missed him?"

"We must have," Marshall said. "He must be here."

"But how could we?" Lydia murmured. "We've been watching. Where is he?"

They scanned the rows, and Lydia felt a sudden fear: that he was not here after all, that he had been somehow lost. It was irrational—they knew he was here—but familiar. Fear had become part of her consciousness.

Lydia had not grown up in this world. The military had been entirely alien to her. There was no long family connection to it, no swords, no photographs, no war stories. Her father's only connection to it (two quiet years on a naval air station in Tennessee, long before she was born) was rarely mentioned. It played no part in her family history.

She had grown up in the aftermath of the Vietnam War, when the military was shadowed by disgrace. As a child she'd seen her parents watching the evening news night after night, their faces grave. They sat before the TV, drinks in their hands, listening in silence to the serious voice of the newscaster. One night her father listened to a general as he blustered and stalled, challenged by hostile questions.

Her father shook his head, swirling the ice cubes in his glass. "The country will never recover from this."

Lydia, who was eight, was alarmed. For years afterward she expected something to happen, dire consequences. It was the military, she understood that. The military was in disgrace. The Vietnam War had been a scandalous mistake, everyone knew it. The advisers had lied to the press, the White House had lied to Congress, the generals had lied to everyone. The military had manufactured evidence, the troops had massacred civilians. The whole thing was a national shame.

Lydia grew up believing that the military had been permanently dishonored by this. Never again would the public trust it so deeply. The lesson had been a terrible one, harsh and costly, but the nation had learned it. This was how history worked, the way nations formed attitudes and policies. This was the school of experience: never again would America allow such a thing to happen—to undertake war so secretively, so recklessly, so duplicitously.

By the time Lydia was a teenager, the draft had ended, and no one she knew enlisted. That whole world receded into vague obscurity for her. The military seemed huge and surreal, like a factory out of Kafka, grinding on endlessly, groaning and rumbling as it produced a vast, dangerous, and incomprehensible product. It was outside the rest of the community, unrelated to civilians or peacetime. Lydia had seldom thought of the military until the spring of Conrad's junior year at Williams, 2001, when he came home to tell them about his plans.

The Farrells lived in the small town of Katonah, in northern Westchester, in an old farmhouse on a hill that slanted down to a dirt road. The house was set on wide, sloping lawns and shaded by huge rough-barked sugar maples; the fields were bounded by lichened stone walls. Across the lawn from the house was a red two-story barn, with an enormous hayloft above and big box stalls below: it had been converted from a dairy to a horse barn before the Farrells bought it. Behind the house, meadows rose up over the crest of the hill. Beyond them, on the other side, the land sloped down and gave way to woods. The original farm contained several hundred acres, though the Farrells owned only six. They'd bought it during a dip in the market in the late 1970s. After that, prices soared, and they'd never have been able to afford it.

The house was white clapboard, with three stories and five bedrooms, comfortable but not grand. On a beam in the attic was the signature of the carpenter: *Richard Inglesby, 1856.* For a hundred and fifty years people had lived their particular lives in those rooms, within those same plaster walls. Prosperous farmers, to judge from the house and its grace notes—high ceilings, elegant moldings, three bay windows, and a back stairs for the help. For all those years people had gotten out of bed each morning in those rooms. They'd set their weight on the slanting wide-board floors. On bone-cold winter mornings they went down the creaking back staircase, put on coats and boots, and went out to the barn to feed the animals. On hot summer nights they slept with the windows open onto the dark lawns, the murmuring sugar maples. During thunderstorms they looked out through the pouring rain toward the barn, revealed in terrifying precision by the flashes. Babies had been born in these rooms, the mother twisting and sweating, holding on to the iron bedstead behind her head, a doctor leaning over her. People had become ill in these quiet rooms. They had died here, their breathing stilled. Someone had watched, her gaze locked on a yellowish face, unable to turn away. All these people, cooking and sleeping and having children and getting ill, having parties and arguments, being confused and happy and grief-stricken, were part of the history of the house. Someone had decided to modernize and put in gas, and they'd had to cut the mysterious pipeline in the wall in order to add the window in the breakfast room. Someone later had put in electricity, plumbing; someone had paved the driveway. The Farrells changed little. They respected the modest nineteenth-century presence of the house. They'd preserved its integrity, protected it from change. They felt responsible for it.

The Farrell children had grown up there, Conrad, Jenny, and Oliver. Marshall commuted, taking the train every day to New York, where he taught law at NYU. When the children were grown-up enough, Lydia had slowly gotten her M.S.W. When the children were older, she set up a family therapy practice in New York, and she began commuting, too. The trip took over an hour on the train, and it was tiring. By the time you reached Valhalla, it seemed endless. But at the end of the trip you stepped out of your car in your own driveway, drew a breath of sweet country air, heard the soft calls of the mourning doves in the lilacs.

That Saturday morning, the weekend Conrad came home from Williams, Lydia and Marshall sat at breakfast, reading the *Times* and waiting for the children to straggle down the back stairs. Conrad and Jenny, twenty-one and eighteen, were usually the last; Oliver, fourteen, was usually first.

Marshall and Lydia sat in the little breakfast room off the kitchen, overlooking the garden. The paper was spread messily across the table, Classifieds and Real Estate already discarded on the floor. On the windowsill stood a jug of spring flowers: bleeding hearts and Jacob's ladder. Beyond the jug lay the brindle cat, Murphy, her eyes shut, her white paws tucked neatly under her chest, feigning disinterest in their food. Lydia was deep in the crossword, Marshall pored over the op-ed.

They heard movement upstairs, and then they heard someone descending. They saw bare feet, legs in loose gray sweatpants, someone jolting down the back steps. Lydia expected Ollie, gangly and loose-jointed, his face shimmering pink with hormones, his mouth complicated with braces. But the steps were light and controlled, the feet tidy. After the gray sweatpants she saw a faded T-shirt that declared in orange letters, WILLIAMS TRACK. Conrad.

"Good morning," Lydia said. "You're up early." She moved the newspapers to make room for him. "Want me to make something to eat?"

"No, I'm good." Conrad went past them and fixed himself a bowl of cereal. He brought it back to the table and sat down across from his parents.

"Good morning," Marshall said, raising only his head. His torso was cantilevered over the paper. He was poised, ready to dive back into it.

Conrad took a spoonful of cereal, then leaned back and folded his arms across WILLIAMS TRACK. "I wanted to tell you something," he said. "I have an announcement to make." He seemed awkward and self-conscious.

They waited, Lydia holding her coffee mug, Marshall poised over the paper. Neither was alarmed. Conrad was their eldest child, an achiever, responsible and conscientious. He trusted the world and had faith in the way it worked. He was always on the honor roll, always captain of the team. He completed the task before him; he moved beautifully through life.

Why would they be alarmed? What he was facing was his future. They'd had many talks about it. Conrad was majoring in classics, and he was drawn to everything in the ancient world: literature, history, art. He'd talked about going on to study archaeology or history; he'd talked about becoming a classics professor himself. He'd talked about law school and following his father's path.

Lydia was proud of his wide interests. She was proud that he'd moved into regions that were unknown to her, mastering knowledge that would never be hers. This was one of the delights of being a parent, wasn't it? Watching your children stride steadily past, outstripping you, knowing that they were carrying on the life of the family—whatever it was, the essence, genes, some kind of tribal presence—into another region, one that was distant, rich, remote. Astrophysics, intellectual property, ancient Greece: places where her mind would never go would be explored by her children.

Lydia waited, ready to applaud Conrad's decision. This was like unwrapping a present.

"I'm joining the Marines," Conrad said. His arms were crossed like a barricade across his chest.

Marshall sat up straight and carefully folded the paper closed. His eyes were pale and intent, like a benevolent hawk's.

"The Marines?" Lydia said, stunned. Her mind went blank. "The real ones?" she asked stupidly. She had no idea what she meant. She tried to think what exactly they were. Why were they called that, *marine*? What connection did they have to the sea? Why did they wear those white gloves?

"The real ones." Conrad looked from one to the other.

"Well," Marshall said soberly. "That's quite a decision."

"When do you go?" asked Lydia.

"Right after school, this summer, I'll go to officers' training school at Quantico," Conrad said. "Next year, after graduation, I'll go in for good."

"Quantico," Lydia repeated, mystified. *For good? How could it be good?*

"That's where the training school for officers is," Conrad said. "It's in Virginia." There was pride in his voice: another shock for Lydia. He was proud of this.

"Tell us more, Con." Marshall folded his hands on top of the paper. "Tell us why you've decided on this."

"So, I want to do something big. I don't want to just go into some graduate school and get another degree. I want to do something that has consequences. This is the biggest challenge I know," said Conrad. "I want to see if I can do it."

Marshall nodded. "I can understand that."

Lydia looked at him, betrayed. Marshall had nearly gone to jail for protesting the war: How could he suddenly understand this strange martial urge? The wish to join the Marines.

All of it bewildered Lydia: the pride in Conrad's voice, the understanding in Marshall's. Suddenly she was confused and excluded. This was something the two of them seemed to have been sharing all along, a private language she didn't speak. She'd thought they'd all shared the same world, but they had not. Her son, her husband: Where had they been leading this secret life? The one that only they knew about.

"This is a big change, isn't it," she asked, "from majoring in classics?"

She tried to sound supportive and interested instead of appalled and frightened. Conrad was an intellectual; how could he choose to enter a totalitarian system? And he was compassionate. She remembered him as a child, coming into the kitchen and carrying a tiny wounded rabbit, soft in his hands, bright-eyed and desperate. Rabbits, chipmunks, snakes—Conrad was the one who tried to save them all. Saving had been his mission. Why would he now choose a world of violence and killing?

And anyway, weren't the Marines a last resort—for misfits, people who were so violent and misanthropic they couldn't function in the outside world? Weren't they for someone who needed a rigid iron rule to suppress antisocial urges? Conrad wasn't like that. Their family wasn't like that. Their family was bookish and liberal, not martial and authoritarian.

But Conrad shook his head. "Not really. It's kind of a continuum. The classical writers love war, that's their main subject. Being a soldier was the whole deal, the central experience. That's what first got me interested. Sparta. The Peloponnesian War, the *Iliad*. Thucydides, Homer, Tacitus. I wanted to see what it was like." He shrugged uncomfortably. "It seems like it's the great thing. The great challenge." He looked at them.

Traitorously, Marshall nodded again. "I see."

"But that was different," said Lydia. "The Greeks were all at war with each other. We aren't at war. Being a soldier isn't central now."

"It's the idea," Conrad said. "Being a soldier is elemental. It's kind of primal. And I want to defend our country."

"Defend it from what?" Lydia asked. "This is 2001, not 1941. We have no enemies."

Conrad shook his head. "It's the idea of it," he said again. "I want to do something serious, something that will make a difference."

It all seemed adolescent to her, that absurd male sentimentality about violence. There were other ways to make a difference, why choose something so hostile, so alien?

"Aren't there other things you can do?" she asked. "What about the Peace Corps?"

"The Peace Corps is lame," Conrad said. "And ineffective."

"But this is so violent," Lydia said. "The military is a culture of violence. Every solution is violent."

"First of all, no it's not," Conrad said. "Second of all, the military is called in only when all other solutions have failed. When it's necessary. Do you think nonviolent resistance would have worked against Hitler?"

There was a pause.

"What does Claire say about it?" Lydia asked. She was hoping for solidarity.

Conrad swallowed. "She's fine with it." He nodded. This was not entirely true.

Lydia nodded, watching him.

"I mean, she was surprised," Conrad admitted, "but she's supportive." Also not entirely true, but anyway they hadn't broken up over it.

Lydia said nothing.

"I can see you're horrified by this," Conrad said.

"No, no." Lydia shook her head. She was horrified.

Conrad began to explain, stroking the cat. Electricity began to crackle in Murphy's fur. Irritated, the cat jerked her head with each stroke, swishing her tail back and forth while Conrad told them about the Marines. The language he used reminded Lydia of ancient myths, Nordic sagas, King Arthur. Courage and loyalty, Conrad said. Commitment, a code of honor. All straight from the ancient world, from Sparta. Semper Fidelis.

Lydia watched him as he talked, the early light flooding in from the window, across his face. He looked like both of them: he had Marshall's wide jaw, his long, straight nose, his light coloring, pale hair, smooth, creamy skin. He had Lydia's slanting eyes, though Conrad's were blue. He was theirs, he was of them, he represented them. He was carrying them into the future. How could he be so wrong, so unlike them?

His body had become solid. She saw that it was, really, now a man's: the chest springing strongly outward, the arms muscled and firm. His face was lit from within by youth; his features were precise. The brave, mournful eyes, the smooth, powerful arms, the slanting cords in his neck: his beauty was borne in on her. *He can't be risked,* Lydia thought.

He talked earnestly, looking up at them, looking down at the cat.

Someone had come to Williams and given a talk about the Marines. It was inspirational. A professor stood up and challenged the speaker, saying that the military shouldn't recruit on liberal arts campuses—that they were trying to militarize the academy. The speaker had argued back: on the contrary, he said, he was trying to liberalize the military. Conrad had been offended by the challenger. Weren't you meant to choose for yourself in college? Weren't you meant to consider everything and then make your own decisions? It was the challenger who had made him think more about the Marines.

Conrad talked about Homer. War was his great subject, how it shaped history, affected families, changed young men. War was the route to nobility. Before Aeschylus died, he asked for his epitaph to mention only his achievements as a warrior, nothing about his plays. War, not art. As he talked, Conrad ran his hand hard down Murphy's spine and her tail sprang up with each stroke.

It was too late for Lydia to say anything, she could see that. Conrad was immersed in this, lost to it, in full spate. He was in love; it was in his voice.

When he finished, Lydia said tentatively, "So is it done? Final? Have you committed?"

"I've signed up for this summer at OCS." Conrad sealed his lips shut over the words. "It's done." He stroked harder. Murphy stood up in a distracted crouch, unsettled, swaying, her coat rippling.

He was leaving the world Lydia knew. He would enter another, alien to her: the strange, violent life of soldiers, where killing was the right thing to do. This was anathema, the very opposite of everything you brought children up to believe. *Don't you remember,* she wanted to say, *what we always said about the military?*

Conrad saw her expression. "It's not dangerous," he said. "Don't worry. This is peacetime."

"It's not just that," she said. "It's a different world." It was as though he were declaring his plans to join another family. *You can't do this,* she wanted to say; *you're one of us.*

Conrad watched her as he stroked the staggering cat. She could see that he could do as he chose. His life would unroll into the future.

And in this way, watching her son stroking the twitching cat, Lydia came to understand that the national memory did not work the way she'd thought. She saw that the shapes of ideas changed, slowly, like clouds, within the public mind. First the shift of an outline, the blurring of edges; then, mysteriously, according to some unseen current, the whole form alters. What had certainly been a high-heeled boot becomes unmistakably a swan. The idea of war as unacceptable, the military as unreliable, which seemed to Lydia fixed, immutable, had changed completely. Those concepts—war, and the military itself—were no longer scorned, not even among liberal intellectuals, not even among classics majors at liberal arts colleges. Somehow, while Lydia and Marshall were not looking, those ideas had become plausible, possibly necessary, maybe even laudable. Anyway, acceptable.

More than that, they had become honorable. It was a mystery to her.

Later, Jenny and Oliver came down, and Conrad told them. Jenny came slopping in wearing a ripped-neck T-shirt and sweatpants, earbuds in her ears. The whistling slither of the music was audible to everyone, and though it was strictly forbidden to wear these at the table, Jenny made herself toast, brought it back, and sat down without removing them. Lydia was too distracted by Conrad's news to say anything, but Jenny started eating and then realized that Conrad was talking to her. She took off her earbuds and said, "What?"

"Pay attention," Conrad said. "I'm joining the Marines."

Jenny stared at him. "You must be out of your mind."

"Or just maybe," Conrad said, "you don't know what you're talking about."

"The white gloves, right?"

Conrad shook his head. "You have much to learn."

When Ollie came down, Conrad waited until he sat down with his cereal, then told him.

"The Marines!" Ollie said. "No way!"

"The ones with the white gloves," Jenny said.

Conrad rolled his eyes, but Lydia could see that he was more confident now.

That night when they went to bed, Lydia and Marshall talked more about it. Lydia closed the door to their bedroom. The room had a bay window and a window seat looking out over the lawn to the barn. The walls were papered with a ferny green print, the curtains white. The furniture was honey-colored—an old maple bureau under a curlicued mirror, two carved side chairs. In the corner was an upholstered chaise longue, comfortable and inviting, on which no one ever sat. A white bookcase stood in the corner holding Lydia's favorite books and photographs of the children. On the floor was a fraying carpet that had never been large enough for the room.

Lydia stood leaning over the bureau to look in the mirror as she took off her earrings. "So what do you think?" she asked. "I'm flabbergasted. The Marines." She looked past herself in the mirror, at Marshall. "I don't think I like it."

"I don't recall being asked if we liked it." Marshall unbuttoned some of his buttons, and pulled his shirt over his head, straining the ones still buttoned.

"But this isn't some summer job. It's dangerous," Lydia said. "We should have some say about it."

"I don't actually think we do," Marshall said. "But it's not dangerous. We're not at war."

"The military is always dangerous," Lydia said. "What about those Marines in Somalia?"

"There are thousands and thousands of Marines. A few died in Somalia. That could have happened anywhere. They could have died in a car crash."

Lydia turned to him. "But they didn't. That was a horrible death."

Marshall said nothing.

"It's so strange of him. Where did he get the idea?"

Outside, the big sugar maples muffled the house in the darkness.

"We're not supposed to know where our children get their ideas," Marshall said. "It's a mystery. If we're successful parents, our children will invent themselves."

Marshall stepped out of his pants and turned them upside down.

He took them by the cuffs and swung them neatly, aligning the legs. He set them over the back of a chair.

Lydia sat down on the bed. She put her hands on her knees. "I really don't like it," she said. "I really don't."

Marshall sat down next to her. He put his arm around her. "It's something we didn't expect. But I think his mind is made up. He's twenty-one, he's an adult. I don't think we have much choice."

"He has a year before he signs up for good. I hope he changes his mind," Lydia said.

"I can understand the appeal," Marshall said.

Lydia frowned. "Why do you keep saying that? You were a protester."

"Because I thought *that* war was morally wrong. I'm not opposed to all wars. Some wars have to be fought, like World War II. And I can see why Conrad wants to do this. It's the big test: I'm kind of proud he wants to take it."

"In our generation, if you acted out of moral beliefs, you were a protester," Lydia said. "Or you joined the Peace Corps."

"So, maybe in his generation, you join the Marine Corps," Marshall said. He stood up again.

Lydia shook her head. "It's just insane. I know I'm supposed to adapt to this. I mean, I'm a family therapist. A mother has to let her children go. I know that." She shook her head again. "But does she have to let them walk off a cliff?"

The colonel snapped his hand down at his side.

"Welcome home, gentlemen. Dismissed," he said. "Go see your families."

At once the platoons broke lines. The men of Dingo Three turned and waded into the milling families as though into the surf, the dense MARPAT brown mingling among the bright colors of the crowd.

Conrad swiveled, looking for his parents, at the same time watching the reunions around him. Haskell, a grunt from third squad, had barely taken a step before he was seized by a beefy teenage girl with heavy arms and long oiled black curls. "*Bobby!*" she screamed. She threw her arms around his neck, leaning against him and knocking his hat back on his head. Haskell drew back, tucking in his chin, raising his hand to his hat. But she was clamped full-on against his chest, and she pressed her meaty lips over his. A group of plump girls in bright tube tops stood nearby, watching and giggling.

Private First Class Jackson, second squad, had begun moving slowly into the crowd when a girl in a red dress came running through it and threw herself on him. She jumped into his arms and wrapped her legs around his hips like a monkey. It was somehow electrifying and obscene, with the small children drifting past. Jackson staggered at the impact, but recovered. He put his arms around her and began turning slowly. Her red dress flared out around her in a rippling circle.

Everyone in the platoon knew who the women were. They all knew names, pictures, stories. The beefy girl kissing Haskell was someone he actually hardly knew, a sort of long-distance girlfriend. They'd gotten to know each other while he was in-country; they'd never even fucked. It got like that, though, people sending hot emails back and forth to people they barely knew back home. All that testosterone had to go somewhere, speeding out onto the Internet.

Jackson's girlfriend, Helena, the girl in the red dress, had been a cheerleader back home in Oklahoma, and Jackson was always talking about how strong and flexible she was. Jackson ate coffee powder for energy when they went out on patrol, and when he got stoked, you couldn't shut him up.

"Cheerleaders, man," he'd say, shaking his head. "You have no fucking idea. They can do anything. Twist into pretzels. *Yes!*" He squeezed his eyes shut. "They bend themselves all around like acrobats."

After that, "cheerleader" became code for anyone who could do something extraordinary. Bad guys, Ali Babas—which was what you called bad guys—Marines, anyone. And here was the cheerleader herself, doing a flying fuck-jump like a monkey as proof. Jackson was proud of it; that's why he was swinging her in that circle, her dress flaring. He wanted everyone to see it.

In-country they talked about women all the time, on patrol in the Humvee, on security, back at the outpost, laughing and lying and sweating and swearing. Once, Jackson had impersonated Helena in a dance contest. He came out from behind a curtain wearing an orange towel and white socks, waving pom-poms made out of white paper he'd gotten from the mess hall. They'd all cheered while he kicked, raising his knees and grinning.

Usually Conrad wasn't part of those things: as an officer, he kept apart. There was a lot he didn't want to see, stuff he left to the sergeant. But the men had invited him to the dance contest. "*The cheerleader,*" Jackson had shouted, waggling his eyebrows, swinging his hips inside the orange towel. "*Take it off,*" they'd yelled back. "*Take it all off!*"

Now Conrad snaked through the crowd, pushing gently past Vasquez: he and his wife had found each other. They stood embracing, locked into each other's shapes. They were nearly the same height, and they seemed fitted together, eyes closed. They were silent, and Conrad looked away to give them privacy.

He was glad Claire hadn't come. He wouldn't know how to greet her. How could he not kiss her? For two years at college they'd spent nearly every night together. But while he was in-country, they'd broken up, or sort of broken up. Maybe they'd broken up before he left. He didn't know where they were. Were they now supposed to shake hands when they met? When he next saw her, he didn't want it to be in public.

Where were his parents? He tried to raise their faces in his mind. Had he seen them without knowing?

Now he saw his father making his way through the crowd. Marshall raised his hand awkwardly to bat at a white balloon that drifted across his face: WELCOME TOMMY. Behind him was Lydia. They were both smiling. Of course, once Conrad saw them, they were utterly familiar: tall and lanky, both slightly gawky.

When Marshall reached Conrad, he put his arms around his son. They hugged, shoulder to shoulder. Conrad was surprised by his father's body. It seemed thin and insubstantial: Had it changed, or had he? Compared with the solid, muscular density of Marines, Marshall seemed almost frail. It was not the way he'd ever thought of his father. Conrad turned, and Lydia moved into him, putting her arms completely around him, and he felt the thump of her sob against his chest.

When she drew away, there were tears in her eyes and she was laughing. She said, "I had the craziest idea. I was afraid I wouldn't *recognize* you. I couldn't call up your whole face, only parts of it."

The crowd was swirling around them, ebullient. Jackson came over to them, his arm around the Monkey. He stood apart, waiting politely to be seen.

"Jackson," said Conrad.

Jackson was short, with a long head and fleshy ears. He had low, beetling brows and gleaming blue eyes, skin mildly pitted with acne.

"LT, I'd like you to meet my girlfriend, Helena," Jackson said formally.

"Hello, Lieutenant Farrell." Helena smiled at him. She had a very red mouth, loose dark ringlets, a small cleft in her chin. "I'm glad to meet you. I've heard a lot about you."

"Glad to meet you, too, Helena."

Conrad nodded politely, not mentioning that he'd heard about her as well. It was strange seeing her in the flesh, lipstick smudges on her teeth, strands of dark hair clinging to her damp throat. Strange to see this physical manifestation of Jackson's other life. His new life, under this darkening California sky, a small evening wind rustling the leaves overhead. Strange to think that this was the last time he would see Jackson in this way. The balance had already shifted: Jackson's arm was around the Monkey. His allegiance was now to her, or to whoever came after her. He'd never again be under Conrad's command.

The last four years were being dismantled around him, subsiding, melting away in a silent cascade. Their shared life was over: from now on, for the rest of their lives, they would share only a past, never the present. It was as though Jackson himself were vanishing before his eyes. Though what they shared would always be there. Part of their life was fluid, part fixed.

"All right, Jackson. Have a good evening."

"You, too, sir," said Jackson.

Conrad thought of the Monkey's legs wrapped around Jackson's waist, that graphic, flamboyant welcome, the public declaration of a different life. He thought of Claire. Everything was breaking up and changing.

As Conrad turned back, he saw Anderson, ten feet away. He was talking to his parents, his arm around his girlfriend.

"Excuse me one moment," Conrad said to his parents. "I want to say goodbye to someone."

Anderson saw him coming over.

"Hey, LT," he said. "Like you to meet my mom and dad, Chuck and Nita Anderson. And my girlfriend, Sue-Ann Hanson." Everyone smiled. Sue-Ann was fat but pretty, with liquid blue eyes and springy blond hair.

Conrad shook hands with the parents. "Your son is a good guy," he told Nita.

Nita was short and stocky, with short gray hair, small features in a wide face. She wore baggy khaki pants, some kind of striped sweater. She beamed at Conrad.

"Well, we think so," Nita said. "We have always thought so."

Chuck Anderson wore a loose short-sleeved jersey with a diamond pattern across the chest. He had a wide, colorless mouth and wore square gold-rimmed glasses.

"Hear you had some pretty exciting things going on over there." Chuck looked at Conrad from under his thatchy eyebrows.

Conrad tried to remember—was he an accountant or a lawyer? Something like that. They lived in a small town outside Minneapolis.

Conrad clapped Anderson on the shoulder. "This guy," he said, "did some exciting stuff. As exciting as anything that happened in the whole country."

Nita and Chuck both looked at Anderson, who grinned and shook his head.

"You're a hero," Sue-Ann said, turning to Anderson. She had pressed herself against his side. Her dress was royal blue, scoop-necked, wide pleats tight against her big legs. She was brimming with excitement. The fact that Anderson was here, that his body was next to hers, that the future lay before them, nearly made her wriggle with delight.

Anderson shook his head again.

"So, now, the dogsled?" Conrad asked.

"Coming soon," Anderson said.

"Dogsled?" Sue-Ann asked. She looked at Anderson, then at Conrad.

Anderson squeezed her shoulders but didn't look at her.

"Okay," Conrad said, "I've got to go. It was nice meeting you," he said to Chuck and Nita. He nodded to Sue-Ann. “Keep in touch,” he said to Anderson. “Semper Fi.”

“Thanks, LT.” Anderson nodded. “I’ll see you.”

Conrad made his way back through the crowd, nodding and smiling. He reached his parents.

“Sorry for that,” he said. “So. Where we headed?”

3

“We’ve got reservations at a place in Oceanside,” Marshall said.

“It’s an Italian seafood place,” said Lydia. “We figured you wouldn’t have had much of either over there, Italian food or seafood.”

His parents waited while Conrad went into the barracks to change out of his cammies. When he came back, they began making their way slowly through the family groups.

The Marines in their cammies, the families in bright clothes, the signs and flags and balloons, the shrill calls, the children yelling and racing—all of it seemed both familiar and unfamiliar to Conrad, possible and not possible, as though he were trying to live two lives at once.

He was among people for whom there was no dark undertow. Here there were no sudden black boiling clouds, no exploding vehicles. There would be no crack of an AK-47, no smell of burning flesh. Here the air was mild, the landscape quiet. No one would round a corner to find something lying on the street, ripped open and gasping, ruby-colored, terrible. These wives and children and parents, with their cameras and rental cars and balloons, were exempt from all that.

Somewhere, on streets Conrad knew well, those things did exist. Those huge sounds (too great to be called sounds, really, they were more like whole days, or years, like weather systems, obliterating everything, taking over the air, your breath, your body) were still being heard. He felt as though those sounds were here, too, somehow, only they’d been blotted out, muted—as though they were all around, but now he couldn’t hear them. How could they not exist here? He felt he was derelict in his duty by not hearing them.

They were moving slowly toward the parking lot. The evening air was warm and buoyant, light and alive, hinting at the unseen Pacific with its briny tingle, its sweep and movement. Long streaks of light from the sunset still filled the western horizon. Above them the sodium lights had turned the landscape dim and shadowy. Sounds seemed amplified: footsteps on the paved pathways, nearby voices.

The skyline of cartoon figures was behind them, the first sharp thrill of the reunion was over. Tired mothers called to rebellious children, *Come over here, I told you to stay next to me*; returning fathers were quick to back up their wives, *Listen to your mother, you do what she tells you*; fathers were asking reluctant children for a kiss, *Come on, now, sweetie, look at Daddy. Look at Daddy.* Mothers were quick to back up their husbands, *Honey, look at Daddy. Give Daddy a kiss.*

The parking lot was full. The cars were in neat rows, their smooth, rounded shapes gleaming under the arc lights. People moved among them, opening doors, setting off the little pinging bells. The lights made radiant tents of the interiors. Children were buckled, protesting, into car seats. Trunks were opened and shut. The men were dispersing, vanishing into the night. Conrad felt a zigzag of reflexive anxiety—but they'd been dismissed. Dispersal was correct. They were home now. Not in his care, not under his command.

"Where'd we leave the car?" Marshall stopped to scan the row. "Do you remember?"

"At the end of a row, near a trash basket," Lydia said. "I dropped something in it. But I don't remember which row." They walked haphazardly toward the cars.

"It's over to the right somewhere," Marshall said.

"I don't even remember what it looks like," Lydia said. "Is it red?"

"Silver." Marshall raised his arm, pointing the key toward the cars like a magic wand. He clicked forcefully. Nothing happened. He pointed in the opposite direction. "Go!" he commanded.

Two rows away, a small black car chirped and blinked its lights.

"Thank you!" Marshall said. "I mean, it's black."

His parents thought it was funny, their running dispute with technology. Conrad found it baffling. It was like arguing with language. Why not just use it?

"How did people find their cars before clickers?" Lydia asked.

"There were fewer people," Marshall said, "fewer cars."

He unlocked the car, and Conrad threw his bag into the trunk and climbed in back. Lydia opened the front door, then shut it. She opened the back door.

"I'm going to sit with you. I just want to be next to you for a while."

She climbed in beside him. The back was cramped, and they sat very close. Lydia turned to look at him. She said nothing, smiling a little. She shook her head, then looked away, her eyes glittering. He could feel her tenderness. Marshall looked at Conrad for a moment in the rearview mirror. He could feel their gratitude that he was back, their gratitude at the end of the fear they'd lived with: the car was thick with it. But there was nothing he could say about being alive. You were alive or you were not. It was too close for you to look at.

The cars were all leaving, backing out carefully and getting in one another's way, forming a glacially slow parade.

"This will take all night," Marshall announced.

"It doesn't matter." Lydia smiled at Conrad, then looked away, out her own window.

Marshall called back, "How was the flight home?"

"Good," said Conrad. "From Germany on, we flew chartered."

"Nice," Marshall said, nodding.

Going over, on his first deployment, he'd flown cargo. They'd left San Diego in the middle of the night. He remembered lining up on the runway in the dark, the men humping their ponderous packs in silence. Above them towered the huge C-5, its dark outline barely visible against the night sky. There were no lights.

Inside, the vast cargo bay was cavernous, smelling of oil and metal and canvas. Rows of Humvees, chained to the floor, gleamed faintly in the dim light. The men's boots rang on the metal floor as they filed past the tarpaulined mounds of equipment, snaking their way to the steep, ladderlike staircase. The passenger capsule was set high against the side of the plane, narrow seats and no windows. The metal seatback hit at the base of his head, and on the floor there wasn't enough room to put his feet side by side. When the engines started, the noise drowned out everything. Conrad sat beside the thrumming metal wall, motionless and solitary as the sky roared past outside.

Sealed and sightless, high inside the plane, he was cargo. Roaring toward the unknown, fear was with all of them, he knew. Not exactly fear of death—that was a blackout, an abstraction. No one could imagine it. What they feared was mutilation. The exploded body, the missing limbs, the horribly scarred face. The wheelchair beside the Christmas tree. The C-5 roared through the dark sky; they put in earbuds and listened to music; they slept, cramped in the narrow seats.

"Chartered! That's good," said Lydia.

"It was great," Conrad said. "Real seats, real flight attendants, and real meals. And a movie."

"What did you see?" asked Lydia.

"*The Aviator,*" Conrad said.

"What is it? We didn't see it," Lydia said.

"Martin Scorsese, Leonardo DiCaprio," Conrad said. "It's about Howard Hughes."

"Any good?" Marshall asked.

Before he could answer, Lydia broke in. "I'll tell you what you have to see," she said, "*Sideways.* It's wonderful. It's so funny. About two guys going to the wine country in California and drinking too much. Red wine, it's all about red wine."

He hadn't seen it, of course. The last four years had been a cultural blank. Everyone here had been watching movies and reading books, and he had not. He was Rip Van Winkle. He'd never catch up with the things he missed while he'd been living in the alternate universe. Even if he saw them, he'd see them in a different context, part of a different year.

When they left the base, they headed into Oceanside. The road was flanked by a bright lineup of national chains—motels and gas stations and fast-food restaurants—but there was a holiday air to it all. The low horizon, the moist air, the palm trees all suggested the presence of the coast. Between the buildings were glimpses of a wild, majestic sunset, scarlet banners melting into the sea, the sea a molten pewter.

The hotel was Spanish Mission–style, two stories high, pink adobe. Heavy wooden beams framed the doorways, with clusters of red chili peppers hanging in the corners. The lobby was pinkish beige: rug, chairs, the hard-looking sofa, the high counter at reception. The girl behind the counter didn't fit in with the Spanish colonial theme. She was Eastern Bloc, with pale skin, heavy eye shadow, and a scary smile. Her dry bleached-white hair was teased back in a rooster tail.

"Welcome," she said to Conrad, baring a row of little gray teeth. "Welcome home. Here's your key." She slid him the envelope with his computerized plastic card.

"Thanks," he said.

They were on the second floor. Conrad's room was next to his parents'. He slotted his key card into the lock and it flashed green. He stepped inside, pulling the door shut behind him.

He was alone in the room.

He hadn't been alone for a long time. He stood still, feeling the air settle around him, hearing the faint singing sound of silence. The room was stuffy, smelling slightly of cleaning fluid.

Against one wall were two double beds with carved and painted wooden headboards. Against another wall stood a painted wooden armoire with double doors. A wide mirror hung over a low bureau: he saw himself standing against the white curtains, the festive headboards. The sunburned face was familiar, but not the rest. He was in civilian clothes—a polo shirt and khakis. He stared at himself. He looked like someone else.

He walked to the window. Below was a small rectangular swimming pool, the water bright turquoise. The pool was empty, and the water lapped restlessly along the tiled sides. The narrow pavement around it was scattered with lounge chairs. On one side was a high stockade fence, easily scalable. On the far side of the pool was another wing of the hotel, and rows of blank windows stared in at his. The other wing was twenty meters away, an easy shot. Though he'd turned in his rifle.

He pulled the curtains closed. He wanted a civilian shower. He began to undress, dropping his clothes on the bed. He kicked off his moccasins. His feet were white and slimy: he had a Godzilla case of athlete's foot. Everyone got it. It was fungus from wearing your boots too long, too much heat, not enough washing.

He didn't actually want to touch his feet. Sometimes when he'd taken off his boots, the skin peeled off in his fingers in long, pale, putrid strips. When he was wearing his boots, his feet didn't hurt. It was when he took them off that his feet started itching and burning.

It was strange walking around in civilian shoes, no boots, no dog tags inside the left one, bunching beneath his toes. The dog tags felt like a good-luck charm, even though they were for the worst-case scenario, ID'ing a dead body. But they meant a kind of ultimate care, like a name and address pinned onto a traveling kid. *This is who I am.*

In the shower he closed his eyes and let the hot water stream over him. The showerhead was a small disk, pale with oxidation. He raised it, training the stream directly at himself, closed his eyes, and turned his head up toward the hammering rush. *All the hot water he wanted, and all the time.* It was unimaginable. He felt something release in his neck. He was here, standing in the bathtub in a hotel in America. He was back. What lay before him was dinner with his parents, nothing more than that, and he was not in danger, there was no threat outside this room, his body was not held tightly on alert, nerves singing, waiting endlessly for the sound of the explosion; he was here in this clean, tiled space, alone, and he was safe, and this was a kind of miracle. The shower curtain drifted against his shoulder and he twitched reflexively, but it was only the shower curtain moving in the current of air made by the shower. It was nothing. He was safe, and at that surprising thought he felt something stinging around his eyes: he was crying. The water drummed against his face, his ears, the back of his calves, his slimy feet.

This would be good for the athlete's foot. Or maybe not: you should dry out fungus, not get it wet. He didn't move. The pounding water felt primally good, like a reward, and he stood under it for a long time, head lowered, letting the water thud onto his neck and shoulders, turning back and forth, offering himself to it, as if the stream could carry everything away.

He turned off the water, got out, and stood on the thin mat. He began to dry himself, rubbing hard. It felt good. There was no sand. He kept expecting to find it in creases, armpits, balls, ass. Behind his knees. No sand.

The thing was that he couldn't see where he was going. It was like heading toward a dam. He couldn't see past it, over the edge. All he could see was air, though he knew about the drop. He was waiting for something to click into place. In the military you had orders, and a task. Now what he had to do was keep moving. Without orders or a task.

He thought of calling Claire, but couldn't imagine the conversation. He'd call later. This was something else he had to figure out, besides what he was going to do with his life. He wasn't sure how to talk to her now. Now that she'd semi–blown him off. Not entirely, of course, Claire was too nice to blow him completely off while he was in-country. She'd gone on writing, but everything had changed, and now he didn't know what tone to take or how they were meant to talk, or if they were supposed to talk at all. Or if she had another boyfriend, which she never mentioned, and which she clearly did not want to discuss before he came home, and which he certainly had not wanted to know about. The thought depressed him.

He went back into the bedroom and dropped down onto the deck, the carpet rough beneath his hands and feet. He did fifty push-ups, fast, his arms pumping up and down, trying for speed. He was determined to stay fit. He kept his face forward, gaze focused, body rigid, arms flexing and straightening, as though he were doing PT. He counted in a loud whisper. What he wanted to do was yell out the numbers at the top of his voice, like during PT. *One! Two! Three!* Everyone rising and falling together, thundering out the words.

When he'd finished he felt better, as though he'd paid off something, shaved a piece off a debt. He thought again of calling Claire. He'd do it after dinner. He didn't want to start the conversation now.

The civilian clothes felt weightless and flimsy, like a costume. This was not real life. It was unnatural not to put on anything more: no flak jacket, kneepads, holster. No CamelBak over his shoulder, no grenades at his belt, no tourniquet. When he left the room, stepping into the hallway, he felt unarmed. Lightweight, useless, walking down the hall in the flimsy pants, as if he were in disguise.

The restaurant was a long, high-ceilinged room. On one side was a wall of plate-glass windows looking toward the beach. The tables were full, and when Conrad and his parents pushed through the heavy doors, the noise closed around them, loud and shrill. Conrad felt his chest draw tight. There were too many people in the room, and too much noise.

They stood at the high front counter, waiting. A young blond woman came over, wearing tight capri pants and white jazz sneakers.

Her hair was pulled back in a wispy ponytail that nodded jauntily when she moved. She gave them a wide, empty smile.

"Three? Follow me, please." Holding big menus, she led them through the crowded room. She rose a little with each step, as though the white sneakers held springs. The ponytail bounced. She stopped at a big round table in the center of the room.

"Here you are," she said.

"Do you have anything smaller?" asked Marshall. "We're only three. This looks like it would hold ten."

The waitress shook her head. "I'm sorry, this is the only table available."

"We did ask for a table for three," Marshall said.

"I'm really sorry, sir." The waitress smiled without apology. There were crow's-feet around her eyes: she was older than she'd looked. Was everyone in Southern California an actor, or was that a myth? "This is all we have. We're really busy."

Marshall looked around the room; Lydia spoke.

"Never mind," she said, "we'll take this. Thank you."

They sat down, widely separated. The waitress dealt out the menus like cards and left, ponytail bobbing.

Lydia cupped her mouth and called, "We'll just have to shout!"

Conrad smiled but did not answer. He hated this.

They were in the dead center of the room, full tables around them in every direction. On one side a wall of breakable glass gave onto a public thoroughfare. Behind him, double swinging doors led to the kitchen, where people pushed back and forth. He didn't like being in the middle of the room. He didn't like having his back to the swinging doors, and he didn't like people suddenly appearing behind him. He didn't like the big plate-glass windows giving onto the beach just beyond them, strangers walking past carrying bags. Conrad began to sweat.

He opened his menu. The name of the restaurant was spelled out across the top in elaborate gold letters. *Italia del Mar.*

At the next table was a group in their forties, with bright clothes, big hair, loud voices. The nearest man was balding and dark-skinned, his open collar showing a nest of black hair. His rosy shirt rose loosely over his swelling belly. He leaned forward in his chair.

"No, she didn't!" he shouted. "She never tells me! That's her little secret!"

The others screamed with laughter.

The woman beside him was deeply tanned, with thick black hair, big glittering blue earrings. She waved her hands. Her crimson fingernails were like talons.

"He never listens!" she shouted back. "How would he know if I told him or not?"

They were all screaming, screaming and laughing, like demons. All around him was the clinking of glasses, silverware, crockery. The room was dense with noise. Waitresses and busboys hurried between the tables, behind his back, carrying trays. A pulse started in Conrad's head.

"What are your thoughts, Con?" asked Marshall.

About this place? Conrad looked up, but Marshall was holding his menu. The waitress stood beside him. His father was asking about food.

Conrad cleared his throat. "Veal parmigiana," he said at random.

The waitress didn't move.

"Ah," Marshall said. "Did you see that on the menu? I think they just have seafood."

"Oh, sorry." Conrad looked down. "Right. Scampi."

When the waitress had gone, Lydia drank from her water glass and looked at him.

"So, Con," she said, "how are you really?"

He looked at her. His father, too, was waiting.

But it was impossible to drag the whole lumbering world of Iraq—hot, smoky, contaminated, the fucking sand, and the sound, that terrible enveloping sound that filled the world—to this table. None of it was transferable. The sound of mortars. The foul black smell of the shitters. Setting out through the narrow streets of Haditha. Waiting for the sound, the giant earth-stopping sound of explosion. The screen you put between yourself and the rest of the world. He had no words for this; there was no bridge between that place and this.

"Glad to be back," he said, and smiled.

4

The difference between a cult and a religion depends on what's being worshipped. It's a question of whether or not the object is divine, and whether or not the worship is excessive. But the definition of divinity is subjective, so the answer will depend on who you ask. Zoroastrians or Jews, for example, might consider Christianity a cult. Civilians might consider the Marine Corps a cult. But true believers know that what they follow is a religion.

Becoming an initiate into anything involves instruction, ceremony, belief. It means yielding certain personal freedoms in exchange for the power, knowledge, privileges, and protection offered by the group.

The city-state of Sparta, in ancient Greece, was organized around the premise of military supremacy. All its components—religion, law, education, the family unit—were part of a system that held the military paramount. The warrior, with his lethal and seductive glamour, reigned supreme. Sparta was the dominant military presence in Magna Graecia for some three hundred years, from around 650 B.C. to 350 B.C. It then lost its dominance but remained independent for another two hundred years, until it was finally conquered by Rome. When Conrad studied Sparta, in his classics courses, he realized it had lasted as a country far longer than the United States.

Conrad wrote his senior thesis on Sparta. He was interested in the extreme demands the military put on the society, how the society responded to those strains, and how to define "extreme."

All Spartan citizens were full-time soldiers. Citizenship was limited to male descendants of Sparta's founders, but only healthy ones. Selection began at birth: male babies were examined by a council of elders, and imperfect and weak infants were abandoned to die of exposure on a mountaintop. Healthy boys lived at home until the age of seven, when they left to start training—the *agoge*. For the next ten years they lived in communal messes where they studied reading, writing, music, and dancing, but primarily military subjects.

Conditions in the *agoge* were deliberately harsh in order to toughen the young warriors. Each boy was given only one piece of clothing a year, a cloak. To make them resourceful, the boys were underfed. They had to steal food to survive, though if they were caught, they were punished. The physical training was demanding. They were trained to fight in phalanx formation: closely linked, shield over chest, sword in hand. They marched so closely that each soldier's shield partly protected the man to his left. This was part of what created such a powerful bond of loyalty and trust between them; also, each young soldier had a close relationship with an older mentor, who acted as his adviser and guide.

Every aspect of their lives was affected. The trainees were expected to speak like soldiers, to be terse and witty: the word "laconic" comes from *laconia*, a Greek word for the region of Sparta.

At eighteen Spartans graduated from the *agoge*. At twenty they became members of one of the *syssitia*, military messes or dining clubs, and it was here that they formed their closest personal bonds. They remained full-time soldiers until the age of thirty, and until the age of sixty they were active reservists. At thirty they were required to marry, and they left the messes to live with their wives and children. The system, with its intense focus on military training, produced legendary warriors who were fiercely loyal to their fellow soldiers and their country.

The business of Sparta was war, and all else was subjugated to that. Since its citizens were full-time soldiers, all other business was transacted by noncitizens. Manual labor was performed by Helots—state-owned slaves who were often captured soldiers and their families, brought back from foreign wars. Sparta's economy was primarily agricultural, and the Helots did the farming, living in small outlying villages. Relations between the two groups were hostile: Spartans were suspicious of the slaves, and in order to prevent mutinous stirrings, Helots were routinely mocked and beaten, to crush their spirits.

Sparta was governed by two hereditary king-priests, as well as magistrates, or ephors. The ephors took office each year, and at that time the state declared a ritual war against its Helots. The act of murder was a serious offense, carrying the burden of blood guilt, but killing a Helot was not considered murder. Helots could be killed with impunity.

The ritual war took place in the autumn. At that time, certain graduates of the *agoge* were chosen for a secret rite called the *krypteia*. These soldiers were sent out at night, armed only with knives, into the Helot villages. Their mission was to stalk and kill any Helots they thought troublesome.

The political purpose of the *krypteia* was to suppress the possibility of revolt: the young warriors on their nocturnal raids struck terror into the Helot community, like members of a secret police squad. But for the soldiers it had another, darker function: the *krypteia* legitimized the kill. It gave the soldiers moral permission from the state, the church, and their comrades to step outside the bounds of humanity. It broke down the psychological restraints against murder.

Humans have a powerful and innate resistance to killing other humans. Something in the heart curdles at the prospect. The sound of screams, the sight of blood, the evidence of pain: all arouse an urgent need to quit. The human recognizes itself in the other. Within the military, this deep empathetic response causes profound problems. To be effective soldiers, men must be persuaded to kill other men. They must be persuaded to give up their recognition of another man's humanity.

There are different ways of persuasion. One strategy is to dehumanize the enemy, making his death seem less significant. Helots were ideal for this dehumanizing, since they were both foreigners and enemies. They lived separately from the Spartans and often spoke different languages. Their work was demeaning. They were beaten and ridiculed. On occasion they were forced to get drunk, and then to sing and dance to amuse the crowd. They were treated as less than human, which made them perfect targets for homicide. Moreover, since Helots were forbidden to carry weapons, these first kills would be easy ones.

All this was invaluable battlefield training: no other city-states offered practice killings. Only certain warriors were selected for the ritual, which gave the *krypteia* a glamorous elitist luster. The dark, bloody bond, forged in secrecy and violence, strengthened the brotherhood between soldiers. It offered a shared sense of godlike power, the belief that they were above the laws of man and of human nature.

Sparta was an unparalleled success as a military power. Its soldiers were legendary heroes: it was Sparta that brought down Troy. It may have been the most successful warrior culture in history.

Part of Sparta's military success depended on its treatment of the family, which was entirely subordinate to the state. The state superseded the authority of parents over their infant children, ordered small boys to leave home, required close male bonding, and banned marriage for men under the age of thirty. The state was a deeply and intimately invasive presence within every aspect of the life of the individual.

The reasons for Sparta's failure were the same as the reasons for its success: everything was subordinated to the military. The stringently exclusionary citizenship requirements meant that Spartans could not replace the warriors whom they lost in battle. The requirement to wait until thirty to start a family meant fewer children and a diminishing population. Since they could not accept non-Spartans as citizens, eventually their ranks became too diminished to fight effectively. The soldiers were outnumbered by their Helots, who were allowed neither to fight nor to become citizens. Sparta's rigidity in obeying its own strict laws was finally the cause of its downfall.

So, wrote Conrad, *do we count them a success or a failure?*

His own initiation took place at Quantico, in Virginia. Officer Candidates School lasted only ten weeks, but in some ways it was just as transformative as the *agoge.* And in some ways the Marine culture was based on that of Sparta.

Conrad expected the physical duress, push-ups and drilling, exhaustion. And the mental tedium, the psychological stress. That was the point, wasn't it? It was a kind of brainwashing, a relentless conditioning process meant to break you down, devalue everything you were so that you could start over with a new body and a new way of looking at the world. A new mind. It was obvious what was happening, but because it was so extreme, and because there was no alternative, it was completely effective. Everything happened right in front of the candidates' eyes, with their acquiescence. There was nothing they could do about it except quit, and the whole reason they were there was that they would not quit, that they were prepared to endure.

On the first day, when the new recruits boarded the shabby white bus that would take them from the airport to Quantico, a young second lieutenant stood up and came down the aisle. He set his gaze into the distance and began to shout over the noise of the engine. There was no preamble.

"Honor, courage, and commitment are the Marine Corps values," he called out. "If you can't be honest at OCS, how can the Corps trust you to lead men in combat?"

No one answered. No one had any idea of what to say. No one their age in the civilian world talked like that. Popular culture was driven by irony; the Marine Corps was driven by earnestness. By belief. It had something to do with the fact that Marines stood so straight that their shirts had no wrinkles. That their gaze was so fixed.

At Quantico, they lost everything.

The first to go was appearance: they lost their faces. Not really their faces, only their hair, but the change was so extreme it seemed to affect their faces. Conrad saw himself in the mirror after his hair was gone: without the face he knew, he felt vulnerable and strange.

Everything familiar was taken away. The candidates became objects of derision and contempt, and so did their families, their backgrounds, their education, any source of pride they might have had. Mockery and abuse were the tools.

Once, the sergeant stopped dead in front of Conrad, who stared past him, his hands rigid at his sides. The instructor folded his arms and glared, rage leaking upward.

"Candidate, you're nothing but a skinny piece of trash, you know that?"

There was no swearing at Quantico, and no physical contact—lawsuits had ended those. But the instructors were still ferocious.

"Yes, Sergeant Instructor!" Conrad shouted.

"How the frig do you think you're going to pass this course, candidate?"

"I don't know, Sergeant Instructor!" Conrad bellowed back. Big mistake: he'd used the personal pronoun. He should have said *This candidate* instead of *I.*

"'You' don't know? You?" the sergeant roared. *"Who the heck are 'you,' candidate?"* He stuck his face right into Conrad's. A big vein in the side of his neck moved under the skin like a snake. *"You think you're some kind of special piece of lowlife trash?"*

His face closed in under the hat brim, his nose nearly touching Conrad's. A gob of spit landed on Conrad's eyelashes, and Conrad blinked instinctively and met the sergeant's eyes for an instant.

"Get your eyeballs off me, candidate!" he screamed. *"What the fug are you looking at?"*

"Nothing, Sergeant Instructor!" Conrad screamed back, his eyes now on the barracks wall.

"Are you looking at me, candidate? Why are you looking at me? Are you in love with me? Do you want to date me, candidate?"

"No, Sergeant Instructor!" Conrad screamed.

"Don't you ever, ever look at me, candidate. I'll make you sorry you were born. I'll make your miserable self into grass. I know what you're like, candidate. I can see right through you. Do you think I want a nasty piece of trash like you in my beloved Marine Corps?"

"No, Sergeant Instructor!" Conrad shouted.

The contempt from the instructors aroused a kind of answering rage. In fact, during training, rage was the ruling emotion. It was always present, though the level ranged from simmering resentment to throat-choking fury.

They had to yell their responses, which meant an investment of energy. The word they had to yell most was "Kill!" They yelled that all the time—on their way to meals, when an instructor walked into a classroom, and when they drew their chairs out to sit down. At first they focused only on volume. Later, when they were more confident, they concentrated on gusto, zest.

One day in the barracks the instructor went after a candidate named Thomas. They were lined up in front of their racks, which was what they called beds. He'd been not quite fast enough in lining his bare feet up along the painted line on the floor. The instructor came over and stood in front of him.

His face red and swollen, he yelled, "What the fug is wrong with you, candidate? How long do you think you have to obey my order?"

"I'm sorry, Sergeant Instructor!" shouted Thomas.

"Sorry isn't enough," yelled the instructor. "You think that's all you have to do? Say you're sorry? You think you can get into the Marine Corps by saying you're sorry?"

"No, Sergeant Instructor!" shouted Thomas.

There was a silence. The instructor folded his arms on his chest and stared at Thomas.

"What the heck is wrong with you, candidate? You still dreaming of having sex with those sheep on the farm at home? Is that what you're thinking of?"

In fact, Thomas had come from a farm somewhere in Ohio. He stood still, staring straight ahead, but a deep red began to stain his neck, rising up to his face.

"No, Sergeant Instructor," he yelled.

"This is no place for sheep lovers, candidate!" yelled the instructor. "Do you have sex with sheep?"

"No, Sergeant Instructor!" yelled Thomas. His face had turned a deep brilliant red. The thought of it was in everyone's mind now. You couldn't help but wonder why this was so painful for Thomas. Had he actually ever fucked a sheep? It was an interesting idea. But they didn't have sheep anymore on those mega-farms in the Midwest, did they? Only two hundred miles of corn.

The drill instructor went on yelling, now about Thomas's sexual activities with other farm animals.

"Maybe it was a cow, candidate. Maybe you're dreaming about a cow."

Thomas was glowing with red. They were all trapped at attention, arms at their sides, eyes straight ahead. All of them were watching Thomas with their peripheral vision.

"No, Sergeant Instructor!"

The instructor unfolded his arms. "Then maybe it's your parents who are dreaming, candidate. Maybe you're thinking about your mother and that horse!"

Thomas stood rigid, arms at his side, head erect. *"Shut the fuck up, Sergeant Instructor!"* he screamed. *"Leave my mother out of this!"*

The instructor's face went dark. He threw himself into Thomas's face, almost touching him. Thomas threw himself backward against his rack. His head made a clanging sound against it. What the instructor wanted to do was kill Thomas with his bare hands; everyone could feel it. He leaned into Thomas's face and shouted at him.

"What the fug did you say to me?" he screamed, so loud and with such an explosion of violence that it seemed that he'd kill Thomas just with his voice.

The rest of them, motionless and silent, watching with their peripheral vision, were all part of this. Secretly they took both sides. They reveled in Thomas's throttling rush of adrenaline, his brave and suicidal rebellion, but they also reveled in the awful excitement of the instructor's swollen face pressed so close to Thomas, Thomas pressed against the rack.

The instructor did not kill him, but Thomas did push-ups out on the deck for most of the night. Somehow the rest of them felt as though he had been killed, as though they'd watched it. Been in on the final, slavering moments. There was no call to civility or reason. Conrad thought of that later, that no one in charge insisted on restraint. There was no sense of restraint. When the instructor lunged at Thomas, there was no sense of limits.

They lived in the barracks, a nondescript two-story brick building with rows of bunks under a low ceiling. They marched for hours at a time. They drilled on the drill deck, a huge flat rectangle of trampled earth. They learned to call cadence, the singsong marching rhythms in which the leader lays out a line and the others respond.

Born in the woods, born in the woods,
Raised by a bear, raised by a bear.
Double set of sharks' teeth, triple set of hair.
I'm lean and mean, I got my M16, I'm a U.S. Marine.

The cadence song dates back to an evening in 1944 at Fort Slocum, when a black soldier named Duckworth began a call-and-response chant with his tired fellow soldiers as they marched back to base. Spirits rose, marching became unified, and the cadence song was born. The first ones were made up of numbers, but soon they became narratives and spread quickly through American military culture.

The song, with its call-and-response form and stereotypical characters, derives from black culture. It harks back to secretly subversive work songs sung by slaves, and later by black prisoners toiling at prison farms. But the subversion in the Marine songs is deliberate and outspoken. It's not directed at the Marines' masters, but at their old civilian lives and all their values.

There were cadence calls about everything, and if *The Marine Officer's Guide* was the official source of Marine culture, cadence calls were the unofficial source. Some of the calls were about the home front and a stock character called Jody. Jody was the sneaking, lying rat who'd steal your girlfriend or your wife and your car as soon as you were out the door. Suzy Rottencrotch was the girlfriend who'd betray you before you even climbed onto the bus, who fucked everyone she knew the second your back was turned. You hated her, and you hated Jody. These calls told the candidates not to trust civilians. According to the calls, there was no one a Marine could trust except another Marine.

Some of the calls praised the Marines and some trashed the other services.

I don't know, but it's been said
Air Force wings are made of lead.

One afternoon they marched along a dirt road beside a swamp. The air was sultry and hot. Mosquitoes drilled into Conrad's face and hands as he marched along, and sweat inched its way down his forehead into his eyes. It was the first time he'd heard the napalm song.

Gather kids as you fly over town,
By throwing candy on the ground,
Then grease 'em when they gather 'round,
Napalm sticks to kids!
Napalm sticks to kids,

French-fried eyeballs and baby ribs—
Marine Corps!

Burn the town and kill the people
Throw some napalm in the square
Do it on a Sunday morning,
While the people are at prayer
Throw some candy in the schoolyard
Watch the kiddies gather 'round
Slap a mag in your M16
And mow those little fuckers down.

They marched in a long double line, boots thudding in the soft dirt, voices chanting in rhythm. They sang things together they would never say alone, in a speaking voice.

Go to the market where the women shop.
Get out my machete and I start to chop.
Go to the park where the children play.
Get out my machine gun I begin to spray.

One day in class, an instructor walked up and down at the front of the room. The classroom was large and bare, and the candidates sat at desks that descended in tiers to a platform at the bottom.

The instructor that day was short, with a big chest, grizzled hair, and a gap between his front teeth. He talked about the rules of engagement that governed military behavior during combat. The ROEs changed according to conditions, varying from engagement to engagement. Fighting a uniformed military unit on a battlefield was very different from fighting nonuniformed insurgents in a city. But fundamentally, the ROEs defined a military code of honor: targets were to be clearly identified as the enemy and clearly engaging in hostile activity. Civilians were not to be targeted for lethal fire.

Conrad wrote this down in his notebook.

The notebooks they were issued were small and cheap, hinged at the top with a metal spiral. The paper was greenish white, with wide horizontal lines and one vertical line down the middle. He had to ignore the vertical line when he took notes, writing across it. While he wrote down the part about not targeting civilians for lethal fire, Conrad thought about the napalm song, but he said nothing about it, nor did anyone else. The napalm song and the ROEs about civilians were like dinosaurs and Christianity: they seemed mutually exclusive, but somehow you could believe in them both.

5

Conrad aimed his seabag ahead of him, up the steep back stairs. The bag itself nearly filled the stairwell, and he went slowly, walking diagonally on the narrow steps. At the landing he turned, heading up the next flight to the third floor.

While he was growing up, Conrad had shared a room with Ollie. They'd been on the second floor, with Jenny and their parents. But at the age of fourteen he'd asked for his own room, and he'd moved up, alone, onto the third floor. There he had the larger of the two bedrooms and his own bathroom. The third floor was his territory.

It was May 2006, and he was home. He was through EAS, the end of active service, home for good. He stood in the doorway. Nothing had changed: His room, tucked under the roof, was long and narrow, with a low ceiling and slanting eaves along one side. At the far end, two small arched windows gave onto the willow trees. Two single beds, with mismatched iron bedsteads and sagging tan spreads, stood against the wall. Between them, on a table, was a big copper lamp, the yellowing shade still crooked, ever since he and Roddy Blodgett had knocked it over, wrestling. In the corner was the small leather-topped desk that had been his father's as a child, where Conrad had never sat doing his homework. Facing the beds was the tall, battered bureau. The top was crowded with sports trophies, tiny gold-colored figures in heroic poses, standing on plastic plinths. There were the photographs: Conrad wearing his dress blues at his induction; Conrad and Pam Outerbury (not his girlfriend) at the high school prom. Conrad at the end of a ski race, grinning, his poles raised in triumph. On the walls were tattered band posters and a large, blurry color photograph, overexposed, of the huge amphitheater at Ephesus.

On either side of the doorway stood tall bookcases, crammed with his people. Tacitus, Ovid, Homer. Pliny and Seneca. Thucydides. Marsilius. He could feel their voices, the presence of that ancient, dusty, sunlit world. The clamor of swords.

He was surrounded by his earlier life. Outside was the dirt road where he'd ridden his bike up and down in seventh grade, doing wheelies and wiping out. In this house he'd called girls for the first time, he'd hidden porn magazines and jacked off. Here, downstairs in the kitchen, he'd argued with his father, shouting, slamming the refrigerator door so hard the shelf inside broke, and when he opened the door, the mayonnaise jar fell out and shattered greasily on the floor. Here he'd stayed up late reading, surrounded by silence. This was the house from where he'd entered the world.

It was strange to know that everything was now in the past. He couldn't change anything. The fact that he was back here where he'd started made it feel almost as if he could choose to start over, undo things.

He remembered going downstairs that morning, to tell his parents he was joining the Corps. He remembered their alarm and his excitement. The more concern they showed, the more elation he felt. He'd thought he'd made a brilliant maneuver. He'd believed that he'd outsmarted the system, that he was about to enter the adult world through a secret door.

Conrad moved to the bureau, looking at the photographs. There was his induction, which had taken place at college, in the library. His parents behind him, smiling, their eyes on him. He stood waiting to receive the ornate Mameluke sword, the symbol of the Marines' campaign in Tripoli; he remembered the surprising weight on his outstretched arms.

That photograph was the only link between the person who'd lived in this room and the person he'd become. There was the time before it and the time after it, no connection between the two. There were two pasts, the past of his childhood and the past he'd just come from. The recent one seemed, here, not like the real past, but some dreamed state. Or maybe this was the dream. They had no connection. He was the connection, but he felt like someone different now.

He set his duffel on the bed and began to unpack, shirts and khakis, cammies, things from the last four years. He opened a bureau drawer to put his clothes away, but it was full of neatly piled sweaters. The next was full, too. They all were, the whole bureau overflowing with the clothes from his other life, clean, preserved, as though ready for him to slide back into them. He looked in the closet: it was full, too. There was nowhere to put what he had brought, the clothes of his current life, and he felt a sudden red pulse of irritation. More than that: rage. He had arrived home, and there was no room for him.

Standing still, the clothes in his hands, he saw himself in the dim mirror—his angry face, the knitted eyebrows, tight mouth, a dark line of vein running up his neck. Behind him, on the wall, was a Led Zeppelin poster, ripped halfway up and mended with yellowing tape. A furious Marine, standing in a kid's room: he was embarassed at himself.

He took everything from his duffel and set it out in piles on the second bed. He folded the empty bag and put it in the closet. Tomorrow he'd go through all his clothes and decide what to keep. What he was going to do right now was stay in control. He got down on the rug and did fifty, fast, pushing off against his hands, thrusting himself upward on the count, his body rising and falling. He whispered the numbers, hissing them fast and loud. When he was finished, he did fifty more.

After that he checked his email—messages from some of the men who were out, home: Molinos, Jackson, Anderson. They were just checking in, *Hey LT,* but it gave him a lift to see their names, to answer, to feel the network still there.

As he went downstairs for dinner, his spirits rose. He thudded fast down the steep, narrow stairs, grabbing the railings and making them creak from his weight, swinging down the last few steps as he'd always done.

The stairs led abruptly to the little ell off the kitchen, the breakfast room. It was small and square, with three windows, side by side, overlooking the back garden. Against the wall stood an old maple table, polished to a warm honey color, and six blond bentwood chairs. On one wall hung a bright patchwork quilt; across from it was a pastel, by Jenny in first grade, of the animals' Christmas tree. Beside that was a bulletin board jammed with cards, messages, a big calendar. Beneath the bulletin board stood a narrow black oak drop-leaf table, holding the telephone. Conrad's parents still had a landline. All this raised Conrad's spirits: the clumsy phone on the table beside a small pad of paper, his mother's battered address book, and an old marmalade jar full of pointless pencils and inkless pens. It was exactly as it always had been, which cheered him.

Around the corner, through a wide archway, was the kitchen proper. Against the back wall was the massive no-nonsense black stove, with red knobs and a broiler that sounded like a car factory. A big butcher-block work island stood in the middle of the room, over it two hanging lamps with translucent green glass shades.

Lydia stood at the stove. She turned to smile at him. "You're down? Okay, we're on," she said, then called, "Marsh?"

Marshall appeared in the doorway from the library, a folded newspaper in his hand. His hair had fallen across his face, and his shirt was rumpled. In the evenings he changed out of his business suit into corduroy pants or khakis, a polo shirt.

Lydia turned from the stove, holding a heavy iron skillet with both hands, using quilted pot holders. "Hot," she said. "Look out." She set the skillet down on the island beside two blue enamel pots, a wooden bowl of salad, and the small stack of their three plates. The hanging lamps cast a mild glow on it all: the deep blue pots, the rough black skillet with the sizzling brown lamb chops, the heavy white ceramic plates, flecked and rimmed with blue. The one on top was chipped. All this was familiar: the black stove, the scarred butcher block, the hanging green lamps. The chipped plate, all of it. Everything was deeply known: the kitchen was part of him. This was both comforting and painful.

Conrad picked up his plate. "So. It's good to be back," he said.

Lydia put her hands on her hips. She was wearing a white shirt, open at the neck. She smiled, pursing her mouth in a tiny, teasing way.

"Really," Lydia said. "You think so?"

The thought came to him that his mother would forgive him anything.

"Make yourself a plate," Lydia said. She handed him the top one, chipped.

The table in the breakfast room was set with the blue quilted mats, the dark blue water glasses, the polished brass candlesticks. Murphy had arrived, as she did at mealtimes, and stretched herself out along the windowsill. She was not allowed on the table, and so pretended that the sill, one inch away from it, was neutral territory. Lydia dimmed the hanging lamp over the table. Marshall lit the candles, little liquid flickers of light. Evening had set in, and the light inside made the windows suddenly black.

"So," said Marshall, unfolding his napkin. "Con. What can you tell us about Haditha? I've read what I could, but there isn't a lot. What can you tell us?"

"It's a small town on the Euphrates," Conrad began.

The Euphrates River rises in the highlands of eastern Turkey and meanders south through a mountain range, then crosses into Syria. It winds in an easterly direction before crossing into Iraq, and there the river flows southeast, running roughly parallel with the great Tigris River, which lies to its north. Between the two rivers, as they approach each other, lies the Fertile Crescent, which has been called the cradle of civilization. Fortunate in climate, terrain, and soil, it is believed by some to be the actual Garden of Eden. Below Baghdad the rivers join, forming a rich alluvial plain before they flow, together, into the Persian Gulf. Mesopotamia, which was the name of Iraq up until World War I, means "Land Between the Rivers."

The Fertile Crescent offered one of the most benevolent landscapes on earth, and it has been settled for at least six thousand years. During the Bronze Age the inhabitants produced sophisticated weapons, intricate jewelry, and beautiful ceramics. The Sumerians, who settled the region around 4000 B.C., were believed to have established the earliest civilization in the world. During the Roman Empire, the Euphrates River was the eastern border of the Roman occupation.

But before that, before humans arrived, the region through which the Euphrates wandered was rich with life. The banks were once lined by riverine forests, plane trees, and Euphrates poplar, tamarisk, and ash. In the wooded Syrian steppes there were long-legged gazelles and onagers, ostriches, wild boars, gray wolves, golden jackals, and red foxes. In the alluvial plain near the Persian Gulf stalked the great predators: leopards and lions. As late as the nineteenth century, European travelers in the Syrian basin reported a rich tapestry of wildlife. The arrival of humans, with their grazing herds, their habits of plowing and reaping, their insatiable need for firewood, meant the destruction of the riverine forests, and most of the animals vanished.

Haditha lay on the western bank of the river, in western Iraq, not far from the Syrian border. It was a quiet agricultural town, with schools and mosques, a market, a hospital, a morgue. At the north end was a small commercial section, but most of the town was residential and most of the inhabitants were involved with farming of some sort.

To the west, toward Syria, the land was desert steppe, but along the river it was fertile, and a patchwork of irrigated fields and orchards ran along the banks. In the fields were herds of grazing sheep and goats, and fruit orchards. Along the water were groves of date palms. Haditha was famous for dates, and in the market there were stalls that sold only this delicacy. They were piled in baskets, honey-colored, mahogany, coppery; fresh and dried, long and heavy or short and light, dense, and almost suffocatingly sweet. In the vegetable stalls were piles of gleaming eggplants, beans, cucumbers, peppers, tomatoes, figs, mounds of apples and sunny apricots. Fresh fish and crab from the river.

Before the American invasion, Haditha had been a resort. Iraqis went there during the stifling heat of the summer to stay among the fruit orchards and palm groves that stretched along the wide blue river. The streets of Haditha were narrow, and the low houses were made of stone, or stucco painted in pastel colors.

Along the banks were the sites of ancient settlements, Kassite and Parthian and Aquilian, remains of houses and temples. The region had been inhabited during the time of the Roman Empire, though no one was sure if the Romans had been in Haditha itself. Traces of ancient waterwheels and aqueducts suggested an early water transportation system, but no one knew whether the water had been sent to Rome or merely to the wide fields flanking the river.

Haditha was Sunni.

The Sunnis and the Shias had split apart centuries earlier over the question of Muhammad's successor. The division had become one of class as well as religion; in Iraq, Sunnis were the ruling class, richer and more powerful than the Shias. Saddam Hussein and his tribal family were Sunni. The western province of Anbar, where Haditha was located, was a Sunni stronghold.

To understand what had happened in Haditha, you first had to understand what had happened in Fallujah. When the American invasion, called OIF, Operation Iraqi Freedom, took place in 2003, American forces arrived in the Sunni city of Fallujah. This was downriver from Ramadi and closer to Baghdad. At the time of the invasion, Fallujah was relatively peaceful, and it welcomed the U.S. forces, which would maintain order after the fall of Saddam. An Iraqi governing council was established, allied with the American forces; the U.S. Army set up bases outside the city; and an equitable relationship was established.

Then, without consultation, the Army moved into the center of the city. It took over a school building, evicting the occupants and setting up an observation post on its highest floor. This was tantamount to an invasion: Muslim lands are considered sacred ground, and the American infidels had invaded their allies' city without permission. This outraged the Fallujans, as it violated the religious mores of the community and meant a breach of trust with their allies. Worse, the observation post enabled Army soldiers to look down into the private gardens, where Muslim women walked about freely, without veils or scarves. The privacy of Muslim women was jealously guarded, and this breach was considered a deep insult to the men of the community.

Moreover, since the Sunni community had lost power after the American invasion, there were factions within the city that did not welcome the American presence, despite the official response. A group of protesters broke curfew and marched on the school, demanding a response. Instead of sending out a representative, the Army made announcements over the loudspeakers, which did nothing to calm the crowd. It shouted back at the barricaded soldiers; and frustrated people began to throw rocks at the building. Faced with an angry and unpredictable crowd, the Army responded with automatic weapons. Soldiers killed an undetermined number of unarmed people (claims ranged from two to seventeen), wounding nearly sixty. Two days later, three more unarmed protesters were shot and killed by American troops.

Iraq is a tribal country, where kinship ties are powerful and permanent. This network runs strong and deep through every community, every relationship and transaction and marriage, running back into the past for centuries. Every person killed or wounded at Fallujah had friends and relatives, and that evening all of them became sworn enemies of the American forces. In one stroke the Army had set off a wildfire of hatred. From then on it blazed throughout the region, leaping from family to family as the story was told.

What had initially been a quiet community became a hotbed of hostility, composed of deadly enemies of the American occupation. Fallujah had turned, and the insurgency movement used this as a rallying cry for the jihad, the war against the infidel. Insurgents from all over flocked to Fallujah to carry on the resistance against the invaders.

The Army did little to dispel the tensions it had created, and a year later, four Blackwater employees were captured by insurgents. They were beaten, set on fire, and hanged. Their mutilated bodies were paraded through the city.

The Marine commander on the ground in Iraq recommended a strategic response. He advised a surgical strike, targeting only the kidnappers. His advice was ignored. A written directive was sent from the Joint Chiefs of Staff, possibly from the White House itself: they wanted a firefight.

If the Marines are the surgical tool of war, the scalpel, the Army is the blunt instrument, the sledgehammer.

In April 2004, American forces mounted an offensive against Fallujah, using bombs and heavy artillery. The strike was meant to be swift and overwhelming, short-lasting—a campaign of shock and awe—but things didn't go as planned. As the Marines say, "No plan survives contact with the enemy." The insurgents responded ferociously and refused to yield. After four days of fighting, U.S. forces had managed to gain control of only one quarter of the city. Moreover, they were coming under intense criticism from their own local ally, the Iraqi governing council.

Bombs and artillery meant heavy civilian casualties. In order to eliminate a single sniper, whole buildings were blown apart. As insurgents moved from house to house, entire neighborhoods were turned to rubble by Hellfire missiles and Spectre gunship rounds and five-hundred-pound Paveway bombs. There was nowhere to take the wounded, as the U.S. forces had ordered the hospitals to close down during the attack. The governing council vehemently protested the fact that their allies were killing their citizens. Moreover, the council accused U.S. forces of using white phosphorus, a substance that had been internationally banned as a weapon.

White phosphorus is a chemical compound that works more or less like napalm. It eats flesh, burning it away from the bones. In Fallujah, bodies were found with the peeling flesh and extensive burn patterns characteristic of white phosphorus.

At first U.S. officials denied using it, but then military reports were discovered that described "shake-and-bake" missions. These cited the effectiveness of white phosphorus, used as an incendiary that creates a blinding white flash and clouds of smoke. It was used on insurgents in hiding, to drive them out into the open, where high explosives were used to finish them off. After these reports became public, U.S. officials stopped commenting on the subject.

The United States had not signed the agreement that altogether banned the use of white phosphorus, which was a legitimate military tool as an illuminant and an obscurant. Later, the Army claimed that it had used WP only for strategic purposes, and that the burns and deaths had been inadvertent. The term "shake-and-bake" was not mentioned.

After six days of battle, in the face of steadfast resistance from the insurgents and growing criticism from its allies, the Army declared a cease-fire. On May 1 it withdrew, turning over official control of the city to the Fallujah Brigade. This was a local militia group that, in theory, supported the American occupiers but in fact refused to confront the insurgents. Wearing Iraqi uniforms that identified their true loyalties, the brigade members briefly manned the checkpoints, then quit the conflict altogether. The city fell entirely under the control of the insurgents. These were by now a mixture of Sunni loyalists, religious fundamentalists outraged by the Army presence, local warlords who were quick to seize a strategic opportunity, and anyone else incensed by the killings of unarmed protesters.

The U.S. command found this situation unacceptable, and in November 2004 it launched Operation Phantom Fury. This consisted of ten thousand U.S. troops mounting a full-scale attack on the city of Fallujah. The force included Marines drawn from bases elsewhere in the region, among them Haditha.

Before the battle, women, children, and the elderly were advised to leave the city; thousands of them did so. Some civilians, as well as the hard-core mujahideen, remained. The battle was long and bloody. The Marines fought bravely, house to house, moving slowly through the city. More than a thousand insurgents were killed, and the rest fled.

Technically, the battle ended in a U.S. victory, but the city of Fallujah was left in ruins. Some 250,000 people had fled, and about half the houses in the city had been destroyed. Of the civilians who stayed, about six hundred had been killed. This meant another explosion of hatred: the tribal families of casualties and homeless refugees also became blood enemies of the Americans. The insurgents who died in battle became martyrs and heroes. The jihad blossomed. The battle of Fallujah became a rallying cry among the mujahideen.

The Marines understood the consequences very well. Later, an officer at Pendleton told Conrad, "Okay, we won at Fallujah. But we made Fallujah happen. We can't do that again."

Haditha was deep Sunni territory. Like Fallujah when the Americans first arrived in the spring of 2003, it was friendly. Haditha's mayor was pro-American, and he welcomed the arrival of U.S. forces. In July, a few months after the shootings of the protesters in Fallujah, the mayor and his youngest son were assassinated, which sent a chilling message to the community. Around this time, strangers—mujahideen—began arriving in Haditha, using brutality to intimidate the local population. In November 2004 Marines were withdrawn from Haditha to fight in Fallujah. In their absence, the local insurgents acted with impunity. Dozens of policemen, who had been cooperating with the Americans, were executed.

By the following year Haditha had become a base for the insurgency. The town was only a day's drive from Al-Qa'im, on the Syrian border, and many Hadithans had family connections in Syria. The town was a convenient way station for mujahideen slipping in from outside the country, and al-Qaeda's feared and shadowy leader in Iraq, al-Zarqawi, was said to be a frequent visitor. "Al-Qaeda in Iraq" was given its name there.

Haditha was small and remote, and during that year the United States effectively washed its hands of the place. It was declared a TAZ, or temporary autonomous zone. Though the alliance still maintained bases there and performed an offensive operation in May, the area was largely under the control of the mujahideen. These were religious fundamentalists, very like the Taliban. They took over all municipal functions and imposed strict sharia law on the population. All Western music was banned, as well as all behavior that was deemed immodest. Public punishments were carried out by men in hoods: whippings, the severing of hands, and decapitations took place on the bridge over the river, where people lined the banks for these events. The punishments were considered public entertainment, and families brought their children to watch. Videos of decapitations were sold in the market.

Haditha was strategically important. Not only was it part of a covert route for insurgents, but it was also the site of the largest hydroelectric dam in Iraq, a major source of electric power throughout the country. The U.S. forces were determined to protect the dam from the insurgent threat, and in 2005 they sent the U.S. Marines back into Haditha.

The events at Fallujah in 2003 had aroused a fury of anti-Americanism within the Muslim world. Fundamentalist zealots stirred it into a lethal stew of rage and kept it simmering.

The fundamentalist mullahs came from poor families that had few options. In order to better their sons' lives, parents sent them to religious school, where the boys studied the sacred text of the Koran, memorizing hundreds of its verses. When the students became mullahs and returned to their towns, they knew the Koran from end to end, but they had never read a word of any other book. They knew nothing of other religions, other political systems, other countries, or other methods of perceiving the world. They could interpret the Koran in any way they chose, and they had absolute power within the community. It was in their interest to prohibit all contact with the Western world.

Haditha, now in the grip of the mujahideen, became deeply hostile to the U.S. occupying forces. During the summer of 2005, before Conrad arrived there, six Marine snipers were ambushed and killed. One was said to have been captured alive and tortured, and his mutilated body was paraded through the streets. Videos of this, too, were sold in the market. Improvised explosive devices (IEDs) were devastatingly successful in Haditha. That summer, fourteen Marines were killed by a roadside bomb.

The mujahideen of Haditha controlled more than the paramilitary and religious systems—they also ran the civic and physical infrastructure. They ran the judicial system and the courts, carried out their own punishments, took charge of the well-being of the citizens, and took credit for the uninterrupted flow of power from the dam. Haditha had electricity, a bounteous supply of local food, and its own civic system. There was little room for the American presence and little tolerance for it among the muj.

In the fall of 2005, the Marines' commanding officers moved upriver. They established a command center outside the town and closer to the dam. The Marines in Haditha itself were left with a skeleton crew in violently hostile territory. Their base was in a school administration building, though some Marines moved out of this into small huts nearby. The base was called Sparta.

Sparta was remote, isolated, and embattled. Its Marines rarely left the compound unless they were in full combat gear and mounted in Humvees. Each time they left the wire they knew they might be hit: IEDs were ubiquitous and well concealed. There was little diplomatic or constructive interaction between the Marines and the locals.

That fall, another initiative was carried out in Haditha: Operation River Gate. The Marines destroyed the two bridges leading to the eastern side of the river, and then they attacked from the west, moving slowly through the town from house to house. This time they were careful not to use bombs and artillery, not to destroy the town or kill civilians. But both sides had learned from Fallujah: this time the Marines met no armed resistance. Most of the insurgents had slipped out of town the night before. At the end of the day the Marines had arrested some six hundred insurgents, most of whom were later released. They called the operation a victory, but it was hard to define exactly what they'd won.

"So, it was a pretty interesting place," Conrad said. "There were some ancient sites along the river, but I never got to them."

"You never got to slip away," Lydia said.

"To look at archaeology?" Conrad laughed. "There was no slipping away, Mom. We were in a combat zone. We never left the wire without full battle rattle, nothing smaller than a squad, twelve or fourteen guys."

"So what did you do when you went out?" she asked.

"Went on missions. Patrols, carrying troops around, different things. There was a local elder we'd meet with. We were supposed to be making an alliance."

"But you didn't?" asked Marshall.

"He had no intention of making an alliance with anyone," said Conrad. "He always had a list of things he wanted from us, and he never did anything we asked him to. It was all bullshit. He never trusted us, and we never trusted him. He'd say, 'Give us back this man, Abdullah, he is innocent. Release him.' We'd say, 'No way, man. Abdullah's in a decapitation video, we've seen it. He cuts people's heads off. He's staying where he is.' The guy would say, 'He is a good man. Set him free.'" Conrad shrugged and shook his head. "Most of the locals didn't like us. We were the problem, as far as they could tell. We worked some with the policemen, but they never knew if they'd get shot just for being seen with us. Some of them were good guys, but a lot of them kept their distance. It wasn't the climate for friendship."

"How did you work with the policemen?" Marshall asked.

"We did some training. And we used to sit on guard duty with them at night in the police station," Conrad said. "Sometimes they'd bring food and share it with us. Theirs was always good. We called it red shit and rice." He didn't tell them what they'd called kebabs: pricks on sticks.

"So what was it like to go out on a mission?" asked Marshall.

"We'd go in a convoy. Every time you left the wire you'd wonder if this would be the day," said Conrad. "Some guys counted the days between IEDs, as if there were some mathematical pattern they could figure out. Lot of superstition. You couldn't eat the Charms from the MREs. They were a big deal. Everyone would get mad at you for that."

"Charms?" asked Lydia.

"That hard candy," said Conrad. "It came in some of the MREs, Meals, Ready-to-Eat. Charms were bad luck. Bad bad."

"Did you ever eat them?" she asked.

"Hell, no," said Conrad, laughing. "I wasn't going to be the one."

They all laughed; then silence fell again.

"So, Con," said Lydia. "Do you want to tell us about the day you were hit? Or would you rather not?"

Conrad looked down at the mat, picked up his water glass, and moved it back and forth on the quilted surface as he spoke.

"There were no Charms, as far as I know," he said. "No mathematical patterns, nothing, though afterward someone said someone else had had a bad feeling that morning." His glass left a faint silvery trail on the mat. "We were picking up some policemen from another outpost. I chose the route, I always did. Haditha wasn't that big, there were only so many ways you could go. We headed south, along the river. When you were in the Humvee, it was kind of like a state of suspended tension. You were tense all the time, waiting. But there was nothing you could do about it. It wasn't like being ambushed. You could have your weapons ready for that, keep your eyes open, figure out the territory. IEDs were different. You couldn't prepare for them. You could only wait for them to happen." The cobalt glass was glittering with condensation, drops pooling along its sides. "You focused on the mission, what you were doing, keeping contact, paying attention. You did all that to distract yourself. It did no good to think about whether or not it would happen. But it was there in your mind."

His parents sat silent, watching him.

"So that day, we were heading down along the river. We always closed off the road wherever we drove, because of suicide bombers. The locals knew that. They pulled over when they saw us coming. We were driving along between houses on one side and some empty land on the other. A strip of empty land, then orchards going down to the river. The buildings were on the other side of a little ditch. I remember looking at the ditch and thinking that I'd seen a stone slab set there for pedestrians, just a slab, a couple of feet wide, for people to cross the ditch on. I thought of the stone and I wondered if I was misremembering where I'd seen it, and then just as I was thinking, *It's been removed, they've taken it away*—that was exactly the kind of thing you paid attention to—the air kind of changed, and things went black."

He paused again, looking down.

"Everything changes. It's like being in a vacuum tube. All the air is sucked away, and everything slows down. I remember thinking that the Humvee was sliding sideways, we were tipping over on a flat road, and what was Olivera smoking? I was trying to stay upright and turn around to see what had happened, but I couldn't move. You feel zapped, too, shocked, as though you've just run into an electric wire. You're surrounded by noise. The sound is too big to understand. The whole world is black noise, and you're floating in it. You can't move or speak, and you may die. Your body knows that. And then it's over, the light comes back, but you have no idea what happened. You still feel lost in the world. You can't figure anything out, but you have to keep going."

There was a silence. The candles flickered, the points of light reflected in the blackness of the windowpanes.

"Hard," said Lydia. "That sounds so hard."

"How did you get through it?" Marshall asked.

Conrad shook his head. "Just did."

"Con," Lydia said, her voice quiet, "are you all right?"

The question, asked in the dim light, there with the sleeping cat, the glowing lamp, took him by surprise.

"I don't know how to answer that," Conrad said. "I'm here." He was ashamed of the sudden filling in his chest, the risk of tears.

"I'm so sorry," said Lydia. "I'm so sorry."

The only way he could be in this world, here, was to turn his back on the other, there. But it was unclear how he could do that when that other life kept circling back on him when he least wanted it.

At the end of the meal Marshall leaned back in his chair. Conrad knew what was coming.

"Con, any thoughts about your next step?"

"I've been thinking about graduate school." He wondered if he sounded audibly false.

Marshall nodded.

"Great," Lydia said. "In what?"

He saw they believed him.

"Political science. International relations," he said. "Or law."

Discomfort appeared on their faces as they realized his uncertainty.

"Which one are you more drawn to?" Lydia asked.

"Not sure," Conrad said. "I've gotten really interested in political science."

In fact his chest tightened at the idea of studying political science or international affairs or law, or anything else. Sitting silently in a crowded classroom, taking notes and trying to concentrate. Studying in the library, people moving behind him, unseen. But also, the idea of starting out again in a whole new field implied that all this, the life he'd been living for the last four years, was finished, behind him. It didn't feel finished. He was still part of it; it was still part of him. It wasn't over. He knew he had to keep going, move on, but the future seemed like a locked gate. He couldn't see into it.

None of this—the dim, enfolding clouds of anxiety, the rise of choking panic, the throttling claustrophobia, the straight-out jolts of terror—had anything to do with the bright, calm world where his parents and everyone else lived. He couldn't tell his parents any of this. He had to move forward. Charlie Mike: continue the mission. You made a plan and carried it out. His plan was to make a plan. Speaking it made it real.

"So what schools are you thinking of?" asked Marshall.

"For international affairs, Kennedy, Columbia, Fletcher. I'll need to take the GMAT or GRE. I'll study for them over the summer, and take the test in the fall."

At the moment, of course, he could not study for them. Whenever he tried to read anything serious, to concentrate, the headache descended on him, sinking its talons deep into his mind. He didn't tell his parents this; he was pretty sure it would stop. He'd get some rest, things would calm down, he'd go back to normal.

"Sounds great," Lydia said again, nodding.

It was strange to think that everything was going on at Sparta without him. In the early evening the cooks would be shouting in the mess hall. Marines were walking into the courtyard to mount up, the sound of their boots grinding into the gravel. At dusk the bats came out, skittering black outlines against the darkening sky, quick, erratic, like scraps of night let loose.

He could not stay here. This house was so thickened with the fragments of his own life that he could hardly breathe. Here his parents had their own adult lives, and he had none. Here there was no room for him as an adult, the closet still filled with his childhood clothes. He was a child here. But where else was there?

"Con," Marshall said finally. "This has to be hard. Is there anything we can do?"

He shook his head.

"Is there anything you'd rather talk about?" Lydia asked. "Anything you want to tell us?"

Conrad shook his head.

"I feel as though we're so far apart," she said. "As though there's something between us."

He said nothing.

"We got a movie," Marshall said. *"Life of Brian."*

The way to get through this was moment by moment. It would get better. It was a question of getting through the moments.

The library was long and narrow, lined with books on three walls. Two small sofas faced each other across a kilim-covered chest; at one end was a fireplace, with a battered leather bench on the hearth. Family photographs stood on shelves and tabletops: Here they were in Kenya, arms around one another's shoulders, thorn trees and savanna in the background. Here was Jenny at her high school graduation, her mouth bristling with braces, smiling, squinting up and holding the ribboned scroll. Here was Ollie in sixth grade, with huge black eyebrows and a pointed wizard's hat, as Prospero. Here was Lydia at five, solemn in a nightgown, glancing sideways at a Christmas stocking.

They settled in to watch the movie. The room was dark except for the bright liquid images on the screen. This was one of his favorites. It was a relief to sink into it, to feel the dark fist of pressure against his chest begin to release. To laugh out loud.

As the movie went on, the fist against his heart began to clench again. Crowds of robed people milled about, pressing bodies, the confusion, growing chaos. He wanted someone to take charge. His heart was speeding up and he felt the swollen surge in his throat. He watched them stand up in the amphitheater, dangerously outlined against the sky, the crowd below shouting and mutinous. Conrad stood up and left the room. He closed the library door and went through the darkened kitchen, on out the back door.

Outside, he stood on the brick walk. The white fence gleamed in the darkness, the dim garage beyond it pallid. Above was the black sky. He counted slowly to ten. He looked around, letting his eyes adjust. It took ninety seconds to get night vision, a long time if someone nearby was trying to kill you. The darkness breathed around him; the willow trees moved slightly, the leaves hissing faintly. He stared into the blackness. There was no one there. He could walk up the hill, across the field, on into the woods without danger. There was nothing.

Something had gotten loose in his chest.

He looked up at the hillside. He could sense the chem lights drifting dimly across the field. He couldn't see them without his night vision goggles, but he knew they were there, glimmering and green. He strained to see them. He listened for footsteps, the brush of cloth against stone.

He remembered the night on guard duty at the police station in Haditha. The day before, an IED had killed three Marines, and everyone was on edge. That night they sat without talking, drinking chai. Two local police guards and two Marines from Sparta. Around midnight they heard footsteps in the street. They looked at one another. It was after curfew, and anyone outside was there illegally. The footsteps stopped outside the building. The Iraqi policeman called out, but no one answered. The footsteps came closer, right outside the door. Nomer Caulfield stood up and aimed his rifle at the door and shouted, first in English, then in Arabic. No one answered. The Iraqi called again. No answer. They heard fumbling at the doorknob, and Nomer Caulfield shot right through the door. They heard a heavy grunt, and then a wild, broken braying. They opened the door: it was a donkey, gotten loose from somewhere. It lay on its side, screaming and trying to lift its head, until Nomer shot it again to stop the noise. The next morning it was in the street, bloody and buzzing with flies.

Here no one was creeping toward him. The night around him was safe. He knew that. He stood still, breathing slowly. He counted to ten. Nothing.

Conrad went back inside, catching the screen door with his hand so it wouldn't slam. The kitchen was dark. The dishwasher thumped noisily. He stood still for a moment, watching the line of light around the door into the library. He started to count again, trying to slow his heart. Against his leg he felt the soft, hideous brush of a camel spider, and he kicked out violently. He caught the cat on his instep and she gave a cry. *Jesus.*

Conrad knelt, reaching for her in the dark. His hand found her, the light, bony body upholstered in fur. He took her, soft but struggling, into his arms and held her still, her tail switching angrily against his chest.

"Sorry, Murph," he said, his heart racing again.

Those fucking spiders didn't bite, they ate. He'd seen the big hole in Stocky Warnock's leg, the flesh red and open, hollowed out like a half-eaten peach.

"I'm sorry," Conrad said again, deep into her fur. "Shh. I wasn't thinking of you. Good cat."

She had stopped struggling, but would not purr. She waited in his arms, ready to leap out.

"Purr," he said. He held her against his chest, stroking hard. "Purr. Goddammit." He thought of slamming her against the wooden counter.

"Con?" Marshall stood silhouetted in the doorway.

Conrad put the cat down and stood up. "I was petting Murphy."

"You okay?" Marshall asked.

There was a silence.

"Yeah," Conrad said.

His heart had been wound up too tight. It was coiled in his chest like fuck. He still had all these hours to get through and there was nowhere to go.

6

Ollie must have come up the drive soundlessly, because Conrad, who was in the kitchen, didn't hear him arrive. He didn't hear Ollie drive up or get out of the car or slam its door shut. He didn't hear Ollie coming through the white gate into the yard. He didn't hear anything until Ollie came through the back door, jumping up the one step into the mudroom. His backpack caught on the screen door on that jump, and he jerked himself free and the door slammed behind him like a gunshot. Conrad, who was standing at the open refrigerator, felt the sound go off inside his head like lightning hitting his heart, and as Ollie appeared in the doorway, Conrad threw himself as far as he could get inside the fridge, pulling the door shut against himself, ducking down, his blood thundering.

For a moment there was silence. No one moved.

Conrad emerged, closing the door behind him.

"Sorry," Ollie said.

"It's okay," Conrad said. He shook his head. "Reflex."

"Sorry, Con." Ollie looked appalled.

"No problemo," said Conrad. He took a breath. "Welcome home."

They gave each other quick shoulder clasps, a thump on the back. Ollie was taller than Conrad remembered, but insubstantial. The bones were just beneath the skin, unclad by muscle.

"Glad you're home, bro," said Ollie.

"Yeah," said Conrad. "Me, too. You want a beer?"

They went out through the library to the porch, a square room added onto the side of the house. On three sides the walls were tall windows: the room faced the side lawn, toward the big ash tree and the barn. The ash tree made a high, graceful canopy. The grass had just been mowed, leaving a pattern of wide silvery stripes in the lawn and a damp, fresh smell lingering in the air. It was the end of the afternoon, and the golden light slanted wide and low across the velvety green.

Conrad sat on the sofa, his back to the wall. Ollie sprawled in a big armchair. They both stretched out, putting their feet on the glass-topped coffee table. The table was made from a pair of printer's trays, and the small compartments held whimsical family objects: a tiny box containing one of Conrad's baby teeth, tiny and yellowing; a freshwater mussel shell, a pearl encrusted in it, found by Jenny; the tarnished brass name tag from Yeats, the beloved childhood dog. Everyone was in there, one way or another.

Conrad stretched his arm along the back of the sofa and took a long swallow of beer. He let it run down his throat, cold and yeasty and dark.

"Man," he said, "this is what everyone dreams about, over there. Sitting down back home, with a beer. Everyone has a dream, the plan of the first beer: What brand. Where you'll be. With who."

"What was yours?" Ollie said.

Conrad waved his hand at the golden light, the green canopy, the fresh-cut grass.

"Here, I guess," he said.

Actually, he couldn't remember. Until he'd gone to Ramadi, his first deployment, it would have included Claire. After she'd made her declaration, he didn't have a plan for that first beer. He didn't have a local bar or a bunch of buddies he'd grown up with. His friends from college now seemed distant, separated from him by something huge and untranslatable. He couldn't imagine talking to them, this whole country lying between them. He'd rather see another vet, someone who'd been there—but now he was trying to get past that.

He didn't want to stay in the world he'd been living in, he wanted to get on. You couldn't come home and still go on living in Sparta.

He took another swallow (the second one never quite as good) and thought, *I'm home. It's over.* There was no longer any need to throw himself under a table at a loud noise. He was safe. Alive.

But instead of being a relief, this was faintly sickening. It led somewhere he didn't want to go. There was some unnamed weight attached to his being here. He was here. Olivera was not, and never would be, and how had that happened? And there were those other lives, the pattern on the wall and the girl, and the man lying in the street, and how was he to read that equation? How was he to learn the somber laws of metaphysics that determined who survived and who did not? How could they be tolerated?

He would reenter his life here. He took another swallow (the third always ordinary) and turned to Ollie. "So, what's up at Bard?"

"It's all good." Ollie nodded.

Ollie looked older, Conrad could see. He'd lost the blurred look of adolescence; his features had become defined. He looked like a blend of the family, Marshall's wide mouth, his wide-set amber eyes, something about Lydia around the nose. Ollie had become handsome. Conrad felt pleased, surprisingly proud: his little brother. Olivetti.

"So you're heading into your sophomore year? What courses you taking?" Conrad tipped back his bottle as Ollie recited them: English lit, anthropology, Mandarin, the Origins of Islam.

"Mandarin," said Conrad. "Whoa. How's that?"

"Seriously hard." Ollie shook his head.

"I bet it is," said Conrad. In a high, hissing voice he said, *"You must be cra-zee."*

It was the punch line from an old family joke about a psychiatrist and a dog. The joke itself had been lost, but the punch line had become part of the children's private language. It was used only among themselves, and delivered in a shrill, manic singsong.

"No shit," said Ollie, laughing. "I don't know what I was thinking."

"No, it's good," Conrad said. "Good move. Europe's over, China's next. The Chinese will be taking over the world, and you'll be all set. Fluent."

"Yeah, maybe." Ollie glanced at Conrad. "You ever study any Iraqi?"

"I know the basics," Conrad said. "'Stop. Put your hands in the air. Lie down. Your ass is grass.' All you need."

Ollie grinned uncertainly, and Conrad regretted what he'd said.

"But you had an interpreter, right?" asked Ollie.

"Sometimes. In Ramadi we had a terp when we went on the school missions. I told you about him: Ali."

"Why did he know English?"

Conrad shrugged. "Why are you learning Mandarin? He was an engineer. He had a graduate degree. A lot of educated Iraqis speak English. They learn it in school, just like you."

But why was he snubbing his brother? He'd made the same assumptions himself.

Ali was tall and thin, in his early forties, with curved shoulders and a hollow chest. His face was long and hawkish, the cheekbones high and sharp. A dense black mustache, sloping hazel eyes, thick black eyebrows, jutting Adam's apple. He wore a kaffiyeh twisted jauntily around his throat, a long-sleeved loose white cotton shirt, and khaki pants. He held himself erect and with dignity.

Conrad met him when he and his first squad were providing security for a visiting officer going to a base outside Ramadi. It was a long trip; Conrad and Ali sat next to each other.

Conrad asked him what he had done before the war.

"I was an engineer. That is over now." Ali drew a line of completion in the air with long fingers. "During a war, a man does whatever he can. I am fortunate to have this job."

Conrad nodded. This was not true for him, nor for any of the Americans here. They were doing what they'd chosen, not whatever they could. That was the difference between himself and Ali, between occupier and occupied.

Ali seemed without resentment, though Ramadi was in chaos. The occupying forces had been there for a year, and still there was no sewage system, no trash removal, no reliable clean water, and only sporadic electric power.

Ali had gone to university in Baghdad; he spoke very good English, with a colonial British accent. He asked if Conrad had gone to university and what he had studied.

The classics, Conrad told him. "The Greeks and the Romans. The ancient world."

Ali nodded politely. He said, "Of course, all that came after us. We think of them as the modern world."

Conrad laughed.

Ali was curious about everything: Conrad's religion, his favorite books.

"What, in your opinion, is the greatest work of literature?" Ali asked.

Conrad told him the *Iliad.*

Ali hadn't read that, but he'd read *Hamlet* and *King Lear.* "I understand that *Lear* is considered the greater of these two, but I prefer *Hamlet.* Ambiguity," he said. "This is something we admire."

They had often gone on missions together after that. When Dingo Three was detailed to oversee a rebuilding project at a local school, Ali became their regular terp. He always brought food and always offered to share it. Ali was Conrad's introduction to Iraqi food—rich, savory stews with sweet currants, sharp citrus, mysterious spices.

Once, Conrad offered him an MRE in exchange. He showed him how to rip open the brown plastic packet and start the chemical reactions to heat it up. It was a vegetarian omelet, though, one of the worst MREs.

Ali took a bite and began to chew, staring at Conrad in concentration. His mouth began to pucker. He swallowed, his jagged Adam's apple shifting.

"Conrad, let me ask you something," he said politely. "Do you Americans call this food? Or is it just what you call supplements?"

"We call it food," Conrad admitted, sheepish. "At least, the military calls it food, and we eat it."

Ali asked about Conrad's family, where he'd grown up, what the landscape was like, what kind of birds there were: he knew a lot about birds. He showed Conrad a photograph of his two daughters. They were small, six or seven years old, arms wrapped around each other, heads pressed together. They were smiling; one was missing a front tooth. They had that honey-colored Iraqi skin, the big, dark, melting eyes. Along the hairline, their dark hair had turned coppery from the sun.

Conrad handed the picture back. "They're beautiful," he said. "Not like you."

Ali laughed. "No," he said. "They are fortunate in that way."

Conrad showed him a picture of his parents on the lawn behind the house. Ali leaned over it closely. "Your parents are very handsome," he said. "And this is where you live? This tree, what is the name of it?"

"White ash," Conrad told him.

"And this?" he asked, but Conrad couldn't tell what he was pointing at.

"Nothing," he said. "What?"

"This," Ali said, "all this green. A carpet? Is it grass?"

"Grass," Conrad told him. "That's a lawn."

"Ah," Ali said, nodding. "Of course. We don't have many of those here. We don't have grass like that. Like a carpet."

It was an odd notion: no lawn. Conrad remembered his brother and sister in their pajamas, playing leapfrog on the grass, singing.

Conrad asked to see a photograph of Ali's wife, but Ali shook his head. Conrad didn't know if Ali didn't have a picture, or if he didn't want to show her to an infidel, or if it was dangerous to show it to an American soldier.

Nor would Ali say where his family lived. Translators were considered traitors by the insurgents, collaborators with the infidel invaders. Terps received death threats; there were kidnappings, decapitations. Ali said nothing about his job being dangerous, though Conrad knew it was.

On the base at Ramadi, the hard manual work was done by locals. They were given low wages to do whatever was dirty and menial—digging ditches, construction, loading trucks. Each morning a group of them arrived early and waited in the clearing room to go through security. Every day there was a line of them, shabby men in grimy clothes and broken shoes. They stood silently against the wall, some sliding their backs down it to sit on their heels.

One morning Conrad came into the clearing room looking for Ali. His gaze skimmed past the laborers, and he went on looking around the room. He heard his name called out and looked back: Ali stood among the shabby men, smiling and beckoning.

Conrad didn't like this. He didn't like seeing Ali standing with them, didn't like him smiling and beckoning. Instead of answering or approaching Ali, Conrad lifted his chin, almost as a command. Ali turned to the man beside him. He was thin and hollow-eyed, with thick, messy black hair, a dirty striped shirt, and worn baggy pants. The man smiled at Conrad, but Conrad frowned, gave an abrupt nod, and turned away to speak to someone else. He didn't like any of it. It irritated him.

Later, on the way to the school, Ali said, "Conrad, that was my friend Mohammed in the clearing room. I had told him about you. I wanted you to meet him. He is very pleased to be offered work at the base. For a long time now he has been unable to get work and could not support his family. Now he is glad to have some salary." Ali spoke cheerfully; he seemed unaware of Conrad's snub.

"That's good." Conrad felt distaste again at the somehow unsavory link between the shabby laborers and Ali. "What did Mohammed do before the war?"

"Mohammed is like me, a chemical engineer," Ali said. "Before the war he was a supervisor, in charge of one of the largest oil refineries."

This irritated Conrad. "What's he doing on the base?"

"I think he is digging trenches."

"If he speaks English, why isn't he a translator?"

"Many people apply for that job. We are not all so fortunate. But Mohammed is well educated. He studied the Greeks, like you. He is very fond of Homer. I thought you would enjoy talking to him."

Conrad didn't answer. He saw Mohammed, the grimy clothes and broken shoes, the hollow face and black eyes, and for some reason Conrad thought of his own father, imagined him like this, standing along a wall, waiting.

There was the question of appropriate behavior. Conrad was an officer; he couldn't talk to every laborer with broken shoes who had read Homer. And he couldn't consider every question that arose and challenged his moral right to be in Iraq. He was there to carry out the mission, to obey his commanding officers in a branch of service he deeply respected. He was doing his duty. There was the question of why the U.S. forces had destroyed this country. The question of why they were treating their allies—the people they had come here to liberate and protect—with such deep and lethal contempt. The question of whether what they were doing was honorable.

None of these were thoughts he could address. He said nothing more to Ali about Mohammed, and Ali never mentioned him again.

Conrad didn't want to remember any of this. He was trying to put everything behind him. He would make a rule: no thoughts of Iraq until the end of the conversation. He was going to hear about Ollie's school year.

"So," he said to Ollie. "Why 'The Origins of Islam?'"

"Just—you know." Ollie jerked his chin and picked at the label on his beer bottle.

"Because of me being over there," Conrad said.

Ollie's eyes flicked up. "Well, yeah," he said. "I've been hearing from you and watching it on the news for years."

"Nothing you see on the news is real," said Conrad.

"I know that," Ollie said. "I just mean—"

"Nothing here has anything to do with what it's like there."

"Yeah, I know that." Ollie seemed both deferential and subversive, as though he were pretending respect while planning mutiny. He shifted uncomfortably.

"You have no idea what it's like," Conrad said.

Ollie nodded, picking at the label, peeling the corner away from the slippery surface. "I know."

"Even what I told you isn't what it's like."

Ollie nodded again, frowning at the label.

Suddenly suspicious, Conrad said, "You're not thinking of signing up, are you?"

"I've thought of it," Ollie said. "Not right now. Maybe after I graduate."

Conrad leaned forward. His heart began to pound. "Don't even think of it. Don't fucking even think of it."

"What do you mean?" Ollie asked, aggrieved. "All of a sudden you think it's a bad idea?"

"I'm saying you shouldn't do it."

"You did it," said Ollie.

"I'm saying you shouldn't," Conrad said.

"You don't think I could handle it?" Ollie asked. "Is that what you think?"

"I didn't say you couldn't handle it," Conrad said. "I'm saying you shouldn't do it. I'm telling you not to."

"Oh, I see. You're giving me an order? You think you're the only one who can do the big things?" Ollie said. "You think you're the only one who's brave enough to be a Marine? Fuck off, Conrad. You can't tell me what to do."

"I can tell you what to do about this," Conrad said, his voice rising. The inside of his head was becoming hot and swollen. He stood up and put his hands on his hips. *"Don't you fucking think about signing up."* He leaned over Ollie and screamed into his face, *"I'll tear your fucking head off."*

"Great," Ollie said. Shockingly, his eyes filled, and he blinked. "Be an asshole. Just be an asshole, Conrad. What the fuck is the matter with you?" He turned his head away. "Are you saying you wish you hadn't joined?"

Things rose suddenly into Conrad's mind like waves. There was no warning, he couldn't stop it. Leaning over his brother, furious. It was like an alarm going off, the horn blaring over and over, and then he was back in Haditha.

In the morning an IED had gone off, hitting the third Humvee in a convoy of four. They'd been on a milk run, delivering food supplies to a small outlying base, picking up some Iraqi policemen who served with their troops. They made the run every morning, taking a different route each time to avoid IEDs. But this one had been buried under the road and concealed by fresh paving. There was no way to detect it.

The blast destroyed the Humvee, splitting it in half and flipping it over into the crater made by the bomb. The driver's head was crushed, and he died on the scene. The man riding shotgun had been blasted out the door of the Humvee: his foot was blown off, and he had trauma to the head. Another Marine was in shock, dazed and unable to speak.

The other Humvees had stopped, and everyone jumped out. Up the road from the convoy was a taxi, which had stopped when the Humvees headed up the street. After the blast went off, the doors opened and five men got out. They waited with their hands in the air. The Marines opened fire on them; they were all shot and killed. There was some fire received from nearby houses. Marine tactics are to lay down superior fire right away, and the fight was over quickly. There were no American casualties in the firefight. Choppers came in to medevac out the two Marines wounded by the IED.

Conrad was on the QRF, Quick Reaction Force, which was called in afterward. By the time he got there, the firefight was over and things seemed under control. Nearby houses had been searched for whoever had detonated the IED. From what Conrad had heard, everything was over. The squad had gone through the houses, and everything was quiet.

Conrad's squad pulled up near the other Humvees on Route Chestnut. He got out and walked toward the row of houses on the north side of the road. They were low, one story, the front doors facing the dirt road. Two Marines stood outside one of them. Conrad walked up to them. They were from another platoon; he knew them.

"Redbank," he said, "what's going on? I'm QRF."

"LT," Redbank said, nodding. "We had an IED go off. One KIA and two wounded. They've been medevaced out. There was some trouble afterward. We took some fire, then cleared these houses. It's over now. We're all set."

He seemed to be standing in Conrad's path.

"Okay, thanks," Conrad said. "I'll just take a look around."

Redbank was a short, burly guy. For a moment he didn't move, but Conrad didn't, either, leaning toward him until Redbank stepped back to one side. Conrad stepped past him.

The house was painted stucco, with straggly plants outside. It was sixty or seventy meters from the road, and not close to the IED. It would be unlikely for snipers to choose such a distant site.

Inside was a big, shadowy high-ceilinged room with a window on one side. Nearly at Conrad's feet lay a man in robes, his arms flung out at his sides. Just beyond him was another man, his hand open on the floor. A sandal lay next to his head. They were covered in blood. At the back of the room lay another man; beyond him was a woman. She was half kneeling by the sofa, one arm flung across it, as if she'd been trying to climb onto it. Her head was dark and glistening. On the pale wall behind her, flung high, were dark spatters in a sickening spray.

Conrad went on through the room and out into the hall. The floor was sticky. In the hall an old woman lay crumpled on the floor in a swirl of skirts. In a small adjoining room on the right was an old man slumped in his wheelchair at a desk. Before him was an open book, spattered with blood. Down the hallway, on the left, was a door into a small, dim bedroom. A young girl, ten or eleven, lay curled on the bed, her arms wrapped tightly around a little boy in striped pajamas. Her body was curved around his, chin tucked over his head. Her eyes were half open, and her hair lay thickly across her mouth, full of blood.

Conrad stood in front of the children. The girl was gone, he couldn't look at her, but the little boy seemed fine, untouched, clean. He had the feeling that the little boy was all right, that he was pretending to be asleep. Conrad leaned over him and spoke.

"You okay?" The boy wouldn't know the words, but they were what came out. The boy didn't move. Conrad could hear the sounds of the town, a few chickens, traffic, at a distance. Voices. He reached out and touched the boy's arm, plucking it from the locked embrace of the girl; he lifted the soft, limp limb. It seemed light at first but then death heavy, and in lifting the arm, Conrad disturbed something and the boy's head lolled horribly backward to show a dark red glistening maw gaping in the neck. Conrad gently lowered the arm again, seeing a dry patch as the body shifted. The stripes on the pajamas had once been blue and white. They were now black and red.

He went all the way through the house to the back door. He stepped into the yard, crouched down on the smoothly swept sand, and vomited over and over. The taste of metal came up sharp in his throat.

The yard was marked by a line of pebbles. Beyond this were tall bushes on which clothes were hung out to dry. The points of the branches poked up into the fabric. The clothes would be there forever, he thought. Who would bring them in? The bile came up against the back of his tongue, coating his teeth.

He stood staring at Ollie while the waves broke over him in his mind. He turned and sat down again, throwing himself back against the sofa as though he were making a point.

The thing, the fucking problem, was all this time, this empty time spreading out ahead of him. He held the beer bottle loosely in his fingers. He knew how it would feel to throw it hard enough to smash it. If he smashed it on the coffee table, the glass top would shatter, too, and the sound of it—the glass shrapnel and the fucking family memorabilia inside flying scattershot through the air—would be like an explosion of everything. Not enough, though.

7

Marshall and Jenny came out to Katonah from New York on the same train, arriving just before dinner. Jenny walked in through the back door, dropped her bag, and shouted for Conrad. He came in from the porch, through the library. When he appeared, she threw her arms around him.

"Yowie! You're really home," she said, and pulled away to look at him.

Jenny was three years younger than Conrad, slight and pretty. Her face was long and narrow, and she had light blue eyes, delicate features, and smooth, pale skin. Her dark hair was fine and shiny, cropped short. She had a sunny smile and perfect straight-edged teeth.

She looked the same, except somehow she'd become surprisingly hip, Conrad thought: tight bright-orange top, wide tan pants, a loose jacket. Stylish. When he first went away, she'd looked like a student, in sweats and cargo pants. When had she gotten so cool? When had she started wearing big orange earrings?

"I can't believe you're really here." She grinned at him, her hands still gripping his shoulders. The thing about Jenny was that she was hands-on.

"I really am." Conrad grinned back. He willed himself not to shake off her hands. It was just his sister. But he didn't like being grabbed. And it was going to be like this, moment by moment. He smiled at her. This was his family. He had to be here. It was great. It was like prison, the seconds ticking away.

At dinner, Lydia gave Conrad the update on Jenny as though he'd never met her.

"Your sister is doing brilliantly at work," Lydia said.

"Big surprise," Conrad said. Jenny always did brilliantly.

One afternoon, when Conrad was in his teens, he and Roddy Blodgett had been babysitters for Jenny and Ollie. They mixed a foul drink made of whatever they found in the kitchen—milk, Coke, Worcestershire sauce, ketchup, orange juice. They filled a glass with it and called Jenny in.

"Here, Jen," Conrad told her. "Drink this." He was the oldest. He was showing off for Roddy.

"What is it?" Jenny asked warily.

"It's good," Conrad assured her. "Just drink it. Drink."

Jenny took the glass. Looking at him over the rim, she began to swallow. He thought she'd stop after the first sip, but she went on. She drank it all, steadily, watching him, her eyes challenging beneath the ragged arch of her bangs. He heard the soft, compressive clenching of her throat as she swallowed. When she finished, she set down the empty glass, still watching him.

"Ahh. Dee-licious." She smacked her lips.

She was ten or eleven then. It was a clear *fuck you*.

Conrad and Roddy had laughed like hyenas, shouting and punching each other's shoulders as though they were laughing at her. But really they were laughing out of admiration. She'd won; they knew it.

"So," Conrad asked Jenny, "how are things with Jock?"

Jock Sawyer was the boyfriend. He was from Atlanta, which meant that he had unfortunate taste in sports teams, but otherwise Conrad liked him. He was tall and thin, with a bony forehead and a slightly protruding mouth. His eyes were ice blue, and his hair was at best ginger-colored: Jenny hotly denied that it was red. Jock was in medical school at Columbia. He and Jenny were both insanely smart and competitive; they rode racing bikes and ran mini-marathons.

"Good," Jenny said, nodding. "I think very good. How are things with Claire?"

Conrad shook his head. "Not sure. Haven't seen her yet."

"Is she coming out?"

"No," he said. "I'm going into New York next week to see her."

This was what he'd told his mother; he hoped it was true. He still hadn't called Claire, though he was going to. Apparently he was putting it off.

He asked Jenny, "So, the job is good?"

"She's already been promoted," Lydia said.

"Already! What's your rank?" asked Conrad.

"Rank beginner," Jenny said. "No one even knows I work there."

"Not true!" Lydia said. "She's doing very well."

Jenny rolled her eyes. "Okay, yeah, I'll be taking over the firm soon."

"Tell about the new account," Lydia said.

"Well, that is kind of cool," Jenny admitted. "They asked me to work on a new account. It's an international company with some really good designers."

"They love your sister," Lydia declared. "They love her."

"We get it, Mom," Ollie said.

The others laughed. Conrad laughed with them, but it was like watching a movie. After a moment Jenny turned to him.

"So, Con, tell. What was it like?"

They all wanted something. They all wanted to draw him home, into their world, and they all wanted to enter his world, but in a safe way. They wanted funny stories and brave ones, scary ones only if they were bearable. They wanted their hearts wrung, but in a tolerable way. They wanted to learn that his world was safe, or, if not safe, that it was livable after all. They wanted to hear stories here, from the safety of the kitchen table, and who could blame them? Why would he impose on them what he knew? Why bring the black bloom of explosions into their eyes? Make them hear the sounds he had heard coming from human beings?

But there were stories he could tell them. He could offer parts of his world. He told them about Johannson and Boccatto and the mink farm.

Marines worked in pairs; they all had buddies. Johannson and Boccatto were buddies and partners, members of second squad, third fire team. Johannson was from Wisconsin and Boccatto from Jersey City. They were both young, nineteen or twenty.

Johannson was skinny, and so pale he was nearly blue. Cloud-blue eyes, blue-white skin, colorless hair. He closed his mouth tightly after he spoke, as if he were sealing something in. A long face and sunken cheeks. Big jug ears that stuck out like cabbage leaves, veiny and pale.

Johannson's plan, after finishing in the Corps, was to start a mink farm back home. It was all he thought about. He said mink coats were recession-proof: there were always rich people, and they always wanted coats. He talked about it all the time, how he was going to go about it. He knew what kind of cages you used for minks, how you bred them, what you fed them. He wanted Boccatto to go in on it with him, move out to Wisconsin.

Boccatto was a big, beefy guy, and he thought the whole thing was stupid. "You want to start a rodent farm?" he'd say. "I'm not running a rodent farm. We've got enough rats in Jersey City to make coats for everyone in North America." He had thick lips, a big nose, a shaved head. "Maybe Central, too." He shook his head. "Plus, you know what, Johannson? No one wants mink coats anymore. They want the fun-fur shit. They want endangered species. Snow leopard. Fucking spirit bear. White tiger. Who wants a fucking mink coat?" He looked around. They were in the mess hall. "Carleton? You want a fucking mink coat?"

Carleton, eating his chow, shook his head.

"What about your mom?" Boccatto asked. "She want a mink coat? She have one?"

Carleton turned to look at him. "We live in Tennessee," he said. He liked playing the redneck card. "Only one restaurant's got air-conditioning, where you could wear a mink coat, and we don't go there. Don't need a fur coat for drive-through."

"You see that?" Boccatto said. "You see that, Johannson? No one wants them. You're behind the fucking fur curve."

Johannson paid no attention to him. "Dude. Mink is the lightest, softest, and warmest fur there is," he said. "Except sable, but we're not doing sable."

"Hey! We're not doing mink! We're not doing anything!" Boccatto said. "We're not starting a fucking mink farm!"

One night in the mess hall Johannson began talking about the kind of cages you used for mink. Apparently you had to use special ones, large and very strong. Mink had sharp teeth and they were nasty creatures, with a habit of biting the hand that fed them.

While Johannson was explaining about the cages, Boccatto started imitating the minks. He talked in a high, shrill voice, shaking his head and flapping his hands, held up like paws. *"No! No! Don't make me live on that farm! Don't make me eat those fish! Oh, no, no! Don't want to do it!"*

Everyone started laughing. Boccatto kept it up, getting higher and shriller, the whole mess hall listening and laughing. The face of one of the Iraqi cooks appeared around the corner, then another. Boccatto carried on in his falsetto. The Iraqis stared at him, then at the others.

As explanation, Johannson stood up and mimed putting on a fur coat. As though that explained anything. More kitchen workers came to the doorway, crowding around it. Johannson pulled on larger and heavier coats, frowning at their weight, while Boccatto chanted in his falsetto, waving his paws. The mink, the coat, and the cooks: the mess hall went crazy.

For weeks after that, at every meal, when the Iraqis serving at the chow table saw Boccatto and Johannson, they gave a ceremonial imitation, flapping paws for Boccatto, pulling on coats for Johannson. They nodded at them, saying something in Arabic. And Boccatto and Johannson nodded back, saying, *"Salaam alaikum,"* because who knew what they were saying, but that was what you always said back. The other Marines, walking past with their loaded plates, called in high, muted falsettos, *"Don' make me eat dat fish!"*

That night, sitting around the table, everyone in the family laughed, and Conrad laughed, too, remembering. It was strange to be telling this as though it were a story, and not real life.

He told Ollie and Jenny briefly, too, about being hit by an IED. He knew they wanted to hear it, though there wasn't much to tell. Being hit wasn't a story like a firefight; it was an existential occurrence. You were driving along and the world was normal, and then it was black and filled with sound, and you were lost.

He told them that, but he couldn't tell them about anything else, about the men who were lost, or the sounds, or the feelings of high desperation, because those stories seemed to have no connection to this place: the warm kitchen, the faces glowing in the candlelight, the bright reflections against the dark window. It seemed impossible to tell those stories here.

They told Conrad their own stories, weaving him into the things that had happened while he was away. Jenny told him about last Christmas Eve. The goose had been roasting in the oven and the grease in the pan caught fire, and the fire alarm went off and they couldn't turn it off, even when they got the tech guy from the security company on the phone and he talked them through it step-by-step. It absolutely wouldn't turn off, it kept on blasting and blasting, and finally they had to ask him to drive all the way down from some town up in Massachusetts, where he'd gone to *his* parents' house for Christmas, and it was snowing, and the roads were worse and worse, and he didn't get there till nearly midnight but finally managed to get it turned off.

During the story, Jenny kept imitating the sound of the siren, *Wah! Wah! Wah!*, loud and blaring. Everyone laughed except Conrad, who winced: the noise was like a hammer striking his head. Apparently he had a limited tolerance for all this noise and talking, even in his own family.

After the dishes were done, Lydia and Marshall went up to bed. Jenny and Ollie stayed, calling good night to their parents with an air of subdued anticipation, the kind of conspiratorial looks children exchange as their parents withdraw from the field.

The table was covered with after-dinner detritus, an air of modest dissipation: the stained wineglasses, the last, near-empty deep green bottle—when did wine bottlers stop using real corks? now they were plastic—the bright Italian pottery water pitcher, the wicker bread basket, still holding a rounded nub of baguette, pale crumbs littering the patterned mats, softened butter collapsing slightly in its dish, everything sinking into a terminal state, declaring the end of the evening.

Murphy lay on Jenny's lap, her body still, her eyes alert for leftovers. There was still a plate of cheese, leaking the semiliquid yellow center from its white patterned crust. Murphy stretched out an idle paw, touching the table as though by chance.

"No cheese, Murph." Jenny stroked her. "You're not getting up there." Murphy yawned elaborately, declaring her disinterest. "Remember the time Mom and Dad were upstairs asleep and Murphy went into the dining room in the middle of the night and started walking on the piano keys, and they woke up and thought it was burglars?"

"Burglars playing the piano," Ollie said, laughing.

"That famous gang of musical thieves," Conrad said, "known all over Westchester."

"Very famous, but not, really, all that good on the piano!" Jenny leaned over Murphy, stroking her. "You're not, Murpho! Sorry!" Murphy closed her eyes.

"And often outdone by that group with the slide guitar and the kazoo," said Ollie.

This was how they reconnected, through family stories. The time the raccoon got into the kitchen and climbed up the wall of pots and stood on the shelf at the top, peering out between the mixing bowls at Lydia in her nightgown. The time Dad opened his wallet at the tollbooth and there was a bee trapped in it and it flew out and he was stung and started swearing, and the toll collector thought he was swearing at him and threatened to call the police. The time Ollie nearly drowned, bobbing for apples at a Halloween party. But Conrad could feel them waiting for more stories from him. He had more: he told them a Marine joke.

"Two guys are arguing in a bar, a Marine and a sailor, about which is the better service, the Marine Corps or the Navy. The Marine says, 'We had Iwo Jima.'

"The sailor says, 'We had the Battle of Midway.'

"The Marine says, 'Not all Navy. Some of those pilots were Marines. Henderson Field, in Guadalcanal, is named for a Marine pilot killed at Midway.'

"The sailor says, 'Well, we had John Paul Jones.'

"The Marine says, 'We were born in Tun Tavern, during the Revolution.'

"The sailor draws himself up and delivers the killer, 'Here's the thing: the Navy invented sex.'

"The Marine says, 'Maybe so. But Marines introduced it to women.'"

Everyone liked that joke; Jenny and Ollie nearly choked.

Then he told them about Carleton.

Carleton was the radio operator for the platoon. He was a solid kid from Nashville, with one thick, dark, bristly eyebrow that went all the way across his face like a caterpillar. His father was a car salesman and his mother had an online cosmetics business. Carleton himself liked snakes. He liked jokes about snakes, and songs with snakes in them. He either had a python at home or he was going to get one, it wasn't entirely clear which.

When they went out on mounted patrol, Carleton would take caffeine tablets and get stoked, and once they were under way, he started talking about snakes.

"Between a python, boa, and cobra, sir?" he said to Conrad. "I'd take a python, any day."

"Is that right, Carleton?" Conrad said.

"Cleaner and safer, sir," Carleton said. "Also big. Largest snake in captivity is a python. Also beautiful. Ball python, sir? One of the great serpent beauties of the world." He gave a thumbs-up.

"I'll show you a beautiful snake," Morales said. He was riding behind them in the back of the Humvee. "Right here in my pants, you want to see it?"

"I thought you already had a python, Carleton," said someone else. "You talking a real python or conceptual?"

"All pythons are real," Carleton said. "Same as all assholes."

That had been in Haditha, and they'd been driving up to the command center, at the dam. The sand blew in fine clouds, twisting and swirling under the endless sky.

"So, Con, do you feel you're back—you're home?" Jenny finally asked.

He leaned back, raised his arms, stretched. "Yeah. Sort of. Hard to say."

"I know it's hard to talk about a lot of stuff," she said.

"I don't talk about the stuff that's hard to talk about," Conrad said. He smiled at her, so as not to sound mean.

Jenny nodded. "Because you think we can't handle it or because you don't want to?"

"I guess both."

She nodded again. "So, well, if you ever want to talk about it, I'm ready." She spoke carefully. "I mean, you can tell me anything."

Ollie nodded, solemn, respectful, leaning back in his chair, his eyes large. "Yeah."

Jenny lifted her wineglass to sip from it, looking at him over the rim. He remembered watching her, drinking steadily from his concoction. She and Ollie waited.

"Thanks," he said. "I mean it."

As a kid, he'd once watched a polar bear at the Central Park Zoo. The bear was close, only fifty feet away. He was walking across a huge outcropping of stone. Conrad was mesmerized by him, his huge padded feet, his narrow, snaky muzzle, his creamy pelt, his massive, dangerous size. The bear stopped and turned, looking straight at Conrad.

The small rounded ears were pricked, the black eyes focused. For a long, locked moment they looked at each other. The deep gaze seemed to link them. The watching boy returned the look. He felt an awed kind of kinship, a primal recognition.

But he'd misunderstood. Between them was a sheer granite drop and a deep chasm, a high metal fence, wire netting. They were in different worlds. The bear, seeing Conrad and pausing in his endless quest, had thought, simply, *Prey.* Conrad realized that later. There was no kinship. Now, when Jenny told him he could tell her anything, there was that same kind of drop between them. A chasm.

Conrad pushed his chair back and stood. "But I'm going up," he said. "I'm kind of whacked. I've got four years of sleep to catch up on. I'll see you in the morning."

They smiled without reproach: they were younger siblings, they were his subjects. They were happy at his return, happy in his presence. Trusting.

He thought of taking Ollie's throat in his fist.

You stupid fuck, he told himself. That was the kind of thought that would do him in. What was the matter with him?

When Carleton was killed, Conrad had to write to his parents. He had wondered then about the python—if it existed and what Carleton's parents would do with it if it did. How did you get rid of a python? Carleton's Humvee had been hit by an IED, but it wasn't the explosion that killed him. He was alive at first, but he couldn't get out. The doors had been soldered shut by the heat of the blast. It was one of the new Humvees, heavily armored, with a new locking system and windows that wouldn't shatter. They couldn't get him out. He was screaming and shaking the door handle, and at first they tried to open it from the outside, trying to unlock the handle, and then to smash the windows with the butts of their rifles, but the fire had bloomed quickly, overtaking them all, and they had to fall back and stand there watching, and hearing him. By then the fire was burning too fast and too hot for anyone to get near enough to work on the door.

Climbing the stairs, Conrad felt exhaustion drop suddenly over him like a muffling blanket. When he reached the landing and faced the next flight, he nearly stalled, and he took hold of the wooden railing, wondering for a moment if he would actually make it to the third floor. He was poleaxed. It felt good.

Four years, two deployments in Iraq—Ramadi and Haditha—and an honorable discharge. He was through, back at home. His parents were asleep in their room overlooking the darkened lawn, and his brother and sister were sitting at the kitchen table, yawning, and he was climbing the stairs to bed, and this made some kind of full circle, the completion of a mysterious equation. As though his family had a deep connection to what he'd finished, or that what he'd done was done in some way for them, and now, because of being here, because of their being here and safe in the sleeping house, he could give in to exhaustion.

He held on to the notion of exhaustion as if it were a reward. He would get into bed and turn off the light and he would lie on his back in the dark, peaceful, closing his eyes in surrender, knowing that this time, finally, as he lay in his room under the eaves, his whole family beneath him, the willows whispering outside his windows, sleep would drift easily over him. It would slide across his mind in a dark, soft tide, carrying him down into a deep silence.

But when he turned on the overhead light, everything sprang again into existence, the low ceiling, the twin beds, the high bureau. Everything was now raked in shadow, and the room looked somber and claustrophobic, something harsh and judgmental about the light. The windows were black holes.

He hadn't actually accomplished anything all day.

He still hadn't unpacked his clothes, they were still lying in piles on the bed. He hadn't called Claire. He'd dialed the number twice, but each time he hung up before it rang.

He sat down on the bed and looked at his hands.

He was too heavy for the bed; he was too big for the room. He felt he might break something if he moved around in it—as if he'd become a giant while he was gone. His younger self inhabited this place. The person he'd become was an intruder. This was like a room in a museum. It was a room he could not use, one he could only disturb. The night was silent, the air motionless.

He thought of that other world: the dawn sweep through the streets of Ramadi. The big black bats flickering through the air like thoughts as the sky went from dark to pale. The gritty sound of footsteps in the empty street. The burning, cindery smell. The rows of date palms along the river in Haditha. The sound of his pulse beating in his head, of Olivera whispering. The spattered walls.

He tried to keep Haditha from his mind, but how could you keep a thought from your mind? The thoughts lived in his mind. The dark spray on the wall. So much of it, so high up. The limp bodies on the bed. The terrible limpness. The boy in the stained pajamas, the girl's arm curled around him.

He looked at the windows and willed himself to think about something else. Just beyond the screens, in the darkness, were the willows, their narrow leaves nearly brushing the house.

In the fall, these silvery leaves dropped messily everywhere. Once, he'd seen a thin, whippy twig draped on a tall boxbush in the garden. At least he'd thought it was a twig, but it was a striped garter snake curved into a serpentine shape among the dark green leaves of the boxbush. Its neck stuck straight out into the air, the mouth wide open. The long, forked tongue waving like a flag, trolling for insects.

That was a good thought, the snake in the bush. You could focus on it safely. If you could keep Carleton from getting in. There were good thoughts, but they ran out. You got to the end of them, and then the others came back.

He sat still and let the silence move in. In a moment he would get up and undress. He looked down at his hands. They lay on his knees, palms down. They looked strange, unfamiliar.

He got undressed and into bed. He lay waiting, the room black, for sleep. Anxiety began rising, and the space around him took on a massed and hostile presence. It seemed as though the ceiling were lowering toward him. Images he had no wish to see began to flicker inside his head. He rolled over, as though he could leave them behind, but his mind had entered a state of crazed alertness, connected now to a jittering web of filaments that led him to places and moments he did not want to visit. Olivera whispering, the pattern on the walls, the girl on the bed, Jesus.

None of these were things he ever wanted to see again or even think of, and how could he erase them from his mind? Wasn't there some kind of therapy that blotted stuff from your memory? Or was that a movie? Wipe it smooth, wipe it all clean of this stuff. How was he meant to get rid of it? Wait until he forgot it? How could you make your brain forget something? There must be a way to force it to forget. There must be something. He'd been trained to make things happen. What you did was carry out the mission: get it done. No excuses.

This was what he had to look forward to; this was every night for the rest of his life. He was lying rigid, eyes open, every muscle locked tight. His jaw was clenched, his calves and shoulders taut, his breath quickening, his pulse rising. Tension had taken him over as completely as exhaustion had earlier. He kept seeing the face of the girl, the little boy's head falling back.

He turned on the light.

He'd gotten another thriller, this one by a better writer. It was about drugs in the projects, with a beaten-down black woman policeman going after a criminal. At least this was a real kind of war, and the characters seemed real. He read until after one; Jenny and Ollie were long upstairs and the house was quiet. When his eyes turned heavy again, he tried turning off the light, but the same thing happened, his brain jumped alive at once, headed for things he didn't want to think about.

It was like an alarm system activated by darkness and silence: as soon as the lights went out, everything came crowding in on him, packed and massing, things he kept out during the daytime. Things he didn't even think about during the daytime, things that should be gone and over and done. Christ.

He turned on the light and sat on the side of his bed. The house was silent. He held the mattress with both hands. He squeezed his eyes shut and bowed his head, swinging it from side to side, bending over low, as if he could somehow get away from his mind.

He would call Claire. He raised his head. This was the moment—right now, when everything was quiet. It wasn't that late. It wasn't even three. Quarter of, not even. Eighteen of, nearly twenty. Practically two-thirty. She'd definitely be awake. They'd stayed up this late lots of times.

He couldn't make the call from here; his cell phone was dying. He'd use the phone in the kitchen, no one would hear. She'd definitely be awake, she'd answer on the first ring. She'd say, *Where are you? I want to see you.*

Is that what she'd say?

He didn't know what she'd say, or what he'd say.

They had been together, at Williams, when he signed up for the Corps. They were still together when he finally went in for good. They'd agreed then that they were separating, sort of. It wasn't clear. The agreement was that they were not tied to each other, that they were both free to connect with other people, but for a while it seemed as if nothing had changed. In the beginning Claire's letters were full of her thoughts of him, and how much she missed him. She never mentioned seeing anyone else. Gradually that had changed, and she stopped saying how much she missed him, or that she loved him. He was sure she was seeing other people, because why wouldn't she, and if she was, he didn't want to know too much.

When he came home after Ramadi, things had changed further. He saw her for a few days in New York, but it was awkward. They spent the night together, but it seemed as though they hardly knew each other. Their bodies were still familiar, but they didn't seem to share a common language. He didn't know what went on when he wasn't there; he didn't want to know.

After that, Claire still wrote to him, but she told him that she had to take a break, whatever that meant. He hadn't argued because you couldn't argue with that, because if she wanted to stop she would stop, and because he didn't want her to say anything more. He didn't want her to tell him anything he didn't want to know.

And he didn't want her to stop writing. In-country, getting mail, real mail, was not something you'd give up. Getting real mail was the way you knew you had another life, that you'd go back to it.

Standing outside the command post, the sand blowing in pale, whirling skeins across the open ground, tiny drifts of it rising around your legs as you opened the letter under the flat, hot Iraqi sky, reading the words and breathing in the black, burning stink of Iraq but being in another place because of the letter, which was from Jenny, about swimming in the reservoir in the late afternoon, the smell of the flat green water, the sun going down through the trees and the way it looked on the water, flickering, gold, stretching in a shimmering path right up to you. Mail was one of the things that kept him sane.

In the beginning, Claire had written about everything. About school, when she was still in school, and later about her job—she was working in the Porcelain Department at Findlay's, the auction house—and about her two roommates and her boss, and things she saw on the street in New York. How much she loved him and missed him. After Ramadi she just told him the other things, nothing about love.

He had told Claire it was okay, they would write however she wanted them to. He didn't want to break up with her, and he didn't want her to stop writing to him.

They all got mail from the send-a-soldier-a-letter programs, letters from teenage girls at Catholic high schools who wrote generic notes full of smiley faces:

> *Hope you are keeping your spirits up, tho' I know sometimes it must be hard!!! I can't even imagine. You are doing good work and we all apprecaite what your doing. Thank you! I look forward to meeting you when you come back!!! Lots of love, Rosalie.*

Most of these letters were thrown out unread, but some of the girls enclosed pictures and some of them were kind of hot, or anyway you could persuade yourself they were, and some guys took the pictures and used them for jacking off. Some of the guys even wrote back to Rosalie and Traci and Tiffany and Lori, and if you got no mail from anyone else, which was true for some guys, then teenage Catholic girls who were complete strangers and writing letters for credit in school or in heaven or both were still better than nothing.

Mail was a fine line connecting you to the life you'd once had. Paper mail was best because it had been held by the person who wrote it. Not just letters from a girlfriend, which you always sniffed, but ones from your family: you knew that when this letter was written, your mother was sitting at the kitchen table looking out the window at the garden in winter. The paper itself had been there in the room while garlic sizzled in a pan; it was there when your father came in the back door from the train, his face and hands cold. You could hold the piece of paper and read it over and over, wherever you were, and it reminded you that the other place was real and that you'd go back there.

That June, in Ramadi, insurgents started sending rockets and mortars onto the base. The perimeter fence kept them at a distance, so they couldn't see where they were sending them. They just lobbed them over at random. Sometimes the mortars missed everyone and everything, exploding harmlessly, and sometimes they were duds and didn't explode at all, and sometimes they took someone's leg off, like Kuchnik, who was in their sister platoon and was on his way over to the mess hall with his buddy Colbert.

Halfway there, Kuchnik remembered a letter he wanted to mail to his girlfriend. He went back for it, and Colbert went on ahead. Kuchnik got the letter and started back to the mess hall and was nearly there when the rocket landed. It didn't hit him, though, it landed right beside him. It hit a utility pole, and the impact detonated the rocket's hot-metal penetrator. White-hot metal shards pierced Kuchnik's thigh, severing the femoral artery. Kuchnik lay in the sand outside the mess hall, screaming and bleeding out, still holding the letter. Doc Whitman came running, but he was on his way to the shower and was wearing only his PT shorts, and he didn't have a tourniquet.

They finally got Kuchnik tourniqueted and medevaced out to Landstuhl, in Germany, where the trauma hospital was. But by then he'd lost a lot of blood, and even though they got him stabilized on the flight over, two days after he got to Frankfurt, he died of organ failure.

He was twenty feet from the door of the mess hall, which had sandbags around it to protect it from blasts. Colbert had already gone inside and was standing in line. Afterward it was impossible to get all the blood out from the sand, and for weeks after, going in and out of the mess hall you walked over a dim stain on the ground from Kuchnik. At the beginning, when he was still alive, you thought of it as blood, but after he died, you thought of it as Kuchnik.

Email and phone calls were not as good as actual letters. In Ramadi at first, there weren't enough computers to use for email, though later they could use one sometimes. At Sparta things were more basic, and they rarely had Internet access. They could almost never use phones, but in any case everyone knew by then that phone calls were never as good as you hoped they'd be. They had those electronic gaps, overlapping voices, the ringing sounds of distance, starting and stopping, misunderstandings. Both of you were trying to put too much into the words, more than was possible. You could never say what was really going on, so you were left talking about scraps of nothing, and you couldn't hear very well. And the calls were always over too soon, before you'd said what you meant to say, and afterward they were gone completely, no way to remember exactly what had been said, what the tone of voice was, and no way to rehear them.

But letters you carried with you, you kept them in your pocket or under your pillow, if you had one. You put them inside your helmet, or just inside your seabag, or in your boot or your locker, someplace where they were safe and you could touch them. Sometimes you just wanted to run your fingertips across the envelope, that was enough; sometimes you wanted to take the letter out, unfold it, and read it again so you knew you'd had another life once, been part of another world.

8

Conrad had met Claire Ingersoll during the fall of his junior year at Williams. They were both in a seminar on Homer. The class was small and hard to get into; it required permission from the professor, who was a medium-well-known classical scholar and majorly finicky. He accepted only upperclassmen who were majoring in classics, and he was fussy about even them.

When he accepted Claire, who was a sophomore planning to be a lit major, everyone knew she had to be smart. They could see that she was beautiful—dark, straight eyebrows and dark blue eyes, a surprisingly red mouth, wide and calm. A broad forehead, narrow, elegant nose, winged nostrils.

After their second class, Conrad asked her out for coffee.

"So how'd you get into Hodgson's class?" Conrad asked. They were at the snack bar, sitting at a table in the back by the big windows. He twisted the top from his water bottle. "It's for classics majors. I thought underclassmen weren't even allowed to apply. How'd you do it?"

Claire shook her head. "I don't know. I love Homer, so I just asked Hodgson if I could apply. I gave him something I wrote in high school." She was drinking green tea, and she raised it to her mouth.

"You wrote about Homer in high school?" Conrad was trying not to stare. She gave off a muted radiance; he felt everyone could see it. It was like sitting with someone who had a spotlight trained on her.

"Not about Homer. Greek myths," she said. "The gods. I've always been interested in them since I was little. Did you ever read those D'Aulaires books?"

"All of them," Conrad said. "Did you have the one about the trolls?"

"We had all of them," she said. "I can't believe you had them, too. I loved them. Remember how everyone kind of glowed, like the sun was behind each figure?" She held her cup in both hands, her fingers wrapped around it. "Anyway, I read that book about the Greek myths, and it hooked me. In high school I read Edith Hamilton. I wrote a paper about Zeus and Hera, how their personalities were complementary. That's what I showed to Hodgson, and here I am." Her smile was faintly asymmetrical, her mouth rising slightly more on the right side.

"Yeah, but the *Iliad*? Kind of a guy's poem, isn't it?" He couldn't stop looking at her. He took a swig from his bottle.

"I guess," she said. "But it's so *major*. I feel like I have to know it. I need it in my head."

"Just so you know," he warned, "it contains violence and some adult material."

"What?" She looked shocked. "I had no idea."

"Fact," he said.

The table next to them was being colonized. Two guys set their backpacks on the floor, dragging the chairs out. They were jocks, in torn sweatshirts and jeans. One glanced over, and Conrad saw his gaze settle on Claire. Conrad leaned across the table, proprietary. He spoke again, wanting to keep her attention.

"You're brave. How's it feel to be the only girl in the class?"

"I'm not," she said. "There are two juniors. Women, actually," she added delicately.

Conrad hadn't noticed the other girls—okay, women—but he didn't want to tell her that. He didn't want to tell her that he actually couldn't take his eyes off her, the way she looked up at Hodgson, her grave brows lifting attentively, and the way she set her lips together and the smooth angle of her wrist when she took notes. He didn't want to tell her that he hadn't even seen the other girls, because then he'd sound either like a complete bullshitter or a complete dork. He leaned closer.

"I didn't see any other women there," he told her.

She looked at him, then laughed. "Conrad," she said.

His name in her voice: he felt a tiny jolt of excitement.

"Claire," he said. Her name in his mouth.

"So what did you say about Zeus and Hera?" he asked, leaning back. "I'm actually writing my thesis on them. How they're both transgendered."

She didn't know him well enough yet to know when he was joking, or what kind of jokes he'd make. But she would come to know him, and they would learn each other. They had that to look forward to, and the idea gave Conrad a giddy lift. He leaned toward her again, to speak; she leaned toward him to listen.

"Kidding," he said.

"I knew that," she said.

Claire's hair hung down her back nearly to her waist. She wore it loose, sometimes outside her parka, where it spilled and drifted, full of static electricity, across the whispery fabric. Sometimes she kept it inside her jacket, a soft, secret mass pressed against her warm back. Just the thought of that, the hidden shimmery mass shifting across her back, used to give him a hard-on. Nearly everything about her gave him a hard-on. The fine, ridged edge of her upper lip, the way it articulated the line of her mouth. The shallow indentation along her upper arm.

Her neck was long and graceful, and when she spoke, sometimes she took her hair in both hands, lifting it away from her face to toss it down her back. As she did so, she raised her chin, lengthening her throat, while looking steadily at him. When she smiled, she looked at him sideways, shyly.

Conrad could make her laugh. She nearly fell off her chair, helpless and twisting, her hand over her mouth, when he told her the story about his roommate and the pizza delivery guy. She liked country music, but he forgave her for that because she liked baseball and was a Sox fan. Her fingers were short and stubby, like a little girl's, and they were double-jointed. She could bend her thumb backward, nearly touching her wrist, and that gave him a hard-on, too.

Six weeks later, they had their first fight. They were on their way back to Conrad's room after a long evening with friends. It was late, and they were walking uphill.

"I don't know why Josh even likes her," she said. "She's an idiot."

"Yeah, well. Maybe not an idiot." Josh was Conrad's friend, barrel-bellied and chubby-faced, cheeks covered in dark stubble. His girlfriend, Lisa, was a junior, a girl from Chicago, redheaded and noisy, with a big, boisterous laugh. Conrad liked her.

"No. She is," Claire said. "I couldn't believe what she said about date rape."

The sidewalk was getting steeper, and they slowed, walking in step. Conrad put his arm around Claire's shoulders and she put her hand in his back pocket.

"Yeah," Conrad said vaguely. He couldn't remember exactly what Lisa had said. Had they even talked about date rape?

"Didn't you think—" Claire asked.

"I don't know," he hedged. "I'm not sure exactly what her point was."

Claire stopped and looked at him. She took her hand out of his pocket. "You're not sure? How can you not be sure?" They were under a streetlight, and the light struck straight down. Claire's eyebrows were beetled. "Conrad, she was basically saying it doesn't exist."

"Yeah," Conrad said. "That's not what I thought she said."

"Well, she did." Claire turned away and started walking again, her head down against the hillside. "She said what happens is that women have sex with somebody and then the next morning they kind of wish they hadn't, so they claim date rape to make themselves feel less like sluts. Which, she implied, they basically are." She turned to him again. "Don't you remember that?"

"I thought we were talking about, uh, sex in general."

"She was showing off, Conrad," Claire said. "Like she's Miss Sex. Like let's all think about how horny she is."

Conrad had not been thinking of how horny Lisa was. She didn't attract him, with her narrow, red-rimmed eyes and bushy, gingery eyebrows.

"I thought she was talking about how horny guys were," he said.

"Well," said Claire. "You're supposed to think she knows that because she's so hot they can't keep their hands off her."

"Uh," Conrad said, focusing on the sidewalk. "I thought we were talking about something else." They walked on for a few moments in silence. Conrad thought they were done, but suddenly Claire spoke again.

"You don't remember we were talking about date rape?" she asked.

"I thought she just said that women should take more responsibility with the whole thing," Conrad said. "Like, from the get-go."

Claire stopped. "Why would you use a word like 'get-go'?" she demanded. "It's not even a word."

"Okay," Conrad said. He wondered if Claire had had more beers than he'd noticed. "I don't know why I would, you're right."

"Honestly," Claire said severely. "It's an idiot's word." She shook her head and started walking again, then stopped. "I honestly don't even know why we're having this conversation if you're going to use words like that."

She stood still on the sidewalk, her legs slightly spread. Her head was lowered and set strangely to one side. She was weaving.

"Conrad," she said, "I'm sort of getting the whirlies." Her voice was now muffled and sorrowful. The streetlamp was behind them, casting her crooked shadow ahead. Beyond her was the deep darkness of a fir tree, dense against the night.

"Hold on." Conrad put his arm around her. "Don't move. Keep your eyes open. Don't close your eyes."

"My eyes are closed, Conrad." Her voice was despairing. "They're already closed."

"Can you open them?" he asked. "Try to open them."

Claire shook her head. "It's too late," she whispered. "I'm going to be sick."

He took her by the shoulders and guided her to the edge of the sidewalk. She swayed, then suddenly bent over. He held her by the waist as she shuddered; he pressed his hips against her butt, holding her against him. He was surprised by the violence inside her frail frame. She retched, convulsive, struggling. He held her blue-jeaned hips. She gagged, and the smell rose up at him. He kept a firm grip on her, keeping her steady. He was touched by her helplessness. She was alone in her body, swept by waves of anguish here in the wideness of the night, the dark sky rising above. What he felt was tenderness. He was grateful to be there, holding her.

She wasn't listening yet, but he whispered, "You're okay. I've got you."

In March, when Claire turned twenty, for her birthday Conrad gave her a scavenger hunt based on the *Iliad*. He handed her the first clue, which he'd printed out in an antique font.

Age—goddess, sing the age of Helen's daughter Claire,
Gorgeous, fortunate, she that turned the heads of countless Williams guys.
Begin, goddess, in the place where our illustrious bard begins and ends
his eponymous journey.

The answer to the first clue, of course, was Homer, the home plate at Bobby Coombs Baseball Field. He had made ten clues, and the hunt took them all afternoon. When Claire wasn't getting it, Conrad whistled and looked away, and when she was getting hot, he shook his hand hard and said, *"Ow!"* in a high falsetto. They went all over Williamstown: the answer to one clue was at the supermarket, among household cleansers.

Mighty warrior from Greece.
Mighty great and mighty little.
O Achaean, once invincible, once your fierce and noble self,
Now your ancient might is altered, now you're always on the shelf.

That was Ajax. Conrad had gone over in the morning and wrapped the clue on the outermost container, hoping it would be there when they arrived. He had brought an extra as backup in case it was gone, but when Claire strode down the aisle, it was still there, tied with a green ribbon, and she snatched it up, delighted.

The last clue of the hunt was:

Proud warriors, you stood your ground,
Upon the ramparts made your stand
You were undone, your walls were breached
The gods here played a dooming hand.

The answer, of course, was Trojans. Since that was the brand Conrad used (partly because of the name), the solution brought them back to his room, and they ended up in bed, his plan from the beginning.

When Conrad first told Claire about joining the Marines, she thought he was joking. They were eating lunch at the health-food store, where Claire had persuaded him to go. They were sitting at a table crammed in the corner near the refrigeration units. The table was tiny, and their knees bumped. Behind Claire's head were the cooler doors, misted pale by condensation, and behind them shelves of strange frozen products in bland packaging.

"The Marines?" Claire said. She cocked her head. "Have you ever tried one of those paintball weekend warrior things?"

"Paintball?" Conrad said, offended. "This is serious. This is the Marines. I'm really planning to join."

She lowered her sandwich and looked at him. "You really are? Why would you do that?"

He shrugged, disappointed. She was supposed to get it. "I want to do something for my country." It sounded totally false, pompous, hypocritical.

Her sandwich was full of sprouts, and they kept drifting out of her mouth. She licked her lips to capture them, and this was distracting to Conrad, who kept watching her mouth and her supple, active tongue.

"What would you be doing for your country?" she asked.

"Protecting it. I don't want other people to have to fight for me."

"But we're not at war," Claire said. "No one has to fight for you."

"We have a standing army," Conrad said. "Someone has to be in it. I believe in national service. It's a patriotic duty."

He sounded like a recruitment poster. Watching Claire's face turn quizzical and wary, distant, he began to wonder if he was making some irretrievable move, abandoning his own peers, his cohort. He'd be stepping across some line, and they'd be staring at him from the other side, the people he knew, all his friends, and why did he want to abandon everyone he knew, and where was the sense of ethical clarity he had thought was illuminating this decision?

Claire put down her sandwich. "This is completely mysterious to me. I never knew you liked to shoot guns."

"I'm not doing this so I can shoot guns," Conrad said, though secretly he was excited about exactly that.

"There are lots of other ways you could serve your country," Claire said. "This is like resigning from the world."

"The opposite," Conrad said stiffly. "I'd be joining the world. The real world. The larger world." Christ, he sounded like an ass.

"You'd be resigning from normal life. The military is not normal life, it's like the priesthood. You'd be turning your back on the rest of the world," Claire said. "How long does it last?"

"Everything you do means turning your back on something," Conrad said.

Claire shook her head. "Not like this." She took another tack. "You think it's glamorous? The uniforms, the tanks, all that stuff? Is that why you're doing it?"

"Yeah, I'm doing it for the uniforms," he said. "The white gloves."

She raised her eyebrows, then picked up her sandwich.

Behind her, a bright-faced middle-aged woman wearing jeans and a fleece jacket squeezed past Claire's chair to get to the freezer. The woman's hair was short and gray, her cheeks pink. She took out a couple of frozen packets and then turned, meeting Conrad's eye. She smiled reflexively. It was a generic health-food-store response, mindless, friendly, like, *We're all family.*

It irritated Conrad. Health-food stores were exactly the opposite of the Marines: soft and gooey, homemade idealism, peace and love, sentimentalism, crunchy raw vegetables and tasteless expensive food. What kind of response was this to mega-farms, supermarket chains, pesticide companies? A bunch of pink-cheeked do-gooders, impractical, ineffective, no hope for their hopes.

Conrad put down his fork. "You know, this stuff is really disgusting. What am I eating? Tofu burger? It tastes like old socks. It's not food."

"It's not meant to taste like hamburger," Claire said.

"It's meant to taste like old socks?"

After that they argued about food, and Conrad behaved badly and demanded that they go to Burger King, where he ordered a real burger. Claire ostentatiously ordered water, and he sat and ate his burger in complete silence and felt like a dick.

They didn't talk about the Marines again until the next morning. Conrad lived on the top floor of an old dormitory building. His room was narrow, with a a single dormer window projecting out of the eaves. A monolithic silver radiator stood below the window, and Claire was convinced that it looked different depending on its temperature. Before the heat came up, she claimed, the radiator looked cold and withholding, frigid. As it warmed, it began to glow, expansive and benevolent, giving off the fine, dry scent of heat. Conrad said that was impossible.

That morning Conrad and Claire lay under the covers of his single bed, their limbs entangled, the covers pulled up to their chins, waiting for the heat to come up.

"I have a biology lab to finish," Claire said, not moving. "I have to be there by nine-thirty."

"Look at the radiator. Does it look hot yet?"

"It looks cold. I can't get up." Her arms wrapped around him, she lay on her side, pressed against him. "But don't you think it's kind of crazy?" she asked. "Four years of your life—what will you be at the end of it? What will you do then?"

"I can do anything afterward," he said. "Graduate school, anything. It doesn't mean I've stopped my life."

"It sort of does. You'll have stopped the life you lead now."

He wasn't thinking of afterward. He was thinking of himself made different, better, more powerful, more effective. He would enter into a state of moral clarity.

"Anyway," he said, "it's not like I know, right now, what I want to do, even if I don't go in. This will give me a better sense of everything. Who I am."

"You'll be a killer." The way she said this did not make it sexy. "They'll train you to kill people."

"It's not about killing," he said. "Don't be a jerk, Claire. You're so melodramatic." He rolled away and sat up, raising the sheet unkindly, letting in a flood of cold air. "Look at it, it's hot."

"Don't do that," Claire said, grabbing for the sheet, but he was up, he was gone.

They'd argued about it for weeks, but they hadn't broken up. They were still together for the rest of that year and after his first summer at OCS. They were still together right up until the next summer, when he went in full-time. Even then they didn't break things off completely, though each told the other they were free to pull away.

"You'll get too busy blowing up things to write," Claire told him.

"You'll be doing too many missions to think about me. You'll have your buddies."

"Right," said Conrad, sort of sarcastic, but also thinking of his new life, which would be exciting and demanding, and that she was partly right. "No," he said, "I won't. Duh."

The night before he left, they were together in Katonah. They sat up late in the library, sitting side by side on the small sofa, drinking beer and talking.

"You're free to see anyone you want," Conrad told Claire again. She was curled up next to him, her knees drawn up against her chest, her feet tucked underneath her.

"I know that." Her eyes were pink around the edges. She'd been crying. She sighed and ran her fingernail along the label on the beer bottle. "But I don't want to see anyone else. I want to see you. I still don't see why you're doing this."

At that moment he didn't know why. At three o'clock in the morning, Claire's warm body next to him, his parents asleep upstairs, the countryside dark and silent beyond the windows, he couldn't remember. There was this life, living with people, in houses, and there was the other, and why exactly had he chosen the other?

"Too late," he said. "It's done."

They both hoped it would last in spite of the distance and separation. Why would it not? They loved each other. They wrote and emailed, and they saw each other when Conrad came home on leave, and they made it work until Claire graduated in 2003 and moved to New York. After that, Conrad saw that things were changing. While Claire was at college, she had still been within the world that had held him, where the two of them had been together. But in New York everything was new for her. She was living in a new community in which Conrad had no place.

That fall she sent him a long email. He was in training then, in the Pacific. *Here's the thing,* she wrote.

> *I can't go on living as though you're still here. It's making me kind of crazy. I still love you, Con, but I can't go on thinking that you and I are*

together, because we aren't. You're off somewhere, doing things I don't know about. And I'm here, doing things you don't know about. I feel disloyal, all the time, because I'm making new friends and entering into a world I never knew with you.

While I was still at Williams it was different, it still felt like our world, but now everything I do is something you and I never did together. Everyone I meet is someone you don't know, and at first I felt like I was sharing everything with you. Every day I couldn't wait to go home and write you all about it. But I can't keep up, I can't tell you everything, there's too much. And I feel guilty and disloyal if I have fun, and if I like people you don't even know, and I'm not sharing any of it with you. But I can't share it with you. You're on a ship somewhere in the Pacific. I can't go on like this for three more years.

When he read that, Conrad looked at the date. She'd written it at 5:38 a.m., October 17. It was a Friday for her, though he was on the other side of the international date line. He looked at the time and date as though they were important. He pictured her sitting cross-legged in bed, typing on her computer. None of that changed the fact of what she'd written.

Conrad wrote back and told her he understood.

You've always been free to let go, anytime, he wrote. *We always said that.* Then he thought that this sounded patronizing, because saying that she was free to do something made it sound as though it were in his power not to make her free. But he couldn't think of another way to say it, because it was what they'd told each other. All of it made him feel heavy and leaden, sickened. He didn't know how to say it any better, and he wanted to get through with it, and he pushed "Send."

They kept on writing to each other. They stopped saying they loved each other, though they wrote *love* at the end of their messages. He often wrote group emails to his family, and after that he usually included Claire in them instead of writing to her alone. But she was still the main person in his life.

At first, when he came back on leave, he saw her and it was all right. It seemed as though they were the way they'd always been. But then he'd gone to see her after he came home from Ramadi, in September 2004, and that was not all right.

He went first to Katonah. There, almost all he'd done was sleep, but somehow he hadn't ever actually relaxed. Every moment included the knowledge that he was going back, and probably back to redeployment. That sense was physically present. Each morning when he woke up, he knew exactly how close he was to leaving again. His departure was like a huge ticking clock hanging over every moment. By the end of his leave he was dying to get on with it.

Claire was in New York then, working at Findlay's and living with friends in a white-brick building on First Avenue. Conrad went in to see her. They went out to dinner, and he ended up spending the night. They didn't talk about it, they just got drunk and went to bed, which was something they knew how to do. They were very good at sex, only this time it had gone wrong. Somehow rage had gotten mixed up in it, and Conrad found himself lying on top of Claire's long body and looking down into her terrified face. She was crying. Afterward, he knew it was bad. He knew he'd made a mistake. He held her, stroking her hair. He whispered that he was sorry.

In the morning Claire lay turned away from him as though she were asleep. He knew she wasn't, because of her breathing. Conrad put his hand on her side, down low, and began to stroke the smooth curve over her ribs.

She took his hand and moved it away. Then she rolled over to face him.

"Con," she said. "I can't do this. I love you, but I can't do this again." She spoke very quietly.

He looked at her face, the broad, smooth forehead, the straight eyebrows. The fine-edged line of her mouth. He smoothed her hair away carefully from her face.

"Sorry," he said. "I didn't mean to be like that." What had he done? He couldn't exactly remember.

"It's not what you did," she said. "I just can't be in two places at once."

"I'm sorry," he said again. "I fucked up."

"No," she said. "I have to be clear. Whatever is going to happen between us will have to wait until you're back for good. I can't do this."

He had no idea what she meant. Did she want to end things? Did she have someone else? Or did she just want to be available in case someone else came along? Some guy from Wall Street, was that what she wanted? Was that what she already had? He had no idea what she meant. He couldn't bring himself to ask.

"Okay," he said, nodding. "Fine. I understand."

Fuck.

Now it was nearly three o'clock in the morning, and it seemed like the right time to call. He was dreading a really bad conversation, a fire wall between them. Stilted questions, *Hi, how are you?* As if they had known each other years ago, not well.

He was dreading the call, but once he talked to her, he'd know more. It might be something he didn't want to know, but he had to do it. If she didn't want to see him anymore, at least he would know that. If she did want to see him, he still had to figure it out. He needed to know, one way or the other. A throbbing started up in his temple. On the right, the bad side. Maybe he could go into New York and stay with her for a while. This house was beginning to feel like a cage.

He got up, in his T-shirt and boxers. The back stairs creaked, all of them, and there was no way to get down them quietly. In the kitchen he switched on the light, and the white glare caught the room by surprise. The blue-and-white tiles on the wall beside the stove, the scarred butcher-block counters, the hanging green lamps—everything was frozen, caught by the illumination. Murphy was curled up on top of the island, lying half on a pile of catalogs. She yawned pinkly.

Conrad sat down and took the phone in his lap. He dialed Claire's number, listening to the electronic sound, the faint busy plinking of connections being made. Just before her phone started to ring, he hung up.

What exactly was he going to say? Was he supposed to beg? Explain that she did know him, that he was the same fucking person he'd been at Williams? Which he was not. Though part of him wanted to be that person—at least he wanted to be part of that person, the part that had been her boyfriend.

What he would say was *Claire.*

She'd hear in his voice why he was calling.

He didn't know what he was meant to say. He was saying, *Let me back in*. He was saying, *Fuck you*. Rage was involved again somehow, though in a way he didn't understand.

He dialed her number. It rang five times before she answered, her voice clotted with sleep.

"Hello?"

"It's me." There was a pause. "Conrad." It irritated him to have to say his name.

"Conrad." She'd been deeply asleep; he could hear her struggling up to the surface. "Con. Where are you?"

"Katonah," he said. "My parents'."

"Mmm."

"I'm sorry to call so late," he said. "I thought you might be up."

The middle of the night was familiar terrain for them. They'd stayed up all night many times, fucking, watching movies, driving around. At college they'd stayed up studying for exams, writing papers. As the hours wore on, he'd watched her face go pale and plain, half-moons darkening under her eyes, her lips turning gray. When she was tired, she got cold: she stretched her legs out and covered them with her parka. That gave him a hard-on, too.

"No," Claire said now. "I wasn't awake. I have to get up in a few hours."

Stupid of him. She had a job. "Sorry."

There was a pause. Finally she spoke.

"Are you coming into the city?"

"Do you want me to?"

She sighed. "Don't be like this. It's the middle of the night."

"I need to know what's going on," Conrad said.

He studied the bulletin board, collaged with notes and reminders. The chimney cleaner's card, CLEAN SWEEP, with a top hat on the logo. An old list of family birthdays, the paper pierced by a million thumbtacks. A photograph of Lydia's mother as a child, wearing a snowsuit, beaming, her own mother's angular old-fashioned writing above it, *A Happy New Year!* His arrival date marked on the calendar: *CON!*

"Come in," Claire said.

"Okay," Conrad said.

"I want to see you," said Claire.

"Me, too," said Conrad.

He felt a kind of elation. He wanted to see her, enter into the world he had with her; he also wanted to wrench himself free from something, pull away from the people around him who didn't know what the real world was like. He wanted both to enter into this world and to cut himself off from it forever.

9

The train station at Katonah was no longer housed in its original whimsical nineteenth-century building, with a shallow-sloping roof and deep eaves, dark red clapboards and small-paned windows. That building was still there, flush with the tracks and right in the middle of the village. But it had been sold by the railway and was now a down-scale Italian restaurant, noisy and crowded, with a neon sign outside and lines for takeout spilling into the parking lot.

When the station was first sold off, it had become an upscale restaurant with a spare, minimalist look, bare wooden walls, Bauhaus chairs, and a pricey menu. The handsome owner came over to each table to describe the specials—fresh crab flown in from Maryland, shrimp from the Gulf. It was amazing that such a restaurant could flourish in such a tiny village in the outlying suburbs, where practically no one went out to eat during the week. And it was amazing that the food was brought in from such exotic locales. It was amazing that the owner used his own plane to bring it in. Then it turned out that the owner was using his plane to bring in other things besides Gulf shrimp, things that were not on the menu. It turned out that the restaurant was a front and the owner a dealer, and he ended up in court on narcotics charges and the restaurant changed hands.

The old station had been sold off when the trains became electrified. A third rail was installed alongside the old ones. This one was solid and angular, a dirty brown, unlike the smooth, curved, shining rails that carried the trains. This one carried a lethal charge of electricity and made it life-threatening to walk across the tracks at ground level. The old station, with its wide sheltering eaves and roomy waiting room, was still a restaurant, and Katonah had no station building at all. North of the old building was an overpass that led over the tracks. In the middle of it, concrete stairs descended to the platform, between the north and south tracks. At the end of Conrad's homecoming weekend, Lydia drove Jenny and Conrad to the train. She parked and got out to say goodbye. When she kissed Conrad, she said, "Give my love to Claire."

"I will," he said.

She spoke into his ear. "You can always come back, Con. You can stay here as long as you want." She looked at him. "You know that, right?"

"Right, Mom," he said. "Thanks."

People were already down on the platform. A teenage girl in tight jeans and blunt-toed sheepskin boots, a middle-aged man in khakis and a windbreaker, two women with small suitcases, standing side by side and not talking.

Conrad and Jenny made their way up the outside staircase, then down to the platform. Everyone stood waiting, occasionally glancing up the track with the air of public travelers, a combination of patience and passivity. The afternoon was warm and balmy. Along both sides of the tracks was a narrow stretch of untended woods, ash and sugar maple, spindly saplings thrusting up under the bigger trees, the ground thick with unraked leaves. The trees had made their annual unfolding, offering their brave, innocent leaves to the air. The concrete platform—flanked by the iron tracks, the wooden ties, the dull stone roadbed—was like an industrial island in a natural sea. Along it foamed the deep green of summer.

When the train pulled in, they walked down the platform and got on the last car. The train had come from more rural stations, and the car was nearly empty. High-backed gray seats stood in rows beside the big plate-glass windows beneath the open racks for luggage. They walked to the end of the car and took the last seats. Jenny slid in next to the window; Conrad tossed their bags onto the overhead rack and sat beside her.

Jenny was wearing kid clothes again, brown cargo pants and a black

T-shirt. More big earrings: today they were black—big, dangling question marks. She leaned back in her seat and propped her feet up. Someone outside gave a call and the train began to glide forward, slowly at first, then, clicking and shuddering, faster.

The view outside was a leafy tangle, the trees too close and going by too fast to focus on, the images quick and broken, like strobe-lit flashes. Then they were out in the open, where the highways ran briefly side by side—the big, wide modern one, with its careful engineering, next to the narrow, curving old Saw Mill River Parkway, designed for aesthetics, with its graceful hanging trees and its riverbank that flooded within minutes of a rainstorm. The wide lanes ran parallel, the cars sliding along in a smooth wave, all at the same speed, as though they were controlled by a distant electronic panel. The highways vanished suddenly, blotted out again by trees crowding against the windows. Near the next village were glimpses of low brick buildings scattered around the old station. It was now a watch-repair shop or a picture framer, Conrad couldn't remember, couldn't quite see the sign.

When he was growing up, these little towns in Westchester had felt like the center of the world. Mount Kisko, with its mall and movie theater, its huge parking lots, its shoe stores and banks and car dealerships, had once seemed pulsing and vital, central. Now these towns seemed quiet and peripheral, with their low buildings and seedy restaurants. They were no longer the center of anything to him.

New York was the center of a kind of universe, pulsing with a focused, self-absorbed energy. It was sort of the center of the family universe, since both his parents worked there, and Conrad had gone into the city all his life. But now it was strange to him. It didn't feel like the center of his life, either. He wasn't sure where it was now, the center of his life.

"So how's it going?" Jenny asked. "Being home." She glanced at him.

Conrad nodded without looking at her.

"Good," he said. "Weird."

"Yeah, I'd think it would be," she said. "You having a hard time?"

"Not really."

There was nothing to complain about. There were these few things he had to get through, that was all. There was nothing he could explain.

"Why are we sitting back here?" she asked.

Conrad shrugged. "I like to sit facing the door."

She nodded, her eyes on him, then turned away to watch the rattling view.

"I hear things are pretty good with you and Jock," he said.

"Yeah, I think we're going to move in together," Jenny said, frowning.

"Hey." Conrad nodded encouragingly. "Sounds good."

"I think so," she said. "He's about to start his internship, so if we aren't living together, we won't see each other at all." She leaned her head back. "I don't know. It feels like a big deal. This sounds stupid, but I really like my apartment. What if I give it up to move in with him and then we break up? I'll never find anything as good."

"That's not stupid," Conrad said. "That's kind of big."

Jenny nodded.

"But don't decide because of your apartment. You'll always find another one. You should decide because of how you feel about him."

"Yeah," Jenny said again. "It's just hard to know how you feel. I mean, you can't measure how you feel against the way anyone else does. How do I know if it's right? What if there are things I haven't even thought of? Like, *Oh, you never asked if he was a serial killer*?"

"Yeah," Conrad said. "Hard. I guess you never know everything about someone. Guess you go with your gut. What did Mom say?"

"She said, Ask yourself two things: Is he kind, and do you trust him?"

"Nothing about serial killers," he said. "So, do you?" He wondered what Claire would say about him. Was he kind to her? Should she trust him?

"I think so. But you know, it's hard to focus on things like that. It's like picking something out of the air. What if there's something about him that will drive me crazy in ten years? And I know there will be. I mean, I know you have to forgive people the little things, it's just . . ." She paused. "I guess I can't figure out what the big things are." She shook her head and turned to him. "What about you and Claire? How are things?"

"Kind of up in the air. I don't know what she wants."

"What do you want?"

"Yeah," Conrad said. "That's the thing. I don't really know that, either."

It flooded around him again, the sense of being back, but lost. He wanted Claire to take him back, but then what?

At Quantico they'd memorized the leadership traits: bearing, courage, decisiveness, dependability, endurance, enthusiasm, initiative, integrity, judgment, justice, knowledge, loyalty, tact, and unselfishness. They'd memorized the six troop-leading steps, BAMCIS: Begin planning. Arrange for reconnaissance. Make reconnaissance. Complete the plan. Issue the order. Supervise. Speed was a weapon. The Marines' method was maneuver warfare; they slipped around the hard surfaces of the enemy, into the vulnerable ones. Never attack in the teeth of the guns. Indecision is a decision. He knew all these things.

Jenny looked at him, then away. "That's kind of how you seem. Out of focus." She paused. "Not too happy." She paused again and flicked a glance at him. "Would you think of seeing a shrink?"

"It's not like that," Conrad said.

As the train rattled on southward, new people got on at every stop and the cars began to fill. It made Conrad uneasy. Faces kept appearing in the doorway, people tossed bags onto the overhead rack with a sliding thud, people walked in and out of the car, the door suddenly rattling open, a new face appearing or someone disappearing.

He'd thought of seeing a shrink, but he had nothing specific to say. Whatever he had was formless, indistinct. And anyway this was military stuff, a civilian wouldn't understand. There were shrinks in the VA, if he wanted to talk to one, which he did not.

During the last month at Pendleton, after coming back from deployment, he'd filled out the mental health forms, the questions about symptoms for PTSD: panic attacks, flashbacks, insomnia. Headaches. There was no point in putting all that on your record. Everything the Marines had ever drilled into him said suck it up. He was back, and he wanted to put all that behind him. And at that point it hadn't all started yet. He'd had insomnia, some panic attacks, but he'd thought it would all stop once he was home. It seemed sort of late to claim it now.

Now that he was really back home, he'd get through it. He'd gotten through it over there, in-country, when it was real. There was no point in raising the issue now, when everything was over. There was the question of objective reality. There were no IEDs on these roads. No snipers in upstairs windows or on overpasses. No one was firing mortars or rocket-propelled grenades. The point was to keep yourself under control. This was the mission: Suck it up.

A man in his mid-twenties pushed open the train door. He was short and burly, dark-skinned, with big, dark, liquid eyes and thick lips. His hair was buzzed short and he wore a basketball jacket and jeans. He held a cup of coffee, and a tiny wire snaked its way up his neck to his ear. He made his way down the aisle and sat down across from Conrad and Jenny, sliding over to the window without looking around. He took the lid off his coffee and began drinking, staring out the window. His head was bobbing to the beat of whatever was coming through his earbuds.

That morning Conrad had done a hundred push-ups on his bedroom floor, his body rock solid, thrusting himself up over and over. He whispered the count as he rose. After that he'd done a hundred crunches, rising easily, hands locked behind his head. Then he'd gone out and run the four-mile circle on the dirt road, the short, steep hills with the twisting corners, the long slope up through the meadows, the short paved stretch coming home. Respecting his body, keeping it strong and ready, was part of something he'd promised himself.

It irritated Conrad that this guy seemed to feel so safe, so comfortable, that he didn't even need to look around, make one single assessing glance, figure out who was nearby, where trouble might come from. Why did he feel so fucking entitled to safety? The car was full of strangers, all of them carrying backpacks, briefcases, bags. No one was checking on anything. This asshole was sitting right next to a piece of plate glass, closing his eyes and sipping his coffee, bobbing his head like a rock star.

"Why are you doing that?" Jenny asked.

"Doing what?"

"Banging your thumb against your knee. Are you thinking of a song, or are you nervous?"

He looked at his hand and stopped it. He shook his head.

Jenny touched his shoulder. "You okay?"

He shook his head again. After a moment she took her hand away, but that didn't stop the way he felt. It swept across him like some kind of mist, this feeling of tingling confusion, as though the molecules in the air were suddenly alive, teeming, in dangerous, suppressive motion around him. There was nothing he could do.

He kept glancing over at Earbuds, drilling him with his eyes, and Earbuds, feeling his stare, glanced over once, then looked away. He took out a pair of sunglasses and put them on, then slid down on the seat, hunkering inside his big jacket, and turned his face to the window.

"Conrad," Jenny said.

"What."

"Why are you staring like that?"

Conrad turned to her. He could feel his chest, tight. *Because he's an asshole. Because he's not fucking paying attention. Look at him. He's one soft motherfucker, lazy and sloppy. He doesn't understand anything.*

He didn't answer. None of this would sound right. It was all true, but it wouldn't sound right. If he said it, he would sound like the asshole.

He said nothing and turned his head toward the front of the car, toward the passengers ahead. With his peripheral vision he was aware of Earbuds, who stayed hunched in his jacket, staring out the window, head bobbing. Every once in a while Conrad turned to look at him, masking his gesture with another, rubbing his chin or scratching his neck, but turning toward Earbuds. When he did, he could see Earbuds glance his way, using his own peripheral vision, noticing.

When the train pulled into Grand Central, everyone stood, reaching for bags and sweaters, collecting the detritus of the trip. Earbuds didn't move. He stayed where he was, facing the window as if there were something important to see out on the platform. He didn't want to stand and meet Conrad's stare: this gave Conrad a jolt of satisfaction. At least the guy had gotten the message.

As Conrad reached up to grab the bags, Earbuds looked up at him over the frame of his sunglasses, his eyes darting nervously. It struck

Conrad suddenly that the guy was actually alarmed. He'd frightened him. Conrad felt pleased: the guy should be afraid of him. The asshole. Earbuds turned, shifting to face more to the window, giving Conrad more of his back. Then Conrad's satisfaction drained away; he felt a sudden twitch of self-disgust.

What was the matter with him? This was just some young guy, a kid, really, who'd gotten the message that a complete stranger would like to punch him out. For what, for getting on the train in his own town, listening to his own music? And what was Conrad doing, trying to eye-fuck someone who was minding his own business, listening privately to hip-hop?

You stupid fuck, thought Conrad. He felt enraged at himself, helpless. The worst was the helplessness.

He pulled the bags down from the rack. He and Jenny joined the line of jostling passengers moving slowly toward the door. Everyone now was too close; everyone, in these last slow, gliding moments, was restless and impatient. In front of Conrad were two girls, twelve or thirteen, in bright tops and tight pants. The nearest one stood close to him, the back of her head in Conrad's face. Her hair was in a ponytail.

Ponytail was talking loudly. Her friend had a narrow charcoal-colored face, fuzzy hair pulled back by a pink plastic hair band. They pushed each other, laughing. Ponytail fell back against Conrad, thudding against his chest. She didn't apologize or even glance around as he recoiled. He drew away, but she moved with him. She kept collapsing against him, shouting with laughter. Each impact felt like a blow. The sudden thud of her body was like an electric shock.

He turned his shoulder so that the duffel bag was between them. Ponytail went on chattering, but her friend looked up at him and got it. She whispered to Ponytail, who turned to look at him. He stared at them. They put their hands up to their faces, giggling, pursing their lips in private hysteria, holding on to each other for support.

Conrad looked straight ahead, frowning, willing the door to open. He felt caught in some way he didn't understand.

When the door finally opened, he and Jenny shuffled slowly off the train at the tail end of the hurrying crowd. Footsteps echoed around them as they walked through the dank, cavernous space of the platform, then entered a more civilized hallway that led into the station itself.

In the great atrium, the painted domed ceiling soared over the hurrying crowds. The sounds rose, fragmented, into the space. This was a place Conrad knew well. He knew just how the constellations were laid out, knew the faint gold stars linked into liminal shapes of gods and heroes against a celestial blue. He knew how the classical past, silent and beautiful, was spread out above the streaming current of the present. Coming through the station, Conrad often used to stop to look at these starry heavens, tilting back his head to gaze up—he knew all the gods, all the heroes. But now he didn't want to tilt back his head, to lose his bearings or let go of his hold on the world. Around him surged the crowd's endless stream, face after face coming at him, all intent, determined, heading for the next destination. Everyone carrying something, briefcases, suitcases, handbags, duffel bags, shopping bags.

In the center of the echoing space, Jenny stopped and put out her hand for her bag.

"So, I'm heading up to the West Side," she said. "You're going up the East. You're staying with Claire, right?"

"I guess so."

"I mean, for the night?"

"I guess so. Things are kind of loose."

"You can always come to my place," Jenny said. "Anytime. You know the address. I'll get you a key."

"Thanks," Conrad said.

"I mean, in the middle of the night, or whatever," she said.

"Okay," he said. "Thanks. I've got your number in my cell."

"Call me tomorrow." She put her arms around him and pulled him tight against her shoulders. She leaned back and smiled at him, then turned away, the black question-mark earrings dangling from her glossy cap of hair. *So cool,* he thought again, marveling.

Conrad headed off through the station, down the long ramp toward the East Side lines. Of course Jenny would be dressing differently four years later. But it wasn't just clothes: she had a whole new life—the job, the boyfriend—and the knowledge gave him a small thrum of anxiety. She was getting on with things, and where was he? Each intimation of change delivered this reminder: he'd missed a lot. How did you go about catching up? There was an empty space in his life, one that was filled for everyone here.

He made his way across the concourse. The crowd surged toward him like a deep stream, dividing and shifting but fluid and steady, moving easily ahead. Young girls with pouty mouths and long legs in cutoffs and flip-flops, brisk middle-aged women in khaki pants and floppy sun hats, gray-haired men in short-sleeved shirts, young, skinny guys in torn jeans and T-shirts—where were they all going on a Sunday afternoon with such speed and purpose?

He had a sense of the world hurtling past him the way these crowds hurtled past, this endless stream. What else had he missed? What had happened without him? Was it important? Could he even reenter this world? He felt as though he were watching from outside, with no idea how to get in. And also: Why did he have to fit into this world? Why didn't all these people have to fit into his?

On the 6 line the subway car was nearly empty. Two Asian teenagers in jeans and sneakers stood talking to each other at the far end, a heavy black woman in a pink jogging suit sat reading a magazine, and a family of European tourists, slight and anxious, stood around a pole, the father holding a map of New York and frowning. The train rattled uptown to Seventy-seventh, where Conrad got off. He jogged up the dank stone staircase to the street, heading toward First Avenue.

The view was framed by the brownstones and the small city-stunned trees that lined the street. One house was entirely blocked off for construction, its five-story face covered with scaffolding. This was New York's endless cycle of renewal, this iteration at the hands of a billionaire. The whole building was being gutted. A two-story-high platform was staged over the sidewalk, creating an alarming metal tunnel for pedestrians. Conrad stepped off the sidewalk to go around it; going under it made him nervous. Ahead of him was an elderly man in a sweater. He was walking unbearably slowly, each step an agonizing osteoarthritic stutter. *Go on,* Conrad thought. *Go the fuck on.* Conrad made a wider detour, skirting him as well as the scaffolding, walking out into the middle of the street. He just wanted to get on with things, get on with them.

Farther east the white-brick apartment buildings of First and Second avenues rose in tiers against the sky. The futurist dream of 1950s architecture, it hadn't aged well. The white walls were stained and grimy, discoloration spreading stealthily across the bricks in continent-size patches. The stepped terraces were all empty and untended. No one, it turned out, actually wanted to sit outside on gritty furniture on a narrow, low-ceilinged, windy, noisy, sooty platform.

He thought of these buildings, how they must have been when they were new, in the postwar dream of rising wealth and plenty. People had come flooding here after the war; they'd come from around the world. America was the success story then, rich, powerful, generous. Everyone wanted their children to grow up American. All of Europe had tried to get in: the country had had to change the immigration policy because so many people wanted to become American. This was the land of plenty, with its spotless white towers rising toward the sky.

Now the white bricks were dull, and the rows of bare, small windows looked mean. The neighborhood was anything but trendy, full of frugal young singles, impecunious families, and the elderly. First Avenue was bustling, even on a Sunday afternoon. This was a residential community: a supermarket, a drugstore, an Italian restaurant. On the corner of Claire's building was a bank.

The crowds were polyglot, though mostly white. The younger people were walking fast, with that rapid, commanding New York pace. An old woman headed toward Conrad, her thin hair ruffed up in a white crown. She was leaning heavily on a cane, though she had not given in to age: she was wearing bright lipstick and big sunglasses, a sleek jacket and pants. She met Conrad's gaze boldly, shuffling quickly along, ignoring the faster traffic that flowed around her, doing her best to keep up. It was all she could do, he thought: wear lipstick and bright clothes, try to keep up. All aging offered was that slow, unfair struggle. You could never win, you could only show your spirit as age won. He wondered what would happen to his mother if his father died. He couldn't imagine her like this woman. Old. He couldn't imagine his parents as anything but what they were now, forceful, healthy, in the middle of their lives.

Caught by the woman's challenging stare, he nodded at her. *Go for it,* he thought.

A tall young blond woman in yoga pants and a stretchy T-shirt moved past her, twisting to avoid collision, her eyes fixed straight ahead, as though the old woman were invisible. A fine electronic cord snaked up to her ear and she was talking earnestly into the air.

"I told her that," she said loudly. "I told her that." She nodded. "I told her I did not respect her position. Like she knows what a position is." She ignored Conrad, ignored the people around her, looking ahead as though she were alone.

When had everyone, *everyone* on the street, started talking on cell phones? And they said anything, the most private and personal stuff, loudly, in front of strangers. It was insulting, really, a declaration that no one around you had any significance. In the military, you took other people seriously. You weren't allowed to walk and talk on a cell phone. He imagined talking on a cell phone and walking past a superior officer: he'd be fucking torn apart.

Claire's building fronted on the avenue. The narrow foyer was separated from the lobby by a locked glass door. Conrad found Claire's name on a long row of dingy white placards and pushed the buzzer. A voice crackled shrilly over the intercom: *Conrad?* He shouted yes and was buzzed into the low-ceilinged lobby. It was empty: a scuffed black-tiled floor, dull gold ceiling, dim mirrored walls with marbled veins. Along one wall was a shelf full of leafy green plants, probably fake.

The elevator was slow and uncertain, finally lurching to a stop on twelve, where Conrad got off. The long hallway was wallpapered in a dim reddish print and carpeted in bright synthetic blue. The trapped air was stale and cloying. Claire's door was halfway down the hall. Conrad raised his hand to press the fat mirrored button to ring the bell, but before he touched it, the door opened.

There was Claire, standing in the doorway, waiting for him, and he felt something in himself lift. Her head was slightly tilted, a tentative smile on her face. The smile pierced him, its hesitancy. Was this how he made her feel?

"Hi," he said, now awkward.

"Come in," Claire said, stepping back.

She led him inside and shut the door. She turned to face him. Her eyes were steady under the straight dark brows. Her hair was still thick and glossy, shorter now; it brushed her shoulders. She was barefoot. Her dress was short and loose, pink, with some kind of wide peasant embroidery around the neck. Beneath it was her narrow body, the long torso, the tiny swelling of her belly. The dress was sleeveless, showing the shallow indentations on her upper arms. He wanted to take her arm in his hand.

She didn't seem to be wearing a bra. The dress was low-necked, the skirt wide and full: she was unbelievably available. He thought of putting his hand on her thigh and sliding it up her leg. He felt his breath shorten. He hadn't been this close to a girl in months. Years?

"Conrad," she said.

She gave him that serious, gentle look, head tilted on her long neck, her collarbones fanning beautifully out from her throat. She opened her arms, and he stepped into her body, folding himself around it. He felt her against him, her ribs arching outward, hard and neat, like a little curving ladder; the thrumming beat of her heart, fast and steady like a bird's; the small, high breasts, which he knew, knew how they felt beneath his hand and under his fingers. She pressed against him, and this gave him a sudden massive hard-on, how could it not, and also he felt, inexplicably, the threat of tears filling his eyes, and that was crippling, and he gripped her too hard and she pulled away.

He'd gone too fast, *fuck,* but he didn't exactly have any control over himself. He tried to hold on to her, keep her in his arms, partly because he wanted so badly to hold her and partly because he didn't want her to see the shameful aspect of his eyes, tears, or the eagerness of his cock. But she put her hand on his chest, pushing him off.

"Con," she said, stepping away. "Please."

"Okay," he said. "Sorry." He stood back, blinking. "Sorry." He didn't say, *I can't help it.* He brushed at his eyes.

A door opened and another girl appeared, thin and blond, in black yoga pants and a purple tank top. Claire and Conrad both turned to look at her.

"Hi," the girl said to Conrad. "Sarah Gibson, Claire's roommate."

"Hi," Conrad said. "I'm Conrad Farrell."

"I know you are." She came over and put out her hand and smiled. She was one of those perfect New York girls, long, straight, thick blond hair, full pink cheeks and narrow eyes; confident and energetic.

Claire had told him about her: Sarah was a smart southern girl who worked for a local TV channel. She drove around the city in a van with a dish receiver on top and stood with a microphone in front of disaster scenes, speaking crisply and looking serious. Apparently the cameraman spent a lot of driving time smoking pot, so the shots were not always steady. But Sarah was headed for bigger things.

"I'm glad to meet you," she said. "I'm glad you're back." She smiled. "I know Claire is."

"Thanks," he said.

"Don't mind me," she said, turning away and waving her hand. "I'm just getting something to drink. I'm going to leave you alone." She slid past them toward the kitchen. "I know you have a lot to talk about."

When she'd gotten her drink and gone back to her room, Conrad leaned close to Claire and said, "What did you tell her about me?" and Claire said, "You don't want to know," and they both laughed, as though they were back at college again, lovers and friends, conspirators.

Claire had written to him about both her roommates. The apartment had two bedrooms. The larger one was shared by Sarah and the third roommate, Gretchen, who worked either at the Museum of the American Indian or the Morgan, Conrad couldn't remember which. A small, distinguished museum. Gretchen had a boyfriend in Brooklyn, where she spent most of her time. Sarah was out a lot, too. Claire liked them, and she didn't mind having the smallest room, since she had it to herself.

Claire and Conrad took beers from the fridge and went to sit in the living room. Big plate-glass windows looked out on another white-brick apartment building. Beyond the buildings, on the left, was a choppy brown rectangle, a glimpse of the river. The long curtains had wide black-and-white stripes. A boxy white sectional sofa stood with its back to the window, flanked by dark armchairs. The room was cluttered, but in a quiet, girl-messy way: kicked-off shoes on the rug, magazines open on the big square coffee table. An empty glass or two, flattened pillows on the chairs.

Conrad and Claire sat at opposite ends of the sofa, facing each other.

"So," Claire said. "How is it, being back?"

She had tucked her legs up beneath her and was leaning an elbow against the arm of the sofa. It was strange to be with her, and to know that she was so distant. He had no right to touch her. He knew that, but it was strange. He'd never been with her like this before, without the right to touch her. Not since he'd first met her.

"Okay, I guess," he said.

"You look kind of . . . uneasy. Or something."

He shrugged.

"Do you want to talk about it?" she asked.

He shook his head.

"Okay." She smiled. "Then I'll tell you some classmate news." She stretched her legs out in front of her, settling in. Her back was against the arm of the sofa, her bare feet stretching out onto the cushions. She now seemed more comfortable, and something inside Conrad began to loosen, seeing her like that, relaxed and easy. "I heard from Lizzie. She's in Sedona, working as a hiking guide for a big resort hotel."

"Cool," Conrad said.

"Well, yeah, but Lizzie?" Claire wrinkled her nose. "She never even wanted to go for a walk, let alone a hike. Remember? She wanted to drive down the hall to the shower. Now she's ready for the Himalayas."

"Maybe she takes the guests on virtual hikes," Conrad said. "Maybe she just drives them around in a van."

Claire shook her head. "No. She's seriously different now. She sends these photographs, like *Sunrise over the Mesa* or *The Soul of the Saguaro.*" She shrugged. "Who knew, right? She's suddenly Eco-Queen. I think there's a guy involved. I think she's living with a woodsman."

"Maybe there's an alien involved."

"She might have been body-snatched," said Claire, nodding. "She might *be* an alien."

"What about Baynor?" Conrad asked. "You heard from him?"

"He's working for his dad, making boats in Maine."

"Not possible," Conrad said, grinning. "Didn't he say that's the one thing he would never, ever do?"

"We have it on tape," Claire said, laughing. "Remember that time? We all said what we were going to do?"

Junior year, late one night, they had passed around a microphone and declared plans for the future. Conrad had said he was either going to be a wilderness guide or teach public policy law, like his father. He hadn't yet said the word "Marine" out loud. Claire had wanted to be an archaeologist.

"How's archaeology?" he asked.

"There's still time," she said, grinning. "I may do it. And you're a wilderness guide already, aren't you?"

Conrad laughed. "So, does he like it, Baynor?"

"I guess." Claire shrugged. "He's there."

"What about Gordon?"

"Go-Go's on Wall Street. Lehman Brothers or somewhere. I see him sometimes. Pinstripe suits. He wears those shirts with white collars and the rest of them striped?"

"Go-Go?" said Conrad, laughing.

Gordon Russell had been a political science major and something of a political radical. He played bass guitar in a very bad grunge band, wore fingerless gloves and torn jeans. His hair was longish, and to promote the black sandpaper stubble terrorist look, he didn't shave every day. He'd cultivated a kind of badass unkemptness. On the door to his dormitory room was a hand-lettered sign that read IF IT HAS RULES, FUCK IT. OR IF IT MOVES.

"Not possible," said Conrad.

"Possible," said Claire.

"Didn't he have an earring? Several of them?"

"He did," Claire said. "Many of them. Once."

"It's good to see you, Clairey," he said. He lifted his beer, saluting her.

He liked sitting here on this comfortable sofa, listening to her talk about their friends.

"So what else is going on?" he asked. "How about you?"

"Well, I've told you about my job at the auction house," she said. She folded her legs neatly at the ankle. "You know about Yvette."

Yvette was Claire's strange Belgian boss, unmarried and unfriendly and incredibly knowledgeable. She was plain, with pale skin and lips and cold blue eyes, but always immaculately dressed: earrings, heels, her hair drawn back in a chignon.

"Yes. Yvette, the scourge of the Porcelain Department," Conrad said.

"I've decided I like her," Claire said, "even though she's so strange and unfriendly. I've decided she has some secret pain."

"Hemorrhoids?" Conrad asked.

Claire waved her hand. "I don't know. I just feel sorry for her. I don't know if she has any friends. And my god, she's so snooty and so fussy, how much fun can she have? When she talks, it's like she's been wound up with a big key on the back of her head."

Conrad laughed. "Sounds fun to me."

"But I don't mind her. She knows everything about porcelain. I mean, everything. And the other woman in my department, Louise, is very nice. She's just gotten pregnant, so the big discussion we have all the time is how much time she takes off, does she take off any time, does she quit altogether. And also morning sickness, and the development of the placenta. I know so much about pregnancy now! I've told you about her. And then you know about my friend Denny, in Oceanic Art."

Oceanic Art was next door to the Porcelain Department. Denny was the head of it, an older gay man, a good friend of Claire's. She had written to Conrad about all these people.

"Yeah, what's up with Denny?"

"Denny's great. He may be the funniest man I know."

Conrad lay facing her on the sofa, sipping his beer, listening to her stories. Some of them he was hearing for the first time, some she'd already told him, but he let her tell them again, for the pleasure of lying there, watching her face and hearing her laugh. *This is how it is to be back,* he thought.

Conrad told Claire his own stories, the ones he could tell. He told her about Johannson and Boccatto. He told her about the market at Haditha, the baskets of golden dates. He told her what the desert looked like beyond Haditha, those long, arid undulations beneath the flat blue sky. The way the powdery sand drifted when the wind came up, lifting and twisting through the air in soft pale skeins.

But even that, even talking about the landscape there, in-country, was oddly painful. There was some kind of pull from it: he didn't tell Claire that. She assumed he was glad to be back, everyone assumed that. And he *was* glad to be back. He didn't tell her there was something he missed. He missed his men, and he missed something more. It was like a dark crack, a crevasse, a sliver, reaching down inside him, deep and narrow. There was something he needed from there, something he didn't have here.

10

Conrad sat sprawled on the sofa in the living room while Claire took a shower. He had asked where he could take her out to dinner. He hadn't asked if he could spend the night, though she must have seen his duffel bag, which he'd slid onto the floor close to the sofa, and she must have known what it meant. Or what he hoped it meant. He was back now, for good: didn't that mean that they were back together? He wasn't sure how the evening would go.

He picked up a gossip magazine from the coffee table and began leafing through it, glancing at the photographs: here was a defiant middle-aged woman wearing harlequin glasses; she was suing her parents because she was ugly. Conrad peered at the picture. It was hard to tell if the woman was ugly or not: she was middle-aged. Maybe when she was younger she'd been ugly, but now she was merely middle-aged, so what was the point? Beside the picture of her was a smaller one of her parents, looking sullen and overweight. Not so good-looking themselves: maybe they should sue *their* parents. There was a story about a hiker who'd been lost on a mountainside for six days and given up for dead. He'd been rescued by someone's dog, not a trained search-and-rescue dog, just a terrier out on a walk with his owner. The hiker was photographed, safe and well, at home, for some reason wearing a clown suit. Next to him was a small headshot of the terrier: a Jack Russell, ears pricked, nose raised, avid. Then a picture of an old woman with greasy hair, sitting at her kitchen table and grinning, holding up a small object. She'd found a packet of old gold coins in her grandfather's trunk in her attic, and now she was unthinkably rich, which was especially heartwarming, since the bank was about to foreclose on her mortgage and throw her out on the street.

There were pictures of movie stars: Getting married, having adorable children, being jealous, splitting up. Behaving badly, nailed for shoplifting, joining cults, getting busted for drugs. Not paying their housekeepers, having the safe cleaned out upstairs by burglars while their security men were having coffee in the kitchen. Delivering racist rants on video. Leaving vicious messages on ex-wives' voice mail, which the ex-wives then sent to the newspapers and the Internet. Story after story, a smorgasbord of bad behavior.

Of course Conrad *got* it. He knew everyone loved this spectacle, the rich and famous behaving badly and receiving public censure. He got it that it made people feel good. Schadenfreude was particularly active around the rich and famous. He got how it worked, how everyone loved to watch the turning of the wheel of fortune, the high brought low and the low, high. He got the fact that the wheel raised collective self-esteem, reminded everyone that famous people were no better than they—in fact, probably worse. He got it that this made everyone feel good because they all knew that they themselves would never be so foolish. They would never shoplift. Never join a cult. Never get caught doing drugs. Never leave Jennifer Aniston for another woman, never leave a stupid message for their daughter on their ex-wife's voice mail. From these pages rose a big, steamy, invisible plume of self-righteousness, superiority.

He got it, but he didn't get it.

What he was holding in his hands, these flimsy pages with the sensational text, the idiotic stories and voyeuristic photographs, was proof of how many people cared about all this and how much they cared. These magazines sold in the millions. People had been reading this stuff in doctors' offices, in airports, on the subway, in bed, in the kitchen, waiting for water to boil. They'd all been reading this stuff, here, while his men were over there, in-country, getting up in the dark, clumsy and tired, covered in sand, loading themselves with sixty pounds of gear, fear clogging their chests. Checking the springs on the magazines, buckling on helmets, getting ready to mount up and head out, ready to be blown apart. Actually being blown apart. Everything over there had happened, real things, while people here were reading this stuff. Feeding on it.

He couldn't fit the two things together. It gave him a jagged, unfinished feeling, like the first pinprick of heartbreak, a tiny pointed lance of light beaming on something you can't bear to see, can't bring yourself to look at, can't look away from.

The door to the other bedroom opened and Sarah appeared. Now she was dressed to go out, in a glossy jacket and tight pants. Her blond hair was sleek, her eyes dark and glittering. She waved at him, holding her hand up and waggling her fingers.

"'Bye. I'm heading out." She gave him a wide white smile.

"Where you going?" he asked.

"Meeting some friends downtown," she said. "See you later."

"See you later," he answered, nodding.

He liked hearing that she'd see him later. He took it to mean he'd been preapproved for an overnight. He sat up straighter.

He wondered where Sarah meant by downtown. He used to come to New York during college, he'd known the places to go then, but things would have changed. He didn't exactly know New York now. He'd heard everyplace was now gentrified, all art galleries and good restaurants.

It was strange, thinking that you had to keep up with things like that. That the places you'd known might not be there, or they might be there but no longer were where anyone went. He'd gone away to Iraq thinking that this country, everything he knew about it, would all be waiting for him. He'd expected it to be just the same when he came back. He'd thought that there was some sort of compact—wasn't there? He was offering his life for his country, and his country would be there when he came home.

Now it felt as though he'd been left behind. Some steady onward movement had continued without him. It was like dropping out of line on a long march. He had to run to catch up, and even so, he couldn't find his place.

Claire's door opened and she came out. Conrad put down the magazine. She looked summery and gorgeous. Her shoulders were bare, her blue dress gathered into a drawstring, taut across her collarbones. She wore a silver circlet around her throat. Her dark hair was smooth and glossy, and her eyes and mouth glinted. She looked charged, electric.

"Hi there," she said.

"You look fantastic," he said.

She tilted her head, smiling, and the long shaft of her bare throat caught the light. He felt the sight of her all through his body.

He thought that this was how it would work. He could feel her body with his body. They still felt the same way about each other; they were the same people as before. This would work because he would make it work. He was here. He would be what she wanted. He wanted to be the person he had been before. Resolution was the thing, determination. He would make it happen. You planned the mission, then carried it out. Continue the mission: Charlie Mike.

The air was warm, and they walked slowly up the avenue, people flowing around them on the sidewalk. The city skies were changing from afternoon to evening. The light was slanting lower, shifting from a harsh overhead glare to long horizontal shafts. Above them, the upper stories of the buildings were still brilliant. Illuminated by the setting sun, the white-brick towers blazed against the darkening sky. But a dark edge of shadow, the echo of the planet's edge, was rising smoothly from below. The shadow flooded through the streets: down on the sidewalks the sun had set, the light was dimming.

The gathering dusk made it hard to see. Crowds flowed steadily along the sidewalk, bodies coming too close in the gloom, faces appearing too suddenly. Conrad's chest tightened, and he took Claire's elbow, steering her through the surge. A huge, grimy truck, thundering along the avenue, slowed suddenly beside them. The brakes gasped explosively, like gunshot.

Conrad felt the sound as if it were an electric shock. Dread rocketed through him, and he ducked, twisting away from the truck and opening his arms to protect Claire, putting himself between her and the blast.

By the time she looked at him, puzzled, it was over. He'd already straightened up; he shook his head, embarrassed. People's glances flicked at him, then away. He felt ashamed doing this so blatantly, in public—being scalded by fear. Fear and shame were mixed together.

The restaurant was a long, low room filled with packed tables. As they stepped inside, the noise rose up, deafening: the clamor of voices, the clatter of cutlery.

"Sorry," said Claire. She looked at him. "I didn't remember it being so loud. Do you want to go somewhere else?"

"No, it's fine." He didn't want her to think he couldn't handle it. But the noise bore down on him like a weight, and a ticking started up in his temple.

They stood by the front door and a young man came up to them carrying menus. He wore a blue button-down shirt with the sleeves rolled up. He was clean and preppy, though his cheeks were dark with a two-day stubble.

"Good evening." He was ostentatiously friendly. "Do you have a reservation?"

"Farrell." Conrad found the dirty-looking stubble distasteful. In the Marines you were required to be clean-shaven at all times. Stubble made you look like a slacker or a terrorist. "We asked for a table by the wall."

"Right. Follow me." Friendly turned with a flourish and began threading his way through the tables. They were set very close together. It was impossible not to brush against the chairs as they passed through, though Conrad tried.

They stopped at a table near the wall. Friendly pulled out a chair and stood beside it.

"I actually asked for a table *by* the wall," Conrad said.

"Right," said Friendly, his face bright. "This is the closest we have right now." He bared his teeth in a professional smile, his pink lips framed by stubble.

"I did call a couple of hours ago," Conrad said.

"As I say, this is the closest we have right now." His voice took on a syrupy politeness.

"So, when I asked for a table by the wall and was told I'd have one, what was that?"

"As I said, sir, this is all we have right now. If you'd like to wait at the bar, we'd be glad to let you know when one of these others opens up."

Friendly's tone was brisk, glazed with a layer of official courtesy. Underneath that lay a deep current of condescension: Why would you tolerate the fact that you were a waiter, and subservient to customers, unless you believed that on some level you were better than they? And here was why you were better: the customer was a dick and you were not. The more the customer protested, the more that fundamental belief became apparent.

Conrad studied him.

"Do you want to leave?" Claire asked.

He could hear in her voice that she did not.

"No, it's fine." He nodded at Friendly with dislike.

Conrad sat down with his back toward the wall. Friendly handed them menus solicitously.

"Have a good evening." He swept away, the heels of his tasseled loafers clicking on the wooden floor.

Conrad looked around: The door to the kitchen on his right, the bar beyond. The door to the street straight ahead and to his left. Outside, beyond the plate-glass windows, the sidewalk streamed with people. Behind him were the two tables, people at them talking. He couldn't see them. This made him uncomfortable, the low, constant rattle out of sight. In front of him was a sea of tables: young couples, eyes locked on each other's faces; older couples in foursomes, leaning back and laughing; middle-aged women in pairs, talking earnestly. The noise was cacophonous.

After they ordered drinks, Conrad asked, "So, tell me something. Was that guy being offensive?"

Claire looked at him. "Do you want to leave? If you want, we'll leave."

"No," he said. "We're not leaving."

"Is this really hard?"

What he didn't want was to seem damaged. "No, it's okay," he said. "It's just different. From what I've been used to."

He was working on two fronts. He was keeping the noise away from his brain, he was focusing on making it small, erasing it, and making himself seem normal. He knew he could do this because he had been normal before.

"What would you like to talk about?" he asked.

He was going to be normal.

He told her more about Haditha, the normal things. He told her about the bridge over the wide blue river. The fruit orchards that rippled across the hillsides, the groves of date palms along the river, with their stiff upright sprays of leaves. The herds of goats that flowed through the streets like a dry, shaggy tide, nodding and bleating.

"It sounds beautiful," Claire said.

"Yeah," he said. "Except they were always trying to kill us. That interfered with the scenery."

He could see she didn't know whether to laugh or not.

"Travel advisory for Haditha," Conrad said. "Food, great; population, homicidal."

Now she laughed outright.

He grinned but didn't go on. You couldn't expect anyone here to get the humor, it would horrify them. In-country they'd made jokes of everything. The Haqlania Bridge, at the entrance to Haditha, had been where all the executions took place. Everyone lined up to watch them. It was called Agents' Bridge because so many locals were accused by the insurgents of spying and executed as agents. Then someone changed the name to Agents' Fridge because so many bodies were left there, ready for the morgue. It wasn't a joke you would tell here.

The drinks arrived, his beer, her glass of white wine.

"Chardonnay," he said. "You used to drink beer. You've gone grown-up."

She shrugged. "I guess."

"Who do you see?" he asked abruptly. "Who do you hang out with? The guy from Oceanic Art?"

"Sometimes," she said. "There's a bunch of people from work. They're fun."

"Your crowd," he said, watching her face.

She shrugged, looking guarded. Obviously she'd been going out with someone.

"Cold," Conrad said. He touched the side of the beer bottle to his forehead. "It's miraculous. You have no idea." He smiled at her, and Claire put her elbows on the table and leaned toward him. Shadowy hollows appeared beneath her collarbones. She smiled back, her mouth widening, the straight, dark eyebrows lowering. There were faint circles beneath her eyes: she'd been living, here, while he was living, there. She was older now. She seemed open to him, warm and compassionate. She seemed beautiful and merciful. She would save him.

He rolled the bottle along his forehead, taking pleasure in the coolness against his skin.

"In Haditha," he told her, "we were garrisoned in a school administration building. There was a little courtyard behind it. The guys rigged up a kind of wading pool, a waterproof tarp with the edges draped over a circle of sandbags. Every so often they'd get water from the river and fill it. Then everyone who could fit would get in and lie down. Wall-to-wall bare-assed Marines, in four inches of water, pretending they were at the beach."

Claire laughed.

"They'd start calling for a striptease."

"Really? From who?"

"One of the guys. Molinos. He'd come out with a towel around his uniform. He'd start wiggling his hips and blowing kisses, and everyone would go nuts."

"My god," Claire said. "I love it."

"He'd strip underneath the towel, unbuttoning his blouse and pulling it off sleeve by sleeve, and everyone would go wild, shouting and throwing water. He'd toss one boot away, then the other, balancing on one foot. He'd end up in his shorts, tossing the towel out into the crowd, and it would be nearly torn apart, everyone lunging for it."

"But is he gay?" Claire asked.

"No. It's just imitation sex. Funny. Nothing."

"I never get it." Claire shook her head. "I never get how it is for you guys. I think I have it, and then I learn something else and it's all different."

"Not for us," said Conrad. "It seems really obvious to us. Like, if you can, then why *wouldn't* you have a wading pool and a striptease?"

"Right, obvious," said Claire, laughing.

"But then we get home and it seems like we're from outer space." He looked at her. "Aliens. No one knows what to do with us."

"I'm sorry it feels like that," said Claire, kind.

Conrad tilted his glass. He held the cool beer in his mouth for a second before swallowing.

"So where are we?" he asked. "You and me. Am I in or out?"

Claire looked down at her wineglass, sliding her finger around the rim. He could see the soft shifting of her eyes beneath her eyelids, like an underwater disturbance.

"I don't exactly know," Claire said. "I don't know what to say. I feel like we've gone back and forth so much. Splitting up after you left, then sort of getting back together."

"Sort of?"

"Yeah," Claire said, "it was sort of. For me it was strange. I mean, I still love you, but it wasn't the same as it was at college. You know that. You know I went out with other guys. I felt like we were—like cousins or something. I loved you, and when you deployed, I wanted to be there for you."

"Until you didn't."

"Well, you were so strange when you came back that time. I felt like I didn't know you."

"So you dumped me." He hadn't meant to say this. He was trying not to be angry.

Her eyes flicked up at him. "I didn't dump you."

"What would you call it?"

"I told you what I called it. I had to pull back. I couldn't write love letters to someone who scared me."

"So you dumped me."

"I didn't dump you, Con. I went on writing you. But I couldn't pretend. And it seemed like we weren't aligned. We were asymmetrical."

"Ah." Conrad nodded. "We couldn't have that. Asymmetry. That would be wrong." He could feel this unrolling ahead of him, how it was going to go. It was going to go wrong.

"Conrad," she said. "What do you want?"

"Were you fucking someone else?"

Her face went bright and stricken, as though he'd hit her.

"What do you want to know?" she asked. She leaned back, away from him. "Exactly what is it that you want to know?"

You stupid fuck, he thought, furious at himself. *You stupid fuck. Now you've done it.*

He paused, trying to steady himself. He was trying to withdraw from anger, trying to unlink himself from the bullying, hectoring, harrying self that took over. The stupid fuck that was going to wreck everything. But who was there to take his place?

The waitress appeared beside the table.

"Ready to order?" She was pretty but haggard, with straggly black hair and dark eyes with huge circles beneath them. "Would you like to hear the specials?"

"No, thanks," said Conrad. "We're ready." He didn't want to hear the recitation. Waiters loved to show off their memory skills. He wanted to get on with it.

"You sure?" The waitress smiled hopefully at Claire, who shook her head. They ordered, and the waitress picked up their menus and set off.

Conrad turned back to Claire.

"What would I like to know?" he said. "I'd like to know that we're calling an end to the time-out and we're resuming play."

"It's not that simple," Claire said. "I don't know how to talk to you now. Everything makes you angry. You're like someone holding a ticking bomb."

"Were you fucking someone else?" He was sure she had been.

"Conrad." She leaned back, pushing herself away from the table.

"What?"

"You make me feel like I'm on trial."

A middle-aged couple had been inching their way through the surrounding chairs toward the table next to the wall, which was now empty. The woman was carrying a huge striped pocketbook. When she reached her chair, without looking, she swiveled to sit down and the bag slammed into Conrad's face. In the same instant he rose to his feet and grabbed it, holding it still, staring at her.

The pair were in their fifties, the man solid, with hooded eyes and heavy, silky cheeks. He wore a thin short-sleeved jersey that drooped off his shoulders like a gangster's. The woman was short and chunky, with coarse black hair and a bold gaze.

She turned, outraged. "Let go of my bag."

"You just slammed it into my head," Conrad said, not letting go.

"That doesn't mean you can steal it." The woman's face was a mask of dislike. "Let it go or I'll call the manager."

Conrad stared at her, holding the bag.

The man with her leaned toward Conrad. "Let it go, Mac."

Conrad said nothing. He stared at the man. It was like being offered a treat, something small and delicious right in front of him.

"Conrad," Claire said, her voice low. "Please let it go."

Conrad could feel his blood thumping through his veins. But this wasn't worth it. Just as he thought this, the woman spoke.

"Yeah, listen to your girlfriend, schmuck," she said, twitching the bag in his hands.

Joy flooded through him in a warm rush; he almost closed his eyes.

"Conrad," Claire said to him again, now urgent. "I'm sorry," she said to the woman. "He's had a shock."

"He's gonna get another if he doesn't give me my bag back," the woman said. She gave another tug, and this time Conrad let go. She staggered back a step. He stood facing her, his whole body ready, everything right there, not that he would touch her, hurt her, but showing her what was not going to happen to her.

In her startled face he saw that she could feel his heat, the great, furious readiness of his body, everything, his muscles, his heart and lungs hammering, the blood coursing through his chest, and she stepped back. Fear finally entered into her gaze.

"This guy's a maniac, Carl," she said, but now not loudly. She drew away from Conrad. "I don't want to sit here."

Carl had seen what Conrad was offering. "We're out of here." He gave Conrad a look that was dirty but muted, offended but not quite offensive. They started off again, aggrievement written in their stiff backs, elevated chins.

Conrad watched them, still standing, his napkin in his hand. He felt a kind of itch in his fingers. He could feel the man's fat shoulder under the cotton shirt.

The two of them paraded toward the door, toward Friendly. Conrad stayed standing, watching, ready. He saw them stop to complain. Friendly listened, glancing discreetly up at Conrad. Conrad raised his hand in a wave. Friendly looked back at the couple. He nodded, solicitous, but they pushed out through the door. Conrad sat down, watching Friendly, but Friendly stayed busy at the reservations desk, not giving people tables by the wall, and wouldn't look over.

"Conrad," Claire said.

"She nearly knocked me out of my chair."

Claire studied him. "You can't do that," she told him.

He stared at her, trying to hold on to the swollen, surging rush of excitement, the way he'd known exactly how to proceed, the sense of anticipatory pleasure. He could feel it draining away. It had been so clear and right, so juicy, but it was going, and it was wrong, and it was going in a swift, flooding rush, leaving nothing, leaving a black, poisonous taste in his mouth. He felt the approach of shame, and he turned away.

"I know," he said.

He looked past her, watching another couple who were making their way through the tables. Not coming his way, but still. Their waitress, in a white shirt, slipped in and out of the tables, carrying trays. She came near and Conrad tensed, but then she twisted away in another direction.

He and Claire didn't speak until the food came.

Conrad had ordered a hamburger. In-country he'd dreamed of them. Occasionally, in Ramadi, they'd had frozen ones, gray and dense, without texture or taste, like hot boiled felt. He'd imagined real hamburgers, thick and running with juices, soft pink inside, darkly charred outside. The great American meal.

It arrived on a spongy seed-sprinkled bun, fringed with lettuce, flanked by a slice of pallid tomato. The hamburger looked swollen and bloody. He took a bite. It was greasy and flavorless, just salt and fat. He thought of the pungent stews, rich, savory dishes with lamb and prunes, apricots and spices. He put it down.

"You scare me," said Claire.

She looked distressed, and he put his hand on her wrist. He meant to reassure her, but he felt a faint reflexive flinch, a withdrawal. This gave him a sinking feeling; also a dark undercurrent of triumph.

"I'm sorry," he said, and he was. "Didn't mean to get so mad."

"What happens?" she asked.

He shook his head. "Sorry."

"I don't know what you want," she said. "I don't know whether you want to talk about it or not. Everything seems to make you angry."

"Right." He nodded. "Sorry."

She leaned toward him. "I love you."

He had no idea what she meant. Did it mean they were back, that they didn't have to take things slowly after all? Or just that they were best friends? Was it platonic love that she meant?

He didn't know which one he hoped for.

"I love you," she said again, "but we're not exactly back where we were four years ago. And yes, I've seen other people since I wrote you that letter. But I'm not going to talk about them the way you talk about them. You don't have the right to talk that way. Maybe I'll tell you about them, when I'm ready to. But I don't think of them the way you do. I don't know if I'll ever tell you about them."

None of this mattered. He wanted to be able to press himself against the length of her and pound himself into oblivion; he also wanted to be able to turn and walk away at any moment, recover his own sense of his world, return to a place where she was not. A wildness was inside him, like a sandstorm, raging, senseless, amorphous.

"I love you, too," he said, because you had to answer that statement, you couldn't let it hang in the air.

Of course she had slept with other people. Four years: she hadn't been sealed in plastic. What was he thinking? "I'm sorry," he said, because you had to respond to the rest of it, and everything she'd said was true. All he could do was hope that there was no one she was seeing right then, that the timing had miraculously worked out and that right now she was available; ready, maybe, to have him back.

But he couldn't focus on her, couldn't keep his gaze on her face. Beyond her was the noisy jangle of the restaurant, the couples leaning toward each other across their tables, shouting over the din. Waiters were carrying laden trays, the headwaiter was winding in and out with his sheaf of menus. The noise was enormous.

What made him so wild, what made his throat swell with rage, was the fact that no one here knew anything, no one here understood about the real world. No one understood what you looked for on the street (risk assessment), how you cleared a room (always moving as a team, though you had to slip through the fatal funnel one by one), how many shots you fired to kill someone (three), how you identified yourself on the radio (company, platoon, individual), how to establish a perimeter, or what the risks were in a room like this, filled with moving people and noise. They knew fuck-all here, everyone.

He wondered if this was what it had been like after World War II, soldiers arriving home from the battlefield to all those beaming civilians. But back then the soldiers had had critical mass, and the war had been a national effort. Not like this, where no one could even find Iraq on the map. No one knew why we were there, no one could remember if we'd found WMDs or not.

He looked down at his plate.

What he wanted was for Claire to understand all this without his saying it, because he didn't know how to say it. He couldn't describe, even to himself, what it was that was hanging low and threatening over his head.

He took a deep breath and started at ten, heading for one. Sometimes it was better to vary it; sometimes it worked better if you shifted things around. Because he didn't have a lot of choice. He could feel the world closing in around him, a kind of invisible tunnel, the air turning more and more solid, impossible to breathe.

At the apartment, the door shut solidly behind them, and Claire turned to look at him. He stepped forward and put his arms around her because this was what he had been waiting for, the deep solace of her embrace. He felt all of her against him, her cushiony softness, firm and elastic.

She stiffened, but he pushed closer, tightening his arms around her, because he wanted this right now more than anything. He felt her resistance, but also something else. Wasn't there some yielding? All those nights in college, spent in his narrow bed in the freezing cold, when they had made their own heat. All those nights of joyful sex, all that shared exhaustion and delirium, the delight they'd given each other, all that trying to get inside each other: once you had that together, wasn't it always there? You could summon it up forever, couldn't you?

Because he wanted now to be with her, he would give anything to press himself against her long, soft coolness, wanted to wrap his hands in her hair, run his lips over the hard ridge of her collarbone, wanted to fuck her senseless, wanted to be part of her. This now was desperation, he wanted the division between them to be over.

He said her name. He ran his fingers slowly across her face, the powdery softness of her skin, the miraculous secret hardness of the bones beneath.

"Clairey, I will never hurt you," he said into her hair. *Save me.*

11

During the night Conrad jerked awake several times, disoriented, his heart thudding against his chest. He had left the bedroom door open a crack, and the shaft of light from the hall fell across the bed. When he came jolting into consciousness, opening his eyes, he saw the dim contours of the room, the black rectangle of the half-open closet door, the dim shimmer of the mirror over the bureau. Dark rectangles, pictures on the wall, clothes draped over a chair. A girl's room: he was next to Claire.

Each time he woke, she woke and put her arms around him. Each time, she drew him close and moved herself against him. She was smooth and bare and warm. He put his face into her hair, her neck. He knew her smell; he drew long, deep draughts of it; it didn't soothe him. The nightmares had unfastened him. Something inside him was running loose.

He was awake as the sky outside the window began to brighten; he watched the room turn gray. He was facing Claire, waiting for her to wake. She lay with her head on the pillow, facing him. He watched until she opened her eyes. When she focused on him, he spoke.

"I want to know more," he said. "What happened after you wrote that letter."

"Conrad," she said, blinking. He could see consciousness coming into her eyes. She was just waking up.

"I want to know."

There was a long pause. Claire looked at him, drawing herself up from sleep. She rolled onto her back and rubbed her eyes. "What do you mean, 'what happened'?"

"I mean, after you decided we were asymmetrical. Did you just start going out with other guys, just like that?" He didn't like saying the words, he didn't like the feel of them in his mouth.

Claire drew a breath. She spoke without looking at him. "I told you. I went out with people. Different guys."

"Are you seeing one of them now?"

She turned to him. "I don't like this. I feel like I'm being interrogated."

"I need to know what happened," said Conrad. "If we're going to go on."

After a pause Claire said, "I've been seeing one guy more than others."

"Do you fuck him?"

She stared at him. "I'm not using that word," she said. "You use it like a weapon. Stop it."

"Okay," Conrad said. "Are you sleeping with him?"

The room was silent. He could hear her breathing, he could hear the rustle of the sheets as she shifted her legs.

"I don't know that you have the right to ask me that," she said. "This is our first night together. I'm not sure you get to ask me to roll out everything in my life for you."

"This is not our first night together," he said.

She put her hand on his shoulder.

"Conrad," she said.

"Okay," he said. Her hand was soft and cool.

"Don't do this," she said. "Don't blow this up."

He breathed evenly, watching her. She raised her hand to his forehead, smoothing his hair.

"Don't pretend this is our first night together," he said.

"Don't pretend that we've been together all along," Claire said. "You know it's different now." She withdrew her hand, turning on her side toward him, laying her hands beneath her cheek.

He lay on his back, raising himself up on his elbows, his head turned toward her.

"So you won't tell me." Frustration was mounting in his chest. "You just decide we can't talk about this. But what if I do want to talk about it?"

"It's not that I won't talk about it—" Claire started to answer.

"But you won't talk about it," Conrad interrupted. "What if I think it's important to talk about it?"

He ripped the sheet off himself and sat up, throwing his legs over the edge of the bed. "Fuck this."

"Con." She put her hand on his shoulder.

He jerked away from her touch. "Fuck that."

Claire sat up and knelt on the bed, naked, her legs pressed closely together, her hands on her thighs.

"Okay." Her voice was not steady. "So, I don't know what to do. I don't know what you want, and I don't know what I should do. You're so angry about everything, and what do you want? You want to just show up and be back at the center of everything, like that?"

Conrad didn't answer. He stared at the wall.

On it was a framed photograph of Claire's parents when they were in their twenties. They were standing in the cavernous reaches of a European train station. They both had long hair, and they were wearing bell-bottom jeans and carrying backpacks. They were smiling, beaming, really, their faces hopeful and innocent. They were making the V sign with their fingers: peace, brotherhood, we're cooler than you, whatever. What struck him—what enraged him, actually—was their complete unfetteredness, the lack of purpose and responsibility. They were just drifting, doing whatever they felt like, going wherever they wanted. They were his fucking age.

"It's been *four years*, Con," Claire said. "You can't just arrive home and move back in. My life is different. Things aren't the way they were before. This is too abrupt."

"It's too abrupt for *you*?" said Conrad. "How do you think it is for me?"

"Okay," said Claire nervously. "I know."

Conrad swiveled to face her. "How do you know? How do you have any idea what it's like for me? To be over there and see my friends die? And then to come home and be told to go slow? That this is *too abrupt*." He paused. "What am I supposed to do? How am I supposed to arrive less abruptly? You want me to just come home from Iraq for weekends? Arrive in stages?"

"Okay," said Claire. She fanned out her hands. "Okay." She sounded frightened.

"No, really," said Conrad. "How do you think I should do this?"

"I don't know how you should do it," Claire said. "But we're both part of it. I can't help how it is for you. You have to do this with me. If you want to be back in my life."

"That's what I'm doing."

"Not like this," Claire said. "I want you to learn what it's like. I want you to meet my friends, I want to get to know you again. You can't just walk in and start giving orders."

Conrad said nothing. Anger was still solid in his chest. And giving orders was how you got things done. You didn't encounter something and then wait around to see what happened. You took command, made a plan, and carried it out. What was inside him was ready to explode, it always was.

He stood and faced her.

"I'm not going to hang around for this," he said. "If you don't want us to start up again, fine. Your call. But I'm not on trial. I'm not being interviewed for this position. I'm not going to wait around while you decide whether or not you want me. Either we're on or we're not."

Claire pressed her hands together, sliding them between her knees. "I can't talk to you if you're like this."

"Like what?"

"This is not a conversation," she said. "It's just you saying what you want."

She had no idea, he thought. How you had to work to make everything happen, push it into the channel you intended. You had to plan everything, you had to take control. Part of what he felt was rage, part of it something he couldn't name, which twisted at him, like pain.

"Okay," he said. "I'm out of here."

At Grand Central, Conrad waited for the next train to Katonah, though it wasn't for an hour. He turned off his cell phone, though he kept checking it, and by the time he reached Katonah, Claire had called seven times. At the station he took a cab, an old blue Chevy that sounded like a motorboat. The driver was a Hispanic woman with dark skin and long black hair. She drove slowly up their dirt road, the car gurgling heavily up the driveway. He paid her and got out, and the car wallowed down the drive.

Lydia was in the kitchen, she had been grocery shopping, and stood by the counter in front of a row of bags. She turned, surprised. "Con! You're back sooner than I expected. I thought you were staying for a while in the city."

Conrad stayed on the far side of the room. He didn't want her to touch him.

"Yeah," he said, "I came back out." He was being graceless.

"How's Claire?" She was putting away the groceries, briskly taking things out of the bags, setting them on the shelves.

"Fine," Conrad said.

Lydia turned to look at him. "Really?"

He shrugged.

"Are you two okay?"

"Yeah, I guess. I don't want to stay in the city with her, though. She's working. She gets up in the morning and goes to the office. I don't really have anything to do there. I thought I'd come back out. I'm going to start studying for the GMAT. It'll be better here. I can go running, do some training."

Lydia nodded, looking steadily at him. "That sounds good."

He didn't want her to look at him that way, focused and searching. All this was embarrassing: That his girlfriend wouldn't take him back and it was probably his fault, since he seemed unable to talk to her without starting a fight, and that his stupidity might be driving her away for good. That he couldn't seem to have a normal conversation with his mother, couldn't even act polite to her. The fact was that he was ashamed, and what was the matter with him?

Lydia picked up the empty paper bag and folded it neatly against her chest. "Con, if there's anything you want to talk about," she said carefully, "you know you can tell me."

"Thanks," he said. "I know that."

Conrad went upstairs and checked his cell: twelve calls from Claire. She'd still be at work and wouldn't answer. He could leave an apology without having to talk to her. He punched in the number. She picked up on the first ring.

He closed his eyes. "Hey."

"Where are you?" she asked.

"Katonah."

There was a pause.

"I've been calling you," she said.

"Yeah," he said. "I've been out. Sorry."

There was another pause; then they both spoke at once.

"Are you coming back?" she asked.

"I was a dick," he said.

There was a silence.

"I was a dick," Conrad said again. "I'm sorry." His chest felt full of barbed wire.

"Thanks," said Claire. "Yes, you were. But it's okay."

He didn't like her saying he was. She could have said, *No, no, you weren't.*

"I don't know how to make this work, Con," she said. "But it's not going to if you just walk out on me. Don't cut me off."

"You cut me off," he said.

"No," she said, "I didn't."

Conrad said nothing.

"Conrad?"

"I'm here."

"I don't know what you want," she said. "I hope you don't think everything can be the way it used to be. I don't think it can."

He said nothing. He thought of the night with her, of waking up over and over, the terror of the darkness, the strangeness of finding her there with him. The way fear filled a lightless room.

"Do you think we can? Just be together again as if nothing happened?" she asked.

"Maybe not," Conrad said.

"So what is it that you want, Con?" Her voice was gentle.

He said nothing. He looked up at the windows and the willows outside.

"Everything's changed," she said. "We've changed."

"And so then what?" he asked.

"I don't know. I think we should go slowly. Maybe it's good that you're out there instead of here," Claire said. "This way we can talk every day. Start to get to know each other again."

He wanted to see her and he didn't. When he was with her, he felt clumsy and powerless. And it seemed like a kind of betrayal that she'd carried on so smoothly without him. She'd been living that other life, the life everyone else had, taking showers, going to the office, having dinner with people, seeing movies, sleeping late on weekends. He wanted to demand that it hadn't happened, all of it. He wanted just to rewind and delete. Everyone over here, living their lives, made him feel invisible. Everything had gone on without him, and his absence made no difference.

But not seeing her was intolerable. He wanted to be back in her life, though he wasn't yet back in his own life. He didn't know what his own life was. He didn't know if he could make the connection between his old life and the one here.

He let out a breath. "So what do we do?"

"Let's talk," Claire said. "We can talk."

She sounded level, as though she were in charge. Part of him wanted to bull his way back into the center of Claire's life and move in with her, and part of him wanted a huge explosion to separate them forever.

"We'll start with today," she said. "What did you do?"

"This sounds like kindergarten," Conrad said, but he was laughing. "Circle."

"You got it," Claire said. "Next we're going to play duck, duck, goose."

He was laughing, but the jangling current was still running through his chest.

The next morning, his alarm went off at five. He was trying to make himself stay on a schedule, getting up early no matter how late he'd gotten to sleep.

He was awake at once, eyes open, looking up at the ceiling. This was the best moment of the day, silent and untouched. Outside his window it was barely light, a pale half-light. The willows were still. He dressed and went quietly down the back stairs and out the back door.

The sun was just coming up, silhouetting the row of trees along the crest of the hill. The grass in the meadow was lush and heavy, silvered with dew. The willow trees hung over the driveway like still green waterfalls, their loose fronds trailing. The air was sweet and damp.

He jogged lightly down the short slope of the driveway, out through the stone pillars, then turned onto the hard-packed dirt road. There were old sugar maples along the road at the bottom of the lawn; after that, the woods drew close on either side. The trees formed a soft green canopy overhead. He ran south, down the long slant of North Salem Road, past the tangle of wild grapevines scribbled around a stand of hickory trees, past a white-fenced horse pasture. He turned onto Mount Holly, heading down toward the reservoir. He had to wait to cross Route 35, jogging in place; it was already humming with fast commuter traffic. Once across, he was back on a narrow dirt road again.

Rounding that corner was his favorite moment of the run: the sudden widening view of the reservoir, the great green space, glowing, breathing, full of light and movement, calm and silent. It always came as a surprise, the shock of spaciousness. At that moment he was aware of himself, his own strength, the way he could run steadily and easily for miles. And he was aware of the beauty before him, the miraculous presence of the water shimmering in the light.

The road became paved across the top of the dam. Along the road on the reservoir side were two small Italianate pumping stations, like fortified medieval towers. The reservoir system had been created for New York City in the early twentieth century, and the dams were built by stoneworkers brought from Italy. Conrad wondered if the engineers' plans had actually called for miniature Renaissance towers with architectural detail—blind arches, rusticated stone foundations, tiled roofs—or whether the stoneworkers had simply made the towers look the way they knew towers should look. The diminutive structures altered the perspective: against their tiny battlements, the reservoir looked hundreds of miles long.

On the other side of the road was a ten-foot-high chain-link fence. It was that high to prevent suicides, he thought. He measured himself against it mentally—where to put his hands, the toeholds, how to swing himself up and over. Below it was the sheer stone wall of the dam, dizzying rows of cut stone, perfectly aligned and set, a two-hundred-foot curving drop to the woods and bottomland. Far below was the narrow creek, meandering quietly through the reeds as though it had no connection to the massive masonry wall above it, the billions of gallons of water retained.

The reservoir lay quiet and glassy, a light-struck reach, glittering, flat, and cool in the early-morning sun, a kind of miracle. A small pock on the water's elastic fabric, small rocking circles measuring outward: a fish, rising. Beneath the green surface was a dim world of secret flashing creatures.

He ran across the dam and then on, keeping to the edge of the reservoir, the road curving along the little bays and inlets, fringed by leafy woods. Then it turned away from the water, past a farm with Black Angus cattle grazing quietly in a sloping meadow, and out to the hard road again. He ran east for a couple of miles on a narrow paved road cut between steep banks, commuters hurtling past on their way to the train station. The houses were old and set back from the road, surrounded by lawns and trees. Between them were woods. The smells of the summer earth came to him as his feet hammered out their message on the road. Dogs barked as he went past. Even here, along the paved road, the tall trees reached together in a cool green clasp overhead. He turned north, then back west along Route 35. He hated that. It was the worst part of the run, heading into traffic, the cars roaring toward him, each one like an attack vehicle. His heart was pounding by the time he could turn off the main road and onto North Salem.

Now he was on a dirt road again, hard-packed under his feet, the smooth humped curve of it sloping into ditches on either side, the woods beyond. Squirrels clattering through the branches, a deer following him with her eyes, motionless but for the nervous flick of her white tail. A possum waddling furtively over a stone wall. The woods were thin here, the understory eaten by deer. Tumbledown stone walls meandered through the trees, marking the old fields and pastures. The last half mile was a slow rise back past the wild grapevines, past the barn and lawn, leading to the short, steep stretch of the driveway. He sprinted the last twenty yards up to the house, everything inside him full and thrumming, heart and lungs, every part working. He came to a stop under the willows and walked around in slow circles. The gravel crunched under his feet. The air was still cool and fresh.

Lydia went into the city after breakfast; Conrad drove her to the station so he could use her car. He came home by the back way, taking the road across the reservoir. It was different, crossing the dam in a car. It was nothing. The water was flat and affectless, the light indifferent. You could barely see over the parapet.

At home, Conrad drove the Volvo into the garage and turned off the engine. He sat for a moment in the shadowy silence, listening to the engine tick. Against the cobwebby wall was an old sawhorse, a snow shovel, stacked cardboard cartons. A two-by-four leaned against the wall beside a rake. Unlike a barn, a garage was meaningless space, a narrow backwater for the slow tidal drift of junk.

He opened the car door. It was stiff, and the hinges creaked drily. He shouldn't be driving around in his mother's old car. He should have his own. He'd had a car in college but sold it when he went into the Marines. He could buy another; he had combat pay. Even Ollie had a secondhand Toyota.

Inside, he went upstairs to his room.

He checked his cell phone: Claire had called twice. He checked his email: a couple of messages from his men, who were now scattered. Some of them were back in Iraq. The platoon had a new commander and had been deployed to a base near Hit, in Anbar Province. Bradley was there, and Gomez and Molinos. They had minimal Internet access, but periodically Conrad sent everyone a blast, just to check in. Today he'd gotten mail from some of the guys who were still there and some who were home.

Bradley wrote him from Hit.

Morning LT. Thought you would like to know what's going on: you'll be pleased to hear that we have had no IEDs since yesterday, and also I just received a shitload of comics, a lot of good ones. Some school got hold of my name, I guess. Or who knows? Maybe they came from God. Where they have put us here, it makes Sparta look like the Bel-Air. Got to go, Semper Fi. CPL Bradley.

Bradley was from Iowa. He had sandy-colored hair, a wide, low brow, sleepy blue eyes, and some goddamn itch. Iraq made him itch everywhere, and it drove him nuts. He couldn't stop scratching, mostly his balls. His favorite pastime was reading comics, any kind. He knew every character and every story line. The other guys tried to come up with ones he didn't know, but no one had ever done it. The Super Heroes were his favorites, but he read *Archie*, too, anything, even the surreal modern ones.

Conrad wrote back:

> *Morning, Bradley. How you doing? Glad to hear about the comics, and sorry to hear the quarters are not so good. I'm up in Westchester now, trying to keep in shape. I'll get you some comics when I go into town.* Little Lulu, *right? Hang in there. Semper Fi. Farrell.*

He couldn't tell the men he missed them—an officer didn't say that—but he did miss them.

Another message from Anderson, his sunburned seatmate on the plane. Anderson was through his EAS, end of active service, and back in Minnesota. Anderson was good-natured and generous, and everyone liked him.

> *Hello, LT, how's it going? Just checking in. Not much happening here. I've been swimming in the lake every day, and every time I go in I think of the wading pool we built at Sparta. I think, now I'm in a real lake! And no one's fucking shooting mortars at me! I can't believe it's for real. It all seems like that. I mean that it's for real. Know what I mean? Okay, over for now, LT. Paul Anderson. (Weird not to write CPL anymore.)*

Anderson had once boosted—thrown, really—Molinos over a wall single-handed during a firefight in Ramadi. They were trying to get into a courtyard. All the houses had walls along the street, then a courtyard inside. The door to the street was metal. It could be kicked in or shot up, but if you were trying not to make so much noise or if a sniper was aiming at the door, you went over the wall, and they needed someone over the wall right then. Anderson was pumped, battle-high, and he threw Molinos over like a football.

Anderson was quiet. They called him the Swede, though he'd told them again and again that he was Norwegian. They called him the Swede, and because he was quiet he stopped correcting him. He was a good kid, always ready, willing. He never complained, though his hands had been badly burned by an IED in Haditha. He'd been sent to Germany for treatment, and when he came back, his hands were still wrapped in bandages. When those came off, his hands were red and boiled-looking, swollen and shiny with scar tissue. They were stiff and clumsy, like mitts. He could barely bend his fingers and hardly clean his rifle. The hands looked painful, as if they were about to burst, but Anderson never complained and never asked for help.

Conrad wrote him back:

Hey, Anderson. It's good to hear from you. Glad to hear about you and the lake. I'm running every morning. It's about eight miles, but it seems less because it's not 130 degrees out here. Can't get used to that. I know what you mean about everything seeming not real, but it will get better. You got the dog team going yet? Keep in touch. Semper Fi.

Anderson used to talk about that dogsledding race in Alaska. He talked about it in-country, where 80 degrees was a cool early-morning temperature and the idea of snow was like the idea of deep space. The guys had teased him about going from 120 degrees above to 120 below.

"Hey, Anderson," Carleton once asked, "what's your deal? Don't you do temperate zones? What about a place where the weather is *nice*? Ever heard of that? *Nice weather*?"

"You've never been on a dogsled, Carleton," Anderson said, shaking his head. "I'm sorry for you, man."

Conrad wondered how Anderson's hands were, and if you could go in a race like that with hands like mitts. Anderson swore his hands were okay, though they didn't look okay, and Conrad was pretty sure he was lying.

Conrad answered all the emails. Some of his officer friends were back home, but most of them were still in-country. His best friend, Bruce O'Connell, the leader of their sister platoon in Ramadi, was in Afghanistan. He was up in the mountains somewhere and rarely got to use the Internet. Today he'd written:

Dingo Three Actual: How's it going back home? I bet you're wishing you were here with the rest of us, freezing your ass off and hiking up mountains after dushman. *Eat your heart out, bro, only heroes are here, all the weenies were sent home. We are a million fucking miles from nowhere. Wish you were with us.*

Conrad wrote him back:

Dogbite One Actual, things are tough here too. Can't decide how late to sleep in the morning. Wish I were there with you freezing your ass off. I miss the camel spiders. Let me know how things go. I'll tell you it's pretty weird being back. Semper Fi. Farrell.

He liked hearing from O'Connell and he liked hearing from his men. Until the GMAT review book arrived, his main focus was exercise, run in the morning, PT in the late afternoon. The thing was to keep to a regimen.

After lunch, he drove down to the commercial strip in Casden. The car dealers were clustered along one section. Shiny cars were drawn up along the road below festive strings of fluttering pennants. Conrad drove into the first car lot he came to, which was Japanese. He wasn't sure he wanted Japanese, but he liked the idea of small and efficient.

Snub-nosed cars were drawn up in a row facing the road. Behind them stood the showroom, with a strange swooping roof and a vast plate-glass wall.

Conrad parked the Volvo and got out. The pavement was dense black, fresh and oily beneath his shoes. Did they repave the lot every few months? He wondered how much that added to the sticker price. He pushed through the heavy glass doors. Three cars were parked on the red carpet. Indoors, polished and immaculate, the cars looked like sculptures, like art, not transportation. You were meant to feel like a genius for finding a car that was beautiful and exciting as well as useful.

Conrad stood with his hands in his pockets, looking at a silver sedan. The sloping windshield reflected the bright, watery stars of the ceiling lights. Its outline was smooth and blurred, like water pouring over stones. He thought of a Humvee, huge, heavy, squat, the color of mud. This was like a toy, glittering, small, playful.

A salesman materialized beside him.

"Afternoon," the man said, smiling. He was tall and pear-shaped, with a round face and thinning brown hair. He wore a blue suit and a white shirt, and a narrow striped tie was clipped onto his shirt above the belly.

Conrad nodded. "Afternoon."

"I'm Jim Harkness. What can I help you with?" He had bad teeth and a murderer's smile.

"Oh, nothing right now," Conrad said, nodding, his gaze drifting across the cars. "I'm just looking around."

"This right here? This is a great car." Jim Harkness put a proprietary hand on the sleek fender.

"Yeah," Conrad said.

"Looking for something sporty?" asked Jim.

"I don't really know," Conrad said.

Jim put his hands in his pockets and jingled something. "This one is sporty," he said. "Handles well, good on the highway. Nice acceleration."

"What's the mileage?" asked Conrad. He didn't care.

"Not bad," said Jim. He leaned back on his heels. "Twenty-one in the city, thirty-two on the road." He rose slightly on his toes. "Great audio system."

"How much is it?" Conrad asked. He didn't like standing in front of the plate-glass wall, which would turn into a million flying knives in an explosion. Outside there was constant movement. Cars, trucks, people.

"Well," said Jim reasonably, "it starts at twenty-two." He paused. "But we can be flexible." He smiled, showing the teeth. It looked as though a brown fluid were seeping between them. "Flexibility is our middle name." He laughed, slitting his eyes.

Conrad said nothing.

"Come on, let's go out for a spin. You'll love the way this car feels." Jim Harkness jingled his metallic possessions and rose again on his toes.

Conrad thought of driving with him, turning out onto the strip. Cars coming in constantly from the right, traffic lights every few hundred feet. No maneuvering room, cars pulling up close beside you, tailgating you from behind. His chest felt tight, and he took a deep breath to open it.

"Not today," he said. "Thanks."

"What'll you be using the car for?" asked Jim Harkness. "City driving? Commuting? Long distances? I could show you another model that gets better mileage."

"Yeah," Conrad said. "I'm not buying anything right now. I'm just looking. I'm not sure where I'm going to be." Outside, a van was backing up, making a series of robotic cheeps. The sounds went through him.

Jim Harkness could feel his withdrawal.

"Here's my card," he said. "It's got my cell. Anytime you want to talk, give me a call." He smiled the awful smile. "Some salesmen don't want you to call them at home, won't talk at night. Hey!" He raised his shoulders, lordly. "That's not my way. You want to talk? I'm ready. Call anytime, we can talk about flexible plans, different models, whatever you want."

"Thanks," Conrad said. He put the card in his pocket. "Thanks a lot."

He pushed out through the door. On the black pavement he was hit by the unmitigated glare of the sun. The red and white pennants hung slack. Beyond the pavement was the midday traffic on the strip, the sun hitting the cars, bright refracted gleams everywhere. There was too much to focus on. He'd planned to visit three or four places, but when he left the lot, he turned up the steep hill onto Green Lane to head home by the back roads.

It didn't actually make sense to buy a car now. If he was taking courses in New York in the fall, he'd just be paying garage fees. The idea of graduate school made something rise up in his chest again. It was infuriating. *Shut the fuck up,* he wanted to say to himself. What was it? The sense of helplessness was the worst, the feeling that he couldn't control this.

He looked in the rearview mirror. There was one car behind him, a small dark red sedan, at four hundred meters. It drove slowly, without gaining. He lost it around curves. As he drove, he checked on it constantly, dropping his eyes to the road, then raising them up to the mirror. He watched the car on the straights. He had no backup here, he was alone. In-country you never traveled alone.

He watched the car and saw it turn off onto The Narrows Road. Probably a housewife picking up a kid from school. He knew that, but it didn't change how he felt when he saw the car following him.

When he arrived home, it was midafternoon and the day seemed flat and old. The cleaning lady's car was in the driveway. Conrad parked in the garage but didn't get out of the car. He didn't want to go inside, though there was nowhere else for him to be. He didn't want to speak to anyone. He didn't want to smile at the cleaning lady and say hello to her.

The cheerful, sloppy Italian woman, Maria, who had cleaned for them during his childhood, was gone. Retired or moved away or something. Now there was an Eastern European woman, thin-lipped and small-eyed, who wore tight, pilled foot-strap pants. She had faded frizzy hair and spoke her own impenetrable language and barely any English. Lydia had introduced him to her, pretending the same kind of friendship she'd had with Maria, whom she'd loved. This woman never smiled; she would never hug any of them, but Lydia acted as though she didn't know this.

"Katia, this is *my son*," she had said, unconsciously raising her voice, the way people did when they thought you didn't understand them. Katia nodded secretively, unsmiling, looking from one to the other of them as though assessing the possibilities.

Wherever Katia was now in the house, she would be disturbing, dragging the vacuum noisily over his foot, leaving the bottle of Windex and a cleaning rag in his bathroom sink, a pile of dirty laundry on the kitchen table. Actually, he didn't want to be in anyone's presence right now.

Conrad backed the car up, turned around, and drove down the driveway. On the dirt road he headed north. Ten miles away was another reservoir, the Titicus, longer and more densely wooded. A dirt road followed its southern edge, a paved one on the northern side. He made his way up by back roads.

There were no houses along any of the reservoirs. Along the shore of the Titicus was a tall mixed forest with scrubby underbrush. He took the dirt road that wound around the southern edge. He could see the reservoir through the trees, the flat reflective surface. The water was a dull, muddy green, opaque and glaring. He drove slowly along the gravelly road.

As he came around a corner he saw a woman coming toward him

with a dog on a leash. The dog was black and curly-coated, a Portuguese water dog, with a wide choke collar. As Conrad approached, the woman pulled back and the dog leaned forward, and as the Volvo drew up alongside, the dog exploded. Barking, frenzied, it threw itself against the leash.

The woman was tall and energetic-looking. She had short black hair and wore jeans and a T-shirt. She leaned back, tugging on the leash. The dog was lunging so hard that it levitated, hanging in the air, suspended by the leash and its big choke collar. Its teeth were bared. The woman shouted at it, yanking, but the dog paid no attention.

Conrad lifted his hand as he drove past, but the woman ignored him. She was using both hands on the dog leash, struggling with the creature. The dog nearly reached the car, its black, furry legs sticking straight out into the air. Its mouth was white with teeth. Conrad drove slowly past. He hated the sight of it, the raging dog, the black lips lifted against the white teeth. Struggling brainlessly against its owner, the person who fed it and cared for it. He tried not to look.

He thought of stopping, getting out of the car, and sending one kick into the dog's chest. One kick. He knew how it would feel against his foot, the whole body rising up, borne into the air by his foot, the ribs breaking with the impact, splintering into the chest. He wouldn't do this. He thought of doing it. *Jesus.* What was the matter with him?

Once, outside Ramadi, he'd been on mounted patrol with Jackson. They were driving through open land and saw a group of Iraqi dogs, their ribs showing beneath their tan coats, long tails curled over their backs. The dogs were worrying at something in a ditch at the edge of a field. As the patrol came closer, Conrad saw what they were after: an Iraqi man's body, the clothes muddied and dark. The dogs were crowded around it, gulping, wolfing. Jackson sighted on the dogs with his rifle.

"I can pick them off, sir," he offered, squinting into the sights.

"We're Marines," Conrad told him. "Marines don't shoot dogs, Jackson."

"No, sir," Jackson said, lifting his barrel and facing forward again.

That had been early. Later on, everyone shot dogs. They all called it Operation Scooby-Doo and thought they'd been clever, choosing that name. But everyone called it that. Conrad didn't approve, but he'd stopped telling the men not to do it.

Now Conrad turned his head away from the dog. Afterward, as he drove along, he tried to focus on the reservoir, the open stretches of calm water. None of it made him happy, and the thought came to him that he couldn't live like this.

12

The cleaning lady's car was gone now; the house was empty.

Conrad went up to his room and called Claire. She'd be at work now; he'd leave a message. At once she picked up.

"Hey." He leaned forward, setting his elbows on his knees.

"What's up?" she asked. He told her about the early run, the car dealership.

"The salesman gave me his cell number," he said. "Told me to call him anytime, day or night. Is that normal, or do you think he's desperate?"

"I think he's hitting on you," Claire said.

Conrad laughed. "That must be it." He'd forgotten it was fun talking to Claire.

"Hold on a second." He heard her talking to someone. She came back. "Sorry, gotta go. I'm at the office, obviously. Call me tonight. I'll be at home."

He hung up, feeling lighter. He'd go to another dealership tomorrow, look at another car.

That night at dinner his parents didn't talk about Iraq or ask about his plans. Marshall told them about an article he was writing on gay rights. They argued about why ketchup was so popular.

"It's a completely strange kind of food, you know," Lydia said. "No other country has anything like it. It's so thick, and so sweet. I forget what it's based on, but it's not like that anymore. Maybe some Indian sauce? Other countries think it's awful."

"It's based on Chinese fish sauce," said Conrad.

"How do you know these things?" asked Lydia.

"Why do you think Americans like it?" Marshall asked. He always asked these questions as though he were talking to students.

"Because it's so inauthentic," Lydia said. "We've acquired the taste; it's all sugar and thickeners and preservatives."

"I think it's the color," Marshall said. "It looks life-enhancing."

"Looks like blood," Conrad said. "We always used ketchup when we made our serial killer videos in seventh grade. It was kind of de rigueur."

"I think it's the fact that you can't pour it," said Lydia. "That's what people like."

"Isn't there a case study of that?" asked Marshall. "I think there is, at Harvard Business School—the problem of ketchup bottles—and they ended up saying that the bottles should stay narrow and the ketchup thick because people liked banging on the bottom."

"Only now they've changed it," Lydia said.

"True," Marshall answered. "Could Harvard be wrong?"

"Is that a metaphysical question?" asked Lydia.

"I'm thinking of buying a car," Conrad said.

"Really?" Marshall said.

"What kind? I love my Volvo," Lydia said. "It's seen me through thick and thin."

"But it's no good in the snow, Mom," Conrad said.

"It's no good in the snow," Lydia agreed. "I still love them. They're safe, they're great-looking, and they get great mileage."

Both Lydia and Marshall had Volvos. Marshall had a rusty-bottomed station wagon, used mostly for driving to the station and back.

"They're expensive, though," Conrad said. "And I'm not sure that's my look."

"Yes, what is your look, Con?" Lydia took his empty plate and set it on top of her own. "I've been meaning to ask."

"Haven't worked it out yet," Conrad said. "Camo. Maybe a tank?" He stood and took the plates from his mother's hands. "I'm doing this," he said, and took Marshall's plate. "I'm just sitting around. Might as well work for my keep. As long as I'm here, I'll do the dinner dishes."

"Conrad," Lydia said, "that may be the nicest offer anyone has ever made me. In my whole life."

"I sincerely hope not, Mom." Conrad carried the dishes to the sink. He raised his voice over the sound of the water. "I sincerely hope people have made nicer offers to you than doing the dishes."

"Actually, Con," Lydia said, "the nicest thing is having you home." She brought the glasses and the water pitcher over to the sink. "That's the nicest thing." She set them down on the drainboard. "That you're here."

Conrad turned to her. She was standing beside him, a faint smile on her face. He thought of her here in the kitchen while he was gone, and he had a sudden sense of what it had been like.

She had been here, moving through her day, waiting, waiting for phone calls, waiting for letters, waiting for emails. Unable to do anything but wait. Waiting to learn once again that at that particular moment he was alive, still present in the world. He had been present to himself, living each second, but Lydia had been here in this silent house, powerless.

The waiting and the fear: he felt sorry that he'd done this to her. She had never complained.

"I'm sorry I was gone so long," he said. "Thanks for waiting. I'm sorry I put you through all this."

Lydia shook her head. "It's over." She smiled at him. "That's all that matters."

After his parents had gone to bed, Conrad went up to his room and called Claire.

"Hey."

"Hey," Claire said. "What's up?"

"Not much," he said. "Had dinner with my parents. We had a debate over ketchup. Why it's so popular."

"What did you decide?" she asked.

"Can't tell you, sorry," he said. "Classified information."

"That makes me feel safer," she said, "knowing that you guys are taking such good care of us."

"Trust me, we are."

"Did you ever get into secret stuff when you were over there?"

"Here and there," Conrad said. "I wasn't part of it, but there were a lot of Special Ops around."

"And?"

"Some weird situations."

"Tell me one," Claire said.

"Well, one time I was taking a Black Hawk out of Ramadi to another outpost. It was at night; we always flew at night so we wouldn't be a good target. There were ten or twelve of us on the flight. A random bunch, guys going to the other base, a reporter or two. I was already on board, and two guys got on behind me. A sergeant was checking the IDs of everyone getting on. He's got a list on a clipboard. He calls out names and people come over to him, verify who they are. Everyone's listed by name and rank. The sergeant looks down at his list and says, 'Bob?' and he kind of frowns, looking down. 'Bob?' he says again, and looks up. He adds, 'And Mr. Stirling?'

"I look around. There are two guys standing next to each other. One is tall and skinny, and he's wearing all black. Not a uniform, just all-black clothes, long-sleeved shirt and pants. The guy next to him is huge and wide, like a giant. He's wearing a big brown cape that comes down to his ankles. Neither of them says anything, they just look at the sergeant. The sergeant says, 'So, Bob, let's see what you've got here.' He opens the big guy's cape, pulling it back on both sides like a curtain and holding it open. It's like a cartoon: Bob's got enough weapons under there for a platoon. I've never seen so many guns—rifles, pistols, grenades, knives, ammo. He's like *double* Bob. He doesn't say anything; he just stands there staring at the sergeant. Armed from ankle to neck.

"The sergeant stares at him for a moment, then says, 'Okay, then! Thank you.' And then he looks at the other guy. Mr. Stirling is carrying a sniper rifle and about five bullets, loose, in his hand, and that's all. The two of them just stand there waiting, staring at the sergeant. After a moment he looks down at his clipboard and goes, 'Right, okay. So, Bob and Mr. Stirling.' And they walk past him and sit down."

"Amazing," Claire says. "So where were they going?"

"No idea," Conrad said. "Could be any-fucking-where. They did a lot of Special Ops missions at night."

"Amazing," Claire said again. "Bob."

"Mr. Stirling."

Telling stories made him feel good. He talked on and on, lying on his back in his bed and looking up at the ceiling, making Claire laugh.

Finally she said, "So, I have to go. Have to get some sleep."

"Okay," he said. "I'll call you tomorrow."

"I won't be home tomorrow night," she said.

There was a pause.

"You sound like something's up," he said.

"I should probably get something straight."

"Okay," he said.

"You wanted to know what other guys I've been seeing."

"Go on," Conrad said.

"Well, I do go out with other guys."

He waited.

"No big deal. But I'm seeing one of them tomorrow. It's no big deal," she repeated. "I've told him about you."

"I see. And what the fuck am I supposed to say to that?"

"If you start swearing at me, I don't want to talk about this anymore."

"Okay. I'm not swearing. What do you expect me to say to that?"

"I don't expect you to say anything. I'm just telling you what's been happening. You asked me. So I'm telling you. I see other people, I have other friends."

Conrad waited. This was like an exercise. His chest was tight, but he made himself breathe quietly. He could hear the pulse inside his head.

"Great," he said. "Really great."

"Conrad," Claire said.

"So, tell me something. Do you have another boyfriend or not? Are we on? Or not?"

"I don't know," she said. "There's really no one else."

"So who else are you seeing?"

"Conrad, you can't tell me that I can't see anyone else."

"What's the guy's name?"

"What will you do, hunt him down? I'm not telling you that."

Conrad clicked off. He stood up and threw his cell phone as hard as he could onto the bed. It bounced nearly to the ceiling, fell on the floor, and skidded under the bed. He put his hands on his hips. He leaned over from the waist and squeezed his eyes shut.

"Fuck," he whispered, leaning down. "Fuck. Fuck."

He punched the bed hard.

He straightened and looked around the room: The cheesy plastic gold trophies in a dim line before the mirror. The photograph of himself in dress blues. The Led Zeppelin poster. The books. All those silent books.

"Fuck," he said, this time out loud. He punched the bed, harder. He could hear himself breathing. He walked to the window. The air beyond the screen was black and heavy. Outside there was no sound.

"The fuck," he said. He thought of her sitting at a table with some other guy, cocking her head and smiling. He wouldn't think of her in bed with him.

He thought of calling someone else, but there was no one he could talk to about this. He wasn't close enough now to talk to any of his friends from college about his girlfriend. His Marine friends were fellow officers, and mostly scattered. Maybe his closest friend had been Bruce O'Connell, but O'Connell was in Afghanistan now. Conrad couldn't complain about his girlfriend to any of his men: you didn't complain to your men about anything.

Conrad thought of Go-Go: he was nearby, anyway. Hadn't Claire said he was in New York? He'd been a good friend. It would be good to reconnect with him. Conrad got down on the floor and swept his hand back and forth under the bed. Finally he retrieved his cell phone. He scrolled through it to see if he had Go-Go's number: he did not.

He didn't really want to talk to Go-Go. Civilians wouldn't understand what it was like to leave your life and then come back to it.

There was nothing for him to say to anyone. What was there to say? He was being a dick, that was the thing.

The house was quiet now. He could go downstairs and watch TV alone in the library. He could sprawl out on the sofa, aiming the remote at the screen, flicking idly from program to program. The room would be dark except for the lighted screen. He could lie there and tune out the rest of the world, close his mind to everything else.

He sat down on the bed and dialed Claire's number.

"Okay," he said. "I'm sorry."

She began to cry.

"I'm really sorry," he said. "Fuck."

He didn't know why he acted like this. There was something, like a veil, between himself and himself.

If he was going to be home for a while, and by mid-June it appeared he was, he needed a plan. He still couldn't see past the summer, but he'd work out a routine that would take him to the end of it. He'd go running every day. He'd keep up with his men, which was still his responsibility, and he'd get onto the grad school thing, even if he still couldn't imagine going.

He asked his mother if he could take over the other bedroom on the third floor as a study, and offered to do some project for his parents, something they needed done. Paint the barn, or clear the brush from the back field. His mother said of course he could use the bedroom, and it would be a godsend if he would clear the field. It was being invaded by bittersweet.

So he had a plan. A mission.

The second bedroom on the third floor was smaller but had more light. Its windows looked out on the other side of the house, over the lawn, toward the big ash and the barn. A single bed stood near the door under the sloping eaves. Next to the window was a table and chair, where Conrad put his computer. He'd bought it on his first leave home, and he was still working out the kinks. He faced the eaves, but if he turned his head, he looked out at the green canopy of the ash. This was part of his plan; now at least he had a place of his own where he could sit at a desk, not just sprawl on his bed.

The next morning, after his run, he sat down and checked his phone: Claire had called him on her way to work, from the sidewalk. Behind her voice were the sounds of traffic. "Hi, it's me. I just want you to know I'm eating a Krispy Kreme doughnut in your name. It is really good. You would be proud."

He called back but got voice mail. She was at her office by now, under the eye of the dreaded Yvette. He left a message. "I know how you feel about Krispy Kremes, and all I can say is I'm honored and proud." He thought for a moment. "Yeah. Nothing out here can equal that. Talk to you later."

When he checked his email, there was a message from Anderson.

Hey, sir, how's it going? Just wanted to let you know I've just got a job, and I'm psyched. I start next week, driving a truck for a big company out here, Nordort. Not a big fucking deal but its a fucking job and in this economy that's a big fucking deal. Things are going pretty good here, but in a weird way I miss the big sandbox, if you can believe it. I'm thinking of volunteering for a church organization, working with teenagers. Or reenlisting, ha ha. That's all for now, LT, hope you are well. semper fi.

Conrad wondered if it was really a joke, about Anderson reenlisting. A lot of guys did it, guys who couldn't make things work out at home. There was nothing wrong with it, just as there was nothing wrong in enlisting. But he didn't like the thought that this war had changed men inside, twisted them somehow so they couldn't fit back home. The joke wasn't a good sign. But why would Anderson raise it when he'd just gotten a job?

Conrad wrote back:

Hey, Anderson, congratulations on the job. Any job sounds good, also the volunteering. I know what you mean about missing Iraq, weird, isn't it? But we're here now. It will take a while for things to feel normal, but all this will get better. Stay in touch. Let me know if you want to talk. Farrell.

Molinos wrote him from Anbar Province:

Hey, sir, wanted to let you know that we hit 120 degrees yesterday. I know how you love the heat, thought I would let you know. Otherwise all okay, LT. We are kicking ass over here. Semper Fi. Molinos.

Conrad answered everyone. It felt strange, writing to the men who were re-deployed. They were still right in the thick of it, IEDs and 110 degrees. (It wasn't 120, everyone lied about the heat.) He was here, living on the third floor, in the same bedroom he'd had since he was fourteen. It gave him a lift to hear from them. He'd gone to the newsstand yesterday and chosen a stack of comics, mostly the heroes, but a couple of other ones for variety, *Archie*, and a strange one called *Boxers* he'd never seen before. He'd stood in line at the post office and sealed and addressed the mailing carton to Bradley. He wondered what the quarters were like: mostly they bivouacked in an existing building. Could be anything, a school, a factory, an unused garage.

There was an email from Captain Glover, his CO during the final months he'd been in service. Glover was just checking in, he said, to hear how everyone was. He asked what Conrad's plans were.

Conrad wrote back:

> *All quiet, sir. Everyone good. I'm doing recon and training: looking at grad schools and running.*

After emails Conrad checked the military blogs.

He read them every day. They were news from his tribe, living filaments connecting him to the life he had known. It felt natural to read them but also oddly shameful. A few days earlier he'd been reading one down in the library when Marshall came into the room. Conrad found himself clicking away from the site as though it were porn. As though this were a secret part of his life, not part of his actual life.

He read them avidly. There were hundreds of them. Some were online journals kept by people on deployment day by day in-country. Some were political forums conducted by people in the States. Some were kept by military wives and mothers. The responses were often volatile, digressive, and full of rage. The rage came mostly from vets back home; discussions usually turned ugly, no matter what the subject was. Anything would trigger it.

He checked a blog run by Joe Reese, the father of an Army sergeant in Baghdad. Reese was levelheaded and well informed, and the blog was like a forum. He insisted that people be civil, and he deleted comments that were not. Today he'd raised the question of the rules of engagement: Under what circumstances should a soldier use deadly force?

The subject was instantly inflammatory, but so was everything on the subject of the war. Everyone had something to say about the U.S. presence in Iraq. Everyone was an expert, everyone felt strongly, and everyone thought everyone else was full of shit.

> Joe, I'm glad you raised this issue, because any institution that requires young men to kill other people in cold blood is asking for trouble. We are brutalizing our soldiers and creating murderers in our midst.

Joe replied that soldiers had to carry out a mission:

> If people were shooting at them, they must be allowed to shoot back. Civilians don't want to think about lethal force. Yet it must play a part in war.

There was a technological pause, and then a response appeared on the screen:

> Joe, I have said this before and I will say it again. The only way we can win this war is to win it. I mean establishing a full military presence there, and not any of this chikcinshit 10,000 troops. What we need to do is to bring our full pwers to bear and that means not only Hellfire missils but curtain bombing if not nuclear. We have to make clear to the entire population that they have no choice in this matter.

Yeah, good, thought Conrad. *Great. If you kill everyone in the fucking country, the war will be over. That makes sense.*

Someone else wrote in:

> The soldier who shot a wounded enemy should be court-martialed as an example. That is exactly what war does, it brutalizes our men. Like my lie. My lae.

The soldier in question had been caught on tape months earlier. He'd shot a wounded man who was lying on the floor. An embedded journalist had caught it on film, and the press went nuts.

Shooting the wounded enemy happened all the time, it was called double tapping. If you shot someone in combat and didn't kill him and he was lying near you, wounded, and if he might still have a weapon on him or was anywhere near one, you shot him again. You didn't want him grabbing his pistol, or even a piece of rubble, and whacking you while your back was turned. You shot him a second time to make sure he wouldn't shoot you first. You were still playing by the rules that required you to shoot him the first time. That was what combat meant: lethal force. It meant killing the enemy.

Under ideal circumstances, of course, you did something else with a wounded enemy: you put him in zips and a blindfold and tied him up in a corner. But during a firefight, circumstances were rarely ideal. In combat, your responsibility was to the safety of yourself and your men. In combat you shot him, maybe twice.

But that wasn't what had happened in this case. The soldier had fucked up.

It had been bad. The man on the floor was not an insurgent, but a wounded civilian awaiting medical attention. The medics had treated the wounded prisoners and were coming back for him. He was waiting for the corpsmen. The soldier had come into the room, seen him lying on the floor, and shot him point-blank. It was very bad, very fucked-up.

Everyone had a response.

AlphaWarrior92 blamed everything on the liberal press:

> It's the fucking media who put all this stuff out there, they are blowing up everything out of all proportion. It is they who are responsible for the deaths that occur over there, day after day, and they should fucking well take the blame.

Thunderhead188 disagreed:

> This is a tyypical claim by someone who knows very little. Do you really think the liberal press is out in Fallujah setting IEDs? Or would that be the mujahideen? Get your head out of your butt and put the blame where it really lays.

Alpha replied:

> You are pretending not to know what Im saying. The press CNN and Time and all of them are bloodsuckers, they only want to stir things up. They have been on that story of the sergeant shooting that

wounded soldier now for six months, too long, they should find something else to write about. Enough is enough.

Thunderhead answered:

January to February is one month, March to April is two, April–May is three, May–June is four. That's four months, not six. Stay in school.

Before Alpha could reply, Geostrategist185 appeared. He identified himself as a military historian who couldn't give his ID for security reasons:

I WILL WRITE THE REST OF THIS COMM IN MILITARY CAPS. YOU ALL DO NOT HAVE AN INFORMED VIEW OF THIS FROM A GLOBAL PERSPECTIVE. YOU DO NOT UNDERSTAND HOW THE INSURGENCY HAS PLANNED THERE LONG-TERM STRATEGIES. I HAVE HAD LONG EXPERIENCE AT THE TOP LEVELS (OF WHICH MORE LATER) AND KNOW MANY OF THE PEOPLE INVOLVED AND THEY ARE PLAYING A LONG AND CAREFULLY CALIBRATED GAME, WHICH PUTS THE US INEXORABLY IN A LOSE-LOSE SITUATION. WE WILL HAVE NO CHOICE BUT TO BE BLED DRY BY THIS LONG-TERM WAR, WHICH IS EXACTLY THEIR INTENTION. YOU PROBABLY DO NOT KNOW THAT MOST OF THEIR TOP-LEVEL AUTHORITIES WENT TO SANDHURST, AND STUDIED MILITARY HISTORY AND TACTICS FROM THE BRITS. I WAS THERE.

The comments went wild, many of them deleted immediately by Joe. Strong and colorful language was used, and many suggestions were made about Geostrategist's bodily parts and how they might best be deployed.

Shortly afterward Joe announced that Geostrategist had lied about his identity and was now banned from the site. *Turns out he's a troll,* wrote the blogger, *and he'll have to make his little trollish way somewhere else.*

But everyone was still enraged, even after the troll had been banished.

It was interesting that the post had generated so much anger; Conrad wondered how much of it was due to the patronizing tone and how much to the all-capital letters.

Was there more rage on the Internet than anywhere else? Or was it everywhere now? Was rage the new black? Or was it only in the military? He'd seen a post someone who was just out of EAS had made. His New Year's resolution was "Not to stab someone this week."

The blogs made Conrad feel alive: angry at the fucking idiots, supportive of the smart posters, but engaged and back in the world. He thought about reenlisting himself: Why stand on the sidelines when the life he knew was still going on? For hours he drifted through the blogs. It was surprising how quickly the time passed.

He went downstairs and made lunch, then went back upstairs. He checked email, glanced at a few blogs to see if anyone had gone nuts online, and then began to look at graduate schools.

This was part of his mission. It was a way to start to focus, even if he wasn't ready to choose one. He began scrolling through the sites, ready to look everywhere: law, political science, international relations. Actually, they all sounded pretty much the same:

> Offering a professional education that simultaneously adheres to the highest standards of scholarship and takes a practical approach to training students for international leadership.

That bullshit language. The phrases meant something serious, also they didn't. Excellence and honor, duty and courage—those things were real. But there was another part of the reality, and what did these phrases have to do with the pattern on the wall, the boy in his pajamas, Olivera, whispering?

The two things seemed unconnected, but they moved together in his mind as though they were caught up in an invisible tide. *What's the first thing you feel when you shoot a civilian? The recoil from your rifle.*

He scrolled through the descriptions, clicking through the pages about the schools. Our campus. Our faculty. Our program. He looked at the application forms. One problem was that he'd need to ask people for recommendations. The idea of getting in touch with his old professors—reconnecting in that hearty, friendly tone—made him nervous. How was he going to translate his own history into something that made sense here? He knew the schools were real, but they didn't seem real. His head felt as if it were slowly being squeezed by a vise.

He clicked on the section on one of the sites that showed the campus. Looking at the old brick buildings, the broad green lawns and big trees, Conrad thought of Ali. It was possible that Ali had made his way out of Iraq. It was possible that he was here. There were government programs for people like him who had worked for the U.S. forces. It was entirely possible. Ali was smart, and it was possible that he'd end up at a graduate school. Looking at the majestic trees with their low, sweeping limbs, Conrad imagined walking among them and seeing Ali. Conrad would show him around, and they'd walk across the lawns. Some of the interpreters did get out. He could be here.

There were a lot of schools. A lot of fields. All right, they all made him feel as if he were crawling into a black box, but this was just the first day of his search.

When he turned off his computer, he sat down on the floor. Exercise was said to help maintain your mental health, and he was going to do whatever he had to. He did push-ups and crunches and mountain climbers, which were like push-ups, only it was running in place horizontally.

He put on a work shirt and went down to start the clearing. He got a bottle of water, and in the garage he found tools: work gloves, the big clippers, a pruning saw, rake, and shovel. He liked hefting them, liked the feel of useful objects.

He climbed up through the tall, silky grass of the meadow. Along the crest of the hill ran a tumbledown stone wall, fringed with hickory, wild cherry, ash. On the other side of the crest was the wide back field, two acres sloping down to the woods. An old split-rail fence outlined the space; pressing against it was the leafy crowd of trees. The slanting field was scattered with curving mounds of foliage: brambles and bittersweet had invaded the grass.

Conrad carried the tools to the northwest corner and set them down. He'd work his way across.

The nearest mound was made of bittersweet. It was a ravenous vine, its long waving tendrils snaking into the air and weaving through the grass. Conrad took hold of a shoot at the base and tugged, pulling up a nest of bright yellow roots. The color was surprising, almost fluorescent. They were damp, with dark soil clinging to them. He ripped up more, each surface shoot leading to a long fleshy string of yellow root, burrowing under the soil. He used the shovel, biting into the hard, dry sod. The roots were everywhere; the whole field was infested. He began to sweat, feeling good. He grabbed another piece at the base and yanked it up. The long, taut line of it rose from the ground like an anchor rope from the waves.

"Come on, you fucker," he said cheerfully.

The vine snapped off near the base, and he picked up the shovel again. The air was hot and still. He worked slowly, yanking out the long green wands and the yellow root clusters and tossing them into a big, messy pile. At first the heart-shaped leaves were green and fresh, but they wilted quickly in the heat. He worked steadily, stopping to drink, wiping his face with the heel of his hand. He liked seeing the mass of green mounting higher and higher. He kept on through the afternoon, until the shadows broke over the crest of the hill, spilling down the field and marking the grass with twilight.

This was how he'd do it, how he'd come back. Step by step, root by root.

13

For years the Farrells had rented a house in Cape Cod for the first two weeks in August. When the children were small, the whole family had gone together. As the children grew older and took summer jobs and went on trips, their visits were shortened and interrupted. But Marshall and Lydia always went during the same time each year, and the children came when they could.

This year, Ollie texted Conrad: *Ur coming, rite?*

The house was an old saltbox cottage, small and shabby, with peeling walls and mossy shingles. It stood on a rise overlooking a small pond. Behind the house was a field, and beyond that, pinewoods. At the edge of the woods stood an old water tower the children were forbidden to climb. Beyond the woods was an abandoned cranberry bog, big flat terraces bordered by narrow ditches.

The house faced a quiet road lined with wild beach plum bushes. Across the road were sandy fields of sparse grass flecked with dark juniper trees. The house stood at the top of a little rise. Below it was the barn, musty and cobwebby, full of the sour smell of bats. Narrow haylofts were on either side of the main space, and a single stall. The floorboards were soft and crumbling. A rope swing hung in the open doorway.

In Conrad's childhood summers, stepping out the kitchen door and letting the screen bang behind you was to enter a landscape of infinite possibility. The air was buoyant and salty, the grass wiry underfoot. Everything beckoned: the dense tangle of honeysuckle leading down to the pond, the hot, tarry road, the water tower among the trees.

Nearby was the beach, salt water slapping against you as you waded into the cold, bracing churn. The hot sun, the limitless blue sky.

He texted back: *4 sure.*

Years earlier, playing some game, he had chased Ollie down the stairs, trying to catch him. The stairs were steep, nearly vertical, and Conrad's fingers grazed Ollie's shoulder as Ollie tripped and fell. He thundered to the bottom, arms and legs in confusion. For a moment he lay still on the floor; then he sat up and looked at Conrad. His face was crimsoned, blood spreading over his mouth and chin. He said, "You killed me." For a moment Conrad had thought he had.

It was only a bloody nose. Lydia made Ollie lie down on the kitchen floor while she pressed a cold washcloth to his face, and the bleeding stopped. But after that, during any game, Ollie would give Conrad a zombie look. "You killed me," he would intone.

"Yes," Conrad would answer, "I killed you, and if you don't watch out, I will kill you again." Then they started struggling again, laughing and choking. Conrad was bigger, and he almost always won.

In the sandy meadows across the road the boys made a fort in a tree-ringed hollow. As they were digging a trench, they were attacked by streams of tiny stinging red ants crawling up their legs inside their jeans. They yelled, yanking off their pants. They slapped and scraped at themselves, jumping and shouting and laughing. "Oh, jeez! Oh, jeez!" they screamed, hopping about in their underpants. "Oh, jeezus! My nuts! My nuts!" They never went back to the fort after that.

The road was made of thick, sandy tar, and in the hot sun it melted, making shiny little black puddles. Conrad and Ollie made oily pellets from these and threw them at each other, dodging behind the beach plum bushes. They used the unripe beach plums as weapons, stripping them from the pungent leaves and pelting each other, laughing.

They all drove up from Katonah. Jenny and Ollie went with Marshall, Conrad with Lydia. Early start, Lydia had told them all firmly the night before.

By eight o'clock it was already hot. The early sun was reflecting off the white clapboards. The inlaid pebbles in the driveway gave off heat underfoot, and the willows hung straight and motionless. They loaded the cars, walking back and forth from the house, carrying suitcases, canvas bags, cardboard boxes of food. Conrad liked having a mission. He strode back and forth, carrying the largest things he could find. In the back seat of Lydia's car was the cat carrier holding Murphy, silent and resentful, her pupils huge with alarm.

When the cars were loaded, everyone stood outside waiting for Lydia. She was famously the last to leave. Resisting departure, she went through the rooms in a last-minute fury, turning off switches, locking windows, carrying things from place to place, writing notes, performing small tasks that could not be delegated or even explained.

"Any sign of your mother?" Marshall asked Jenny.

"I'll see if I can help," Jenny said. She came back in a few minutes, shaking her head.

"She said if we were ready, we should go, not to wait." She looked at Conrad. "Do you mind being abandoned? We'll open the house when we get there."

"Nope," said Conrad. "See you up there."

"If we don't break down," Marshall said. "Stop if you see us on the side of the road."

Conrad nodded, and Marshall, Jenny, and Ollie climbed into the laden car. It rolled slowly down the driveway, and Jenny waved and called, "See you up there!"

Conrad waved back, watching them descend the short slope and turn cautiously onto the dirt road, Jenny's arm still waving.

When the car vanished, the place was restored to silence and everything seemed to expand: the willows, with their cascade of leaves, the deep green lawns, cool and sumptuous despite the heat. Conrad thought of Ali. He'd have liked to show him this place. *That's a white ash.* Ali had looked so closely at the photograph.

Conrad climbed into the driver's seat. He left the door open, one leg stretched outside. It was getting hotter, but this was not real heat. Here it was humid and enervating, the heat like a burden, but it wasn't real heat. Conrad turned the key in the ignition and skimmed the radio stations, then turned it off and sat with his head tilted back, eyes shut. He felt pretty good. He'd cleared two-thirds of the meadow, working all of July, tugging out the roots, dragging the branches into big piles of wilting leaves. He was looking forward to kicking back.

Lydia appeared in the mudroom, calling out, "Okay! Sorry!" She turned to lock the door, then pushed out through the white gate. She wore a wide, floppy hat and carried a canvas bag. "Sorry to take so long," she said. "There was a load in the dryer and I couldn't leave it in there. And I had to write notes to Katia." Her face changed as she saw that he was in the driver's seat. "Are you driving?"

"I offered," he said.

"So you did," Lydia said, and got in. "Okay, then, we are off, off, off." She fastened her seat belt and turned to the back. "Hi, there, Murph, you beautiful pussycat. Are you all right?"

Murphy gave her a smoldering look.

"Con?" She smiled at him. "All set?"

"Locked and loaded," Conrad said. "Full battle rattle, ready to roll."

She gave him an uncertain smile. They started down the driveway, the tips of the willow branches trailing faintly against the roof. Lydia leaned back.

"I love this," she said. "I love this moment when we really leave. I love this house, but I love the feeling of leaving it, leaving everything behind and heading off into the summer." She turned and smiled at Conrad. "Con, I'm so glad you're here."

"Yeah, me, too." He smiled, his eyes on the road.

"I mean, back from Iraq, of course," she said, "but also right here, right now, in the car with me."

Conrad nodded slowly in agreement, feeling vaguely guilty. He felt as though he should be offering something, doing more than he was. "Me, too," he said again.

Their narrow dirt road sloped gradually through the woods, down a long hill. At the bottom it reached a fast paved road that led to a big six-lane highway. Conrad turned down the ramp, and the car slid into the stream of traffic heading north through upper Westchester County.

In places the highway had been drilled out of standing stone, and high man-made bluffs slanted steeply away from the road. The open cuts revealed the bare interior: Skeins of strata drifted in pale galactic swirls through the dark stone. Igneous, sedimentary—and what was the third kind? Dropped from outer space? He couldn't remember. He liked these bluffs, they were like a giant geology lab, demonstrating exactly the way the earth had been formed.

As they drove north, the highway cut through hilly woodland and overgrown pastures. Up here, too far for daily commuters, the land was mostly open and undeveloped.

In the nineteenth century it had all been farmland, but when the railways opened up the Midwest, the big agriculture of the era moved out to the great fertile plains. The local farms turned to orchards and dairy herds. Dairy farms survived until the forties and fifties, when refrigeration made local milk unnecessary. Now the dairy farms had failed and the land was either abandoned or being developed, the old apple trees suffocated by bittersweet and the fields gone to weeds and saplings.

Lydia had told them all this a hundred times, her voice reproving, as though her family were somehow guilty, responsible for the twin juggernauts of commerce and technology. As a teenager, Conrad had resented this burden. Lydia felt responsible for everything—every one of her patients and everyone in their families, the environment, and every plant and creature on the planet. How could anyone live like that? And why did she want to share the burden with her children? It made him resentful and impatient.

From the highway the old farmhouses were visible, solid white clapboard colonials, the handsome barns nearby. No animals, though, no tilled fields.

But he wasn't so different from his mother, actually. He'd been sort of trying to save the world, joining the Corps. Now he couldn't remember exactly why. At the time it had seemed unarguable. Now his own ideas seemed as confused and childish as his parents' idealism, all that naive sixties bullshit. How could they have thought anything was so simple? How could he?

Driving onto the highway, Conrad had moved at once into the fast lane. There was a lot of traffic. He didn't like being constrained or having other cars around him. He especially didn't like cars coming too close. When a car moved alongside him in the middle lane, he sped up, keeping a constant eye on the rearview mirror. He actually didn't like having any other cars at all on the highway. He preferred driving in convoy, on a road that had been cleared of other vehicles.

"The first time we rented the house at the Cape," Lydia said, "I think you were three or four. We went up there in the first place because Marshall's family had always gone there, so he loved it. They had a big house on the water in South Yarmouth. You remember it."

His grandparents' house had been sold years before, but he had memories of it: the big sunny rooms, the croquet lawn. They'd driven past it many times, though it was hidden now by pines and a high stockade fence. They could see the upper part, white clapboards, glossy black shutters. Beyond it was a lawn and a path down to the water. The driveway was made of clamshells.

"We used to come up and stay with your grandparents. You were probably too young to remember that. Then one day when it was raining, we called a real estate broker, just out of boredom, and drove around to look at rentals."

He had never heard this.

Lydia looked ahead. "Your father always said he didn't want to inherit his parents' house. He didn't want the responsibility of looking after a second place. And he couldn't spend the whole summer there, the way his father had."

Behind Conrad, in the left-hand lane, was a small white sedan. Nearly every car in Iraq was a small white sedan. Everyone drove them: taxi drivers, businessmen, and insurgents. Suicide bombers. The sight of the car made Conrad's pulse quicken, though he wasn't in Iraq and he knew this wasn't a suicide bomber. The car was moving fast, coming up on him from behind. Streams of cars were sliding along all three lanes; directly ahead of him in the fast lane was a big black SUV.

"So your father was already looking around. Even if we'd kept the family house and just used it ourselves for a couple of weeks and rented it out for the rest of the season, he'd have had the responsibility. He said he never wanted to drive up in the middle of winter to get the boiler fixed or the chimney patched. He always said, 'Never own if you can rent.' Of course, he meant a summerhouse, not our house."

Beside Conrad, in the middle lane, was an opening. The next car back, a bullet-shaped silver sedan, was driving badly, wallowing back and forth. Some idiot, texting.

"I remember we saw several houses that day. Most of them were awful. Brand-new little bungalows, cheek by jowl beside other horrible little houses in developments or else right on top of the road."

Lydia had folded her arms on her chest. She sounded dreamy and abstracted.

"It's sort of terrible, going around and looking at other people's houses. You see their lives, everything they've chosen, the lamps, the bedspreads, the chairs. I mean, not that they're so awful, only that the people are so exposed, so naked, for you to walk through passing judgment. Which is just what you do. If you don't like the houses, the owners feel they've failed. You voted against their taste, their choices, everything. I felt so bad for the owners. They were always there, lurking around in the kitchen or the hall, moving out of each room as you walked in. I walked around saying loudly how beautiful each house was, admiring the curtains."

"Only you, Mom," Conrad said.

The white car was closing the gap. In the front seat were two military-age males wearing dark glasses.

"No, really," Lydia said. "They knew we were judging them. It's a horrible feeling. I read once that when people's houses have been robbed, the first stage is being frightened and angry, but then people get indignant because the thieves didn't take other things that the owners thought were valuable. They're upset that the thieves didn't take more."

The white car was hanging back now, just out of rifle range.

"I remember one house. There must have been a mix-up about the appointment. We got there, and the broker went to the front door and then came back to the car and said we'd have to wait for a bit. We sat and waited. The broker kept going up and knocking, and then she'd come back and get into the car again."

Conrad kept his eye on the rearview mirror. It looked as though one of the males was using an electronic device. It was how you detonated an IED—you could use a cell phone, a remote-control device for a TV or a toy airplane. All it took was one click.

"Finally the broker called to us to come in. Inside was a young couple standing side by side in the hall. They were furious. Especially her. We said hello, and then they stood there glaring while we walked through the house. It had just been neatened up. It didn't feel really clean. You had a sense of things stuffed under the sofa, jammed under the mattress, crammed into closets. I didn't dare open any doors; I thought everything would fall out on top of me."

The male in the passenger seat was using a cell phone. He was talking into it and staring straight at Conrad. The white car was coming up fast, closing the gap.

"You could feel the tension radiating from them. Each time we went past the hall, they were standing there, arms crossed, not speaking. I thought they'd just had a fight about the house. They kept cleaning it up to be shown, and then people didn't take it. It would be so insulting."

The silver car in the middle lane was driving erratically, but Conrad thought that if he shifted suddenly into its lane, the car would drop back. There was no other way. Then he could slide over into the far-right lane, drop back himself, and slow down, leaving the white car trapped in the far-left lane.

"I kept saying, 'Oh, how interesting,' about everything," said Lydia. "The place was pretty awful, actually, full of cheap, trendy furniture. These awful swagged curtains. The woman was furious, her eyes all squinted up." Lydia squinted her own eyes. "She wouldn't look at her husband."

The white sedan drew closer, right behind him. Conrad watched it in the mirror. The two men were staring straight at Conrad. When they were ten meters away, without warning Conrad swerved abruptly into the middle lane, nosing in front of the wobbling silver sedan. It shifted wildly into the right-hand lane, nearly hitting a car in it, then veered back into the middle lane, barely under control. Conrad swerved over again into the slow lane, shoving between a green car and a pickup truck. The silver car blared its horn furiously, and the pickup truck, now behind him, did the same. Conrad straightened, speeding up, then slowing, so the driver in the pickup truck could calm down.

"Conrad!" Lydia leaned forward, grabbing the dashboard.

He said nothing, watching the rearview mirror, checking the road ahead, and watching the white sedan. Still in the fast lane, it kept going, behind the black SUV. Conrad watched it move out of sight. Up ahead was an overpass; he focused on that.

"Conrad, what is it?" Lydia said. "Seriously, don't do that."

"Sorry," he said.

He was only partly here with his mother. He felt her sitting there in her batik-print shirt, her wrinkled green pants. She was real, and he knew that what she was saying was real, but at the same time he was in another real place, where cars on the road were deadly risks, carrying this threat: the exploding bloom of darkness. The two places were not connected.

"Conrad," Lydia said. "I mean it. Please let me drive if you have to do things like that. This is dangerous."

He said nothing, watching the cars around them.

"Con, can we talk about this?"

His chest tightened. Talking about it was the thing he would not do. What he kept inside him was the real thing, the world he knew, carried inside his chest. Letting it out was the risk. He wouldn't talk about this, couldn't tell his mother about the suicide bombers in the small white sedans, couldn't tell her about cell phones used as detonators, couldn't tell her about IEDs thrown from overpasses. The words would make no sense here. There was no way between the worlds.

Conrad drove ahead without answering. The white car had gone on, vanishing into the long line of cars. When he saw a rest stop, he pulled off the road.

"I want to stretch a bit, Ma. You want to drive?" he said.

"Happy to," Lydia said.

She got out of the car and stood on the pavement in the sun, smoothing her hair with both hands. Conrad went into the bushes to pee, and she climbed into the driver's seat. She put her hands on the steering wheel and flexed them, opening and closing her fingers. She'd been clenching them hard against the dashboard. She turned around to look at Murphy.

"How are you doing, my gorgeous girl?" she asked. Murphy was crouched and motionless, her pupils enormous and black. She stared back at Lydia.

"You thought that was kind of scary," Lydia said to her. "I know. I thought so, too."

14

The house and barn both faced the road, but from different places on the hillside. The barn was low, and close to the road. The house was farther back, and up the hill.

The house was eighteenth-century, small and weather-beaten. On the front, the house was only one story high, though up under the roof peak, it rose to two. The shingled sides had once been white, but the paint was peeling off and turning the walls to a shimmering gray. The lawn sloped from the house toward the barn. At the bottom was a stone retaining wall, holding back the hillside. In a gap were three wide stone steps and a rickety wooden railing.

Conrad pulled the car up before the barn. The big doors were open onto the shadowy dimness. Against the far wall squatted an ancient icebox; the wooden swoop of a scythe hung beside it. The rope swing was looped up to one side.

"Here we are," he said. "Everything looks the same."

"It always does," Lydia said. "I don't think they've done a thing to it in twenty years. Which is kind of why I love it."

Marshall's car was beside them, doors open, the back half full of bags. Lydia got out and opened the back door.

"How are you, my beauty?" she crooned to Murphy. "We're here, it's over."

Conrad opened the rear door to the solid mass of bags.

Lydia said, "I'm going to take Murph up to the house, then I'll be back to help."

"Don't worry about it," he said. "I've got this."

He loaded himself up, suitcase in one hand, canvas bags in the other, and headed to the house at a rapid jog. His body knew this—the three stone steps, the slope of the lawn going up to the house.

No one used the front door. It was old and solid, with a heavy brass knocker. It faced the road, but everyone came in through the side door, which opened into the kitchen. That door was relatively new, with a glass panel and a modern lock: the kitchen and the bathroom had been added in the twenties or thirties, when plumbing and electricity came in. An outside shower was on the wall beyond the door.

As he approached the house, Jenny appeared. She held the door open.

"Welcome." She made a sweeping gesture.

"Glad to be here," Conrad said.

The kitchen was long and meandering. In the center stood a square wooden table with a linoleum top; on the far wall was the sink, overlooking the back deck. The stove stood against the back wall; above it was a row of blue-and-white porcelain jars, labeled in French: RIZ, SUCRE, THÉ, CAFÉ. The smells were familiar: old dry wood, sun, a faint hint of kerosene.

The kitchen was cluttered. Bags of food stood on the counter, suitcases clustered on the floor. Marshall was looking for lightbulbs, Lydia was unpacking food. Conrad unloaded the car, and then picked up his duffel bag from under the table. He started up to his room.

As he left, Lydia called, "Con, why don't you take the blue room this year, instead of sharing with Ollie?"

Conrad had reached the living room and paused. "The guest room?"

"Well, yes." Lydia sounded self-conscious.

Of course he got it. The guest room had a double bed, and Claire was coming up the next weekend. But the family rule had always been no cohabitation at home.

"Okay," Conrad called back. He climbed the steep staircase slowly; the steps were so narrow he had to turn his feet sideways. This was cool, but wasn't it a little weird to have your mother publicly enable your sex life?

The guest room was off the upstairs landing. The walls were a faded blue. The room was bright with sun: a big double window faced the meadow; a dormer looked over the back. The double bed faced the window; a bureau next to it. Spindle-backed chairs stood against the walls. Filmy white curtains hung at the windows. Clean and spare, the room smelled of old plaster and wood, baking heat, and summer.

Ollie appeared in the doorway.

"You're in here? How come?"

They had always shared the room at the other end of the hall, overlooking the barn. It was long and narrow, with sloping walls, stretching from the front to the back of the house. Jenny had the middle room.

"Mom told me to take this. Claire's coming up." Conrad waggled his eyebrows.

Ollie visibly considered making a joke about sex with Claire, then decided against it.

"Yeah," he said.

"Mom's lifted the ban," Conrad said. "I guess she thinks twenty-six is the age of consent."

"The ban?"

"On us sharing rooms with our girlfriends. Or boyfriends."

"Oh, that. She lifted it a while ago. After Jenny got out of college. Mom said she felt stupid. She gave us a lecture on taking responsibility, but she lifted the ban."

"She *did*? She lifted it and I *missed* it?" asked Conrad. "I can't believe that."

"You've been away, man," Ollie said. "You missed a lot."

"You brought girlfriends home to sleep in *your room*?"

Ollie's room was famous; Lydia called it the Boar's Den.

"Actually, no," Ollie admitted. "It would be kind of weird."

"Don't know why," said Conrad. "It's Seduction City in there, all those lacrosse sticks and baseball mitts and old athletic socks. All your electronic crap."

"Yeah," Ollie said. "What I thought."

"Shit. I can't believe I missed out on that," said Conrad again.

"Well, you did. But now you're catching up, and I don't know what I'm going to do with all that empty space," said Ollie. "It'll be a big stadium in there with just one person."

"Why don't you just leave your shit all over the place?" suggested Conrad. "Strew stuff around. Filth the place up. That'll make it homey."

"I know what I can do," Ollie said, and jiggled his eyebrows.

He went on down the hall.

Conrad moved to the window. He could see the water tower at the far side of the meadow, a blue-gray cylinder with its slanting hat. The meadow was dry and pale: it was August. The grass shifted mildly in the wind. It made a dry rustling sound.

Beneath him was his parents' bedroom. They were unpacking, and the murmur of their voices came up through the floor: there had been no insulation in the eighteenth century. He wondered who'd built this little farmhouse, the barn with its wooden floor, its narrow haylofts. The one stall. Horse or cow? Ox? Farming here must have been hard: sandy soil, long, brutal winters, the only heat from the fireplaces downstairs.

He started unpacking. The floor creaked as he walked back and forth, the soft pine yielding under his weight. He wondered if his parents would hear him when he did push-ups and crunches. Mountain climbers. Had sex with Claire.

The whole point of the Cape was the beach.

They set off in the morning and stayed for the day, coming back salty and sandy, sun-stunned, silent. There were several beaches to choose from: the closest was West Dennis, sheltered and south-facing, with mild surf. Nauset was distant and more challenging, set on the eastern edge of the Cape, on the Atlantic. Huge pounding waves rolled straight in from the ocean.

The day after their arrival the Farrells went to West Dennis, with its flat shoreline and low waves. When they got there, the big parking lot was nearly full, and they had to park in the farthest line of spaces. They carried their things in over the dunes, walking slowly across the hot sand.

The beach was dotted with encampments. Each family claimed its territory, setting up umbrellas and flinging down towels. Small children sat with buckets and pails, building structurally unsound castles. The Farrells walked past the crowds, farther up the beach to a stretch that was relatively empty. Ollie went first, carrying the furled umbrella. He reached an open area and turned to the others.

"Okay?" he called.

Marshall waved; Lydia shouted, *"Yes!"*

Ollie drove the stake end of the umbrella deep into the sand with a swift, triumphant stroke, as though he were claiming the continent for the queen. When the others reached him, he was cranking the creaking handle, spreading the faded green-and-white-striped cloth in tiny jerks, making shade. Jenny set down the aluminum beach chairs and began to struggle with their rusted joints. "Owie, owie, owie," she whispered, her feet scalded by the hot sand. They set about establishing their own colony, spreading out the faded towels, getting out drinks and books, hats and sunscreen.

When they were settled, Ollie pulled off his T-shirt.

"Hi-yah!" he yelled, and ran toward the water. He exploded into the flat green surge, kicking up droplets of flying white foam. He ran deeper, the water slowing his strides. Waist-deep, he made a low, wallowing dive, plunging into the surf. Coming up, he turned to the others, now gleaming, water cascading down his face. "Come on!" he yelled.

Lydia and Marshall stayed, but the others followed, splashing into the cold green soup of the Atlantic. Jenny ran straight in with a thundering rush, her arms raised, kicking her feet high and wide. Conrad ran behind her, blinking against the spray. He felt exposed out here. He struggled through the knee-deep water, plowing into it. As soon as he could, he dove.

He swam underwater, moving away from the others. He kicked hard, pulling himself through the water with big strokes, sliding through the green underworld until he was alone. He came up to breathe and went back down. He kicked, slowed and drifted, stopped. Hanging motionless, he felt himself rocked, felt the movement of the waves overhead. Below him the light shattered, flickering into soft trapezoids on the sandy bottom. An underwater plant, deep neon green in the murky light, shifted in the rocking current, its long tendrils loose and weightless. Shafts of light slanted through the aqueous dusk. He kicked on and on, moving through the silent weed caverns, leaving everything behind. He surfaced to breathe, gasping for a moment and filling his lungs, then plunged down again, immersing himself in something larger than him, something vast and unknowable, an element more intense but more forgiving than air. This was what he needed, this deep green silence.

He was the last to come back up onto the beach. The others were all there, still damp, sandy, exhilarated by the plunge. Lydia spread out the food, and everyone began to eat lunch. They ate and talked, and then they took their books and lay down, and they stopped talking and turned quiet and somnolent in the sun.

But sitting out on the beach, out of the sheltering presence of the water, Conrad was having trouble. He kept trying to bring the day back into the focus it should have had. He'd remembered the beach as paradise: all that motion and space, all that possibility. The baking dazzle of the sun, the thick, briny air, the seagulls wheeling and calling, the endless insistence of the waves. He'd loved it.

But now he felt exposed, and he couldn't set himself against a wall for protection. Around him people in bathing suits and sunglasses trekked up and down, carrying baskets, towels, trays of food and drinks, hampers, canvas bags. There was no way to keep track of them. The stream was apparently endless. He looked up from his book every few seconds. There was motion all around him; from the corner of his eye he kept catching the quick rush of the waves onto the beach, each one a sliding carpet of foam moving up the sand. All that fucking sand. He'd had enough sand to last the rest of his life. He couldn't believe they'd all trekked out here to sit in the sand.

Ollie and Jenny were stretched out in the sun, Ollie on his stomach, Jenny on her back, eyes shut. Lydia lay beneath the umbrella, arms at her sides, her floppy pale green hat pulled over her face. Marshall sat in a creaky low chair, his hair standing in little wild damp tufts, squinting at *The New York Review of Books*. Conrad sat with his back against the tilting wooden shaft of the umbrella, his book open in front of him. A small gusty wind came off the water, carrying bursts of spray and the strong scent of the sea. He was sweating, though it wasn't really hot. He started the chapter again.

He looked up to see Jenny standing over him. She wore a white bikini, very white against her tanned skin. Her arms and legs gleamed brown, and her glossy hair was being tossed lightly in the wind.

"Come on, Con," she said. "Let's go for a run." Ollie stood behind her. He lifted his chin in invitation. Conrad put down his book.

They set off in a row, heading east at a slow jog.

The beach lay along the south shore of the Cape, the long bottom side—the triceps of the upper arm—the muscled arm clenching itself at the North Atlantic. This beach was the northern reach of a sheltered sea basin, protected to the southwest by the drifting mass of Martha's Vineyard, to the southeast by Nantucket, and due east by the long, casual slide of low-lying rocks and reefs that stretch down from the elbow, on the Cape's southeast corner. Here the dunes were low, the beach low and flat, the waves mild.

The three runners held a course along the water's edge. On the left were low, sandy dunes, on the right the flat green Atlantic. The waves flooded up under their bare feet in a long, unrolling surge, then ebbed, seething and hissing. Flat and affectless, the water sank swiftly into the porous sand, whispering into bubbles, then vanishing.

Ahead, the shining strip of beach stretched to the horizon.

Slowly they began to speed up. They always did this, and Conrad always won. Now he wondered: he was fit, but he was heavier, carrying more muscle than he used to. Ollie had been in training all year. Jenny was a distance runner and might outstay them both. Her legs were shortest, but she kept up with their strides.

They pounded through the soft sand.

Conrad liked this: liked breathing in the salt air, liked running beside his brother and sister, feeling his legs work. His chest began to open, and he felt his heart pumping. The beach became emptier; ahead was the gleaming vanishing point, a ribbon of glitter. The small waves curled idly up onto the sand, slid smoothly back, sank into nothing. Overhead, white gulls wheeled through the bright sea air, making high mewing cries.

Ollie lengthened his stride. Conrad could see his shoulders beginning to move, fists pumping. He slid a half stride ahead of Conrad. Jenny lengthened her stride, then Conrad his. They increased the pace, one speeding up, another matching it, faster and faster until they were all sprinting, feet flying, chins raised. For twenty yards they all ran abreast, thundering and in stride.

Ollie began to pull ahead. His back was slick with sweat and muscled like a man's. *Ollie's like a man,* thought Conrad. *He is a man.* The idea elated him. He ran across the choppy sand beside the wide reach of green water, through the salty air. Around him stretched a sense of spaciousness and possibility. The rhythm in his body and the fact that Ollie was growing up. He thought, *This is how it was. I'm back.*

He began to push faster, his feet pounding the damp sand, arms pumping, fists clenched. He drew closer to Ollie, who felt him drawing near and went faster still, his tempo rising.

Jenny slowed suddenly, her feet thudding to a stop. She couldn't last at a sprinter's pace.

"I'm done," she called, but the other two didn't slacken. Now it was just the two of them, and they kept going, Conrad running in a fury to catch his brother. *One more step*, he thought, gritting his teeth, pounding faster and faster, speeding his racing heart, but Ollie felt each of his strides, and with each closing step of Conrad's, Ollie sped faster, his chin high, arms rocketing like pistons.

Conrad was going all out. They were half a step apart, hurtling down the sand. *I can't,* Conrad thought. He couldn't catch his brother. He could feel it in his own body, he could see it in Ollie's lifted chin, his tight, pursed mouth. It was elating. Conrad slowed to a jog, then stopped, breathing hard.

"Okay," he called to Ollie, "you did it. Yah."

Conrad turned and jogged back to Jenny. She was watching them, bending her knees, doing sideways stretches. Ollie wheeled in a swift half circle and came loping back.

"You're fast, bro," Conrad said.

Ollie shook his head, and Conrad jumped him.

He put an elbow around Ollie's head, twisting it down into a headlock; Ollie grabbed him around the waist and tried to lift him, trying to throw Conrad off-balance. Conrad was already off-balance, snorting and choking, laughing. For some reason it killed him, set him off, that Ollie was so strong, so confident, so fucking fast. He slipped an arm over Ollie's head and shoulder, then shoved his hip, hard, into Ollie's side and pulled him over his own hip, pulling him right off his feet. Ollie started to go over, but Conrad caught and steadied him, then stepped away, grinning.

Ollie straightened, panting.

"You killed me," he said.

"You killed *me*," Conrad answered, grinning. He raised his hand and Ollie slapped him five.

They set off again, heading back along the waterline. They ran more slowly, not racing. They skirted the people walking toward the waves. There were more of them now. As the three drew nearer to their own encampment, they had to swerve constantly.

"I think we should walk," shouted Ollie. "Too many people."

A young boy darted in front of them, shouting at someone in the water. Ollie dodged left and Conrad right, but Jenny had nowhere to go. She shouted as she ran into the boy, her legs flying and pinwheeling, arms flailing, the water splashing up in bright spindrift. They collided in an explosion of foam, going down together in a shallow wave.

Jenny stood, pulling the boy up with her. She leaned over him, steadying his shoulders.

"I'm so sorry. Are you okay?" she asked.

The boy looked at her silently. A man ran toward them, shouting.

"Are you okay?" Jenny asked again. The boy nodded but said nothing. He was eight or nine, blond and skinny. His chest was narrow, his ribs visible.

The man reached them and knelt abruptly in front of the boy. Jenny drew back, and the man grabbed the boy's shoulders.

"Timmy! Timmy, are you okay?" he asked urgently, staring into the boy's eyes.

Timmy nodded slowly, not looking at him.

"You okay? Sure?"

Timmy nodded again, turning away.

The man looked up at Jenny. He was in his forties, stocky, with a wide bullying face and thick dark hair. His mouth was drawn into a small, mean V.

"I'm so sorry—" she began, but the man interrupted.

"I want your name," he said. "I want all three of your names. You can't run on this beach in the afternoons. Not when it's crowded like this. I can have you arrested. You can't run little kids down. What kind of idiots are you?"

Jenny stared at him, her cheeks turning pink.

"What do you think you're doing?" He looked at Timmy again,

who twisted his head to look over his shoulder. "You okay, son?" The man looked up at Jenny. "I want your name. You're going to hear from me about this."

"I said I was sorry," said Jenny. "I don't think he's hurt."

"I want your name," the man said.

"Excuse me." Conrad stepped between the man and Jenny. "Let me give you my name. Lieutenant Conrad Farrell, United States Marine Corps."

The man stood at once, facing Conrad. He was pale and fleshy, his loose belly hanging slightly over his pink bathing trunks. His eyes were small and green.

"Oh, really?" the man said. "Oh, really?" He leaned closer to Conrad so Timmy couldn't hear. "You think that fucking matters to me? I will have my lawyer call you, Mr. Fucking Lieutenant. You give me your card, and we will see what the law has to say about a U.S. Marine running down an eight-year-old boy."

Conrad stared at him.

The checkpoint was outside Ramadi. It was a flat stretch of land, broken desert and rising hills beyond. The checkpoint was surrounded by HESCOs—big containers filled with sand—and barbed wire. There were big signs telling all vehicles, in English and in Arabic, to stop. But checkpoints were spooky places. When people got rattled, they didn't read the signs; they drove faster.

Conrad was in a small convoy. They were slowed to a crawl, about to go through the check. They could see cars coming from the other direction. He was in the second Humvee in the convoy, and he watched the lead car approach. It was a small white sedan, like almost every other car in Iraq. It wasn't slowing down. It came toward the checkpoint at highway speed, barreling toward them, a cloud of dust swirling behind it. The Marines at the checkpoint stepped into the opening, rifles raised. They shouted in English and in Arabic for the car to stop, but it kept coming, speeding toward the narrow opening of the checkpoint. The Marine fired a first warning shot over the car, then a second. The car kept coming. The next maneuver was supposed to be a bullet into the engine block, but if this was a suicide bomber, the whole thing might go up in flames, and the car was coming too fast for anyone to think, and the Marine fired straight into the windshield. The car skidded and fishtailed, then slowed to a skewed stop. No one spoke or moved. There was no sound from inside it.

Everyone watched what happened next. Four Marines went cautiously toward the car, rifles aimed at it. But almost everyone inside was dead: the father in the front seat and the two children in the back, though for some reason not the mother, who sat motionless in the front. Conrad had gone over to the car afterward, had seen the small bodies slumped in the back.

In Ramadi they'd helped rebuild a school that had been damaged by a mortar barrage. It was part of the Hearts and Minds initiative. The school's teacher was aloof at first, but after a few visits she turned friendly. She smiled when she saw them. Each time Conrad went to look at the construction, he visited the classroom afterward to see the kids. He brought candy, crayons, comics, whatever he could find. When they saw him, they shouted, jumped up, and crowded around him. They called him "Mr. Leftenant." That was from Ali: he'd learned British English.

One little girl clung to him each time, smiling up at him. She was missing two front teeth and had a wide, gappy smile. She wore a bright tiger-striped head scarf; her name was Leila. "Mr. Leftenant," she would call, grinning.

Each time he thought of Leila, he thought of the others, the two small bodies in the back seat.

Pink Trunks weighed about a hundred and ninety, and Conrad could have taken him down with one sweep of his arm. The man stood right in front of him, his face tense and outraged. His feet were spread and his hands clenched, as though he was about to start boxing.

Conrad stepped back. He was still here—still here, on the beach, and still there, outside Ramadi. He could feel a pounding in his throat, rising waves inside his head.

But they had, actually, run over this kid. They'd knocked him down in the water. Conrad folded his arms over his chest and said nothing. He gave a little shake of his head, feeling sickened.

"Look," Jenny said, "we're sorry."

In the evening they had drinks out on the splintery deck behind the house. The sun was setting behind the pine trees, turning the landscape scarlet. The tall grass glowed and the pine trees were soft and dark, the sun burning behind them.

They sat in a loose circle, Marshall and Conrad in chairs facing the sunset, Lydia and Jenny on a low bench, Ollie on a stool. Their faces gleamed, ruddy from the day at the beach. Marshall sat leaning back, his knees apart. He wore white pants, a striped Greek fisherman's shirt, and thick-strapped leather sandals. Beside him on an old table was a bowl of peanuts. Marshall held his drink in his left hand and ate the peanuts steadily with his right. He picked a little cluster of them, put them one by one into his mouth, then took another little cluster.

Lydia sat beside him. Her hair was still damp. Her face glowed, her dangling earrings catching the light. Jenny was next to her, looking polished and glamorous in a green silky top and white pants. Ollie, hunched on the stool, was barefoot. He wore a faded T-shirt and khaki pants that dragged, fraying, at the heels.

"So, Con, what do you think?" Lydia asked. "How is it, coming back here after all this time?" She wore a loose blue blouse, and her neck and throat looked sunburned against the collar.

"Good," he said, nodding. He sat in an unreliable canvas sling chair that swayed when he moved.

"Different?"

"A little," he said.

"How?" asked Ollie.

"Everything's smaller," Conrad said. "The ceilings are lower. The rooms are, like, not big enough to stand up in."

The others laughed.

"Maybe you're bigger," Lydia said.

"Maybe you're older," said Jenny.

"Maybe you're a pod person," said Ollie.

"I am a pod person," said Conrad, nodding.

"Speaking of pod people, I thought that guy was going to clock you," Jenny said. "That horrible dad, at the beach." The sun burnished her hair, and she wore big earrings with a black-and-white checkerboard pattern.

"He was nuts," Ollie said, shaking his head. "What was he thinking? You're a Marine!"

"I shouldn't have said anything," Conrad said. "Marines get in trouble here every day for stuff like that. They think they can do anything."

"They can," Ollie said loyally.

"They can't," Conrad said.

"Sounds like a good move," Marshall said, "walking away."

Conrad said nothing.

"On the set we have a guy who's a fixer," said Ollie. He was changing the subject deliberately, Conrad saw. This touched him, his little brother offering protection.

Ollie was working for the summer as an intern on an independent movie production. The movie was being shot in a grand old decaying house in western Massachusetts. The plot involved a beautiful refugee from Kosovo, a drug runner, and a redneck libertarian. Other than that it was hard to explain, Ollie said, because the director kept rewriting it. "It's a fast-paced, action-packed zombie love story," he told them.

"We should have had this guy there on the beach. Anything that goes wrong, he fixes it."

"Like what?" asked Jenny.

"Anything. If we don't have a permit to park somewhere or to shoot at night, something like that. Or if someone has left a truck in someone's driveway or opened a gate and let the dog out. Anything that goes wrong, they call Mick."

"What's he like?" asked Marshall. "His manner. Is he conciliatory? Brisk? Threatening?"

"He's really friendly, but also kind of stern underneath. He apologizes, but he never says it was our fault. He just fixes it. He says, 'Sorry that happened, we're going to move the truck right now.' 'Tell me where to get that application for the permit.' 'What does your dog look like?'"

"Did he really find a runaway dog?" asked Jenny. She reached for some peanuts. "How?"

"He didn't actually find it. He told me later that was something he didn't know how to fix, he just hoped the dog would come home, and it did. But he was really nice to the owner."

"And is he a Mick?" asked Lydia. "Is he Irish?"

Ollie shrugged. "I don't even know his last name."

"Blarney," said Lydia.

"Stereotype alert," Jenny said, holding up her fingers to make a cross. "You don't even know if he's Irish, and you're branding him."

"Those are not stereotypes," Lydia said, "they're cultural characteristics. Do you think everyone in the world is alike? Don't you think the Spanish are different from the Norwegians? Of course they are. There's nothing derogatory about that. You shouldn't be derogatory or demeaning, but you can say there are such things as cultural characteristics."

"No," said Jenny, shaking her head, "you can't. It's stereotyping. It's like racial profiling."

"Hey," Lydia said. "I'm not pulling someone's car over. I'm commenting on the fact that the Irish are charming. Have you ever been to Ireland?"

"The point is—" said Jenny.

"The point is," said Lydia, "that if you go to a foreign country, you find it's different from your own, there are cultural differences. Why would you not want to admit that? That's why you go other places! Because there are cultural differences!"

"Mom. Look," said Jenny. "Any kind of categorization is demeaning. It depersonalizes everyone. 'All black people have rhythm. All Italians can sing.' Those are offensive because they deny individuation."

"I'm not saying all Irish people use blarney. I just mean that it's a cultural trait, being charming. There are national physical traits—being redheaded, for example. Why is that offensive?"

"Because those claims are used in offensive ways," Marshall said. "It's too easy to move into racism if you start out by saying, *All so-and-sos do such and such.* If you agree that everyone does one thing, then you can make that one thing demeaning, and no one can argue it. It's a rhetorical issue."

"Thank you, Dad," Jenny said.

"Well, I'm not being remotely demeaning to anyone," said Lydia.

"And I'm talking in my own backyard, not on national television. I am fascinated by cultural differences. It's what I like about people." Lydia turned to Conrad. She sat very straight, her blouse polished by the setting sun. "Con, help me out," she said. "Maybe you noticed some cultural differences between Iraqis and Americans."

They all looked at him.

Was it his imagination or had his mother raised her voice slightly when she spoke to him? As though he were deaf? Or old, or slightly incompetent?

Conrad shrugged. "There are so many different kinds of Iraqis," he said, "it's hard to say."

He knew he was meant to say something funny. He thought of Ali, and the grimy laborers lined up along the wall in the clearing room.

"The Iraqis I saw, the ones I saw face-to-face and spent time with and talked to, were interesting and mostly good-hearted," he said. "The ones I couldn't see were mostly trying to kill me. Sometimes I did see them, and then I tried to kill them."

He hadn't meant to say that.

With the sunset, a light evening wind was picking up and the air was cooling. The grass in the meadow moved, rustling. The sun was dropping behind the darkening pines. The deck was now in a soft evening shadow, though the upper floor of the house was still illuminated, shimmering white. Why had he thought he could change this by clearing a field of brush? He was back where he'd started. Nothing had changed.

"I'm sorry, sweetie," Lydia said. She looked stricken.

"This must be hard for you, Con," Marshall said. "Being home. Trying to get back into the life here."

Conrad nodded, not looking at him.

"We don't mean to make it hard," Marshall said.

"But you do make it hard," Conrad said. There was a silence. "I know what you're thinking."

Marshall cocked his head. "I don't think you do."

Conrad could feel them not asking.

"If you want to know if I killed anyone, yes, I did," he said.

"You don't have to talk about any of it," Marshall said. "You don't have to say anything."

"Did I fire my rifle? Yes," Conrad said.

They were all silent. Ollie watched him nervously, and Jenny dropped her eyes, bobbing her foot, her sandal dangling from it.

"What do you want us to do, Con?" Lydia asked. "Do you want us to ask you questions? Are there things you want to tell us? What would make this easier?"

He shook his head. "That's all I have to say."

There was a long silence.

"Please don't do this, Con," Lydia said. "Don't make us feel so shut out. We can't help you if you keep us away."

"You can't help me," Conrad said. He leaned forward in his chair.

"There must be something." Lydia stood and came over to him.

Conrad jumped up and moved away. He didn't want her to touch him.

The thing lay all around them, the black weight of it. Jenny stared hard into the dimming meadow. Ollie looked uneasily at Conrad. Lydia and Marshall looked at him, distraught.

Conrad stood up.

"Con," Ollie said. He stood up, too, and his head and shoulders were suddenly bright, caught by the rays of the sun. His face looked stricken.

"You can't help me," Conrad said again, and turned to walk away.

"I'm coming with you," Ollie said, and Conrad turned back to him.

"Get away from me," he said, furious.

Ollie stopped, his face pale and shocked.

"Get away," Conrad said again.

Conrad walked down the steps onto the wiry grass and along the side of the house, out of their sight. He walked down to the road, a dark ribbon in the twilight. There were no cars, there was no sound. Down the road was only one house, the lower windows glowing in the dimness. Nothing else, no other human presence in the landscape.

But he could sense the chem lights moving around in the meadow across the road. He could sense people over there, shadows sliding between the dark, upright shapes of junipers. He listened, straining for the subtle scrape of stone, the faint clink of metal. His heart had begun its crazed clatter again, his chest tight and swollen. He wanted an end to this. He looked back and forth in the darkness.

15

The irony of this, his staying in the guest room with its double bed, was that apparently Conrad no longer wanted sex. Not even with himself, his most skillful and practiced lover. He stayed limp and soft, no matter what secret whispers he summoned up to his inner ear, no matter what lurid images he paraded through his head. Nothing.

He was caught on the surface of his mind. He couldn't let go, couldn't sink down to that hot, private place, couldn't leave the glaring surface of the world.

Claire arrived late on Friday evening.

Conrad was in the kitchen when he saw the headlights coming slowly up the road, then turning in. He went out to greet her, walking down the lawn through the darkness.

Claire had turned off the engine, but the interior light was still on. She was in a little illuminated capsule, unaware of her visibility. Her head was down, and the light fell on her glossy hair. She was doing something with her bag, and when Conrad opened the door, she looked up, startled.

"Hi." He waited for her face to turn pleased.

"Hi," she said, her voice tentative. Her face did not change.

Was this how he made her feel? Ashamed, Conrad squatted beside the open door.

"Hey," he said softly.

She was rumpled and untidy from the drive. A few fine strands of hair were pasted to her cheek by sweat. Her pink linen blouse was wrinkled, and she looked tired and apprehensive.

"Clairey." He was nearly whispering. "Do I frighten you?"

She shook her head. He reached out and smoothed her hair, gently pulling the strands away from her cheek. Her skin was hot and soft.

"Maybe a little," she said.

"Sorry," Conrad said. "Jesus."

Her face was faintly silvered with sweat. Tiny freckles stood out, dark points along the ridge of her cheekbones. The column of her throat was straight and fine.

"I know you don't mean to," she said, and smiled at him.

"Jesus," he said again, shamed. "I'm glad you're here."

"Me, too," she said.

He carried her bag up. Inside, Lydia gave her a welcoming hug and sent her up to get settled. Claire went first up the steep stairs, Conrad behind her with the bag. His face was close to her legs and he could see her smooth bare calves, her ankles, with their mysterious bony knobs and tendons. He could smell her, warm and clean and slightly fruity.

In the room he said, "Here it is, the honeymoon suite." He'd told her about the ban, Lydia lifting it.

"I'm honored," she said, looking around. "It's lovely."

Claire stood in front of the bureau, with the fraying white cotton scarf over the top of it. She touched the silver luster jug, the soft-bristled hairbrush. She looked at herself in the heavy gilt-framed mirror and smoothed her hair abstractedly. She turned to the window and looked out into the darkness over the meadow. The lilac bushes brushed against the screen, and the curtains lifted in the evening breeze.

"It's so quiet," she said, turning back.

"Very," Conrad said.

She pointed down at the painted floor, with its scattering of faded rag rugs.

"And they're right there?" She mimed the words, barely whispering them. *"Right below us?"*

Conrad grinned and nodded.

"We'll be very quiet."

"Yes. And also, they'll have their hands over their ears."

Claire clamped her own hand over her mouth to keep from laughing out loud, snorting, the laughter getting out anyway. It was contagious. They both tried to hold it in, shuddering, bending over, trying not to make a sound. Ripples of laughter were traded back and forth, each setting the other off again. Finally Claire straightened, her face red, her eyes shining.

"It's a lovely room. I'm sure we'll have—" That set her off again, and Conrad, too.

So he was glad she was here.

They went down for dinner; everyone was in the kitchen. Marshall was pulling the spindle-backed chairs up to the table. Ollie was pouring ice water, and Lydia and Jenny had begun putting food on the plates.

"How was the drive?" Marshall asked.

"Horrible getting out of New York," said Claire. "Not too bad after that."

"Have you been here before?" Lydia asked, stopping suddenly, two loaded plates in her hands.

"Never," Claire said.

"But why not?" Lydia set down the plates on the table. "Sit here, next to Marshall. Why did you never come here when you were in college?"

Claire shook her head. "I went to India one summer, another I worked on an Indian reservation in Montana. I don't know. One year Conrad didn't come, anyway. He was at Quantico." She looked at him.

"Ta-*dum*," said Conrad forebodingly. "The beginning of it all."

"Well, it was," said Lydia. She put her own plate on the table and sat down. "Everyone please sit. It doesn't matter where, except for Claire, I want you next to Marshall. Place of honor." Lydia wore a silky striped shirt and fancy earrings, tiers of glitter that chimed faintly when she moved.

The table was covered with a festive tablecloth, bright red, with yellow stylized roses. The wineglasses were mismatched, and so were the water glasses. The plates matched—white, with blue flowers around the rims—but they were faded, with chipped edges. Lydia had put candles on the table. The flames fluttered in a faint breeze: both doors were open, and the scent of the summer night came in on the mild air.

"We're so glad to have you here," Lydia said to Claire, raising her wineglass, beaming.

"It's so nice of you to ask me," Claire said politely. She'd changed her clothes and looked pretty and glowing. She wore a black blouse and a string of red beads. Her thick hair was held back with a barrette.

"Oh, no, it's nicer of you to come," Conrad said. "It's much nicer of you to come than it is of us to ask you."

There was a moment's pause. Jenny, lifting the wooden salad bowl, held it still, narrowing her eyes at her brother. Ollie, reaching for the salt, froze, his eyes flicking at Conrad's face. Marshall, settling his napkin in his lap, looked up. Lydia turned to look at her son, her face filled with alarm.

Conrad grinned. "Joke," he said.

Lydia frowned at him.

"Conrad," she said. "Claire was nice enough to come all the way up here. Don't tease your girlfriend. Isn't that one of the cardinal rules of relationships they tell you on *Car Talk*?"

"I think theirs is about wives," said Marshall. "It's 'No matter what your wife says, you say "Yes, dear."' I've memorized it."

Lydia nodded. "Good that you have."

"That's it?" asked Ollie. "That's all? That's the whole secret of a happy marriage? Just, the husband says yes, no matter what the wife says?"

"That's it," Marshall said. "Great ideas often look simple."

"Gandhi," Jenny said, "Jesus, and Click and Clack."

Ollie shook his head and picked up the saltshaker.

They were all relieved. Conrad could see it in their faces. They thought he was on a knife-edge of sanity, ready to go over.

That night after dinner Conrad and Claire creaked up the stairs and shut the door to their room. Their steps were loud on the wooden floor. The room was lit only by the small bedside lamp. The shade was yellowed, dark with age, and the room was bathed in a rich amber glow.

"It's nice of your parents to put us here," Claire said. She took off her beads and put them on the bureau. "Broad-minded."

"Yeah," said Conrad. "I guess my mom suddenly had an epiphany."

Claire stepped out of her sandals and set them side by side under a chair.

"What did your parents tell you about sex? When you were in high school?"

"My mom's a therapist," Conrad said. "She was all over it. She and Dad sat me down when I was about fifteen and had a talk." He took off his shirt and put it on the chair.

"What did they say?" Claire asked.

"They told me I always had to take responsibility for whatever I did. I mean, *really*. I got the message." He took off his pants and dropped them on the rug. He glanced at them and picked them up, draping them on the chair. "Then my dad drove me to a drugstore at the mall and waited while I went in and bought condoms. I wasn't even having sex, but I didn't want to tell him that."

"Your *dad* took you to buy condoms?" Claire asked.

"It was a big deal," Conrad repeated. "But we didn't talk in the car."

"My mom told me to be careful, and she gave me the phone number of her doctor," said Claire. "I think the whole thing scared her."

"Yeah, well it did not scare my mom," Conrad said, shaking his head. He sat down on the bed in his boxers and waited for Claire to come to him.

Claire stepped out of her skirt and there were her lovely curvy legs, suddenly bare all the way to her crotch, neatly hidden by her underpants. Then her torso was bare as she pulled off her top. In the dim light her skin was luminous. It was miraculous the way she could use her body, walking around so easily, standing by the bureau to take off her earrings, raising her hands, turning her head. The way her hair shifted, stroking the tops of her shoulders.

"I wish you hadn't cut your hair all off," he said, pulling back the sheets and getting into bed. "I liked it long."

"It was too much," Claire said. "It was taking over. It was, like, Me and My Hair. I realized I couldn't do a job interview with the hair, and that was it."

She took off her bra, then her underpants, and climbed in beside him. He slid his arms around her. She was cool and smooth. It was remarkable how cool and smooth her skin was. Beneath the skin was her body, warm and pulsing with her mysterious energy. She was mysterious, all women were mysterious, and why was that?

Conrad ran his hand over her face, then moved down her long

neck, her throat. He traced the smooth curves of her breast, the slope of her side, but something kept him apart from it. He couldn't focus on her body, couldn't make it central. His mind kept sliding away from it. His own body was slack at the center, though his muscles were tight. He stroked her, the long, sweet rises, hoping everything would return. *Jesus,* he told himself, *what is the matter with you? Do this for her if you can't do it for yourself.* But he could not. He was waiting for his body to create its own energy, a kind of wildfire, rising and swallowing him up, taking over.

Nothing happened. Nothing, nothing. His hand lost its purpose.

At last he took it off her breast. He touched her arm.

"Sorry," he whispered.

"It's okay." Claire ran her hand along the side of his face. "Con, it's okay."

"No, it's not," he said, furious.

"It's okay," she said. She rolled over onto her stomach and put her head on her pillow. She closed her eyes.

Lying next to her in the dark, he had the sense that she was falling into something new with him, not love exactly, something else. Something more like concern than passion. It wasn't what he wanted, but right now he didn't want passion, either.

Later in the week, one morning they lay in bed, awake but not yet speaking. It was early, and the light glowed through the papery white shades. The curtains lifted, rippling as the air fell away. Claire turned on her side, propping her head on her hand.

"How are you feeling?" Her voice was quiet.

"What do you mean?"

"Is it getting better?"

He stared past her, uncomfortable. It was his business, not hers. "There's nothing I can do. It's always the same."

Claire ran her hand across his chest, rubbing gently. Her hand felt strange.

"Do you want to tell me anything?" asked Claire. "Would it make you feel better to talk?"

"What do you have in mind?" he asked. "What could I tell you?"

"Whatever's bothering you," she said. "I want you to come back. You're not really here. I think you should talk to someone. If not me, someone."

"The things in my head," said Conrad, "are not things I could tell you."

Claire's hand slid back and forth, smoothing his skin.

"How bad could it be?" she asked, murmuring. "Okay. I guess you killed someone. Or a lot of people. But you were meant to. You had no choice. You were trained as a soldier. It was your job to . . . do that."

"It's not that," he said. "You wouldn't understand."

"Try me," she said. "Why can't you tell me part of it? You can't carry this around anymore. It's tearing you apart."

He looked past her at the window. The shade breathed in and out, the curtain belled. There was nothing he could tell her. There was nothing about there that was connected to here.

"Tell me something," she said.

There was a long silence. He looked at her face, the wide cheekbones, the straight eyebrows, her deep-set blue eyes, her grave gaze.

"Whatever you did is okay," she said. "You had to do it." She moved her hand up to his chin, caressing his face. "You did it for a reason. You were there to protect the Iraqi people."

He shook his head. The mother, stunned, in the front seat. "We were trying to get away from the shooting," she had told the terp.

"If you won't tell me, tell someone else," Claire said. "You need to talk."

He shook his head again, and now he shifted in the small bed, moving away from her hand.

16

It was the third week of August, and the city had a ragged, breezy air. The summer was mostly over, and whatever happened now was out of bounds, overtime. No one was really working, and no one really cared. The traffic on Twenty-third Street was just as noisy as usual, but it didn't seem to matter.

The VA hospital was on East Twenty-third Street, a group of tall modern buildings made of mud-colored brick. They faced south, set in an angular horseshoe. A semicircular driveway curved from the street to the main entrance. In front of this stood a tall flagpole, the Stars and Stripes fluttering from it briskly. A massive porte cochere extended over the drive, a heavy, flat roof topped with three small glass pyramids. Conrad, approaching, wondered if they were meant to suggest the Louvre. If so, it was a strange reference. Why not something martial, something that would offer a sense of community?

But next to the driveway was a sign establishing that very community: NOTICE: NO FIREARMS OR WEAPONS ALLOWED ON THIS PROPERTY. Images of a stylized gun and knife were canceled by a diagonal red bar. Another sign warned that guide dogs and service dogs were allowed on the premises, but only PROVIDED THEY DO NOT LOOK MENACING OR DANGEROUS, AND ARE UNDER CONTROL AND RESTRAINT BY THEIR OWNER AT ALL TIMES.

There you go, Conrad thought, *those are my guys.*

Good idea, to arrive at the VA with your ravening pit bull. Or your automatic rifle.

The driveway was lined with parked cars and vans, ambulettes. A polished black sedan with government plates stood at the curb, a driver at the wheel. Trash blew in little whirlwinds along the pavement. Three employees, plastic ID cards hanging on long cords against their chests, were walking toward Conrad on their way out: a heavy young woman in a tan sweater and tight black pants, her hair a thick mass of tiny braids, and beside her two burly men in jeans.

"She just a beginner," one of the men crowed, glancing sideways at the woman.

The woman smiled and frowned, looking straight ahead.

"She get high on wine coolers!" he said. "She just a beginner! I know her!"

The woman shook her head.

"She don't know *how* to drink!" He gave a shout of laughter.

As they passed Conrad, the woman began to sing in a high, faint falsetto. *"How do you know-ow-ow."*

"Man, we get her started," said the man, grinning. "We show her the way."

The entrance to the building lay through a huge revolving door, slowly circling. The door's interior was divided in half, each large enough for a wheelchair or a gurney. Conrad shuffled through this into the high-ceilinged lobby.

A glass wall divided the room, running side to side. On the left was a checkpoint with two doorways, labeled U.S. MILITARY and VISITORS AND PATIENTS. Straight ahead, a large dome hung from the ceiling over a low oval counter. Behind the counter stood a man with dark, polished skin and a thick beard. He wore a dark blue uniform and a beret angled precisely on the side of his head. An ID card hung on his chest. He was leaning back against the far counter, holding a wrapped sandwich. He had just taken a bite when Conrad approached him. The man swallowed discreetly and concealed the rest of the sandwich behind his leg.

"Morning," Conrad said. "This is my first time here. How do I get started?"

"You a U.S. veteran?" he asked.

Conrad nodded.

"Right over there," the guard said, pointing to the checkpoint. "Give 'em your ID and they'll start the process. Get you registered and squared away."

A businesslike black woman at the checkpoint took his information and sent him up to the fourth floor. The ponderous elevator rose slowly, swaying in its shaft, its doors opening after a pause. Conrad stepped off into a waiting room.

The woman behind the counter was black and middle-aged, with bleached orangey hair pulled behind her head. Her mouth was thin and pursed, and she wore narrow black-rimmed glasses. A limp beige sweater was draped over her shoulders. She sat behind the high counter, watching a computer screen. She glanced up at Conrad, then down again. Overhead was a bank of fluorescent lights, one of them blinking.

"You need a full medical assessment," she told him. "Fill out the form, then bring it back to me."

"Thanks," Conrad said, and took the clipboard she held out for him.

The jutting counter cut the room into two sections. Shabby metal chairs lined the walls on both sides; a few small tables held dog-eared magazines. Most of the chairs were taken by men in jeans and T-shirts. Some of them sat, leaning back, knees splayed wide, hands folded in their laps. Some leaned on an arm and flipped through a magazine. Some played with cell phones or stared down at the shabby tiled floor, arms crossed, legs stretched out before them. No one spoke.

Conrad took the clipboard to the right-hand section. He sat down beside a big-chested man in his late twenties who had a protruding chin, beetling brows, and a buzz cut beginning to grow out. Conrad nodded in his direction as he sat down; Buzz Cut gave a noncommittal nod.

Conrad filled out the first page, then riffled through the rest. The form was eight pages long. Military history, date of entering the service, MOS (Military Occupational Specialties) training, deployments, dates and places where he'd been stationed, commanding officers, all that, and his medical history, description of combat, and finally the questions on The Issue.

Had he been in-country when he first experienced symptoms? What was it, exactly, that he felt? He was to fill in the appropriate box: Extreme anxiety, Panic attack, Mild anxiety, Ambient or free-floating anxiety. Normal fear response to real stress-producing perilous situations. Recurrent flashbacks or vivid memories of particular moments. Sudden episodes of rage or fear. Violent nightmares. Sleeplessness. Weight loss. Weight gain. Breathlessness. Headaches. Raised pulse rate. Disorientation. Feelings of disconnection and isolation.

Reading the questions, he could feel his pulse begin to quicken.

What he felt—"the symptoms"—was exactly what he did not want to describe or think about: the way things turned suddenly dark, the thundering rage, or the avalanche of terror that swept over him. The crumbling free fall of shame, the floor dropping away. The feeling of disconnection and isolation. None of those were things he could control. None of them were things he cared to put down on paper.

You couldn't admit to any of this while you were still in service. There was no way forward once this had been let loose into the spoken air. Everyone felt fear. No one mentioned it. Admission of fear was betrayal of trust. You had to trust one another. You had to trust your superior officers, the chain of command. You had to trust the importance of the mission. That lay at the center of everything—trust and loyalty.

Pride was the prize for never admitting to these feelings, the award for holding the mission above yourself. Pride was the prize for loyalty. Shame was the punishment for breaking trust.

At Quantico, in Officer Candidates School, there had been a candidate named Carrera. He was tall and solid, with a big, fleshy nose and very white teeth. He wore military-issue glasses, BCGs. They were actually basic combat goggles, but everyone called them birth-control glasses because they made you so ugly you couldn't get laid.

Carrera was kind of odd, and kept to himself. He was shitty at making decisions, and making decisions was the whole point of OCS: you were learning to lead. But Carrera couldn't make up his mind, and when he did, he changed it. He couldn't handle pressure, couldn't lead, and didn't project any confidence. Once, during a nighttime maneuver when he was setting up an ambush, he positioned everyone in his team spread out across a hillside. Then he changed his mind and called them back and sent them up over the crest and down the other side and had them set up all over again. You could make a bad decision, but you couldn't let anyone know you thought it was bad. He was made platoon sergeant and given responsibility to see if he'd rise to the challenge. He didn't.

One morning during drill the instructor called him out.

"Carrera!"

"Yes, Sergeant Inspector Drill Instructor!" Carrera shouted, staring straight ahead.

"Carrera, get your ass up here!" yelled the instructor.

Carrera broke ranks, moving unhappily up to the front. He saluted and stood at attention.

"Give me a wide stance, Carrera!"

Carrera stared at him, uncertain. He was a nice guy, with something needy about him that made you want to punch him.

"Wide stance! Spread your fucking legs, Carrera!"

Carrera straddled a bit.

"Wider!" yelled the instructor. *"Nice wide stance!"*

Miserably, Carrera shuffled his feet farther apart.

"Good. Now slide your hand down inside your belt."

No one knew what was coming. This had never happened before. Carrera looked like a beaten dog, his eyes slitted behind his BCGs. He slid his hand down his pants.

"All the way down. Put your hand right on 'em and grab ahold. What do you feel?"

Carrera didn't know the right answer. He knew there was no right answer.

"You feel two of 'em?"

Carrera nodded, then remembered, and shouted out, *"Yes, Sergeant Inspector Drill Instructor."*

"I don't believe you, Carrera."

There was a pause. Carrera stared straight ahead, his legs still wide, hand down inside his pants.

"I think you're lying, candidate." The instructor paused. *"I don't think you have any. I think what you feel is a little slit."*

There was a long hush.

Carrera was gone by the end of the week, and they told themselves it was a good thing. Carrera had shown he wasn't a leader. He was slow and indecisive, he'd have let his men down in combat. An officer can never let his men down. It was better that he was gone.

They didn't tell themselves they'd just watched the use of shame as a weapon. They didn't say they'd just witnessed a public execution.

> Describe the incident, if applicable, that is the source of your symptoms. Describe the flashbacks that you experience. Describe any supporting contextual evidence.

What he didn't want to do was call up all this stuff. Write it all down. It was bad enough having the images in his mind; the words would be worse. What he did was try not to let all this get loose in his head; writing it down would be turning it free. He tried to keep the flashbacks, even the thought of them, away from the center of his mind. They'd take up all the space, they'd rise up and take over. His chest was getting tight.

Anything he wrote down would be on his record forever, right up the chain of command. He thought of his battalion commander's face.

An officer's task was to set an example for his men. You upheld a shared conviction. As long as you believe, they believe. Your men depend on you.

Writing any of this down would be failing as an officer. This would be on his record. People would feel disgust toward him the way they'd felt toward Carrera. They'd draw away in disgust. He'd be dismissed.

Conrad looked around the waiting room. The men were mostly in their twenties and thirties, vets from Iraq and Afghanistan, but some were older, from Vietnam, stubble-faced and gray-haired. Most of them were skinny, their bodies slack. T-shirts tucked into clean, faded jeans. The younger men were solid, fresh-faced but somber. Everyone had a problem.

Buzz Cut shifted, setting his ankle on his knee. His leg jiggled.

Across from Conrad, a man took out a pack of cigarettes, stood, and headed out to the hall. He was thin to the point of illness, his jeans and T-shirt hanging on him. His movements were slow and deferential: he nearly tiptoed in his work boots. But everyone there was quiet. No one was in command; they were all supplicants here. Conrad remembered the silent workers lined against the wall in the clearing room at Ramadi.

Conrad lifted the clamp at the top of the clipboard and pulled out all the pages. He crumpled them into his fist with a crackling sound.

Buzz Cut looked at him. "Change your mind?"

Conrad nodded.

"How long you been back?"

"Four months. May."

"Even if you start today, it'll take three months to get an appointment," said Buzz Cut. "At Home Depot, you buy a hammer, and later, if you need it, they can find your receipt in ten minutes. I spent four years in the Army, and it takes them three months just to locate my records."

Conrad didn't answer. He carried the empty clipboard to the counter, the crumpled pages in his hand.

"Thank you," said the black woman. She glanced at him over her glasses but didn't reach for the clipboard. "Please take a seat. We'll call you." She looked down again, pursing her mouth.

Conrad turned and left, holding the balled-up pages. His name and ID number were on the form. He didn't want to throw it away here. He didn't want any record of himself in the building.

The whole place was black, crushing in on him. He could feel the walls, or some kind of solidified space, crowding against him and he felt his throat go numb as the noise began. The noise was larger than he could survive, the noise filled his body and his mind, and he heard himself begin to scream, but his voice was soundless in that larger sound, and he could feel the explosion starting, the moment when his body lost control, was no longer in charge of itself, the sense of drift and terror. The shock wave of the explosion coursing through his system, roiling the blood in its vessels, all the liquid matter in his being, the sense of being weightless and blown away. He found himself in a different darkness, a kind of patterned light on a wall, an awful divide between shadow and shining, something soft twisted in his hands, and someone was screaming.

"Conrad." It was Claire. "Wake up."

He said nothing. Now there were two places, and he lay still, trying to distinguish this darkness from the other, the day of the IED and Olivera. *Okay,* he thought, *okay.* His heart was thundering. *I'm here.*

I'm safe. I'm not there. He stayed silent, still angry. Fury raced up and down inside him. *What the fuck?* He was holding a pillow, twisting it in his hands. Claire was a little away from him, on her hands and knees, hair hanging in her face.

"Stop it," she said. "Wake up. You're here. You're okay. Wake up."

He was awake, he knew that, but he was still there in that other blackness, feeling the roaring wind come through his body, feeling the sound all around him, lifting him up into some lost place. He still felt rage that this was happening, an astonishment of grief that it could. He could hear himself breathing.

"Conrad," Claire said. She didn't touch him. He rolled over, away from her. She settled back, now kneeling. She put her hands on her thighs.

"I'm awake," he said.

She didn't answer.

One good thing had happened: sex was back. After the VA he'd moved in with Claire. It was temporary; everything was temporary. Some of the nights were bad, but some were good. Things were getting better.

Claire woke up before the alarm and reached out to turn it off. Her movement woke Conrad; he felt her slide away. He reached for her, eyes shut, pretending to be asleep, curving his arms around her. Claire paused, but when he slid himself closer, pressing against her back and sliding his hands around to her breasts, she began to move again, shifting out of reach.

"Got to get up," she said. "Sorry."

She stood, naked, and reached for the bathrobe on the back of the door. Raising her arm made her skin go taut along her side and back. Her ribs stood out like curved shadows beneath the silky skin. She wrapped the robe around herself, then turned.

"Sorry," she said again.

He shook his head, as though it was nothing. But he thought, *How long would it have taken?*

She left for the bathroom, closing the door behind her. The door was lightweight, hollow core, flimsy, like everything else in the apartment. Conrad could have put his fist through it. He sat up in bed, though he couldn't get up until the others had finished in the bathroom and cleared out. He could hardly even stand up in here while he was waiting.

The room was barely big enough for the double bed and bureau. Most of one wall was taken up by the bed and the door. On Claire's side stood a bedside table and lamp, though there wasn't room on Conrad's side. There was barely room for his duffel, which he'd crammed next to the bed. On the facing wall was Claire's bureau, the top littered with stuff: jewelry, little animals, cosmetics. Over this hung a mirror, cards and photographs stuck in the frame, beads and necklaces hung from the corners. Next to the bureau was a chair, clothes draped on it. Facing the bed was the closet, and beside it a framed Matisse poster from some exhibition Claire had been to. Conrad had been in Ramadi then, driving the brown streets, locked and loaded, while she'd been jogging up the steps of a museum, on her way to see art. She took forever going through an exhibition; she stared at each picture. Conrad had wondered if she'd gone to the exhibition alone, or with that guy. He hadn't asked her; he didn't want to know.

Now he heard the thunder of rushing water as Claire turned on the shower. He lay back down, hands folded behind his head. Sometimes he felt good, it seemed that things with Claire were good, things were settling down, that he'd be able to move on. Then something would tip, and everything would be the opposite: the panic would start up again, and it was like the *shamal*, and he couldn't see his hand before his face. Then he didn't know what was going on with Claire, or himself; couldn't bring himself to take a single step, that swirl of panic rising all around him.

The drone of the shower ended abruptly, and after a moment he heard the waspish whine of the hair dryer. When Claire came back, wrapped again in the robe, she looked bright and polished, her hair shiny.

"Hi again," she said. "Sorry about before. If I don't get into the shower first, I have to wait for everyone else, and then I'm late."

"No problem," Conrad said.

"So," Claire said. There was something prim and careful about her voice. She began to dress, facing partly away from him. Her movements were quick. It seemed as though she were concealing herself as a kind of punishment, or statement. Though he couldn't be sure of that. Hidden modestly by the robe, she pulled on her underpants. "What are your plans?"

"Plans?" he repeated.

She turned her back, took off the robe, and put on her bra. Her hands met deftly at her spine to hook it, shoulder bones flaring out suddenly like wings. "What are you going to do?"

Conrad hadn't told Claire about the trip to the VA, which had been a failure. He had nothing new to report. He didn't like having to tell her that. "You know what my plans are. I'm going to start looking at graduate schools, see if I should take some courses before I apply to any."

Not looking at him, Claire pulled at the closet door. It slid unwillingly open and she took out a hanger. She unclipped a white pleated skirt, leaned over, and stepped into it.

"Good," she said carefully, "but I don't mean like that. I mean living arrangements. A plan." She pulled up the skirt zipper, sucking in her breath to narrow her waist. This made her chest rise, and her breasts swelled upward like ribboned gifts.

"Living arrangements," he said, irritated. She sounded as though he were an idiot. Did she think he was moving in? That he wanted to stay in a room he couldn't even stand up in?

"Because I have to say," Claire said. She opened a bureau drawer and took out a yellow sweater. She pulled it on over her head, covering her breasts, her silky skin. He was multitasking; he was pissed off and turned on at the same time.

"You have to say?" Conrad prompted.

Now Claire was entirely dressed, covered by the loose sweater, the prim skirt. She was no longer a lover; she'd become a citizen. She sat down on the bed and looked at him, armored, untouchable.

"We have kind of a rule here," she said.

"Who complained?" he asked. *What the fuck?* He'd hardly even seen Gretchen, and he thought he and Sarah were buds.

"No one complained," Claire said. Obviously not true. "It's just that you've been here so much. Like you're living here."

"Five days," Conrad said. "They weren't even here over the weekend."

"Six," Claire said. "I mean, it's obviously okay with me." She looked distressed. "But do you have a plan? I mean, you can't stay here indefinitely."

"I haven't moved in," said Conrad. This was such bullshit.

Claire looked at him helplessly. "You kind of have. Your stuff is here. You're staying here. And you're using their stuff."

"What stuff? Their yogurt? Their nail polish?"

Claire shook her head. "Conrad, don't get mad at me."

"Don't tell me I'm using their stuff if you won't tell me what stuff I'm using." He threw the sheet back and got up, naked.

Claire waved her hand. "Okay. Towels."

"I'm using their towels. You want me to do their laundry? Is that what you're asking?"

"No," Claire said. "But they don't want to do your laundry."

"Really? That's the problem here? Laundry?"

"Look, just use my towels. They're the green ones. Just use them," Claire said. "But it's not just towels. If you spend the day here, you know—" She stopped. "This is their apartment. If they come home and find you stretched out on the sofa and your dishes in the sink, it feels like they're in someone else's place. Why should they do your dishes?"

"Fine," Conrad said. "I'm out of here."

"That's not the point," Claire said, shaking her head.

"What is the point?" Conrad crossed his arms over his chest. "What is the point?"

Claire stared at him. "Conrad, what do you want?" Desperation was coming into her voice. "I don't know what you want. You get mad at me no matter what I say."

"I'm not mad," Conrad lied. "Why do you think I'm mad?"

"You don't know how you sound." Claire shook her head and stood up. "I don't know what to do. You won't talk about anything." Her face was unhappy. "Okay, I have to go. I'll see you later." She opened the door.

Conrad took her by the arm with one hand and pushed the door shut with the other.

"Don't walk out on me, Claire," he said.

Now he was focused: he was furious. The red rose up in his head and he held her arm tightly. It was so slight he could crush it.

Claire turned and looked at him. "You're hurting my arm." Her eyes filled with tears.

At once he was ashamed.

"Sorry," Conrad said. "I'm sorry." *Christ.* He let her go and stepped back. He held his hands up. "I'm sorry, Clairey."

She shook her head, blinking.

He'd scared her. *Christ.* He moved forward and put his arms around her, remorseful. "I'm sorry," he said into her hair. "I'm really sorry. I would never hurt you."

"I know that," Claire said.

"I'm sorry," he said again. "I'm a fucking idiot." He rocked her, kissing her hair. "Claire."

"It's okay," she said.

It was strange to hold her clothed body against his naked one. His bare skin was pressed against her pleated skirt, the sweater. It felt wrong, as though they weren't speaking.

After a moment she pulled away.

"I'm sorry," he said again.

"I know," she said, half whispering, "but you have to let me go. You can't hold me when you're naked. I mean when I'm dressed."

"What do you mean?"

"I'm afraid you'll get come on my skirt," she said, smoothing the pleats, looking down at them. Then she looked up, eyes glinting, and started to laugh. She couldn't help it, and then he started.

"Yvette," he said, and then both of them got it, both of them helpless with fits and waves of laughter, doubled over.

"Okay," Claire said when she recovered. "Now I really have to go. We'll talk later."

She kissed him and left. He heard the front door open and close, and after a few moments the low thrumming of the elevator.

He was a fucking idiot. Not only had he behaved like an idiot and frightened Claire, he'd also lost the moral high ground and his position on the Roommates and their fucking towels. He'd have had a perfectly legitimate argument if he hadn't turned into fucking Rambo. Now he'd lost, he couldn't even raise the subject.

He had to wait for the Roommates to leave before he could come out. One of them was in the shower, he could hear the drumming.

Conrad dropped to the narrow space between the bed and the wall and began to do push-ups. He did a hundred, then a hundred more. His heart began to pound in a good way. He began to sweat. He whispered the numbers out loud for moto.

When everyone was gone, when he'd heard the front door click twice, heard the elevator rise and fall, Conrad came out of the bedroom. He was barefoot and naked. Now the apartment was his. He liked being at liberty here, walking around, nude and at ease, his morning woody bobbing ahead of him. The Roommates would hate it if they knew.

It was funny getting a chub in such a girlie place. In-country, they got them during combat. During action, when the Cobras flew past overhead, their machine guns racketing down onto the bad guys, everyone got hard. The guys joked about it afterward, boasting. They'd come back once after a firefight in Ramadi, and when Carleton came back from the shitters, he said, "Ho, man! I smell like I just been fucking! Smell me," he said generously to Molinos, who was walking past.

Molinos looked disgusted. "If I wanted to smell hot cock, I wouldn't smell yours," he said. But Carleton was stoked and proud, and thought everyone would want to know.

Conrad padded into the bathroom. The room was small, the air humid. The back of the door was humped and heavy with damp bathrobes, the wall racks crammed with limp towels, the walls and floor filmed with moisture. A bath mat lay rumpled in front of the shower. The mirror was silvered, opaque, the air steamy and scented.

He took a long shower, steaming the room up more, filling it with thick, hot swirling mist until he could hardly breathe. It was still a luxury, the water drilling pleasantly against his skin, cascading onto his head, his face. The drumming, the steam, the embrace of the water itself.

When he got out, he took a towel from the rack and dried himself off. Not all the way. It was still a luxury to feel wet, to feel the droplets making their way down his arms and legs. He stood naked in front of the sink and began to shave. In the mirror he looked at himself surrounded by girl stuff. The back of the sink was lined with tubes and jars; a hanging shelf was crammed with them, face creams, hand creams, cosmetics. A striped glass held pencils and tubes. The mysteries of the face. An open plastic bag of cotton puffs, a box of Q-tips, throwaway razors. It was unbelievable, the amount of stuff women used to anoint their bodies. Shampoo bottles stood along the back edge of the tub. Each time he washed his hair, he chose a different one, a different color and smell. Did they know this? Maybe that was what had pissed them off.

In the mirror he watched his cheeks and throat slowly appear, swath by swath, from under the white landscape of the shaving foam. He kept his eyes carefully on his face, his hands, the razor. He pulled the razor smoothly through the white clouds, making exactly the tracks he wished.

This, right now, was the best part of the day, shaving and getting dressed, full of purpose. Every morning he started new, and right now, sweeping weightless bits of white from his face, doing exactly what he intended, the rest of the day stretched ahead, ready to be mastered. Right now he was making bold, clean slices through the foam.

He wore the towel (not green) back into Claire's room, where he dropped it, wet and heavy, on the bed. Someone would be pissed. His duffel bag was on the floor by the wall, his clothes muddled inside it. He found a clean shirt and a pair of khakis. He dressed, still glowing from the shower and the mild abrasion of the shave. He would apologize again to Claire. The day lay ahead, unopened. He let himself out of the apartment, glancing automatically up and down the hall as he locked the door.

Outside, the air was fresh. The sky was patterned with clouds, big, handsome thunderheads, glowing and shapely, rolling confidently across the blue. The avenue was lively, imbued with an early-morning briskness. It was the start of the new season, and everyone seemed purposeful and focused. Even the traffic, rattling northward, seemed to be governed by courtesy and intent, unlike later in the day, toward rush hour, when a casual hostility spread throughout the streets. But now drivers looked straight ahead, their faces calm, believing they'd arrive on time, that the day would go as they hoped it would. It was possible for all this to come true. On the sidewalks people walked quickly and confidently. Dogs trotted happily behind their owners, tails high, tongues out, on their way somewhere they wanted to go. Everyone's clothes were crisp, their faces neat, their hair tidy. New York was putting its best foot forward.

Conrad walked up First Avenue toward the coffee shop. He bought a copy of the *Times* from a metal stand. He liked having the actual paper. He didn't like reading news on the computer, didn't want to find himself skipping from link to link, site to site. Didn't want to end up reading something he didn't want to read. When he read the actual paper, he felt more in control. If he saw something he didn't want to read, he just kept his eyes away.

At the coffee shop he nodded to the girl behind the counter. She was Indian or Pakistani, young, with dark skin and lightless black hair pulled back into a bun. She smiled at him, her white teeth even and brilliant. He ordered coffee and a blueberry muffin, as he did every day. He took them to the far end of the counter, where he stood with his back to the wall, sipping at his coffee until the corner table was free. When it was empty, he sat down with his back to the wall and spread out the paper.

He read it all, front to back, taking his time, aware now of the gathering presence: the rest of the day. He read nearly every article in full: the school in Queens closed for asbestos removal, the man jumping into the East River to save a dog and nearly drowning himself, the mayor under attack for his management of the police department. More bad behavior in Albany. He skimmed the news about Iraq. He didn't want to let anything in without a filter.

He read the article about Bush and Tony Blair. BUSH WAS SET ON PATH TO WAR, BRITISH MEMO SAYS. He skimmed it. Apparently Bush had never thought there were weapons of mass destruction. Apparently he didn't care that there weren't any. Now he claimed to have thought the struggle would be brief. He thought it "unlikely that there would be internecine warfare between the different religious and ethnic groups." Bush thought there would be no struggle between the Shias, the huge and resentful majority that had been oppressed and humiliated for years, and the Sunnis, who had been powerful and entitled for decades under Saddam? How could anyone, anyone with access to intelligence reports—or who had even looked the place up in Wikipedia—have thought this? Conrad hadn't much trusted Bush, but he'd trusted Colin Powell.

Bush in his fucking Air Force jacket, posing on the destroyer for his victory announcement and photo op. *Mission accomplished!* That was early, before Olivera, before Kuchnik, before almost anyone had been lost.

Fucking Rumsfeld, telling the troops to suck it up, to go to war with the army they had instead of the army they wanted. Go out into the streets in fucking unarmored trucks. The greatest fighting nation in the world sending its troops out over roadside bombs without armored vehicles, in Vietnam-era flak jackets that wouldn't stop bullets. Some of the men without ammunition. Humvees and men blown apart, day after day.

And for what?

Now there were no WMDs. There never had been. There had been no connection between Saddam and al-Qaeda.

Conrad wasn't ready to think about this. Everything was based on trust, trust in the chain of command, rising to the top. But this was the opposite of trust, a cynicism so deep he couldn't consider it.

He folded the paper. The moment of finishing the paper was always bad. Today was particularly bad. He straightened the central seam, quartering it into a small packet, knowing the rest of the day stretched out in front of him, languid, empty.

On his way back to Claire's apartment he passed a crosshatched metal trash basket. He flipped the *Times* neatly into it. Fucking Bush.

By now the street vendors had set up their folding tables along the avenue, colorful spreads of costume jewelry, fake African masks, odd-lot books. Passersby leaned over the tables, picking up earrings, staring at a carved mask. No one seemed interested in the books, which were actually strange nonbooks about coming to Jesus or getting your child's test scores up or how to decorate your house in the South of France, by nobody famous. Behind the book table sat a young black man with toned arms, wearing a knitted watch cap. He was slumped on an empty crate, bored. He wasn't going to recommend any titles.

Passing the tables, Conrad walked on the inside of the sidewalk, near the buildings. He didn't like getting too near the tables, which were covered in long, loose cloths, boxes concealed beneath them. The people near them carried bags and knapsacks.

Almost everyone was carrying a bottle of water, just holding it in their hands as they walked along the sidewalk, taking a swig in mid-step, twisting the top back on.

Jesus, he thought. Why were they all carrying water, here in New York City, as though they were at constant risk of dehydration? How long would it be before they could get to a faucet if they needed one?

When they first arrived in Ramadi, there was no local source of water. Later they rigged up a purifying system and drew from the Euphrates, but at first they used bottled water. It was shipped over from the States through the Mediterranean to Kuwait, then trucked into Iraq. Deliveries were erratic. By late March the temperatures were well over a hundred, and heatstroke was a big risk. People died from it. Conrad couldn't send his men out on patrol without water, but he was often told he wouldn't have enough to give them.

One afternoon Conrad was on guard duty downtown at the government center. He was with Stone, a lance corporal from third squad: he liked doing shifts with his men. They were up on the roof, where they had rigged a camouflage net overhead, which broke the brunt of the sun, though it didn't cool off anything. The temperature was around 110, and Conrad and Stone were crammed into a plywood sentry box, watching the streets below.

Stone was a nineteen-year-old from Atlanta, good-looking, with carved features and dark eyes. He didn't talk much except to swear, and he swore all the time. He always seemed angry, though not toward the other men. They liked him. He was a good Marine, always ready to step up. He was just pissed off.

They sat under the net, looking out over the souk and sweating. The heat pressed against their lungs like a huge, soft creature. It beat against their minds, draining their energy, swelling their limbs, and slowing their hearts. Sweat pooled and trickled; Conrad felt it everywhere, moving down his chest, into his groin, slicking the back of his neck. He felt the prickle of salt against his skin and the suffocating soft powdery sand everywhere.

"Ever notice how slow everyone walks here, sir?" Stone asked. "It's like they're fucking underwater."

"It's the heat, Stone," he said. "You can't walk fast when it's this hot."

"You think they ever dance, sir? They do anything fast? These fuckers are, like, hypnotized."

"Yeah, they dance," Conrad said. "But not like dancing at home.

Not like what you're thinking of. You can't make hot moves wearing robes. No one could see them."

"Then what would be the point, sir?" Stone was a Metallica fan.

"It's different here," Conrad said. "In robes, the moves would be in the footwork. The women do belly dances—now, there are some hot moves—but they don't do them for you. With the men, it's the footwork."

Stone shook his head disgustedly at the idea of hot footwork, and they fell silent. Below, the narrow streets were crowded with stalls. People moved slowly among the makeshift tables, ducking under the clothes hanging on lines, picking up produce, bargaining.

"Ever gone deer hunting, sir?" Stone's voice was intent, as though this were an important question.

Conrad said no, and Stone nodded, scowling.

"Any fun?" Conrad asked.

"I've never done it, sir. I just wondered what it was like." He scowled harder.

"Does your dad go deer hunting?" Conrad asked.

Stone took an audible breath. "I don't exactly have a dad, sir. The fucker left before I was born." He was taking strange breaths, long, deep ones, like gasps.

"I'm sorry, Stone," Conrad said.

"It's okay, sir," said Stone. "He was an asshole." His face was bright red, and crumpled. He looked furious.

Conrad thought Stone was upset about his father. He looked away, to give him privacy.

After a moment Stone said, "Have you ever done any kind of hunting, sir?" His voice had risen. It seemed strangled, and it was then that Conrad realized something was wrong.

"What is it, Stone?" Conrad turned to him, but Stone didn't answer. He leaned forward to kneel on the tarry roof. He began to retch, slowly but violently, going into a spasm. Then he collapsed, sprawling sideways. His eyes were shut, his face purple.

It was Conrad's first heatstroke.

He called Molinos on the radio, then knelt beside Stone on the scorching roof, pulling the rifle off his shoulder, tugging the blouse from his sweaty skin. Molinos came pounding up the stairs, and they got Stone downstairs, out of the sun. They stripped him and sprayed him with water and called a corpsman. The doc used the silver bullet on him, the rectal thermometer, dreaded by all Marines, to see if he needed to be medevaced out and packed in ice. Stone wasn't that bad, and after a while he came around, but for a time he was dazed and confused and couldn't stand up.

What had bothered Conrad was that he himself still had some water left in his CamelBak. It was one he'd bought back home, the commercial kind, which held more than the military issue. He should have offered some to Stone. It was a shock to realize that Stone might have died because of his thoughtlessness. It kept coming back to him. Your men trusted you: you took responsibility for their lives. That was your first task as an officer. In the Marines, officers eat last.

After that, Conrad kept thinking of how people used bottles of water at home. How they talked and drank idly from them, taking long gulps, tipping up the bottles, not finishing them. There were those plastic bottles all over the place, on benches in parks, on sidewalks, on counters. Still partly full of clean water, like little comments, little boasts, saying, *See! We have so much of this we can afford to waste it.*

Even after what happened with Stone, the platoon still wasn't issued enough water when they went out on patrol. Often Conrad had to send someone into the mess hall to steal extra bottles.

He let himself into the silent apartment.

The refrigerator had different hums, different notes and keys, some soft, some very loud. The sound of the city outside was always loud, day and night, though at night it had a different quality—faster, more muffled and secretive. The daytime sound was a roar, rushed and imperious.

The living room was lit by the harsh light from the big plate-glass windows. Another dingy white apartment building stood beyond, with its horizontal lines of windows, the slice of shifting gray river to one side. He didn't want to go into the bedroom, where he had held Claire's beautiful arm so tight that she had pulled away as though he were going to hurt her. Shame spread through him.

The room, with its bright slumped pillows, its tall lamps, was full of a life lived by other people, one that had nothing to do with him. He was invisible here. He had no place here. And what about Kuchnik, Carleton, Olivera?

17

Out on the sidewalk, he turned left, heading south. Traffic was heavy; it was midmorning now. Trucks were heading uptown toward the bridges off the island, great square-cabbed behemoths roaring up the avenue, air brakes gasping, diesel exhaust pipes spewing stench, gears thudding and stuttering. A convoy of city buses groaned along one side of the street. Trucks and vans studded the lines of cars.

A fence of orange netting cut off part of the street and sidewalk. A blue and white Con Ed truck was parked there, its rear doors open. Inside the fence was a hole in the pavement, where men with blue helmets were working belowground. At street level a man in an orange jumpsuit was working a jackhammer, making a driving rattle like gunfire. Farther down the avenue a siren started up, high and whining.

Conrad watched the faces coming toward him. Usually people stayed to the right, just like cars, but not always. Some fast walkers tried to pass slower ones, dodging in and out of their own lanes. Or they appeared suddenly on the wrong side, in your lane, right in front of you, heading at you. Or they walked steadily and heedlessly along in the wrong lane; there was no way to address this. Or they walked along in front of you and stopped abruptly, suddenly seized by a thought.

Conrad didn't like it when they stopped in front of him. He didn't like any of this. Everyone was too close, and they were changing their minds and directions and speeds. He particularly didn't like people stopping right in front of him.

When you were out on a convoy in-country, all other traffic had to pull off the road so that suicide car bombers couldn't drive up next to you and detonate. And because IEDs were usually planted on the side of the road, military vehicles drove straight down the middle. They could use any lane, and that fact had saved one of the Humvees driving on Route Chestnut, Haditha. The sergeant in command was in the fourth vehicle, and just before the blast, it pulled out into the left lane. So the explosion missed his vehicle, though it got the one in front of him, the third, in the right lane. Conrad saw it afterward. The whole Humvee was split in half and blackened, its front end nosing down into the crater the blast had made. Two Marines who'd been in it were killed.

Ahead, First Avenue sloped down toward the dip around Sixtieth Street, where it rose to meet the tall pylon of the gondola to Roosevelt Island.

He began to walk faster, maneuvering around the people on the sidewalk. Impatience drove him. He nearly walked into a woman talking on a cell phone who made a sudden left turn without looking. *Look where you're going!* He wanted to scream it into her face. He didn't say it. He was used to walking as he wanted.

His cell phone chirped, and he pulled it out and looked at the ID. He clicked it on.

"Hi, Mom."

"Con? How are you?"

"Good." He paused at a stand selling kebabs, to let someone move past him. The spicy, smoky smell rose at him: *prick on a stick.* He turned to look at the man enclosed in his tiny cabin: dark, honey-colored skin, a thick mustache, black, piercing eyes. Conrad met the man's gaze, holding his phone to his ear. He nodded, as though to a friend. The man nodded back, aloof but courteous. Conrad thought of stopping and asking the man where he was from. Maybe he was Iraqi. He could be Iraqi.

"What are you doing?" Lydia asked.

"Walking," Conrad said. "Going down First Avenue."

"That sounds nice," Lydia said. He could hear the uncertainty in her voice. "Anywhere in particular?"

"Nope," he said. "Just out for a walk."

"I wanted to tell you that I sent for some brochures." She sounded apologetic. "You said you were thinking about graduate schools."

"Right," he said.

"Well, I asked for some of them," she said. "They arrived. So whenever you come out, I mean, they're there." She was embarrassed.

"Thanks, Mom." He couldn't think about it. "That's good."

"So," she said. "When do you want to come out? What about this weekend? Do you want to bring Claire?"

"Don't know yet," he said. "I'll let you know. Thanks, though."

What filled him, when he talked to his mother, was a sense of failure. A sense of how great the divide was between them now. He remembered himself sitting at the breakfast table years ago, telling his parents what he was going to do. He'd been like them then.

"Mom?" he asked now.

"What is it?"

"It's hard for me to come out there."

There was a silence, and then his mother began to cry. "I know that," she said. The crackle on the line made it hard to hear. He hated hearing her cry. "We want to help, Con. Please don't stay away."

"Mom, I'm losing you," Conrad said loudly. "I can't hear you. I'm hanging up. I'll talk to you later." He hated hearing her cry, hated knowing he'd made her do it.

Impatience drove him. In-country you knew what you were doing. You planned the missions and then carried them out. You knew what you were doing. You had a purpose.

He walked faster, moving in and out of the crowd.

He wasn't meant to be here. He shouldn't be here on the street, among all these people who didn't have these things inside their heads. He was separate. He wanted to get these things out of his mind: the pattern on the wall, the boy in the striped pajamas. Olivera whispering from the driver's seat.

That day they had been on their way to the government center. They were driving down Route Michigan, the American name for the big east-west road across Ramadi. Olivera and Conrad were in the second Humvee in the convoy. The platoon commander was not meant to ride in the lead vehicle, though Conrad would have preferred to be there. He changed the order on every mission so the muj wouldn't know which was the command vehicle. He planned all of it, varying the configuration of the vehicles, the route they took. Mix things up, keep the muj off guard. Michigan was swept every day for IEDs, so theoretically it was the safest road. But it was also the most targeted, since it was the one most used by the Coalition Forces.

This time Conrad had chosen the Michigan route. They passed the Al Haq Mosque. This was in a hostile part of town. Al Haq was a violently anti-American cleric who spewed vituperative diatribes over the loudspeakers instead of prayers. The Marines called it Haji Hate Radio. The Al Haq Mosque was an old one, flanked by narrow minarets, each with a small balcony around the top. The muezzin had once made his calls from these, though now he made them from inside, over a loudspeaker.

Olivera was the driver that day, and Conrad sat behind him, watching the window. Leaving the wire, passing the red-and-white-striped barrier, they had all been silent. That was the moment, passing from safety. The radio crackled, the Humvee rattled around them. They headed down Michigan, between high mud-colored walls. Men stared at them boldly.

The Humvee bounced hard over a pothole. Molinos muttered, "Fuck. I nearly bit my tongue off."

"Wish you had," said Jackson. "Shut you up for a while."

"Fuck you, Jackson," Molinos said without animosity.

Then they were silent again, everyone watching the road ahead.

Once you left the wire, you started picking up what was in the air. You had some kind of extra sense, and you could feel the tension surrounding an ambush, an attack. It was real. You felt it physically, the hair on your arms and the back of your neck turning electric. Sometimes you weren't paying attention and missed it, or sometimes you picked up on it too late to do anything but shout *We're getting hit!* As though just calling it before it happened counted for something.

As they thundered past the mosque, Conrad could feel something wrong. The road was too quiet; he felt the hairs rise on the back of his neck. When he realized that the street was emptying of people, the sidewalks clearing, he leaned forward to shout *We're getting hit!* That was when the sound came up, huge and dark and breathtaking, crowding out everything. Something entered into him, closing him down.

When the world returned from darkness, he lay motionless and stunned. He seemed unable to move. He heard Olivera whispering. There were echoes inside his own head, a ringing noise, and he was dizzy. He couldn't remember where he was or who Olivera was or what they were doing there. Olivera kept whispering. The space was filled with smoke, and outside the Humvee there was the jittering sound of fire, and people shouting. Inside he could hear Olivera whispering. He smelled something he didn't want to smell. His leg hurt, and he wasn't sure he could move it. The radio was crackling. He couldn't grope his way toward action, couldn't figure out what it would mean. His brain felt numb. He tried to clear it. Olivera whispered. Conrad couldn't see him.

The ringing cleared, and then he could make some sense of what Olivera was saying.

"Where am I? I can't see," he said.

"You're okay," Conrad said. "You're right here."

"Am I going to die, LT?" he whispered.

"No." He still couldn't see him. "Hold on, Olivera, I've got you."

He put his hand out. The air was thick with smoke. His hand found Olivera's shoulder. It was wet.

"Are you in pain?" he asked.

"I can't move."

When the smoke lessened, Conrad saw that everything in front had changed. The windshield was shattered and opaque, the frame tilted. It was much closer than it should be. Olivera was still in place, but everything else had shifted. The steering wheel was gone. Inside Conrad's head was a great ringing sound, as if something huge were in there. Also, something had stalled, and he couldn't remember exactly how to move his limbs. When he leaned over the front seat, he was still confused. The crazed windshield bellied like a tent. The dashboard pressed against Olivera, and the shaft of the steering wheel seemed to vanish inside his chest, which was covered with a dark glistening sheen. Someone outside was shouting to them, but Conrad couldn't answer. The door was wrenched open and Haskell leaned inside, shouting that they were okay, but when he saw Olivera he stopped shouting.

"Okay," Molinos said. "I've got you. I'm calling in the docs." He didn't dare move Olivera, didn't dare touch him. He moved back to call, and Conrad waited with Olivera.

"Will I die, sir?" Olivera kept whispering. He couldn't speak in his normal voice. His breath was whistling in his chest.

"No," Conrad said to him, each time. "Hold on, Olivera. I've got you."

He would die. Conrad found Olivera's hand and gripped it.

The corpsmen were delayed by an attack on another patrol.

This was in April 2004, a few days before the whole city erupted in jihad, when they had to call every Marine off the base to fight, even the cooks. The whole city had filled up with the muj, and it took twenty-four hours of nonstop fighting to stop them, and by then they'd lost eight men in their platoon and fifty-four in the company. But that hadn't happened yet.

When Olivera was killed, it wasn't part of a citywide campaign. It seemed like just a bad day with an IED in it, someone standing in an alley with a cell phone in his pocket, pressing the button and watching, then slipping away down the alley, unscathed, unfindable.

"Will I die, sir?" Olivera whispered.

He wasn't looking at Conrad. He was looking up at the roof of the Humvee, which was blistered by the blast. A piece of fiberglass hung down over his head. *"Will I die?"* His breath made that strange whistle.

He'd gone into shock then, and after that Conrad wasn't sure if Olivera could hear him or feel anything, but he kept asking his question. Olivera's face was ashen, and there were tiny drops of sweat on his forehead. The blood smelled rich and ferrous. There was something dark and moist in the corners of his mouth, little bubbles forming there. Olivera didn't seem to notice.

There was a firefight somewhere nearby, snipers were hitting another squad, and Conrad was listening to the radio and to the peppering rattle of M16s and AK-47s while he was squeezing Olivera's hand.

"Hold on," he said. *"Hold on, Olivera. I'm right here. I've got you."*

Motherfuckers!

But Olivera, his chest caved in, died before the medics could arrive.

You believed in the mission and you believed in your men.

And what were these people in New York doing, here on the sidewalk, walking all over the place, not paying attention, and stopping like this right in front of him?

A man in a short raincoat halted abruptly before him, and Conrad grabbed him by the shoulders. The man turned around, ready to complain. He saw Conrad's face. He stepped back, and Conrad kept on going. *Motherfuckers.*

His father was here in the city. He should have lunch with his father; that might help. He couldn't tell these things to his mother, though she kept telling him he could. He couldn't tell her any of these things. What would be the point? He would still have them in his head, and then she would have them in her head. He imagined her face, how it would look if he told her. How was he supposed to do this? How was he supposed to get through the rest of his life?

He stopped suddenly, and when someone touched his shoulder from behind, he wheeled around as if it were the start of a martial arts contest. But it was only a messenger's bag bumping against Conrad as the man turned away from his padlocked bike, unaware that he'd violated Conrad's personal no-fly zone. Conrad saw his black, impassive face and turned away as well.

He took out his cell phone and called his father.

"Conrad?" Marshall said.

"Dad. Could we have lunch?" asked Conrad. "Today?"

There was a pause. Conrad could feel him recalibrating.

"Sure," his father said. "How soon do you want to meet?"

Conrad took the subway. It was nearly empty at this hour. He sat at the far end of the car, braced for impact, feeling the high-speed rattle as the car shuttled far too fast through the narrow subterranean passages. He was aware of everyone in the car. He sat with his back against the wall by the door that led into the next car. The sign over the door read IF YOU SEE SOMETHING, SAY SOMETHING, with a picture of a duffel bag tucked under a subway bench. The same message in Spanish. Fucking worthless. They had no idea, here, how to make a ten-meter check for safety, or what to do if you found something. There was no one in the subways to tell, for one thing, and for another, this whole system, with its long trains of rolling metal cars trapped underground in tunnels, was straight-out fucked if anything happened.

Watching for everything was impossible, though he was aware of everything. Or anyway he was watching everything. Pushing out of the turnstile at Bleecker, he saw that the man ahead of him was Middle Eastern. He wondered for a second time if the man he was seeing was Iraqi—he looked it. Those features had become so familiar, the honey-colored skin, black hair, the hawk nose, the piercing dark eyes. The girl who survived the shooting in Haditha had amber eyes, light brown. He'd seen the photographs, her somber face, her hands tucked between her knees. She wore a turquoise plastic hair band. She'd been shot, too, but not killed. She lay next to her sister, pretending to be dead, while the soldiers went through the house. It was another girl, not the one he'd seen.

He wanted to turn to the man and ask, in his faltering Arabic, if he was from Iraq. He wanted to tell him that he, Conrad, had roots there. The man wouldn't be able to tell that by looking at him, the way Conrad could tell by looking at the man, but he did. That was how he felt—he had roots there. He'd gone there to try to save the people of Iraq. That's why they were there.

He thought of Ali, and the teacher in Ramadi whose school they'd helped rebuild. The part of him that was still there was like the ocean, huge and moving and unseen. It was really all of him. That's where he was; that's where he still was. They'd been helping the people, that was what they had tried to do, Olivera and Carleton and Kuchnik and all the others. He thought of the men in the taxi, and the boy in his pajamas, his head falling back.

He pushed on up the stairs to the street, ahead of the man. He was young, with a narrow hatchet face and those staring zealot's eyes. Marines had zealot's eyes, too, that stern, fixed stare. No one was more zealous than Marines. The mission had been to liberate the Iraqis from a dictator. *Liberation.* So what the fuck had happened? Why was he walking along the street trying to get this mess out of his head, and why had any of it happened? How could he get rid of it?

He thought of his mother hugging him that first night, and the look on her face, ready to forgive him anything. Though not this, not any of this, none of which could be told, none of which could be spoken here, in this country where there was no sand, where people left half-full water bottles on the street, where they read gossip magazines while their young men were driving over hidden bombs. It couldn't be spoken there, either, in-country where it had happened, but over there people understood it. You didn't have to speak it. All the people there understood it. They'd seen it. No one who wasn't there could understand it.

His father was waiting when he arrived. It was a Japanese restaurant, with a low ceiling and pale blank walls, very quiet. The waiter wore a black suit and white shirt. He bowed politely and took Conrad to the back.

Marshall was sitting at a corner table. He sat with his back to the side wall; he'd left the chair with its back to the rear wall for Conrad.

"Con." Marshall was wearing a suit and tie, reminding Conrad that he had a professional life. He was not only a father.

The waiter hovered, and Marshall asked, "Something to drink? I'm having a Virgin Mary."

"Great," Conrad said.

The restaurant was mostly empty, it was early for lunch. The waiters were small, their movements quiet. The walls were unadorned except for one long scroll with a picture of a crow on it. The atmosphere was calm. It was a relief, after the onslaught of the subway, the hurrying crowds on the street.

Marshall folded his hands on the edge of the table.

"How are you doing?"

"Fine," Conrad said.

His father waited, the lock of hair hanging over his forehead, his head tilted forward.

"Shitty," Conrad said.

His father nodded. "What's going on?"

Conrad shook his head. "It's hard to describe. It's like I can't get in here. It's as though I'm standing outside. I can see everyone in here, rushing around and doing things, and I can't get in."

Marshall nodded again. "I'm sorry," he said, then waited again. "Do you have an idea of what would help?"

Conrad had no idea of what would help.

There was too much of everything, too much noise and color and choices, too many ads and people, too many cars and trucks and cabs clogging the streets, too many pedestrians on the sidewalks, everywhere was crammed and jostling. And it was all pointless, trivial, everything people were doing was unnecessary. Going to the grocery store, going to work.

And everything was filled with fucking irony, everything was sarcastic. *Like I care:* that should be the national motto. Every ad, every overheard conversation, every exchange was full of sarcastic animosity. What was the point? What was the fucking point? Why go through all this every day if that's how you felt—sarcastic, disengaged, distant, ironic? How about watching someone you're responsible for die, his chest caved in, blood seeping out of the corners of his mouth? How about him asking you if he's going to die and you lying to him, telling him he'd be all right? What about *Like I care* then?

It seemed this was the way the whole country felt.

So what had they been doing over there for three fucking years and no end in sight, while people in-country were getting their arms blown off and their faces torn apart and losing their wives and girlfriends and their marriages and their lives, and then coming home to people who were all saying, *Like I care.*

He couldn't say any of this, because really, most of what was wrong was his fault. It was his fault that he had those pictures in his head, the things he didn't want to see ever again, that rose up every night, screening out everything else, and he wondered if this was how it would be forever.

"I don't know what would help," Conrad said.

"Can you talk to your mom?" asked Marshall.

Conrad shook his head.

"Claire?"

"Some. Not really," Conrad said. "I can't stay there anymore. I'm moving out."

"Where are you going to go?"

"Jenny's." He had just thought of this.

Marshall nodded. "What about a therapist?"

"It wouldn't help," Conrad said. "The stuff in my head is permanent. It can't be erased." He hadn't meant to say that.

Marshall watched him. "Have you talked to any of your friends? From the Marines?"

"There isn't really anyone I want to talk to."

His platoon was dispersed. They were gone, though he could still feel them, like a phantom limb. He couldn't talk to the men he'd led, though, and his officer friends were scattered, too. Some had extended their active duty to redeploy, some were out and through the EAS. None of them were nearby, and he didn't want to tell this to any of them. Fear was a secret you kept forever.

Marshall nodded again. "This must be hard."

Conrad looked up. "Did you talk to Mom?"

"I did. Why?"

"She always says that. 'This must be hard.'"

"Well?"

"Nothing."

"I'm sorry you're going through this."

Conrad nodded.

What was happening was that the air around him was building up. All this calm, light Japanese air was building up, denser and denser. It was becoming intolerable. What would happen if he could no longer breathe?

He drank some water. The restaurant was beginning to fill up. It was mostly men in suits. The table next to them was taken by two young law firm associates, from the look of them. Dark suits and white shirts and dark silk ties, an unmistakable sense of self-satisfaction. They were a few years older than him, not much. They seemed completely at ease, talking and laughing. What had they ever done in the world? But here they were, in suits, unfolding their napkins, ready to order sushi-grade tuna steaks, and headed for long and rewarding careers. This was the parallel universe, where he was absent.

How could he start over? He was at the bottom of this ladder. Claire was right; he had left the world. Now that he was back, he couldn't get in. And he didn't want to get in here, with these fucking flap-eared monkeys congratulating themselves on their salaries.

"Dad," he said.

Marshall looked at him. He smoothed his tie, laying it down against his concave chest with restless fingers.

"What if I don't know how to say any of this?" Conrad said. "What's on my mind."

"We can wait until you do," Marshall said. "I can wait. I'm only worried that you need to say it, not that I need to hear it. You can say anything to us."

The waiter arrived. He had an oval face and narrow, merry eyes. His thick black hair fell jauntily across his forehead.

"Do you like to order?" he asked.

Marshall ordered chicken yakitori, Conrad the sushi-grade tuna steak.

When the waiter left, Marshall folded his hands again on the table. "It looks as though you feel bad about something," he said, "but everything you've done you should feel proud of."

"Yeah," Conrad said. "Thanks."

Pride was not a possibility, since Carleton and Olivera were in his mind, and he had lost them. He was their platoon commander and he had allowed them to die. They had died in his charge. To say nothing of the other deaths that stayed with him: the family in Haditha, the father and children in the car, and Ali. He had vanished. One day he didn't come in to work, and no one seemed to know what happened to him. Conrad had asked the other terps, but no one would tell him. Forty percent of the translators who worked for the Americans were killed by the muj as traitors. They were killed horribly.

He could tell his father none of this. None of it.

At the next table, one of the young lawyers ordered something more. Conrad couldn't hear what he was saying, only his voice, which was so courteous that Conrad wondered if it was ironic. Or was it patronizing? He couldn't tolerate someone being patronizing. The waiter stood still, head cocked.

He's a real person, Conrad thought. *He's your fucking equal, you stupid prick. He goes home at night and takes off his suit, like you, and talks to his wife. He has dinner and makes jokes about his day, he teases his daughter. He laughs, he has stomach problems.* Conrad felt as though there were a monstrous drum around him, the drumbeat echoing through him everywhere, his mind and body.

After lunch he called Jenny.

"Hey," he said.

"What's up?" she answered.

"Can I come stay with you for a while?"

"Of course," she said, so quickly that he wondered if she'd heard from Marshall. "I'll be home around six. Meet me at the apartment."

"See you there."

"Con," she said, "are you okay?"

"I'm fine," he said. "Why do you all keep asking?"

Now he wanted to be gone before Claire got home. Back at her apartment, he packed his clothes. He took the towel off the bed, folded it, and hung it in the bathroom. He made up the bed with tight Marine corners, smoothing the bedspread exactly. He realized it was the first time he'd done that, made the bed there.

When he was through, he called Claire at work.

"Hi there," she said. She sounded distant and wary.

"I'm sorry about this morning," Conrad said. "You were right."

"I'm sorry I sounded like—so picky." Her voice was now warm. "It's just—"

"No, you were right," Conrad said. "I'm moving out."

"Con," she said. There was a pause. "What's going on?"

"It's not fair for me to stay here," he said. "Sorry I was so rough."

"But don't just leave," Claire said. "That's not what I meant."

"I'm going to stay at Jenny's," he said. "Across town. I'll be in touch."

Now he couldn't wait to get out of the apartment, with its bottles of shampoo, its steamy mirror, its fridge full of soy milk and strawberry yogurt and ice cream. Now he felt trapped here. He couldn't explain that to Claire; he couldn't explain anything to Claire. He had to move on; something was hurrying at his back.

At six o'clock he was on the sidewalk in front of Jenny's building.

18

Conrad sat on a battered folding chair in Jenny's kitchen, holding a beer and watching her cook. He leaned back, tilting the chair against the wall.

Jenny stood at the stove; she was wearing a loose yellow blouse and black tights. The sleeveless blouse exposed her birthmark: a small, dark strawberry shape on the back of her upper arm. The tights just covered her rounded knees, leaving her smooth, pale calves bare. On her feet were flip-flops with glittery straps; her toenails were painted dark blue. She held a spatula in one hand; the other was set on her hip. Steam rose from the pan, and the sound of sizzling.

"You crack me up," Conrad said.

She glanced at him. "Me?"

He pointed with his bottle. "Blue toenails. When I left, you were wearing footed pajamas."

She laughed and looked back at the pan. "Blue's nothing. I used to paint them with cocaine."

Conrad took a swallow. "Did you?"

"No," Jenny said. "Joke."

He waited. "But you've done some drugs." She had to have. Another thing he'd missed—his brother and sister growing up.

"Just weed in college. Nothing drastic." She looked at him. "You checking up on me?"

"I guess I am," he said. "Trying to figure out who you are. You're so grown-up. I'm not used to it."

"You've been away," she said. "We're both different now. It's kind of weird, trying to get to know your own brother again."

"You feel like you don't know me?"

She looked at him. "Do you think I know you?"

He didn't answer.

"I feel like you want to make sure I don't." She lifted a lid and stirred. "You don't want anyone to know you."

"No," he said, "that's not what it is."

But that *was* what it was, as if something had slammed shut deep inside him. He didn't want anyone to come near. But how would he live?

"Up to you," Jenny said. "But it makes it hard for the rest of us. Hard on the parents." She looked at him again. "We all know you're having a bad time." He said nothing, and Jenny looked down again at the stove and changed the subject. "What about drugs for you? You used to smoke some weed, as I recall."

Conrad shook his head. "Not many drugs over there," he said. "It's a combat zone, plus it's a Muslim country. For R and R you go to another Muslim country, like Qatar. Though not us, not combat units. The Vietnam War was different, it was full of drugs. Iraq's not. Sand, yes; drugs, no."

She nodded. "So what'd you do for fun?"

"Nutty stuff. On the base, guys would think up practical jokes. They'd have costume contests. Dance contests."

"Dance contests? Really?" She smiled.

"Yeah. They'd have routines. Sometimes costumes."

"Would you compete?"

He shook his head. "I was the boss. Sometimes I'd watch."

"So they have no idea that you can't dance."

An old joke. He shook his head and took a swallow. "I see you haven't moved out of here yet."

Jenny sighed. "I can't bring myself to give up this place."

"What's Jock say?"

Jenny narrowed her eyes against the steam. "I don't know what he says. He's so tired all the time, we don't talk about it. When we do, we fight." She unscrewed a bottle and shook some flakes into the frying pan. "He says, 'What's the big deal? Why is an apartment more important than we are? What's your message?' "

"And? What is your message?" Conrad asked.

"How do I know? Why should everything have a message? He's coming over for dinner tonight, by the way. He has a night off, and he's going to stay here." She shook her head and stuck out her lower lip, blowing upward to lift her bangs from her eyes. They fluttered, then settled again on her damp forehead. "How's Claire?"

Conrad shrugged. "Good."

"So what happened? Why'd you move out?"

"The Roommates were getting restless," he said. "Time to move on."

"More real estate issues." Jenny nudged the spatula against what was in the pan. "You can stay here as long as you like."

"Thanks."

The tall window beyond Jenny overlooked the street. This was a galley kitchen—the stove, sink, and fridge all in a row. Green-painted cabinets hung over the sink and counter. On the facing wall was a board hung with pots and pans, over a narrow wooden table.

Jenny's apartment was the third floor of an old brownstone. The house was made of solid chocolate-colored stone, with wide steps and heavy double front doors. It had once been a dignified one-family house, but now it was cut into apartments, and had long been in a state of benign neglect. Decades of grime had settled into its cracks and interstices. Inside, all the cornices and moldings had been blurred and muffled by decades of paint, the edges softened as though by snowfall.

The front hall was dim and lofty, with high ceilings and gloomy wooden trim. The walls were a sooty white, with huge faint stains on them, like continents. The black-and-white marble floor tiles were stained and cracked. The space had its own mysterious smell, burning, slightly acrid.

Outside, along 103rd Street, cars were parked tightly along the curb, bumper to bumper. They looked as though they had been neatly set in place forever, solid and motionless, not as though they all dispersed magically each day during ticketing time. Then the street was empty for the huge, lumbering street cleaner that came bobbing and whirling along the curb, while the adjacent blocks were full of double-parked cars, their drivers waiting patiently for the moment of return.

All the houses along the street made brave gestures toward nature. Some of the doorways were flanked by pots of geraniums, now shrunken and wizened after a summer of erratic watering, or faltering neon-pink impatiens, fainting in their planters full of baked earth, or, more trendily, stands of tall dead grasses, which, even dead, rustled beautifully with every breeze. On one house a clambering wisteria had taken stealthy possession of the entire façade, throwing out what had been tiny friendly green tendrils but had become, over the years, giant brown python-size trunks, covering the whole building with a shaggy green pelt.

Jenny's apartment, two stories above the high-ceilinged parlor floor, was long, narrow, and modest. The kitchen overlooked the street, as did the living room beside it, with its bay window. In the middle of the apartment, halfway down the hall, was the bathroom, and at the back was Jenny's bedroom. This was large and square, with two windows overlooking the backyard, and it was the reason she could not give up the apartment.

The front door slammed. "Hello!" Jock called.

"Yo!" said Jenny.

Jock appeared in the doorway. He was tall and gaunt, with pale skin and short, thick reddish-brown hair. He had a narrow, pointed nose and wore small round metal-rimmed glasses. His neck was long, and he had a prominent Adam's apple. He was somehow cool, with an easy, quizzical manner. He grinned at Conrad, who stood up. They clapped shoulders.

"Good to see you," said Jock. "How 'bout them Braves?"

"Still on the wrong side. I'm sorry for you, man. How 'bout them Yankees?"

They grinned at each other.

"So, Jen told me you'd be here," Jock said. "How's it going?"

"Good," said Conrad. "How's the world of medicine?"

Jock squinted and rubbed his eyes behind his glasses, pushing his fingertips into the sockets. "You don't want to know."

"He gets a little time off every two weeks," said Jenny. "But only to sleep."

"Sounds like us," said Conrad. "Only for us it was every three weeks."

"In the sleep-deprivation competition," said Jock, "you guys win. In fact, you guys win in every way. I have to admit, Iraq beats Mount Sinai." He raised his hands in surrender. He moved past Conrad to kiss Jenny. He was much taller than she, and when he leaned down, he put his hands on her shoulders as though to steady her, or himself.

"What's for dinner?" he asked. "God, it smells good."

"It's called tilapia," Jenny said. "Which is either the name of an exotic species from the South Pacific or a made-up PR name for Mississippi catfish."

"Catfish is delicious, you know," Jock said. "I've had it."

Jenny made a face. "With or without whiskers?"

"Don't be a fish snob," said Jock. "You're meant to make a sauce with the whiskers." He opened the fridge for a beer. "Man, I stink. I'm going to take a shower. Back in a mo."

Conrad took another swig. Jenny's face was intent, and the steam rose around her. She leaned over, sniffing, then poured olive oil into the pan. She shook out more flakes, then turned the heat down.

It reminded him of a cockpit, his sister's tiny space, where she checked and monitored, turning dials, summoning up heat and fire, sending up clouds of steam, sizzling drops of fat, the smell of herbs and garlic.

"How did you learn to cook?" he asked. "Did Mom teach you?"

"I guess," she said.

"You like it?"

"When I have the time, and if I'm having someone over. Otherwise I eat cereal or scrambled eggs. Grilled cheese sandwiches." She glanced at him. "Can you cook?"

He shook his head.

"You should learn. Maybe that would make you feel better."

He took another swig. "You think I don't feel good?"

She glanced at him again.

"You don't seem very chipper," Jenny said.

"I'm chipper," he said. "I'm very chipper."

"Could you talk to someone? A therapist?"

He gave a dismissive wave, using his hand holding the beer. The bottle slammed against the wall. "Oops."

Jenny said nothing. She shook the frying pan, sliding it heavily back and forth over the burner.

When Jock came back, he looked damp and fresh, his hair slicked and dark. He rubbed his hands together.

"Now," he said. "Let me have a beer. Then let us have the meal. Then let us watch bad TV, and then let us become unconscious."

When the food was ready, they took their plates into the living room. This was long and narrow and dim, high-ceilinged, gloomily elegant, though the furniture was random and shabby. Two ponderous mismatched upholstered chairs faced the inner wall and the worn red sofa where Conrad would sleep. Near the doorway was a round table with two high-backed wooden chairs. Conrad brought in his chair and set it at the table.

Jock took a bite and shook his head. "Hmm-hmm. That's mighty good catfish!"

"Don't." Jenny lowered her fork and looked at the white flakes distrustfully.

"Okay, it's not." Jock raised his hand in apology. He had pale slender fingers. "It's jalapeño, right? I know that."

Conrad poked at his fish. "Do you have a bowl to put the whiskers in?"

"Very funny," Jenny said. "Tomorrow, you cook."

This gave Conrad an odd, complicated lift. *Tomorrow.*

"Actually, it's pretty good," Conrad said. "Whatever it's called."

"Pescado de gato," said Jock.

Conrad said to him, "So, you're in rotation? What are you doing now?"

"ER," said Jock.

"Intense," said Conrad.

"That's the word," said Jock, nodding.

"How you finding it?"

"Some ways, good," Jock said. "Everything happens at once. You go in with the whole team, working at top speed on a patient, you all work your asses off, and then you're done. You hand the patient off to another department, and you start over with someone else. It's an eight-hour adrenaline rush."

"How do you come out?" Conrad asked. "What percentage do you save?"

"Huge," Jock said. "Half the people coming in are just scared. Bandage 'em up, give 'em Tylenol, send 'em home. Or send them to see their primary physicians. Half the others need attention, but they're not a big risk. Bites, burns, falls, but not fatal injuries."

"But the rest . . ." said Conrad.

"Are serious. Out of them, we save half, maybe three-quarters. The numbers are still really good. Yesterday a guy came in while he was having a stroke. His wife brought him by cab, didn't want to wait for the ambulance. He couldn't stand up straight. He was leaning against the wall. Double vision, slurred speech, just walked in the door. Jesus. He was right in the middle of it. We had him down on the table within ninety seconds, hooked up, IVs, monitors, everything." He shook his head.

"And he was okay?" Jenny asked.

"Fine," Jock said.

"At Quantico, during IOC, we went to the local ER as observers," Conrad told Jock.

"What's IOC?" Jenny asked.

"Infantry Officer Course," said Conrad. "It was so we'd get to see what trauma was like."

"Takes getting used to," said Jock. "The sight of pumping blood is a physiological shock. Your blood vessels dilate, your blood pressure drops just to see it. Some people hit the floor. Men, women, anyone."

"Yeah," Conrad said. "It's tough, seeing that stuff. Your mind kind of refuses to process. You think, *No, that can't be right. All that blood can't be coming out of his chest.* Or, *That hand can't be lying there on a different gurney from the arm.*"

Jock nodded. "Shock can paralyze you. Someone else can end up dying because you didn't act fast."

"It took us a while to get over it."

Later they'd made jokes about it. *Where did I leave that hand? I just had it. It was right here at the end of my arm. Did you take it? Hand it over.*

In-country they made jokes about everything. Politically incorrect, seriously offensive jokes about bodies in ditches, wounds, missing limbs, babies. Black humor.

It was a way to name what was happening, to speak the horrors, to render them powerless. It was the only way you could say how bad it was. He wondered what the ER jokes were, but he didn't know Jock well enough to ask.

After dinner Conrad did the dishes, filling the sink with steaming hot water, snowbanks of soapsuds. He scrubbed the plates, the silverware, the pots. He set the clean dishes in the rack to dry, drained the sink, sponged it clean, and turned over the heavy iron skillet and left it in the sink. He dried his hands with a feeling of accomplishment.

They watched bad TV. Jenny had TiVoed something she wanted to see, but she couldn't get it to work, so they watched a survival show about a bunch of idiots on an island in the South Pacific. The competitors shinnied up ropes and jumped into the water; they clambered through a tropical forest and tried to build fires.

"Jesus," Conrad said, "look at them trying to put up a tent. I'm glad they're not protecting our asses in Iraq."

"They're probably glad, too," said Jenny.

"What kind of asshole goes on a show like this?" asked Conrad.

"Someone without a job," Jenny said.

"Someone without a higher brain," said Jock.

"Seriously," Conrad said. "Who would do that?"

"Oh, I don't know," said Jenny. "I can see someone wanting to do it. It's exciting and exotic and you get to go far away, and it pays money. And they'd feel famous. It's a big adventure. Like going to Iraq."

"Right," Conrad said. "We had a lot of crossovers from survival shows to the Marine Corps."

He was actually glad to watch this, irritating though it was. It was a relief just to give his head a rest, to fill his mind with different images from the ones that lived in his mind. The guy with the mullet sliding down the rope into the water. The blond girls who hated each other but pretended to be friends. The snake moving through the underbrush. The skinny guy trying to put up the tent, swearing each time it collapsed.

"Do they vote on who they like? Or do we vote?" He wasn't up on reality shows, something else he'd missed. "Can you vote to disqualify everyone?"

When it was over and the wrong person had lost, Jock stretched and stood up.

"Okay, guys," he said. "I'm dead. I'm more than dead. I'm hitting the rack. Anyone want to join me?"

"Con?" Jenny asked. "You or me?"

Conrad laughed. "You go this time."

"Night, Con," Jock said. "Good to see you. Sorry we don't have a guest room for you. We will when we move. Into our own apartment." He looked at Jenny, who shook her head.

"No problem," Conrad said.

Jock went back into the bedroom, but Jenny stayed, curled up on the sofa. She looked at Conrad and made a face.

"See what I mean?" she said.

"Dude wants a commitment," he said.

"I'm dragging my feet," she said. "What do you think?"

"Indecision is a decision," Conrad said. "You've got to decide."

"That's the Marine way," Jenny said.

"How we're trained," Conrad said. "How it is."

"Yeah," she said. "You say that like you know what you're doing. But you seem . . ." She faded away.

"What? I seem what?"

"I don't know. You seem like you're saying it, but you don't mean it."

Conrad was sitting in one of the huge square chairs.

"You keep going no matter how you feel," he said. "You just go ahead. Charlie Mike, continue the mission."

Jenny looked at him. "Are you going to be okay?"

"What do you mean?"

"Can you sleep?"

He made a seesaw gesture. "You might hear the TV on, late. I'll keep it low."

"I'm not worried about you keeping me awake."

"I'll be fine," he said. "Thanks for letting me stay."

"As long as you want," she said. "But I wish you'd see someone. I can get you a name. Or Jock can."

"Good idea," Conrad said. "I'll think about it."

"Anyway." Jenny yawned. "You're sitting in the good-luck chair, by the way. I found it out on the sidewalk, and some friends helped me carry it back. When I was cleaning it out, I found an envelope stuck down in the crack between the back and the seat, with two hundred dollars in cash."

"Whoa," said Conrad. "What do you think? Drug money?"

"No idea. No name, no writing, no address. By then I didn't even remember exactly which building it was in front of, just the block. There was no way to return it. I thought maybe the person had died and no one else knew it was there, the apartment was cleaned out, and the chair was put out on the street."

"You lucked out."

"I know. At first I felt guilty, like I should find out whoever it was who had died and give the money to the family. They had to be poor. I thought of some old person, living alone and getting wacky. Then I thought it was a drug dealer and he'd stuffed the money out of sight when someone came in, and before he could get it, he was arrested. Or killed. I had a lot of stories. For a while, every time I saw the chair, I felt guilty. Like, what should I have done differently?"

"Jen," Conrad said.

"No, I know I wasn't *bad*, but it wasn't my money."

"And so what happened?" asked Conrad.

"Then one day I thought, *Okay, that's it. Stop. You can't give the money back. There's no way you can undo this, and you didn't do anything wrong. So just quit.*"

"And so that was it?"

"More or less. I hadn't taken the money, and I couldn't return it. I stopped feeling guilty. I just thought, *Okay, this is what happened. It's not my fault.*"

"Right." Conrad nodded slowly.

"Con," Jenny said. "Are you okay?"

"I'm good," he said.

There was a pause.

He nodded again.

"I feel like you're trapped inside yourself," said Jenny. "Like there's something in there with you."

"I'm okay," Conrad said. "I'm fine. It's over." He stood up. "Okay, it's late. I'm going to hit the rack."

Jenny stood, and they began to take the cushions off the sofa, piling them on the floor. Conrad unfolded the metal frame, lifting it in an awkward arc as it reared and then settled jerkily onto the floor. Conrad and Jenny made it up together, tugging the sheets onto the corners. The pillowcase was covered with faded smiling Dumbos; Conrad remembered it from home. It was Jenny's; no one else was allowed to use it.

"I can't believe you're letting me use this," he said.

"Special circumstances," she said. "Honored guest."

The sheets were clean but unironed. He thought of Jenny at the Laundromat, reading a magazine, waiting for the machines to finish churning and whirling. It was strange to think of her living on her own.

"Thanks, Jen," he said.

She smiled at him. There were dark circles under her eyes. "Glad to have you here," she said. "Wake me up if you can't sleep. If you want to talk."

"Thanks," he said.

What was so mysterious was the fact that she would stand up and walk away. Just a few feet from there she'd open a door and enter another place. She'd move into a realm of shared intimacy, lowered voices, the touch of skin on skin, comfort, sex. Someone she trusted absolutely. Then silence, and then the deep solace of somnolence.

He was alone. What he dreaded was the struggle to reach sleep. To get through the blackness of the night. When he tried, he slid sideways toward sleep but was jerked upright by images, a racing pulse. The night was a minefield. He had begun drinking to get through it. Not a lot.

He got into bed and lay stretched out on his back, looking up at the dim ceiling. The room was dark but not black; the urban night was never black. Ambient light came in from the window: there were streetlights up and down the block, headlights from passing cars, and overhead was the great high wash of light, the city's nocturnal glow, a strange, muted pink.

He closed his eyes, drifting. What he saw was the bloody pattern, so high on the wall, and now it had a mysterious significance. The spattered drops were some kind of writing that he understood but could not bear to read, horror flooding through him as he saw it. Then Olivera's voice whispering in the darkness, asking for something Conrad couldn't quite make out. Now he couldn't reach him, Olivera's shoulder was sliding away, carried by a current that was pulling Conrad down into darkness. A man in the firefight in Ramadi, only now it seemed to have happened at night instead of day. The street was full of shadows, and there were footsteps behind him, and hissing whispers. Now the man was pursuing him. He was filled with dread and fear, and he had no weapon.

When Jenny finished in the bathroom and went into the bedroom, Jock was already in bed, motionless, his face turned toward the wall. He could fall asleep immediately, dropping at once into unconsciousness. Sometimes he was asleep before she got into bed. Sex had become secondary. She didn't know what had become primary.

Jenny slid in beside him, moving herself along his back. She could feel the soft knobs of his vertebrae. He grunted; he was lost already.

"I'm scared about Conrad," she whispered. She pressed herself against him and slid her hand over the top of his sharp shoulder. "Listen to me."

Jock's breathing changed from long, slow breaths to silence. She felt him shifting reluctantly out of sleep, listening. Outside, a garbage truck labored along the street, giving out sharp pneumatic noises, metallic yelps, deep mechanical gasps.

"I'm worried," she whispered.

"What would you like me to do?" Jock's voice was low. He rolled over to face her. "Recommend someone for him to see? Doesn't he have the VA?"

"I don't know," she said. "It's so hard to get anything out of him. This just goes on and on. It's been months since he got home, since last spring, and he's not getting any better. He's getting worse."

Jock ran his hand along her shoulder, down her arm. Down her birthmark. "It must be hard, coming home," he said. "We'll keep an eye on him. I can get him sleeping pills. It's good he's here with us." His hand slid down over her shoulder and onto her breast. His finger touched her nipple and lingered there.

Conrad, flung into wakefulness, lay propped up on the sofa. He held the remote, flipping from channel to channel. The sound was on low, and he could still hear faint noises from outside.

In the street, a garbage truck labored up the block, yawning open and then cranking closed, shrieking into gear. At the end of the block it hit something with the deep echoing rumble of an incoming mortar round. Everything in Conrad flew up into red alert: heart pounding, brain flashing, lungs pumping, adrenaline flooding through his system, and fear. Fear broke through him everywhere and he lay still on the sofa, rigid.

Jesus, he thought. *Jesus.* He began to sweat.

19

During the night he kept waking. Each time, he was roused by a sense of clamor and confusion: shouts, clanging metal, explosions blooming in the darkness. Once, he heard someone speaking Arabic, close and urgent. He was about to respond, or maybe he already had (it seemed he was fluent), but when he opened his eyes and listened, everything subsided into silence.

Sometime after dawn he found himself lying on his back, looking up at the shadowy ceiling. His arms were spread out, his legs tangled in the sheets. The iron crossbar in the bed frame pressed against his spine and shoulders. Something had shifted in his mind; he woke knowing something new. *He would not go on living like this.*

Powdery morning light seeped in around the window shades, making a pale glow around the tall, dim rectangles. Outside were the noises of the city waking, the distant aggregate hum of engines, the proximate metallic rumble of a car driving up the block. A dog barked twice, staccato, peremptory. On the sidewalk were the sounds of rapid footsteps, someone walking fast, breaking into a run for a few steps, then falling back to a hurrying determined walk.

He would not go on waiting to be ambushed by fear.

He disentangled himself from the swirled mess of sheets and sat up, swinging his feet over the side of the bed.

He would make a plan and carry it out. He'd leave all this behind: fear, anxiety, rage. The panic attacks, the headache. He'd get started and keep going, he'd outpace it. He'd pull himself out. He'd reconnect with Claire. His parents. It was a question of focus, will.

There was no sound from Jock and Jenny. Conrad slipped into the little mildewy bathroom, where he showered, shaved. He came out and dressed, then made the bed. He'd learned this at Quantico, where a bed was called a rack. He'd learned to make it perfectly, sheets even, blanket smooth, a flawless envelope, tight and taut as a drum. The things you learned there you learned forever. Pulling the sheets tight, making a straight line with the blanket, gave him a tiny hit of pride. It was a matter of execution. Nothing was too small to do right.

When he'd finished, Conrad lifted the foot of the bed frame, starting its creaky angular arc upward, then scissoring down into the bowels of the sofa. He replaced the big square seat cushions and spaced Jenny's bright pillows across the back. He set his duffel bag on the far side of the sofa, out of sight. It was no longer a bedroom but a living room when Jock and Jenny appeared.

Jock was dressed but ratty-looking, unshaven, in a long-sleeved T-shirt and khakis. He thrust out his stubbled chin. "Hey, Con. I'm out of here. Good to see you." He kissed Jenny and waved at Conrad and was out the door. They heard him thudding quickly down the staircase.

Jenny stood in the doorway, yawning. She was barefoot, in a rumpled T-shirt and sweats, her hair messy and flyaway.

"Want some cereal?" asked Conrad.

"I'm going to brush my teeth," she said. "Be right back."

In the kitchen they leaned against the counter, eating cereal.

"So, I've got a new plan," Conrad said. "Today's the day."

Jenny raised her eyebrows. "What are you going to do?"

"Look into grad schools. Everything."

Jenny looked at him. "Good, Con," she said. "Good for you. I'm glad you're back."

"I'm back," he said. "I'm on it."

When Jenny left, Conrad cleaned up the kitchen, and then settled down with his computer. BAMCIS: Begin planning. Arrange for reconnaissance. Make reconnaissance. Complete the plan. Issue the order. Supervise.

He still couldn't see himself in graduate school, but now he didn't care. Applications weren't due until the end of this year, and he wouldn't be starting anywhere until a year from now. By then everything would be different.

He needed more econ credits to apply anywhere, he knew that. He found a macroeconomics class at Columbia, in post-bac. Miraculously, he was in time to get in. Today was the twenty-ninth, and registration lasted until the thirty-first. Class started on the fifth.

He spent the morning online in the great electronic state of limbo. He clicked to open screens. He entered information: his name, his social, his address, his email address. He talked to the computer as he worked. "Okay, now, go!" he said, "Dog, go! Go, go, go!" He clicked "Enter," clicked it again.

The promise of the Internet is that you, still in your pajamas, lying on the sofa, can function as a presentable, responsible member of society, somewhere else. On the Internet, magically, you can have a material effect on the world without actually entering it. Or this is what it promises.

Conrad's computer kept having failures of confidence. After he had entered all the data, and after he'd clicked "Enter," the computer froze. "Fuck," Conrad said mildly. "Fuck, fuck. Okay."

He had to close it down, wait for its confidence to build up again, and start over. Conrad didn't mind this. He was used to dealing with uncooperative equipment. M16s used to jam because of the sand, because they couldn't get enough of the oil they needed to clean them with, and a jammed M16 in a firefight was a lot worse than a computer that forgot what it was going to say.

"Okay, dog, *let's go*," he said under his breath.

Conrad ordered his transcript. He signed up for an online orientation session. He studied the map of the campus to learn where his class met. He ordered textbooks. He ordered the study guide for the GMAT and registered to take the test in early December. That would give him the whole semester to study for the exam, and he'd have the scores for his graduate school applications. In the meantime he'd have three months to figure out where he wanted to apply.

By the time he'd finished, it was afternoon. Flat midday light flooded onto the big armchairs, making long trapezoids on the rug. A nearby construction site was in full swing, jackhammers drumming their nasal beat, a generator droning steadily. A truck, backing up, sent out high, rhymthic beeping—such a soprano voice for such a bass presence.

Conrad called Claire, but got voice mail. *Hey there, you've got Claire. Tell me something.* When he heard her voice—intimate and confiding, audibly smiling—his heart rose. "Hey there," he said. He tried to think of something intimate and charming in response, but only managed to add, "Beautiful. Call me. I've got some news."

He was on a high, as though he'd won a race.

Checking email, he found a message from Adam Turner, a friend from The Basic School. Turner was a lanky guy from New Hampshire, with hooded eyes and a hatchet nose. When he laughed, he slitted his eyes and shook, completely silent. He'd been stationed in Hit while Conrad was in Haditha. He was back now, and out, and living in D.C.

I'm sharing with three other guys. We have a house in Potomac. Chris Abbott, who was at TBS with us, is one of them. I don't think you know the others, both vets. It's pretty sweet, a four bedroom house. We're all taking classes, headed for grad schools. But Abbott, remember how straight he was? How he would never swear or anything? Okay, but his girlfriend is a stripper. A real no shit one, she works in a club called Aladdin's Cave. She's around all the time. The moral dilemma: should we go and see her show, and if so do we tell Abbott? Would Abbott think we were showing fraternal support or checking out his girlfriend's tits? Stay tuned.

Conrad wrote back:

How could Abbott think that would be anything but fraternal support? Swelling the ranks of the audience (in a manner of speaking) could only be supportive. Go for it! Is she hot? Maybe I'll take a road trip and come down to join you. I love the theater as you know.

He sent Anderson a blast.

Hey Anderson, haven't heard from you lately. What's up? I hope things are going well—let me know your news about the job. I'm hitting the books again, signing up for an econ class. I'm planning on going to graduate school next year, see if that will keep me out of trouble. I'm in the city right now, and for exercise I'm running the track around the reservoir in Central Park. It's about a mile and a half, so I do four laps. It's crowded—like running with the whole souk. About half of them are women, which makes it nice for the other half. Hope you're doing well. How are the hands? Keep in touch. Semper Fi, Farrell.

He liked hearing from everyone in the platoon, even Haskell, who was kind of an asshole and whom he never really trusted. But especially Anderson.

The night Anderson had saved Conrad's life, they'd been in Ramadi.

They'd been on QRF, Quick Reaction Force, that night, and sometime after midnight they were called out to back up a platoon that was taking fire. When they got near, they could hear the firefight from blocks away. They were on foot, and Conrad sent first and second squads to the right, to flank it. He'd gone on ahead with third, fourth following behind them. As they neared the fight they started taking fire. Conrad and Anderson were last in line. The others went one by one, covering each other, but a grenade exploded in the street in front of Conrad. He and Anderson ducked into a doorway. Smoke and dust filled the street amid the chatter of gunfire. Conrad got third squad on the radio: they'd taken cover in a house down the street. He and Anderson were cut off from them by cross fire. They were outside a shop, and they kicked in the metal door and headed for the rooftop.

In the open stairwell at the top they looked out at the low skyline of Ramadi, lit up under the night sky by tracer fire and explosions. Across the street, in the greenish glow of their night vision goggles, they saw a darkened three-story building lit up like a fireworks display. Tracers flashed from all over it like shooting stars, brief and blazing—from the roof, from the windows on every floor. The night echoed with the racketing staccato of gunfire.

"Fuck me," Conrad said. "Look at that."

"There's a million of them in there," Anderson said.

"I'm calling in air," Conrad said.

"Roger." Anderson slid down against the doorjamb, his rifle raised.

Conrad crouched, his back against the wall, to call the CO. The radio jittered with static, and he raised his voice. "Dingo Six, Dingo Six," he called, "this is Dingo Three Actual." He called in the request, putting his hand over his other ear to block out the gunfire and the static.

Anderson was turned away, facing the roof. Conrad was down on one knee, his head bent, listening. And then he was lying on his back on the floor and something heavy was pressing against his neck. He was looking up at a man's silhouette, and he could feel a foot braced against his jaw. A shadowy muzzle was pointed at his head.

The moment stopped. It bloomed around him, pure and vivid, like joy. He was aware of everything, the whole nighttime sky exploding beyond the roof, and Anderson, unaware, three feet away, and the dark stairwell. He felt everything: the heavy, abrasive surface against his jaw, and he was aware of the trigger. AK-47s were clumsy and inaccurate, but it wouldn't matter at point-blank range. It would take only the slightest crook of a finger, the merest, slightest pressure, for this rifle to fire. All these thoughts ran through his body like quicksilver. He was thinking about the Cobra pilot he'd just called, and also about what he was going to do, which was to grab the muzzle and shove it aside, kicking hard to bring the man down. And in that long, frozen moment before anything happened, he heard the sound of the rifle going off.

He waited for what came next: pain or darkness, and he wondered why the AK-47 sounded like an M16. Then everything started up again, and something was crashing down on him like a mountain, liquid heat coursing over him. Conrad was already rolling away, and the man was down, and Anderson was leaning over Conrad, saying, *"LT, you okay?"*

Conrad put his hand up to his face: he was covered in blood. It wasn't his. Amazingly, he could see beyond Anderson's head to the night sky, filled with stars. Everything was still going on. The tracers were still flashing past, though right then Conrad could hear nothing.

He scrambled up onto his knees and picked up the radio. His request had been granted, the Cobra had been diverted, and the pilot was calling.

"Dingo Three, Dingo Three," said the pilot, his voice crackling. "This is Bushmaster Eight, over."

"Bushmaster Eight," Conrad said, "I've got you Lima Charlie. How me, over." Lima Charlie stood for loud and clear.

"Roger, got you same," said Bushmaster Eight. "I'm checking on station with ten Hellfires and guns. How can we be of assistance?"

Conrad had heard the chuddering clatter of the Cobra over the radio, and now he began to hear it in the distance, approaching through the night.

"Be advised," Conrad said. "I have numerous insurgents in a building." He gave the grid coordinates. "Building is three-story, north side of street, near the intersection of Peter and Jennifer, how copy?"

"Good copy," said the pilot. "Searching now." The whacking rattle of the rotors grew louder. After a moment he said, "I copy sparkle at that location." He read the numbers again. "Do you tally my mark?"

The ghostly glow of an infrared spotlight illuminated a building two doors down. It was a cone of pale green, nearly white, shining down on the wrong side of the street. It was lighting the building where third squad was holed up.

"Move your sparkle north," he told the pilot, "one hundred meters. Other side of the street."

"Roger," said the pilot. The glow shifted to the roof across the street. "How tally?"

"You're on target," Conrad said.

"We recommend we engage with rockets, then follow up with guns."

"Good copy," Conrad said.

"Dingo Three Actual, are we cleared hot?" the pilot asked.

"Bushmaster Eight, you are cleared hot," Conrad said.

"Roger," said the pilot. "Coming in hot."

The Cobra let loose with a deafening, triumphant roar, lengthy and sustained, and the entire building disappeared into a slowly unfurling gray cloud lit by sulfurous red glares. The sound of it enveloped the night. Conrad felt his pulse beating in rhythm with the pounding thunder. His whole body was beating: wild survivor's glee.

"Yes!" Anderson yelled.

Roiling smoke billowed up, mounting against the dark sky.

Hours later, the Humvees drew up inside the wire, back at the firm base. Conrad dismissed the exhausted men as they dismounted. Anderson walked past him.

"Anderson," Conrad said. "I owe you one. Thanks."

Anderson took off his helmet. His face was black and filthy, his eyes pale and liquid against the grime. He shook his head and grinned. "That's not how it works, LT. We don't owe each other out here. We just do our jobs."

He was right and not right. Conrad owed Anderson that wild survivor's glee; he'd never forget it.

Now Conrad thought of Anderson swimming out into the blue lake in Minnesota. Heading across the water, going past the raft, nothing beyond but silence, shivering ripples of light. Anderson's hands would work in the water. Even if he couldn't bend the fingers, he could swim.

When Claire called back that afternoon, Conrad told her what he'd done.

"Fantastic!" she said, her voice full of excitement.

"Want to have dinner?" he asked.

He was certain he wanted to see her, but he hadn't worked out the rest.

First of all, there was the problem of venue: he didn't want to go to Claire's place and deal with the Roommates of the Sacred Towels. But it wasn't ideal bringing her to Jenny's apartment, either, where all he could offer was the rack, the foldout sofa in his sister's living room. But even if the venue weren't a problem, it raised the more prickly (so to speak) question, which was whether or not he could raise himself. Sometimes his cock worked and sometimes it didn't, which meant he didn't want to risk it.

"What if I come there?" Claire said. "I haven't seen Jenny in ages. I'll come over and bring Chinese takeout."

"Sounds good," said Conrad. "You bring, I pay."

"Perfect. See you later."

Conrad hung up, wondering about sex. Was she hoping to spend the night? Because she couldn't. The only thing worse than having wild sex on an iron-framed torturer's device, with his sister on the other side of the door, her pillow over her head, was being unable to have it.

Okay, he thought, *focus. Don't go there.* He changed into running clothes and headed off to the reservoir.

That evening, when the doorbell rang, he heard Claire's voice on the intercom, rough and staticky.

"Hello there!" she called cheerfully. "It's me!"

Conrad felt a lift, and he went down to meet her. He could hear her coming up as he went down, and they met on the third flight. She was running up toward him, her face raised. Her glossy hair was tumbled around her shoulders. She was wearing a blue jacket and carrying big white bags of takeout, and smiling at him.

Conrad took the bags and put his arms around her. He felt the strong curve of her back, her soft breasts against his chest. She was out of breath. He felt her breathing and glowing against him, her ribs lifting. She smelled sweet and tangy.

"I'm glad you're here," he said. He felt himself stir and harden against her and wondered if he should ask her to spend the night. Though he didn't dare; the little fucker couldn't be trusted.

Jenny was waiting in the doorway. When they came up, she threw her arms around Claire. "I'm so glad to see you!"

Conrad got a kick from women hugging. There was something sweet and mysterious about it: it came so easily to them, and they were so good at it. Claire and Jenny talked quickly and excitedly, affectionate, fizzing gently like little kettles. He wondered if they were friends on their own, apart from him.

Jenny brought out plates and they opened a bottle of wine. The little white cartons were full of clumped white rice, stewy messes of duck and chicken and pork, slithery vegetables.

"Oh, my god, I am starving," Jenny said. "This is so great."

She was sitting sideways on her chair, her knees pulled up close to her chest. She'd changed into a red T-shirt and gray sweatpants, but she still had on her earrings: tiny kites, bright red.

"I like your toenails," Claire said.

"Twilight in Moscow," Jenny said. She spread her toes wide like a monkey. The nails were deep purple.

"Twilight in Moscow?" Conrad repeated. "How about Late Afternoon in Namibia? Breakfast in Fallujah?"

"I know, really," Jenny said. "The names are bizarre. Who thinks them up?"

"The ad companies," Claire said. "Interns on pot. Did you do your nails yourself?"

Jenny shook her head. "A Thai place on Broadway."

"Why do you do that?" Conrad asked. "Why do women get their nails done?"

Jenny grinned. "It's someone taking care of you. You lie back and feel glamorous. You feel like a movie star."

"I'll give you one sometime," Claire said. "A mani-pedi. You'll love it."

Conrad looked dubious. "I'll let you know when I'm ready."

"One of our clients, a guy, got a pedicure. They took off too much cuticle and went too deep, and it got infected," Claire said. "He got blood poisoning. He was on crutches for months, and he's still on a cane. He could have died."

"The shame," Jenny said. "Dying of pedicure."

"You've got to give him credit," Conrad said. "The guy risked his life. He put it out there."

"True," Claire said, licking her fingers. "So, what's the class you're taking?"

"Macroeconomics," Conrad said, and shrugged. "What can I tell you?"

"I can hardly get my mind around economics," Claire said, "let alone macro."

"You develop models that show the way national economic systems work, figure out the way unemployment, inflation, savings, income, all that stuff works together. To produce the macro-vision."

"Better you than me," Claire said.

"I love this stuff," Jenny said. She sucked a finger. "Short ribs may be the perfect food."

Claire put down her fork and sighed, licking her lips. She had taken off the blue jacket and was wearing a black tank top and tight jeans. Her feathery earrings made a little fluttery cascade against her neck. "So," she said, "how are you, Jen? How's work?"

Jenny shook her head. "Bad. I'm going crazy."

"Why?" asked Conrad. This was news to him. Why hadn't she told him?

"My boss," Jenny said. "Ted Waits. He does this passive-aggressive thing. If we're in a meeting, he won't look at me. If I make a presentation, he doesn't pay attention. Sometimes he gets up and starts walking around, so everyone looks at him instead of me."

"What a nightmare," Claire said. "Is he like that with everyone else?"

"No. Only me," Jenny said.

"Did he hire you?" Conrad asked.

"That's the thing," Jenny said, pointing her fork at him. "No. I was hired by this totally cool woman, who left. Waits doesn't even like me."

"Bad," Conrad said. "You can't let him undermine your authority. You have to stand up to him."

"How?"

"If he stands up, look at him and ask him if there's something he would like to say."

"I can't do that," Jenny said. "He's my boss."

"Gotta show him your balls," Conrad said.

"That's the problem," Jenny said, nodding. "I haven't shown him my balls."

She and Claire began to laugh.

"You have to learn how to deal," Conrad said. "There will always be shitty bosses around. You have to know what to do."

Claire leaned toward him. Her neck and shoulders were bare, and in the hollows at the base of her neck were little blue shadows. She was sitting in that impossible girl way, one thigh crossed over the other, her feet facing different directions. She leaned toward him and put her hand on his arm.

"You're right," Claire said. "Until you get out of school, you're so used to having people around who will help you. You assume everyone will. But in the real world it's not like that. It was a shock for me to realize it. You're way ahead of me. You've been living in a different kind of world."

"Yeah—well," Conrad said. "Always assume someone's out to get you. Always be ready to use offensive strategy. Call in air support. QRF."

"What's QRF?" asked Jenny.

"Quick reaction force," Conrad said. "If you need help. It's like a Mayday call."

"Why is everything in the military called by acronyms?" asked Claire.

"Just to mess with your head," Conrad said.

"What I thought," Claire said. "It's all so insular, the military. Everything is kept from civilians. They keep everything from us, but I kind of have the feeling they also blame us for not understanding them. But how can we?"

"It's tribal." Conrad shrugged. "You're not part of it. And no, civilians can't understand. And we can't explain. It's not sayable."

"Because you don't want to say it?" asked Claire. "Or because you can't."

"Probably both," said Conrad. "Probably we don't exactly want to, because what we know, we've earned. But even if we try, we can't. It's like intraspecies communication."

"Very nice," Jenny said. "What are we, dolphins?"

"Don't be testy," Conrad said.

"Don't be smug," Jenny said.

"But, Con, you can tell us whatever you want," Claire said. "You know that."

"Thanks," he said. This kind of talk never went anywhere. There was nowhere for it to go. He got another bottle of wine from the kitchen.

The headache was hovering off his right temple, though he was ignoring it. He was ignoring it, though his head was beginning to pound as if someone were beating on it with a stick. He wondered if Claire would want to spend the night; he couldn't manage sex when the headache was there. And he didn't want to tell Claire that he didn't want sex because he had a headache. He opened the bottle and filled everyone's glasses.

"Let's talk about Go-Go," he said. "What's he up to? Claire, you need to send me his email address."

"Done." Claire pulled out her phone and tapped at it. "He's around. You should call him." She turned to Jenny. "This is a friend of ours," she began, "who was the most radical, out-there guy we knew."

"Let me guess," Jenny said. "He's now on Wall Street. Maybe we should all be on Wall Street."

When they had finished the second bottle, Claire pushed back her chair.

"Okay, guys," she said, "I'm going home. Early day tomorrow."

Relieved, Conrad asked, "You sure you don't want to stay?"

"No, I've got to go."

"I'm paying, remember," Conrad said, getting out his wallet.

"Okay, I'm whacked," Jenny said loudly. "I'm heading to bed right now." She stacked a load of dishes and took them out to the kitchen. "Good night, guys."

"What do I owe you?" he asked, feeling awkward.

"Forty," she said.

Paying made him uncomfortable. And now that Jenny had so ostentatiously given them privacy—she was banging loudly in the kitchen—now that he and Claire were left alone and it was the moment to ask her to stay, his cock was curled and inert against his leg. The headache beat sullenly at his temple.

"Sorry you can't stay," he said.

"Me, too. But not tonight." She smiled at him, pulling on her jacket. It was padded, with a high Chinese collar and little twisted tie-things instead of buttons.

"I'll take you down and put you in a cab." Conrad picked up the takeout bags and stuffed the empties into it.

On the sidewalk, they walked without speaking. The street was dim and shadowy, the air cool and damp, with a faint autumnal undertone. Their footsteps echoed against the stone housefronts. The streetlights shone down, bright stars on tall black columns. Above them the nighttime sky held the powdery glow that came from the city itself. The sidewalk was lit by the streetlamps, and the sky was illuminated by the city, but between them were the brownstones, dim and obscured, their dark façades rising up in the darkness to high black cornices against the sky. The lighting was dramatic, the acoustics intimate: it was like a stage set. Claire was close beside him, the light glinting off her hair.

"Do you ever see Jenny alone?" he asked suddenly. "I mean, apart from me?"

"No," she said. "Why? Would you mind?"

"No," he said. "I just wondered."

A man came toward them. He was in his thirties, unshaven, with a bland, open face. Despite the stubble he looked affluent: khaki pants, white T-shirt, dark blue running jacket zipped halfway up his chest.

When he was past, Conrad said, "What's the no-shaving deal? The stubble? All these guys look like losers."

"It's European," said Claire. "Or South American or something."

"One of the rules in the Corps is 'Eccentricity in mustaches will not be tolerated,'" said Conrad. "We take facial hair seriously."

"We?" said Claire. "Do you still think you're one? I thought you were out."

"I misspoke," Conrad said. "I'm out. I'm a former. I still don't like stubble."

He listened to their footsteps. He wondered suddenly if Claire was going on afterward to meet up with the Wall Street guy. He looked at her sideways. Once the idea was in his head, it seemed certain to be true. She hadn't looked at her watch, but why had she said she had to leave? It wasn't late, only just past ten.

Wouldn't she want to get laid at the end of the evening? Or didn't women care as much? You couldn't tell. You heard everything: women didn't care as much about sex as men did, which was a problem among lesbian couples, because each waited for the other to initiate. Or you heard that women actually cared exactly as much about sex as men did, but just didn't let on, because men didn't like women to initiate. Or that the big secret was that women actually liked sex more than men did. It was one of those things that was impossible to know. It was one of those things everyone lied about, so how would anyone know?

He'd read that women thought about sex two or three times a day; men, two or three times a minute. That sounded about right. Even in a combat zone. At Haditha, up the dam, it had been a lot quieter than at Sparta. The guys there mostly just stood guard duty, and it was boring. Two of them sent away for penis enlargement pills. They had a competition, measuring themselves every day, and then decided to take all the rest of the pills at once. They ended up with dicks so swollen they couldn't walk. What amazed everyone was not that they'd done it, but that the pills worked. The guys were actually in pain, but of course no one felt sorry for them. There were a lot of nicknames.

There he was again, thinking about sex.

"How's your brother doing?" Conrad asked.

"Howdy's fine," Claire said. "He's at Swarthmore."

"He always was a brain," Conrad said.

"He's an idealist," said Claire. "Wants to save the world."

"What do your parents think about that?"

"They support him." She looked at him. "Like your parents."

"Yeah." He didn't exactly think of himself as an idealist now.

"How are your parents?" she asked.

"Good," he said. "I'm going out to see them this weekend."

At the corner, Conrad stuffed the empty bags into a trash can and stepped off the curb, raising his hand. He looked at Claire. "Thanks for coming," he said.

"My pleasure," she said, and gave him a little smile.

Now he got it: she was making such a point of leaving on purpose so that he wouldn't have to worry about sex. She wanted him to know that she liked his company, she'd come over just for that. It was a gift she was giving him, and when he realized it, he felt again the lift of his heart.

A cab swerved toward them, sliding across the lanes and cutting off a delivery van and a small red sedan before jerking to a stop not quite in front of them. The chassis rocked, and the driver stared at them.

"Do you want this one?" Conrad asked. "Will you survive?"

Claire nodded, and he opened the door.

"I'm paying for the cab," he said, and pulled out his wallet again.

Claire slid past him, onto the back seat. Settled, she turned and smiled at him through the open door.

"No," she said. "You're not paying. That would make me feel like a hooker." She raised her hand and gave an odd wave, palm flat, her fingers opening and closing like a starfish. She waited for him to close the door, but he leaned in toward her.

"Thanks for coming." He meant for all of it, for thinking of it in the first place and bringing over those aromatic white bags of food, and for running up the stairs and turning her face up to him, smiling, and for the way her earrings made little whispery sounds against her beautiful smooth jaw, and the way her skin looked, supple and gleaming, and for the way she had put her hand on his arm, which had felt like a kind of forgiveness. He wanted to say he was sorry for not being able to get it up, sorry not to ask her to stay the night.

She smiled again and shook her head, and he kissed her briefly, just a child's kiss on her soft, sweet mouth, he couldn't risk anything else. Then he drew back and closed the door. She leaned forward to tell the driver where to go, her dark hair falling over the blue jacket, and he wondered again if she was going home or somewhere else. The driver pulled out right in front of a black town car that honked furiously and slammed on its brakes, and then the cab sped up and was lost in the weaving lanes of traffic.

Conrad turned and walked back down the street. When he reached Jenny's block, he saw the woman from next door standing on the sidewalk. The first time Conrad had seen her, he'd thought she was homeless, or maybe crazy. She had short whitish hair and she'd worn a raincoat over her nightgown, the folds showing below the hem. She'd stood motionless, staring down with a fixed psychotic gaze. It wasn't until Conrad was nearly past her that he'd seen the leash leading from her hand to the small, shaggy terrier straining at the end of it, nose pressed intently against a tree.

Now she was wearing her trench coat and her nightgown, flip-flops on her feet. He wondered if she owned any daytime clothes. The light from the streetlamp gave her a halo, irradiating her wild pale hair. One hand was sunk deep in her pocket, the other held the leash. The terrier was parked meditatively next to the streetlight, staring straight ahead, his ears pricked, his hind leg lifted.

Conrad nodded to the woman as he passed; she nodded back.

There you go, he thought. *I'm a member of the community.*

On the morning of his first class, Conrad woke early.

It wasn't quite light. It was September, and the days were growing shorter. In the dimness, Conrad pulled on a T-shirt and shorts, then sat down to put on his running shoes. He remembered putting on his boots at Sparta. In the dark, his hand knew exactly where they stood beside his bed. He knew the feel of the leather: smooth side in, rough side out. He thought of Carleton's boots at his memorial service, side by side on the gritty floor, helmet and rifle beside them. The roll call, and Carleton's name called out in the silence. By then Anderson was at Landstuhl.

The past, Conrad told himself, standing up. *That was the past.*

The thing was to stop letting these things into his mind. Unless he could just let them flow through until they ran out, dried up. Would they stop, eventually? Would he find himself living wholly in the present, getting dressed like this in the early dimness and finding this moment the real one, even though the past was so much more vivid? Even though the past was painted in those unbearable colors and the present was shadowy and colorless? Even though the past carried so much more weight and meaning?

But if the past was not so important, if he was meant to forget it and close himself off from it forever, then what had been the point? What was the point of what he'd done there? Olivera, Carleton, all of them?

Okay, though. That was the past. He was putting it behind him, he was pushing on.

He moved quietly to the front door, holding the knob so it wouldn't snap noisily shut. He jogged down the creaking stairs and landings. In the front hall, the light from the transom made a wide stripe on the stained marble floor. The hall was high-ceilinged, shadowy and secret. He opened the heavy door and stepped outside. It was a good moment: The cool air, the run waiting for him. The moment before the plunge.

He headed up the block. The street was quiet now. There was no traffic and only one or two people on the sidewalk, footsteps tock-tocking sharply in the crisp air. The woman from next door was standing outside. They nodded to each other and Conrad jogged up the block toward Broadway. He was heading east, toward Central Park, and the sun was still down near the horizon, its rays slanting low across the city. He ran toward the light. The streets were quiet, and once he passed inside the big red stone gates of the park, the air changed. It became soft and rich with the scents of autumn: damp earth, the deep, complicated smells of mold. *Season of mists and mellow fruitfulness.*

He reached the reservoir at its northwestern corner. A path led up the bank and onto the raised track that circled the water. On the track, he slid into the stream of runners.

A lot of people ran the reservoir in the early morning. They were mostly men, many in serious running gear: fancy shoes, crisp shorts, bright shirts with bold logos. Techie stuff: stopwatches and little strapped-on contraptions to measure distance and monitor heartbeats and cholesterol and every other thing.

There were women, too, most of them lean and taut-limbed, looking great in their running gear. Their clothes were more varied, regular loose shorts or black spandex shorts or knee-length tights. Tank tops or T-shirts, or those stretchy running bra–shirts with crossed straps that went halfway down the torso, flattening but revealing their breasts.

Girls always looked great, that was the thing. They always looked great, with their supple bodies and their flying hair. Even if they didn't know you and didn't want you and didn't want to know you, they still had those bodies and their unknowable interior selves, and unbelievably, they didn't mind showing you their wonderful bodies. They ignored you absolutely as you passed them or they passed you, headsets on, some private music or audiobook driving secretly into their brains, not giving you the time of day, but giving you, amazingly, complete privileges for looking at their entire bodies, top to bottom—tight, rounded asses; flat mounds of breasts; long, clean legs and pumping arms; smooth, supple backs. They jazzed up the whole world just by running around the reservoir in those tight, stretchy things, not looking at you, their expressions concentrated, their faces and necks slick with sweat, their arms and legs moving fast, their feet pounding on the soft track.

There was one woman he watched for. She had short blond hair and wore a pale green headband. She had long legs and wore loose, silky, colorful shorts or long spandex ones, usually one of those crossover tops. Conrad watched for the green headband among the bobbing heads. The crowd was loose, everyone bobbing along at their own pace. But when Conrad saw the green headband ahead, he began slowly to increase his stride until he caught up with it.

He'd been nearly through his first lap, up on the straight northern stretch, heading west for the stone pumping station, when he saw the bright flash of green. In front of him was a loose configuration, two women running side by side (women often ran together, men almost never), then several people alone. It was a slalom course. Conrad lengthened his stride and moved on the inside past the first two, then pushed on until he was parallel with the next runner. This was a short guy in glasses, wearing a white handkerchief tied around his forehead and an expression of desperation.

"Sorry," Conrad said, and the guy moved over. His mouth was open, as though he were being tortured. Conrad wondered if this was his first run ever.

Conrad moved past Desperate, then slid around the next runner, a plump woman with thick, dry hair and bright red matching shorts and jacket. She was barely running at all, just moving at a lively shuffle along the dirt track.

"On your left," Conrad said, and she gave him a heroic smile without moving her head. He ran past, then around the next runner. He kept moving through the fluid crowd until he was behind Pale Green. He liked watching her run. She had smooth tan legs, a floating stride, and a fast pace. She looked focused and committed. Most people looked as though they were in agony. Conrad had never spoken to her; he'd hardly ever looked her directly in the face. You didn't, running, you were always facing forward.

He ran behind her. They were following the long curve of the water's edge as the sun rose, sending bright shafts across the water. The massed trees along the western shore were suddenly illuminated, the sun striking them into green clouds of glory. Ahead of him, the girl ran without slowing, her brown arms bent loosely, pumping hard, her stride long and tireless. Her back was brown, and gleamed moistly. She never slackened. Her face, when he'd glimpsed it, was sober and expressionless. She didn't wear a headset, either. She was just there, pounding along fast, carrying out a goal. Right in the thick of it, running fast, pushing herself. He loved that.

Conrad followed her for five laps. When he approached the pumping station again, he swerved right, swooping down off the raised track that stretched around the water. He ran down the little bank and onto the grass. He felt good.

He liked pushing himself. At OCS, being pushed felt at first like harassment, but as they'd grown stronger, it became a matter of pride. And pushing yourself, striving, was part of something larger. Conrad, alone, just doing this, just running the New York City reservoir, was part of a long history of Marines pushing themselves, sweating on the PT deck, climbing the ropes, storming the heights. It was the challenge. Conrad liked this, his body sweaty and hot and loose, heart pounding, lungs pumping, everything working.

He ran back across the park, through the stone gateway, and onto the sidewalk. He kept running. When he reached a red light, he jogged in place, waiting for it to change, unwilling to give up the thrumming beat throughout his body. Once, he'd seen a runner in the park meet a pair of friends who were walking. The runner stopped to greet them, but he wouldn't stop running, and he jogged in place as they talked. The walker introduced the runner to his girlfriend. The bobbing jogger put out his hand to shake hers, and the woman took it and out of courtesy began to jog in place, too. For a moment the two of them faced each other, hands clasped, bobbing up and down. Then he released her, she stopped jogging, he went on with his run, and the couple went on with their walk.

When Conrad reached Jenny's block, the day had begun. The sounds were louder and brasher: the roar and clank of trucks and buses, the honks and panting of traffic. The city was awake and at work. Conrad let himself into the dark front hall and took the stairs two at a time.

Jenny was in the kitchen. She was wearing oversize pink flannel pajamas, standing at the table and holding a bowl of granola close to her chest. She raised her spoon at him.

"Hola," she said.

"Hi there." Conrad sat down to take off his shoes.

"How was it?" Jenny asked.

"Good," Conrad said. "I like running the reservoir. Half of New York is out there. It's cool."

Jenny nodded.

"Are you about to use the shower?" Conrad asked. "I can wait."

"I'm about to jump in," Jenny said. "If that's okay."

"No problemo," Conrad said. "I'll wait."

"Today's your first class?"

He nodded. "Four-ten. Mathematics Hall."

"Sounds good," she said.

When she came back out, she was dressed for the day: black T-shirt, bright blue tights, and a striped miniskirt. The big earrings were neon-blue concentric circles.

"I'm heading out," she said. "I'll see you later. Good luck with the class."

"Thanks," he said.

She was gone, clattering down the stairs.

Conrad showered and shaved. In his underwear, he fixed cereal and sat down to read his email. Answering the men was still the main event of his day, though from now on it would be different.

There was a message from Anderson.

Hey LT. I'm still on the job. Glad to have it, cuz I hear a lot of vets are having trouble getting work. It's ok. I don't have to see many people or talk to them, most of the day I'm alone. Kind of weird being out on the roads alone, can't imagine doing that back in-country but its ok. I tried the volunteer thing but it didn't work out. I had to be certified in some way or other, if I was going to actually talk to the kids. They asked me to come and give a speech about being in Iraq at the high school, but I didn't want to. I don't know what to say about it, any of it, is the fact. Do you ever talk about it? It's like a giant country, like a whole fucking continent, that I'm carrying around on my back and don't know what to do with. Let me know what's happening in New York. I miss everyone, weird but true. Anderson.

Conrad answered everyone right away. He still felt connected. He was no longer planning duty rotations and missions, but he still felt responsible and he liked hearing from them.

He was puzzled by what he was hearing from Anderson, who was not a complainer; Conrad couldn't tell if he was in trouble or not. He wrote back.

Anderson. Hey, it's good to hear from you. Glad you're still on the job. Driving a truck without worrying about IEDs and the muj must be hard to imagine. Actually I find myself doing evasive action without realizing it. I scared my mom, driving out on the highway. A white sedan came up on one side and I started swerving like a madman at 70 mph. She nearly jumped out of the car. I felt bad for scaring her, but that still feels like normal driving. I have to keep reminding myself it's not. It's an effort. And I know what you mean about finding it hard to talk about. I hardly talk about it at all. It's hard being back and trying to think like a civilian. I hope you're having an ok time with it. I know some guys are struggling. Keep in touch. Farrell.

There was a brief message from Ollie:

Yo, bro,, wassup? This semester is way better, way. Like my profs, like my classes. Have you heard the Blood Lambs? Vry cool I think. Why don'[t you come up? Yah, O.

Conrad had no idea who the Blood Lambs were.

Yo, O. Cant keep up w/ yr music. Don't know the Blood Lambs. Glad to hear the semester is better. Are you in Mandarin II? Better housing? What? All quiet here. My class begins today. Glad to get started. Yah, C.

When he was finished with the emails, Conrad officially started the day. He got dressed, made the bed, and sat down in one of the giant upholstered chairs with the GMAT review book. It was a big fat heavy paperback with a blue cover and ocher-colored lettering. A red starburst announced that it was *The Official Guide*. Conrad planned to study two hours a day with it, more if necessary. He began flipping through the pages.

If ^ represents one of the operations +, −, and ×, is k ^ (l + m) = (k ^ l) for all numbers k, l, and m?

1) k ^ 1 is not equal to 1 ^ k for some numbers k.
2) ^ represents subtraction.

Okay, he'd need to brush up on math.

He'd start off with the Diagnostic Test—that would let him know which areas he should focus on. Quantitative: money being spent over a period of months, water flowing into a reservoir, integers and prime numbers. The way that mathematics turned the world into a magic realm of quantities, a huge turning face made up of millions of tiny tiles that clicked into place. He could hear that infinitesimal sound as the right answer revealed itself, set perfectly in the vast mosaic of logic. It was logic that drove all of this, a perfect celestial chorus of logic, calm and absolute. There was no margin. There was only one right answer to any of these. You were with the system or you were against it. He felt as though he'd gotten inside the mechanism of a clock, tiny thrumming wires strung taut all around him. He needed to take a breath, get outside this. Make the logic his own.

> The average (arithmetic mean) of the integers from 200 to 400, inclusive, is how much greater than the average of the integers from 50 to 100, inclusive?

He took out a pen.

He could do this, it was just logic. It was just figuring out the approach. He could do it all right. The headache was beginning to hover over his right eye. He could do this. Something had gotten inside his head and was beginning to rattle around in there, something silent and weightless, like a black laser light that flickered and glanced. He reread the question, squinting at it. It was better if he kept his right eye closed. He put one hand over his eye. He knew he could do this. It was a question of focus.

After forty minutes he closed the book, though he had done only three problems. The headache had moved in and taken over the territory. Inside his head it was like a factory, crowded and noisy, throbbing and thundering. He could hardly hear anything else, the sound drowned out everything. It was painful to turn his head. He closed his eyes and set his hands on the arms of the chair as though he were about to be electrocuted. All this—making himself follow that complicated pathway of logic—had started a pounding drumbeat in his brain. The headache was in full stride now, the throb strong and steady, like a silent engine. He sat still and waited for it to subside.

Okay, he told himself. *Okay.* He counted, breathing. Long, slow breaths.

Later he washed the dishes and set off early for the campus. He wanted to be the first in the room.

Conrad walked up Broadway and in at 116th Street, where the passageway led to the Morningside campus. In the interior was an open space several blocks long, grass and paved walkways. Around the perimeter were tall brick buildings with neoclassical details: busts, cornices. Names were carved on their façades: Socrates, Homer, Leonardo, Shakespeare, Milton. The Williams campus had been huge, more or less the whole of Williamstown, buildings and fields and lawns sprawled out across the landscape. This felt like an urban cloister. The sense of enclosure made him uneasy: there were few escape routes. Crowds were bad enough; crowds in an enclosed space were worse.

A loose surge of students moved along the paved walkway. Conrad joined them. They seemed decades younger, with their fresh faces and sloppy clothes, untied sneakers, careless gestures. These crowds were different from the ones on the street. On the street, people were guarded and composed, self-protective. But here the students were relaxed and inattentive, heedless. They walked along, listening to headsets, talking on cell phones, texting, ignoring everything around them. He wanted them to pay attention. There was no cover along this walkway.

A girl walked toward him. She was wearing a ruffled pink blouse and skintight jeans, looking at something in her hand. She had tousled black hair and wore a headband with a big polka-dotted bow. She walked with quick, small, sure steps, not even looking up. As she neared him, she smiled at what she saw in her hand, and started to laugh. Conrad came into her peripheral vision, and she looked up, her face blank. She swerved around him and looked down again at her hand.

It was none of his business, how she walked. No one had asked him to tell civilians how they should act. But why didn't they know?

He began to sweat slightly. He could feel it on his face, the shirt starting to stick to his back. It was September, still hot. The sun was lowering, but the day's heat had gathered in the bricks and mortar of the buildings, and now they were radiating, giving it back. It wasn't really hot here, not compared to the real heat, but Conrad began to sweat. He didn't like the crowds, and he didn't like the way the kids were so reckless, and he didn't like the way he couldn't ignore that. And he was frightened by what had happened to his mind while he was taking the Diagnostic Test.

He was headed for Mathematics Hall. He could see it now, a tall, handsome neoclassical brick building with white doors and trim, on the northwestern side of the campus. Conrad was about halfway across the quad, on the exposed walkway. Next time he'd walk along the side or up along Broadway.

Something heavy crashed against his back, and Conrad whirled, crouching, his hands raised and ready, his heart racing.

A kid in jeans and a T-shirt had staggered backward into him. His back was to Conrad, and now he lurched against Conrad a second time. Another kid was pursuing him, a taller kid with wild dark hair and black-rimmed glasses. The one who'd crashed into Conrad was short and solid, with sleek mouse-colored hair and too-long khaki pants. He was trying to evade his pursuer, twisting and writhing, falling backward.

"Hey," Conrad said. He stepped forward. Mouse Hair had given up, his shoulders hunched, his head down. His hands were raised like paws in front of his chest, trying to fend off the other's pummeling. Conrad moved between them and reached for Black Glasses, who was punching and flailing at Mouse Hair. Conrad grabbed Black Glasses by the shirtfront and saw his face change from feckless grin to frozen, frowning consternation. Conrad was still moving, still in the process of lifting Black Glasses up into the air when it hit him: Mouse Hair was laughing. He was choking and breathless with laughter. They both were. They weren't even fighting. They hadn't even noticed Conrad. Black Glasses looked horrified.

Conrad raised his hands, palms out. "You guys fighting, or what?"

"No," Mouse Hair said, moving away from him. "Sorry."

"Careful where you're going," Conrad said. His chest had become too small.

"Sorry," said Black Glasses. He looked as though Conrad had suddenly declared himself Martian.

"Okay, okay," said Conrad. He bowed his head, blinking, his hands still held high, to make some sort of formal ending to this. He felt sick to his stomach. The two students moved stiffly away ahead of him, awkward, watchful, as though they were not allowed to look at each other.

The adrenaline was still pumping through his chest. Around him everyone kept walking, flooding along the pavement. No one paid any attention to what had happened. Actually nothing had happened: these were just kids, roughhousing. Conrad stood motionless for a moment, his heart racing. He'd been hit from behind, he'd been ready to go. He wanted to shout, kick someone's ass, but there was no one to shout at. They were kids, fooling around. He stood still on the sidewalk while everyone flowed around him as though he weren't there.

Inside Mathematics Hall was a long corridor with a high, curved ceiling. The sound of voices bounced shrilly, high and distorted. Conrad headed down the hall to the stairs, in the midst of a milling crowd. They pressed around him. *Relax,* he told himself. *These are your people now.* They didn't seem like his people, they seemed part of another race. He suddenly had the feeling that he was wearing cammies, sweaty and filthy MARPATs. So everyone could see he wasn't one of them. He had to glance down surreptitiously to reassure himself.

The stairwell was large and square, open all the way up to the top floor. The steps were worn linoleum, and wooden handrails lined the walls. Conrad joined the throng going up. The stairway was the most dangerous place in any building. You could never see around the next corner. The point man on a stairwell was at greatest risk: the stairwell was where you got shot.

As Conrad went up, he found that he was holding his textbook in front of him, his arm tilted at a familiar angle. He was holding his book the way he would carry his rifle. Embarrassed, he lowered it. A few steps later he found he'd raised it again.

The classroom was empty when he arrived. It was a modern interior, a long, windowless rectangle with three projection screens. The room was lined with desk-armed chairs. There were about a hundred, he thought. There were eighty students in the class.

Conrad sat in the last row. He had planned to sit in front. He had planned to introduce himself to the professor, but now he didn't want to go up there. He was still feeling uneasy, and he didn't like the fact that there were no windows in the room. There was no way out except through the back door. At the end of class he'd introduce himself, but right now he wanted to stay where he was, with his back to the wall, near the door.

He watched the students as they came in. It was an advanced course—intermediate macroeconomics—so the students were pretty geeky. Most of them wore glasses, short-sleeved shirts, the proverbial plastic pen protector in the breast pocket. So did that mean he himself was geeky? Could you be both geeky and a Marine? He was pretty sure they were mutually exclusive. Still, he was here taking an econ class, and not in Afghanistan, climbing a mountain after *dushman*. He had to admit this was a swerve toward geekdom.

The students were mostly men, which bore out the stereotype. He wondered if women were really less good at math than men were. Or were they secretly really good at math but somehow intimidated by it? Or by engineering programs, physics labs, investment houses? This seemed unlikely to Conrad, since he thought that women were generally not intimidated by anything. Of course, you couldn't come out and say that women weren't good at math, because if you did, they would rip you limb from limb. Which would further demonstrate that they were unintimidated, but not that they were good at math.

A dark-skinned guy, maybe Indian, wearing black pants and a short-sleeved white shirt, turned into Conrad's row. He shuffled past to sit down on the far side. He nodded at Conrad. Definitely geeky: metal-rimmed glasses, a pen protector. Conrad nodded back, geek to geek.

Just before class time, someone who could only be Dr. Titchmarsh came in from the hall. She was plump and middle-aged, with a round head and short brown hair. She wore narrow glasses and carried a briefcase. She wore a red dress with a full skirt, and a dark sweater was draped over her shoulders. She was physically rather maternal, but her manner was brisk. She walked up to the podium. The room quieted. She took a few moments to take out her notes, adjust the microphone, and look around the room. Then she began to speak.

"Good afternoon," she said. The room was now nearly full, the students silent, their notebooks open on their desks. "Welcome to intermediate macroeconomics." She spoke with a slightly nasal Midwestern accent. "This semester we're going to explore some of the large issues that drive international economics. In order to understand them, we're going to develop models that explain relationships between such factors as national income, output, consumption, unemployment, inflation, savings, investment, international trade, and international finance."

Professor Titchmarsh spoke into the microphone, looking up periodically at the students.

"Output, employment, and inflation," she said. "Let's start with them."

Conrad felt the headache hovering near him. For an hour and a quarter he listened, carefully taking notes. Most of the time he understood what she was saying and wrote it down, but when she began to explain a theory about international trade reciprocity, something went wrong in his head, as though a gear had suddenly missed a tooth and didn't connect. He couldn't get traction on the idea. He watched Professor Titchmarsh talking. She gestured with her right hand and pushed her glasses up on her nose. On the screen was a graph with an angular rising line. He knew the words she was using, but he couldn't make sense of them. He could feel them streaming over him as though he were lying in a river pool. As he listened and struggled with the meaning—as though she had begun speaking Chinese—he understood that he was losing these moments, losing forever whatever it was she was saying. He knew that the longer it took him to get back to the place of comprehension, the more he was losing. He fought the rising panic and kept writing down the words she was saying, though he didn't know what she meant. He kept writing in the hope that later he'd be able to make sense of the notes.

As he wrote, he made himself breathe slowly. Then he looked up and listened hard. He made himself focus on what the words meant. In a moment he entered again into the stream, to his immense relief, and he could understand it. She had switched back to English. What was frightening was that he could slip so easily out of comprehension. It seemed there was no safety net; he could slide over the edge, right off the mountain.

By the end of the class, Conrad had fifteen pages of scrawled equations and comments, and a pounding headache. He stayed at his desk, waiting for everyone to leave. He looked down at his notebook, flipping back and forth as though he were finishing up something. The Geek, beside him, was clearly waiting for him to rise. But finally the Geek stood up, nodded, and shuffled past. Conrad stayed. He didn't want to be part of the crowd bottlenecking at the door. He wanted to be the last to leave. He'd introduce himself next time.

20

Adam Turner wrote back:

We went to see Abbott's girlfriend, the stripper. Her act. We sat in the back and she did a kind of pole dance. I don't think she saw us, but now we know her tits. So now it's really weird seeing her. She's here all the fucking time. We come in to the house and she's lying on the couch watching Oprah.

Conrad wrote to Turner:

Dog, I think it's time for an intervention. All of you get together and meet with the stripper and tell her nicely that she can't be ly9ing there on the couch in the afternoon when you come in. At least nott with her clothes on.

Conrad emailed Go-Go and two weeks after classes started they had dinner together. They met at a small Italian restaurant in the East Sixties, near Go-Go's apartment. The restaurant stretched along First Avenue, though the entrance was on the side street. When Conrad arrived, the headwaiter stepped toward him from the bar. He was Romanian, thin and hollow-chested, with a bulging forehead and black vampire's eyes. He wore a black suit, a limp black tie, and an unpressed white shirt. His manner was both fawning and sinister, like an unctuous Dracula who'd be grateful for the chance to slit your carotid artery. A lock of heavy, dull black hair hung over the disturbing forehead.

"Good evening," Dracula said with an awful smile.

"Good evening," Conrad said. "My name is Farrell. I'm meeting Mr. Russell. I see him over there, thanks." He waved to Go-Go, and Dracula bowed.

Go-Go stood up as he came over, stepping forward to clap his shoulder.

"My man! You're back!" he said. "How've you been?"

Conrad grinned and looked him up and down.

Go-Go had, spectacularly, morphed into the enemy. He wore round horn-rimmed glasses, a tweed jacket, and a gleaming silky white shirt from somewhere much fancier than Brooks Brothers. His khakis had a knife-edge fold, and his brown tassel loafers were polished and gleaming. He wore no socks.

"Who is this guy?" Conrad asked. "I thought I was going to see my old radical friend Gordon Russell, who so violently hated the Establishment. Where is that man, the one with the sixteen earrings and the grunge band?"

Go-Go grinned. "That man is no more." They sat down. "He is no more. I have taken his place."

Dracula appeared before them, his hands folded like a nun's. "Could I bring you two gentlemen something to drink?"

Conrad ordered a beer, but Go-Go leaned back and smiled at Dracula. He wanted a Bombay Sapphire martini, with three ice cubes and this much tonic, only this much.

When Dracula left, Conrad laughed. "Bombay Sapphire," he said, shaking his head. "You are a new person, dude. So tell me, how's it going on Wall Street?"

"I have to tell you," Go-Go said, "it's actually very cool. To my amazement. Very very cool. Cool as shit."

"You love it?" Conrad asked.

"I love it. Love the action," Go-Go said.

Go-Go had smooth skin, very pale, and thick dark brown hair. He had a short upper lip, which revealed, when he smiled, straight, large beaverlike teeth. The horn-rimmed glasses made him look like a professor in an old movie.

"What about the guys you work with?" Conrad asked. He couldn't imagine Go-Go hanging out with Wall Street guys. "Are you in the shark tank?"

"I am one with the sharks, dude," Go-Go said solemnly, and they both laughed. "I swim with the sharks."

"You always swam with the sharks," Conrad said.

"Always." Go-Go nodded.

Go-Go had been a kind of radical, but also kind of a weenie. He was too likable and friendly, too good-natured, to be a real radical. Hard to believe that he'd become a real shark.

"You still playing music?" Conrad asked.

"Not anymore, man." Go-Go shook his head regretfully. "Sharks don't like it."

"What do you actually do down there?" Conrad asked. He wondered if he was sounding contemptuous. Was he contemptuous? Was he actually jealous? Before Go-Go could answer—and he was too nice to notice it even if Conrad was being contemptuous—one of Dracula's minions arrived, a small, unshaven, balding fiend, and they ordered dinner.

Their dinner arrived, tepid risotto and congealed pasta. Go-Go said, "Sorry about the food. I told you, it's not a good restaurant. That's why it's so easy to get a table."

"Gotcha." Conrad nodded. "So, what's up on Wall Street?"

Go-Go explained, though Conrad followed only part of it: derivatives and bundling and mortgage-based securities.

"It's a gold mine, actually," Go-Go said. "A license to print money."

"So why didn't anyone do this before?"

"Securities law," Go-Go said. "The Feds finally got smart and let the banks do what they're best at. Now everyone wins: anyone can get a mortgage, and we can lend them the money. You can't lose with it. It's genius."

Conrad was only half listening. He was wondering if this was what he should have done, gone to B-school and then to a Wall Street bank or brokerage house and started printing money. And he was distracted by the noise and the people, the waiters moving back and forth through the crowded tables. He told himself to relax and get used to it. Walk the walk.

Wasn't something wrong with this picture, though? That Go-Go, whose ear still held all those multiple piercings, should be sitting across from him now, wearing a shirt made of Egyptian cotton, his handmade tassel loafer dangling from his bare foot while he talked knowledgeably about mortgage-backed securities, while Conrad was struggling with panic attacks, worrying about a single econ course, and trying not to dive under the table when a delivery truck backfired in the street? It wasn't Go-Go's fault that this was the way things were, but wasn't something fucked-up here?

When they were sitting over tiny cups of bitter, lukewarm coffee, Go-Go cleared his throat, and Conrad knew what was coming. In a different voice, slightly tense, he asked, "So, how was it over there?"

Conrad shrugged and smiled at him. "Hard to say."

"You must have some stories," Go-Go said.

"Yeah," Conrad said. His smile now felt like someone else's, clamped onto his face.

Go-Go waited, his loafer jiggling, but Conrad said nothing more.

"Okay, sorry," Go-Go said. He sent Conrad a serious look, to show he got it.

Conrad nodded, to show he got that Go-Go got it.

He didn't like being asked, though he didn't like not being asked. He didn't like scrutiny, though he also didn't like invisibility.

Okay, he was a dick. He was working on it.

The following week, Conrad asked Jenny to come out to Katonah with him for the weekend. He would be under less scrutiny with her there, he thought, and it worked. On Friday night they all watched a World War II thriller, and on Saturday he and Jenny ran the reservoir together in the morning, thudding along in companionable silence, passing the shimmering water, blinking through clouds of gnats hovering in the still air. In the afternoon he and Jenny played Scrabble. On Saturday night they all had dinner together. They finished eating and sat on, talking, the green lamp throwing its intimate glow over the honey-colored table.

"So, how's Claire?" Lydia asked.

"She's good," Conrad said.

"How are things between you?" she asked.

"Mom, just because you're a therapist it doesn't mean Conrad's your patient," Jenny said. She crossed her two index fingers at her mother to ward her off. "Intrusive question."

"I'm his mother!" Lydia said. "I'm allowed to ask him how he's doing."

Jenny rolled her eyes and shook her head.

"It's okay," Conrad said. "I don't know how we're doing, Mom. I think it's good. It's hard to say. We see each other a lot, but not all the time."

"It must be hard to keep things going through everything," Lydia said. "Deployment, then coming back."

"It's hard to keep things going no matter what," Jenny said.

"So how are you and Jock doing?" Lydia asked, turning to look at her.

"Okay, sorry I mentioned it." Jenny flapped her hand in front of her face. "I'm not answering. I just mean, of course it's hard. Getting together with anyone is hard."

"Give me a break, Jen, okay?" Lydia said. "Let's just suppose I'm trying to let Conrad feel comfortable if he wants to talk about it."

Jenny looked at the ceiling.

"Yeah," Conrad said. "A lot of couples break up when the guys come home. Marriages, too."

"Did you have guys in your platoon who were married?"

"Some," Conrad said.

"Wow. So young," Lydia said.

"Some of them were sergeants, so they were older and had been in for a while. But some of them were really young. It was a tough way to start a marriage. The guy is living a whole different life, and he can't say anything about it to his wife."

"I hadn't thought of that," said Jenny.

Conrad shrugged. "What's the point? 'Our convoy was blown up yesterday, and a guy lost both his legs?' I didn't tell you guys much. You just scare everyone at home, and it doesn't do any good. So the guy writes about some joke someone played, or how he remembers going swimming with his wife, or whatever. Nothing about his real life there. Sometimes the wife hangs in, sometimes she doesn't. She doesn't know what the guy's going through. Sometimes they hardly even knew each other before he left. She doesn't know what's coming home to her. One guy came back and found his house empty. His wife, kids, furniture, all gone. Bank account cleaned out."

"Holy moly," said Jenny.

"What happened to him?" asked Lydia.

"The guys in his team took turns, kind of kept him on a suicide watch until they figured he was okay."

"Suicide watch," Marshall said. "Jesus."

Conrad shrugged. "Occupational hazard."

"Doesn't the VA do something?" Lydia asked. "Offer counseling or anything?"

"When you come home, you fill out a mental health form that asks if you've thought about killing yourself," Conrad said. "Everyone says no."

"What if they say they're fine then, but later realize they're not?" Marshall asked.

Conrad shrugged. "The whole Marine ethic is that you're tough. You can take anything. You don't ask for emotional help. That's the one place you're on your own."

Marshall nodded. "So there's no way out. You can't ask for help."

"Not really," Conrad said. "Marines can't say they're in trouble. Not if they still think of themselves as Marines."

Lydia leaned back and crossed her arms on her chest. "I really don't like hearing this."

Conrad shook his head. "Not much you can do, Mom."

"But if you were in trouble, Con, could you go to the VA?"

"Sure, anyone can," Conrad said. "But I've heard they have months-long waiting lists, and then what they do if you see someone is give you drugs."

"If one of your guys was in trouble, what would you do?" asked Lydia.

Conrad shook his head. He rubbed his palms on his thighs. "I'd talk to him, try to get him some help. But I'm not sure how much the VA really does." His neck felt hot, and he twisted his head from side to side as though to loosen the joint.

"Okay," Lydia said. "What about dessert?" She stood and began to stack the plates.

"Who won that Scrabble game, by the way?" Marshall asked.

"Con did," Jenny said. "Three out of five. But only by using some very iffy words."

"Iffy?" Conrad said, raising his eyebrows. "Oh, and how would you describe 'oxer'?"

"A totally real word," Jenny said. "Totally normal and legitimate."

"Though not in the dictionary."

"Everyone who rides horses knows what it means," said Jenny. "It's a jump. It's a famous and very well-known jump."

"Oxer." Conrad shook his head.

The weekend went pretty well. Conrad made himself talk to his parents, made himself pretend there was no gap between them. If he acted as though it didn't exist, eventually it would disappear.

Things went well, except for the nights.

There was still the problem of sleeping. Each night he woke up sweating and frightened. He turned on the light and found himself in that room, with the low beds and the uneven lampshade, the crammed bookshelves and tattered posters. It was like a cave: he hated the long, narrow space, hated the low, uneven ceiling, the slanting eaves, the small windows. But he told himself to focus. He breathed slowly, counting, and the minutes kept ticking past, each one bringing him closer to dawn.

21

One Saturday in mid-October, Conrad met Claire at the Metropolitan Museum on Eighty-first Street. The air was chilly and damp, the sky gray and overcast, with a pale scumbling of clouds. Conrad arrived early.

The museum stretched alongside Fifth Avenue for three blocks, a long, low, massive building on a heroic scale. A series of wide, shallow flights of steps led up to the entrance of three triumphally arched doorways. The Italianate architecture declared its connection to Rome, the Renaissance, and an imperial culture. The handsome façade, elevated and removed from the street, suggested power, discretion, and entitlement. This sort of museum, which owned vast quantities of art and objects from elsewhere, was rooted in the period of cultural colonialism, when anyone from a rich country could buy anything they liked from a poor country and carry the booty home and call it a collection. Now things were different: poorer countries were not so poor, and they had changed their minds about who owned what. They declared ownership of their cultural heritage, and they wanted everything back. But had it become part of the cultural heritage of the country that had housed it for so long? Who was to say how ownership is defined? Who is the real owner of the great horses of St. Mark's Square in Venice? How far back does ownership reach? The tides of booty surge back and forth across the globe, rising and falling in the wake of warfare and conquest. In Iraq, museums were looted immediately after the invasion, and who knows where the collections went, and under what conditions? Protection was never certain. Hadn't Bill Gates bought the

Bettmann Archive and then buried it under Iron Mountain in western Pennsylvania to protect the photographs? What if there was an earthquake or some underground leak? Lord Elgin had taken those marble carvings from Athens and put them in a safe place in London.

In any case, the museum now housed one of the great collections of the world, stretched out between Fifth Avenue and Central Park like a great bulwark of culture. Conrad was on his way to see an exhibition of Scythian gold, on loan from the Hermitage. It was Claire's idea.

He jogged up the steps and stood outside the closed doors. Below him, knots of people gathered on the steps and on the sidewalk—faintly festive, anticipatory, all waiting for the museum to open. A school group clustered in a corner, teenagers, all eyeing one another and pretending not to. The girls were wearing skintight jeans and those sheepskin boots that everyone wore, their heads anxiously lowered, everything fixed and rigid, hands jammed into their pockets, jackets zipped up to their chins. The guys were loose and shambly, in hooded sweatshirts, unzipped or half zipped. Their too-long jeans dragged on the sidewalk.

The trees along Fifth Avenue were losing leaves, the striated trunks and twisted limbs standing out a vivid black against the dull grays of the cobblestone sidewalk. Across the street was a line of elegant town houses, all detailed and ornamented: molded cornices, curving stone steps, glossy painted trim. On the avenue, buses droned past heavily, lurching to a stop in front of the museum. People clambered awkwardly down the steps onto the sidewalk; others stood waiting to board. The buses panted, pulled themselves together, and thundered southward. On the sidewalk, passersby moved briskly. A dog walker passed, at the center of a loose constellation of dogs, all of different breeds and sizes, all trotting peacefully, silky tails up, silky ears down.

Claire was early, too. Conrad saw her as she stood on the far side of the avenue, waiting for the light. She wore a long down jacket, dark red, and jeans. Her hair was loose on her shoulders, and around her neck was a bright red scarf. *Look at me,* he thought, willing her to feel his thought. *Look at me.* She turned and looked downtown, then up again at the light. When it changed, she started across. Behind her was a Latino couple, teenagers, holding hands. *Look at me.* Claire crossed the street, peacefully unaware of his scrutiny. Reaching the near sidewalk, she skirted the high school students and started easily up the stairs. Her hands were in her pockets. As she started up the last flight, she looked up suddenly, as though his thought had finally reached her. She looked directly into his eyes and broke into a smile.

"There you are," she said, and held him in her gaze as she walked on up the steps.

She came close, and they kissed briefly. Her cheek was silky and cool. He thought of how her long hair used to hang down over her parka, shimmering. He wasn't sure how he was going to begin this conversation. He wished she had looked at him when he'd first sent her the thought. A guard pushed open the heavy bronze outer doors and locked them into place with a reserved and imperial manner. He didn't speak or look at anyone, but the crowd outside understood that they were now permitted to enter the museum.

The entrance hall was huge, with stone floors and walls and a lofty, echoing ceiling. The scale was vast and godlike; human voices were lost in the great space. It was both overwhelming—individuals had no power here—and exhilarating. The institution, which felt very much like a temple, seemed powerful and distinguished. If you were someone who trusted museums, you were in the right place.

They paid the entrance fee and were rewarded with small metal buttons that they fixed to their collars. They set off up the triumphal marble steps under the vaulted ceilings. The scale and the great spaces were silencing. No one spoke; Conrad wondered if this was the right place for their conversation. Reaching the second floor, they followed signs through hallways and galleries, past huge historical paintings, panoramas of wars and rapes, coronations and weddings and peace treaties; past cases of glowing china, greens and pinks and blues, platters and bowls; past walls of photographs, someone's project on Appalachia, ruined hillsides and lively faces—finally arriving, through a narrow off-center doorway, at the exhibition of Scythian gold. At the entrance was a stand of catalogs and books, posters, bright commercial clutter. Headsets for rent. Conrad asked Claire if she wanted the headset.

She shook her head. "I just like to look at the objects."

A relief: What if she'd said yes? How could he have the conversation?

They moved into the first gallery. Rows of transparent cases stood along the walls, glitter within them. Near the doorway stood a dignified black guard, tall and heavyset. He wore a brown uniform, and at his belt was a walkie-talkie. Conrad wondered who he had for backup: What if a SWAT team showed up for all this loot? Russian gangsters? Who did the Met have on call?

The gallery was not full. Maybe a dozen people moved about, leaning quietly over the cases, reading the wall placards. He wondered when to have the conversation. He didn't want anyone to overhear. He'd thought the museum would be the best place: he didn't want to do it in a restaurant or anyplace where he was sitting alone, across from her. He didn't want to look directly into Claire's face.

Claire leaned over the first display case. Pieces of jewelery were laid out against a white background, dangling earrings, small pendants, heavy bangles. It was a surprise, how bright gold actually was. They moved slowly from case to case: amulets, rings. A bridle ornament. The Scythians drew heavily on animal imagery. There were stylized lions, panthers, bears, bulls. Near them stood another couple, leaning over the case. A woman with angular black-framed glasses and very short hair was next to a man with a small pursed mouth and a European leather jacket. They were speaking quietly in a foreign language—Dutch? Conrad couldn't quite hear.

The Scythians were nomadic warriors around the time of the classical Greeks. The art showed Greek influence, but it also influenced the Greeks. When the rulers died, their wives, servants, and horses were required to follow them into the grave, so the gravesites were extraordinary caches of ceremonial treasure.

"I love these things," Claire murmured, leaning over the case. "I love the idea that treasure has to be portable. Tiny and valuable. These are so beautiful."

A gold plaque showed a battle scene between a horseman and two foot soldiers. The rider sat on a plunging animal with a smooth curved neck and powerful haunches. On either side of him was a foot soldier carrying a short sword and a round shield. They looked familiar: they looked Greek. Conrad felt an odd twinge of something like homesickness.

He had wanted to see this, but he couldn't focus on it. He wanted to start the conversation.

"I kind of love the fact that the women wore these things, things that represented all the wealth," Claire said. "They were the bearers of wealth."

"Men carried the shields and daggers," Conrad said.

"Oh, men had all the power." Claire waved her hand. "That's a given. But women had a part in it. I'm always interested to see what that part was."

"Yeah," Conrad said. It was distracting, the array of glittering gold, the heavy brilliance of the medium, the confidence and intricacy of the execution. And the warriors reminded him of all the stories he knew. But he was here only for conversation. He was waiting for it. The Dutch couple were lingering, absorbed by the plaques, the battle scenes. Conrad willed Claire to move along. *Go,* he told her. *Go.*

She straightened and looked around. At the far end of the room were larger cases holding larger ceremonial objects. In the center was a pitcher in the shape of a swan or some kind of bird. On either side were round platters, their surfaces carved and chased. Everywhere the cases glittered with gold and energy, the ancient residue of a long-vanished empire. *Look on my works, ye mighty, and despair.*

Claire moved toward the swan pitcher. The Dutch woman said something to her husband, and he straightened. The couple turned toward the swan pitcher; Conrad could feel their intention mirroring his. He moved next to Claire and took her elbow, stopping her in her tracks. The guard at the doorway coughed, raising his hand to his mouth.

"Claire," he said, and she turned to face him.

"I want to talk," he said.

She waited, her face open.

This was like rolling a boulder down the mountain. Once he'd said it, he couldn't take it back, couldn't slow it down, couldn't steer it. It would be out of his hands.

"I don't know how to say this," he said.

She shook her head.

He took a breath. "Okay. I want to keep on seeing you."

Claire nodded.

"Okay. But what about this other guy?"

"What other guy?" she asked.

"The Wall Street one," he said. "Whoever he is."

She shook her head. "What about him?"

"Okay, that's not what I meant to say." He paused. He was screwing this up.

"What is it?"

"Look. If you want to quit this, I don't blame you." His voice sounded suddenly loud. The ceiling was very high, and the blank white walls threw back the sound. The guard glanced at him, then away.

Claire frowned. "I didn't say I wanted to quit."

"I mean the sex," Conrad said. Also not what he'd meant to say.

"Forget the Wall Street guy," Claire said. "I'm not really seeing him."

"What does that mean?"

"What I said," Claire said. "I'm seeing you. Not him. I don't sleep with him. Okay? He's a friend. I don't sleep with him."

"Or me," Conrad said.

Claire shook her head impatiently.

"Well?" he asked, angry.

"What do you want me to say? I don't sleep with him," she said.

He waited.

"I told you, I don't care about the sex," she said.

"But I don't believe that," Conrad said.

Claire shrugged her shoulders. "Maybe sex isn't the center of everything."

"Maybe it's pretty close, though," Conrad said. "Maybe it's really important."

Claire looked away from him, and her mouth turned down. Her face crumpled, her cheeks tightened. She was crying, tears spilling down her cheeks. To his horror, she gave a sob.

"Don't do this to me, Con," she said. "It's bad enough without you acting like this."

"Shit," Conrad said. "I love you."

"Yes," Claire said. She closed her eyes. "Don't do this to me."

Conrad put his arms around her. "God, I'm sorry, Claire," he said. "Stop crying, please stop crying. I don't know what to do."

"Just stop it," Claire said into his chest. "Just stop."

Stop what? he wondered. *Stop telling her he loved her, stop seeing her, stop being impotent?*

"We'll just go on like this until you get better," she said. "Just stop talking about it. Stop talking about it. I can't stand it. *Don't talk about it.*"

Beyond her the Dutch couple stood in front of the swan, speaking quietly. Conrad held her close, rocking her slightly.

"Shhh," he said into her hair. "Shh, shh."

But he didn't know what he'd accomplished, after all that.

Toward the end of October, Conrad gave up running. The light came later and later. He didn't like running in the dark, and he didn't like setting out when the city was already in full daily gear, noisy, crowded, ordinary.

He was keeping to the rest of his schedule, though. Every day he spent two hours on the GMAT and two hours on his econ course. It was getting easier to understand the problems, he thought. His brain was beginning to focus, to enter into the strict rhythms of logic. But the headache had not gone away. The headache might have been getting worse. As soon as he opened a book, he could feel the headache approach, hovering, ready to set up its horrid factory. Sometimes he was able to last for two hours without it interfering. Sometimes the hammering was too bad for him to continue and he had to close the book and put his hands over his eyes. When the headache came on, it was more than pain: something happened to his mind; he couldn't think in a straight line.

The nights were getting worse. He woke often, and now the nights seemed endless. The dreams kept coming. Olivera whispered, asking if he was going to die. Sometimes Olivera whispered, *You lied to me, LT.* Before Conrad could answer, Olivera's hand became some soft, gummy substance he couldn't bear to touch or even look at. Then shame flooded through the dream like ink in water, dark clouds blossoming slowly.

To stave off both the insomnia and the nightmares, Conrad took to staying up later and later. Long after Jenny had gone to bed, he lay stretched out on his sofa, drinking beer and watching TV. He held the remote control device like a scepter, clicking impatiently from channel to channel, flipping through old movies, game shows, talk shows. He kept the sound turned low so it wouldn't disturb Jenny. To get to sleep, he drank, sometimes rum but mostly beer. He started each evening with a six-pack sitting on the floor beside the sofa. When it got late enough, he felt his eyelids drifting heavily down, his head dropping forward, his mind sliding off the edge of consciousness. At once he clicked off the TV and the light and lay down, bunching the pillow under his head and stretching out across the thin mattress. He closed his eyes, ready to sink into sleep.

Within moments, the darkness and somnolence had receded to some distant place. His eyes were wide open and his heart rate rapid. It was as though a switch had been turned on. Slowly his muscles began to clench, and he found himself lying on the mattress, his whole body completely tense: his stomach, his fingers, his neck, all taut, anticipatory. The night was another country. Lying in the darkness, willing himself to sleep, finding himself with clenched muscles and careening mind, thoughts came to him that weren't present in the daytime.

Tools, process, opportunity. The words appeared, crisp and factual, like a phrase from a training manual. He didn't know where it came from, but he knew what it meant.

Sometimes he lay awake until dawn seeped around the edges of the shades. When he saw the first light, some internal line of tension snapped. It was as though he'd been on night guard duty and his shift was over. He'd been relieved, and after that he could sink into a confused sleep for an hour or so. He was on a shitty rotation, since he never got anything but night duty. He could have used all that red-alert adrenaline during the daytime, but it seemed he was wired for night and alarmed against sleep. Only in the mornings could he drop off, though not for long. When he woke, he was heavy with exhaustion, like a sack filled with sand.

One morning, after finally drifting off to semi-sleep, he heard Jenny stirring. He was still half asleep; he heard her as though she were on another planet. He heard her door opening, water sounds in the bathroom. He fell asleep. Later he heard her come out into the living room. She stumbled, and then there was a thud, and the musical clunk of something skittering on the bare floor. It would be a beer bottle, one of his. *Shit,* he thought. He kept his eyes closed.

"Shit, Con," Jenny said. He heard her pick up the bottle and walk into the kitchen, heard the clink as she tossed it into the bin. He lay still, his eyes shut. Jenny got breakfast noisily and kind of slammed the door on her way out, to make her point.

Okay, I get it.

Conrad sat up and leaned back against the sofa, legs spread, sheets tangled. The air smelled close and sour: that was him. His eyes felt heavy. He was tired and wired. He had class that afternoon, he had to get up. He rubbed his face hard with both hands, as though he could pummel his mind into activity.

He fixed himself cereal and went back to the sofa to read email. This was still a good moment, sometimes the best of the day. Hearing from his men made him feel good. When he wrote back, they couldn't see him sitting in his underwear on his sister's foldout bed. They pictured him in his cammies and Kevlar, in combat crouch, running down a street, under fire.

Anderson had written again:

So, LT, I don't know if I can go on with this job. I mean I know I can do it, but I don't know if I can make it. Do you ever have the feeling that people are all looking at you because you're a vet? I have that feeling all the time. Not that Im a psyhco I don't mean that but I get a funny feeling and I know I'm right. Fuck em. Maybe its differnet in New York. I don't know, its not getting any easier I thought it would be by now. My parents think I should stick it out they dn't know what its like. What do you think, LT? Best, Anderson.

Conrad wrote back:

Hey Anderson. I can't know what's happening at work for you, but I think you should look around before you quit. See what else is out there first. Are there chances for advancement within the company? Maybe if you stick out this first part it will get better. To be honest, I think it's hard for all of us to come back home. My advice is to hang in there. It's hard, I know, but I promise you it will get better. Charlie Mike. How are your hands? Are they still giving you problems? I've started taking a course at Columbia, and studying for the GMAT test in December. It's finally getting cooler here, a relief. I think about the sandbox, and I don't miss 120 degree heat. Semper Fi, Farrell.

Turner checked in again.

So we had an intervention, with Abbott, not the girlfriend, who's called Dail, by the way. That's how she spells it. (Not her stage name. Her stage name is Angel Cake.) Anyway Abbott says she's his girlfriend, and he can't tell her she can't come over. He got upset about it. We said she can come over but she can't lie on the sofa and she can't be in the kitchen. She can't hang out in the kitchen. She can get coffee but then she has to go upstairs to his room and wait for him there. She can't hang out anywhere but his room. He was pissed. He said you're acting like she's a housepet! Williams and I didn't dare (dair) look at each other. Well?

Conrad answered:

I think you're missing a bet here. You should befriend her. This may be your only chance to get to know a stripper. It's knowledge you might need sometime. You could ask her to teach you her moves, that might come in handy. Widen your experience, Turner.

Ollie wrote about school:

Hey Con: Things are pretty good. Some kid in my dorm set fire to his room at 2:00 in the morning. I don't know how he did it, there are a lot of rumors going around, all related to drugs, big surprise. Anyway the fire was a real scene, firemen in hats and boots dragging big hoses up and down the halls. We all had to go out in our underwear and stand on the lawn. We stood under Sean's window and yelled, Jump! Jump! Of course he wasn't still up there, he was down on the lawn with us. Nothing was damaged, it was just a fire in the sink, it turned out, but he;s in trouble. That's all for today, when you coming up? Yah, Ollie.

Conrad wrote him back:

Watched football all weekend, did you see the Cowboys' game? They put the wrong guy in at the half, I can tell you that. About the fire, you college kids are really something. I may have to warn you about rowdiness. NYC is quiet by comparison though someone drove a taxi into one of the trees outside our building. A lot of honking and yelling and all the dogs on the block began to bark. The cabbie was Russian and he started swearing, or at least it sounded like swearing. No one could tell what he was saying but it sounded pretty ferocious. When the policemen showed up they yelled at each other in two languages. You couldn't tell who was winning until the policeman pulled out cuffs and then the Russian shut up. School here is going well. Yah, C.

Actually, school was not going well.

He had to keep going, as he'd told Anderson to do.

He set the cereal bowl on the floor. He could study just as well on the bed, in his underwear. He'd get up later, take a shower, get dressed, turn the bed back into a sofa. Right now there was no point, and he was whacked.

That afternoon in class the headache began to hover just over his right eye as soon as he sat down. It was disturbing to have the headache when he was in class. It usually came while he was studying at home, when he was tired or trying to figure out something complex. When it happened at home, he could close the book and wait until it went away. But in class he couldn't wait, and he had to cover his eye with his hand. He tried to make it look as though he were just leaning his head in his hand. By the end of class his whole head was throbbing, and he walked home with his hand over his eye, as though he'd gotten something stuck in it.

Jock came over for dinner one night. When he arrived, Conrad was studying in the living room. His books and notebooks were spread out on the sofa.

Conrad looked up. "Hey, there." His head was pounding. He'd had a headache all day.

"My man," Jock said. "The scholar."

Conrad stared at him. Was that condescending? Did Jock think he, the doctor, was in the real world, and Conrad, the scholar, was in some inferior place?

"Aren't you studying, too?" Conrad asked.

"Am I not," Jock said. "Am I not. Though it's more like boot camp, at this point, than graduate school."

"Yeah," Conrad said. "But of course boot camp's different. In boot camp you're learning to kill people on purpose."

Jock laughed uncomfortably. He took out his wallet.

"By the way," he said, "I've got something for you." He opened his wallet and handed Conrad a prescription.

"For me? You've already got doctor's handwriting," Conrad said, squinting. "I can't read it. What is it?"

"Zolpidem," said Jock.

"What is that?"

"Sleepmaster," Jock said. "Ambien. The most widely prescribed drug there is. I give you the gift of sleep."

Conrad raised his eyebrows. "Whoa! Thank you, my man."

Jock shook his head. "Glad to help. But this is only for three months."

"I will be happy for three months." Conrad shook his head. "Man. Okay, I'm just going to step outside for a few moments. That drugstore on Broadway is open till ten."

Outside it was dark, and the streetlights were on. He headed up the block toward Broadway. The woman from next door was on the sidewalk, taking slow, patient steps as her dog explored a little patch of grass. Conrad nodded and she nodded back.

The slip of paper was like money. Sleep was like money.

He reached Broadway just as the light was changing, and he ran across, dodging the traffic. A Duane Reade was on the corner, its window crammed with stuff, stacked with boxes of diapers and mouthwash. He went inside and was hit by the heavy smell of synthetic plastics. He went up the narrow aisle to the back, where a heavyset black woman, her hair in cornrows, stood behind the low counter. He handed her his slip. She took it disapprovingly, without meeting his eyes. She turned and handed the slip to the druggist behind the high counter. Without speaking to Conrad, she looked past him at the person next in line, a girl with dyed orange hair and black-ringed eyes.

The white-haired druggist peered at the paper through his glasses, then looked at Conrad.

"Fifteen or twenty minutes," he said.

"That's fine," Conrad said. He felt euphoric. "I'll wait." He walked up and down the rows, cans of deodorant, boxes of gauze bandages, bottles of shampoo. Racks of candy, soda, potato chips: so much food. He should bring something back for Jenny, the household, he thought. Everything was processed, plastic-wrapped. He thought of buying something for Jock in appreciation, but nothing seemed right. Toothpaste was not a present, and deodorant was an insult. The thought of sliding down into sleep made him feel rich and happy. He walked around, cruising, until fifteen minutes were up. He came back and stood by the counter, waiting. The black woman frowned as she handed him the package.

Conrad smiled at her. "Thank you."

He felt a surge of goodwill. She was saving his life, in a way.

Walking back to the apartment, the little plastic bottle in his pocket, he felt unfathomably rich. Before him were nights of sleep, spreading out before him like miles of treasure.

He stood waiting at the light while cars slid past in an endless current. A homeless man came up to the corner. He was in his sixties, long-haired and bearded. His face was seamed and tanned. He wore a grimy woven tunic and gray institutional pants. He looked like Tolstoy, broad-browed, intent, handsome, his face surrounded by a bushy mass of hair.

Conrad was thinking of Jock reaching for his wallet. *I've got something for you.* The smile on Jock's face, wasn't it a bit self-satisfied? That little turndown at the corners. But Jock was always like that, a bit self-satisfied. Like he was the Man.

Tolstoy moved next to Conrad and leaned over the metal trash can. He put his hand into it and began pawing gently. Conrad heard the rustle of paper.

He wondered if that was actually how Jock felt. As if he were in charge of doling things out. Had Jock been patronizing him? Like, *Here you are, my good man.*

Tolstoy looked up at him, holding an empty bottle.

"Hey, man," Tolstoy said.

Conrad nodded to him. "Hey."

"I think this is the only bottle in this whole fucking trash can," Tolstoy said.

"Could be," said Conrad.

"I have to go all the way down, though," Tolstoy said. "You gotta go all the way down."

"Right," Conrad said.

Tolstoy stared at him. He had narrow blue eyes, and his mouth was surrounded by the streaming beard. His teeth were surprisingly white against his dark skin. "You ever done this?" he asked. "You know what I'm talking about?"

"Not exactly," Conrad said. "But close enough."

Tolstoy wet his mouth, running his red tongue over his lips, staring. "So you know what it's like," he said. "It's for shit."

He stared straight into Conrad's eyes.

"What I do," he repeated. "It's for shit."

He was old. He smelled bad, a rank mix of body and dirt, some kind of animal scent. He was old and he had nowhere to be. On his feet he wore thick sandals, no socks. His life—wounded, shattered—stood around him like an aura. Conrad wondered where he had been when he was twenty-six, in what city, with what plans. This, now, wasn't what he'd wanted, but it was where he'd turned up. Somehow his whole life had miscarried, veered off onto this faint, wandering line. It was a mystery, a loss. He'd lost his own life.

"I know," Conrad said. "I'm sorry." He raised one hand, as though to touch him, but made the gesture into a wave/salute. Probably touching the guy was not a good idea.

Tolstoy stared, holding him in his blue beam, the bottle still high in one hand. "It's better than being inside," he said. "That's where they fuck you."

The light changed. "Yeah," Conrad said. "Good luck."

He walked across the avenue, now starting to feel angry. What was the point of things if people ended up like this, old and homeless and destitute? No socks, and pawing through the filthy trash. What was the matter here? What was he supposed to do?

He headed down Jenny's block. The dog woman was gone. The sidewalk was empty, just the streetlight's cone of light. A car drove slowly past, blasting out a dull, booming bass line.

He wondered again about Jock, if he had been patronizing. The more he thought about it, the more he thought it was condescending. He didn't want charity from Jock. If he wanted prescription drugs, he could fucking well get them from his own doctor. He didn't need to get his little sister's boyfriend to sneak something out to him. Jock was treating him like some kind of charity case. Opening up his wallet, as if this were a birthday treat. The tone of his voice.

Now he owed Jock something. Was that it? Jock had put Conrad in his debt.

When he came in, he was no longer smiling. Jock and Jenny were already sitting at the table. Jenny waved her fork at him.

"Your plate's in the kitchen," she said.

Conrad filled his plate and sat down. He resented the fact that they had started eating.

"All set," he said to Jock. "Thanks."

"No problem," Jock said. He looked down at his plate.

Not looking at Conrad was also condescending.

"So, you do this a lot?" Conrad asked him.

Jock looked up.

"Hand out prescriptions?" Conrad elaborated.

Jock frowned. "No. What do you mean?"

Conrad shook his head. "Nothing. Just wondered."

"As a matter of fact, it's kind of difficult," said Jock. "I may not be able to renew it. But Jenny said you were having trouble sleeping."

Conrad didn't like the idea of Jenny talking to Jock about him. Telling him about his problems. He wondered if she knew about his nightmares. Had he told her? Had she told Jock? It was no one's business.

"Yeah, well, thanks," he said.

After that night, Jock began to piss Conrad off.

He thought that Jock pressed his lips together when Conrad said something, and wouldn't answer. He thought Jock acted supercilious, as though Conrad were a child. Conrad knew he might be overreacting. He couldn't be sure, and that pissed him off, too.

A week later Conrad spent the afternoon at the library, studying for an econ test.

The problem was that he couldn't absorb the information. He read it over and over, and some of it stuck and some of it refused to. When he came to something he couldn't get into his head, he underlined it and read it to himself in a whisper so that the words were formed and spoken. What he didn't want to do was panic. He could feel the headache hovering, and he put his hand over his right eye. What he was afraid of was failure. What if he went ahead, step-by-step, but couldn't make his mind work? What if he failed the class or had to drop out? He couldn't fail. Even if he took the class over next semester, the failing grade would be on his record. He couldn't fail. But what if he couldn't succeed?

The problem was making his mind work. The headache, and not being able to grasp ideas. But he couldn't abandon the mission just because it wasn't going well. You carried on. And in any case, what other option was there?

Tools, process, opportunity.

He was surrounded by a carnival of opportunity, a feast, a smorgasbord. And tools were everywhere, it was like a secret language. Once you understood it, you saw the message written everywhere. It was all around you. The distant star of the subway car bearing down on you through the darkness, rattling toward you, larger and larger, breathtakingly lethal. Jenny's kitchen, with its rack of knives, each of them, even the smallest, fully effective. The vacuum cleaner hose. Tools were everywhere.

Jock came over that night. They had dinner at the table in the living room. Jenny had made lasagna, and the cheesy smell of it filled the apartment. Jock took a swig of beer and looked at Conrad.

"So, how's it going?"

"Going okay," Conrad said.

"What are you taking, again?" Jock asked.

"Just one class," said Conrad. "Prerequisite for grad school. Macroeconomics."

Jock raised his eyebrows. "Serioso."

"Yeah," said Conrad. "But it'll be okay."

"Must be hard to get your brain back into school mode." Jock took a big bite of lasagna. His Adam's apple worked as he chewed.

"Actually," Conrad said, "in the Marines we're always in school mode. Acquiring new information, using it to design strategy. We actually use our brains quite a lot. Contrary to public opinion."

Jock looked at him. His Adam's apple stopped moving. "Hey," he said. "I know that. I just meant that studying—" He didn't finish.

"Actually, there is a very strong intellectual streak in the Marines," Conrad said. *Fucking doctors.*

"Is there?" Jenny asked. She sounded serious and interested.

"Yeah," said Conrad. "A lot of smart jarheads. They read the *Iliad*. They read *War and Peace*. They read history. They come back here and they're treated like idiots."

Jock stared at him. He picked up his beer and drank again. Conrad could hear him swallowing, could see the gulps going down his gingery speckled throat.

"Okay, so, Con," Jenny said carefully, "you make it sound like it's our fault."

Conrad squeezed his eyes shut, then opened them. "Okay, sorry," he said. "Not your fault. Okay? Sorry. I'm a little on edge tonight."

They ate in silence. Jock finished his meal and set his fork on his plate. He leaned back in his chair and looked around the living room. It was a mess.

Conrad's clothes lay draped on the chairs and the arms of the sofa. There was nowhere else for him to put them: no closet, no bureau. His books and papers were stacked on the coffee table; there were more on the floor.

"So, what's the deal?" Jock asked Jenny. "Are we ever going to move?"

Jenny frowned at her plate. "I don't have time to look for another place right now."

"Yeah, but when will you?" Jock asked. "When will you not have a job? When are you going to call a broker or look at the ads in the *Times* and then actually go out and look at the places? Or do you want me to look? Because I'll be happy to. On my day off every two weeks."

"I know, I know," she said.

"Jen, come on. We've been having this conversation for months," Jock said. "What's your point?"

Jenny shrugged. "It's just I hate to leave. I don't know. It's so awful, moving. This place seems safe to me, I know it."

"Safe!" Jock said. "Come on. I'm not suggesting we move someplace dangerous."

"No, I just mean I'm here, I know it," said Jenny. "This is like my burrow, it's mine."

"So you'll never move?" Jock asked. "This is it? Is that your message?"

"Maybe that is her message," said Conrad. "Maybe you've got your answer. She doesn't want to move. If she wanted to move, she'd move."

"Is that her message?" Jock said, looking at him.

"Yeah," said Conrad. "Why don't you get it?"

Jock raised his eyebrows. "Why don't I." He nodded, looking across the room. He looked back at Conrad. "Why don't you mind your own business? In fact, why don't you get your own fucking apartment?"

Conrad stood up quickly, knocking his chair over behind him. He looked down at Jock, elated.

"Great," he said.

"Con." Jenny grabbed hold of his arm with both hands. Conrad pulled slowly away from her, looking at Jock.

"Stop it," Jenny said. *"Sit down."* She put her hands over her face. "You are total jerks. Both of you."

Conrad stood waiting.

Jock stared up at him. "I'm not going to fight with you," he said. "You know that, don't you."

After a moment Conrad said, "I do know that. Yeah."

Jenny stood up. "Both of you shut up." Her voice was raised. *"Shut up!"* I can't believe you're doing this. What is the matter with you?"

Conrad said nothing. He folded his arms, breathing hard.

He was fucking sick of Jock. Jock acted like he was in the trenches just because he was working at a hospital. He thought he should be treated like a fucking hero just because he was tired and working hard, but the truth was that he slept in clean sheets every night and no one was shooting at him or trying to blow up his car.

That night, Jenny and Jock went to his place for the night. Conrad drank beer and watched TV until midnight, then took a pill to get to sleep.

When he came home from class the next day, he heard Jenny on the phone in her room. He put down his books and went into the kitchen for a beer. The bedroom door opened and Jenny came out. Conrad brought his beer into the living room.

"Hey," he said.

"We have to talk," she said.

"Okay." Conrad sat down on the sofa. He took a swig and looked up at Jenny as though he had no idea what was coming. But okay, he felt like an asshole: It was her apartment, after all. Her boyfriend. Still, Jock himself had done pretty well on the asshole front, swanning around like a hero and doling out favors. The skinny little arms, the hollow chest. The fucking Adam's apple and the skin like pink sandpaper.

"Look," Jenny said. She sat down on the arm of the sofa. She was still wearing her clothes from work, black pants and a wide-striped gondolier's jersey. Today's earrings were little red globes.

"Okay," he said, waving his hand. He didn't want to hear this.

"No," Jenny said. "I have to tell you. You can't yell at my boyfriend." She crossed her arms on her chest and looked straight at him. Now he saw that the earrings were little plastic tomatoes, cut in half, showing the sections.

Conrad waited for a moment. He wanted to say that Jock couldn't be an asshole to him, but that might start them down a road he didn't want to travel. He nodded.

"Got it," he said.

She sat still, waiting. He knew she wanted an apology. But he wasn't going to apologize for identifying an asshole.

"I didn't walk in and call him an abortionist," he said.

"What?" Jenny screwed up her face as if he were speaking Martian. "What are you talking about?"

"When I came in, he called me a student," Conrad said.

"What's wrong with that?" Jenny asked. She sounded outraged. "What is wrong with calling you a student? Isn't that what you are at the moment?"

Who he was, was a Marine. Okay, he was a former, but he was still a Marine, he wasn't a fucking Continuing Ed student. What he didn't want to go near was the fact that he was not only a student but very possibly a failing student, a student who was fucking up so badly he'd be fucked for life.

"Let's say I didn't like his tone of voice," Conrad said. "You can make anything into an insult with your tone of voice."

"Yes, but he didn't," Jenny said. "I was here. I heard him. Con, he didn't insult you."

"Jock thinks he's a master of the universe because he's in medical school," Conrad said. "But he's not. That doesn't make him master of anything." The headache was starting to close in. It gathered itself somewhere overhead like a kind of miasma, and now it was beginning to descend.

Jenny shook her head. "You're being an idiot." She stared at him. "You are welcome to stay here, Con. I love you. But you can't stay if you're going to start fights with my boyfriend."

Conrad raised his hand, but he didn't want to cover his eye in front of her. "I didn't start anything," he said. He could feel the thumping throb settling into his skull.

"You did, too," Jenny said. "You completely and totally started it. *What is the matter with you?*"

Conrad put his hand over his eye and closed it.

Jenny stared at him, waiting. After a moment her voice changed. "Are you okay, Con? Is something wrong?"

"No, I'm fine," Conrad said, because how could you tell someone—your sister—you were failing? And where could he go?

22

This time he filled out all the forms.

He was sent to the same waiting room, but this time a different woman sat behind the desk. This one was young and fat and white. She was wearing a red-and-white candy-striped blouse. Her greasy blond hair was strained into a tiny curved ponytail.

Conrad handed her the clipboard when he was done.

"Thank you." She didn't look up.

"So, now what?" Conrad asked.

"Now what?" She looked up.

"Could you tell me what happens next?" he asked.

"First you need a medical assessment. We'll contact you for an appointment. Then, if you need further treatment, we contact you for that," the fat girl said. Her wide cheeks rose up against her eyes like little hillocks, making them squint.

He waited, but she said nothing more.

"Could you tell me when I'll hear?" he asked.

"When the paperwork has gone through," she said.

Looking down over the high counter, he could see that she had a little private nest back there. Her computer was on a ledge. Beside it was a big plastic mug, a couple of framed photographs. A little basket with a ribbon tied to it was full of miniature-sized chocolate bars. She had everything she needed.

"I mean, can you give me an idea of how long it will be?"

She shook her head. "Could be months."

Behind Conrad someone said, "It'll be three months. It's always three months."

Conrad turned to look. It was a Vietnam vet, thin and grizzled, wearing faded jeans and a baseball cap. He raised a hand, nodding. He closed his eyes politely. Conrad nodded back.

"Thanks." Conrad turned to the striped woman. "So it'll be three months before I can get an appointment to see someone?"

"Are you suicidal?" The woman's voice was loud and indifferent. He felt it in his chest like a blow. "If you're suicidal, if you're a danger to yourself or others, put it down on the form. Then we'll be in touch sooner."

She was in charge, and the space around her was filled with power. Her body, spilling out over the edges of the chair, weighing down the rolling wheels: all this was set up in opposition to him. She was the obstacle to what lay beyond, something that was waiting for him somewhere in the long corridors, open doorways, lighted rooms. Whatever he wanted was beyond her. Without looking down, she slid open a drawer at her waist. She reached inside. Still holding his gaze, she took out her hand and secretively popped something into her mouth. She began chewing. Her teeth made a crunching noise.

"Okay," Conrad said. "I'll wait to hear, then."

Three months would be late January. He turned to leave.

The Vietnam vet was watching him. He'd leaned forward, his elbows on his knees. His flat face was raddled and red. His faded blue eyes were watery, his cheeks covered with gray stubble. The flesh beneath his chin had collapsed down his neck in accordion folds. *Thirty years,* Conrad thought. *He's been coming here for thirty fucking years and he's still no better.*

"Thanks, bro," Conrad said.

The vet nodded, solemnly holding Conrad's gaze, as if it were a way to help him.

He was in the back row of the classroom. It was nearly dark; Professor Titchmarsh had dimmed the lights. A little glow came up from the podium, lighting her face from below. All three screens showed graphs. She was talking about international trade, and the way countries used political methods to limit one another's economic activities. She used a small laser as a pointer. The point of light rose uncertainly on the nearest graph, wobbling up and down the jagged line to show the intersections, the crossovers, the rises and falls.

"Take international airline routes, for example," Professor Titchmarsh said. The point of light vanished, then reappeared on the next screen. In the dimness, Conrad could see the ranks of students, the rows of their backs stretching out in front of him. He didn't like taking notes in semidarkness. He couldn't really see the paper; it felt like writing on water.

"Countries use these for negotiation. They offer permission to land in their airports in exchange for something else—political or economic status. Not all international airlines are permitted to land at JFK—this is actually a 'most favored nation' situation."

The three screens were troubling. She was pointing at the one on the far right. He tried to focus on the jagged line, where it climbed and plunged. He should have his NVGs. He thought of slipping them on, pulling them down from the top of his helmet over his eyes, and the landscape turning dim and greenish. In-country they owned the night. Though he wasn't wearing a helmet. It was like double vision: he was here, in khakis and moccasins and a sweater, his parka at his back, but at moments he was also still in his cammies and boots, Kevlar. There was something troubling about the three screens, about having to shift back and forth. When he looked at one, he was aware of the other two. It made him uneasy. The headache hovered just over his right eye.

"Here you can see the intersections," Professor Titchmarsh said. The point of light began to flicker. There was something sickening about the way the tiny brightness moved up and down, silent and loose, on the light screen, and there was something unsettling about the three screens side by side, glowing against the darkness, and as he tried to take all three of them in, the headache descended like night and he had to put his hand over his right eye. But covering his eye made it hard for him to hear. What she was saying was now dim and confused because of his clouded eye. Or there was something else wrong, something was going wrong, he was having trouble concentrating on her words. He was writing everything down, but something was wrong with the way he was hearing it.

Professor Titchmarsh changed the right-hand image to a new chart showing a varied pattern of response. A series of bright red circles glowed against a pale background, and in the darkness Conrad saw the pattern on the wall. The spatters high on the wall of the house in Haditha. That room flooded over him again, the smell of the bodies on the floor, and the blood. The awful way they lay, so heavy, so final. The woman, still climbing onto the sofa. His heart rose up in his chest as though some kind of alarm were going off. It was like an echo chamber, because there was the pattern on the wall again, and his whole body was reverberating as though he were right there in that room, and he put his hand over both eyes and closed them and tried to let blackness come over him and not to think and not to move and he willed for that room to be over. Three more months.

The Ambien took forty minutes to work and lasted three hours. He took one pill to get to sleep, usually around eleven. Sometimes he waited until twelve or one, trying to stretch the sleep. It was like a blanket, never big enough or long enough. He pictured himself pulling at it, tugging to make it cover him completely, make it last all night. When the pill wore off, he woke up again. He'd made a rule: after four o'clock it was too late to take another. If he woke after that, he lay awake.

This morning, when he looked at the clock, it said 4:18. He'd gone to sleep around twelve-thirty or quarter to one, so a little over three hours. He wouldn't take another. Another rule was that he couldn't let himself turn on the light or watch TV. He lay in the dark, his eyes sharpening.

The windows were always paler. The three tall shapes in the bay window glowed faintly. He had put up blackout shades, standing on a chair to hammer into the hard old plaster, chips of paint flying. Still, the light seeped around the edges like water. It came in, rising from the streetlights below.

He looked at the shapes outlined in light and then rolled over, turning away. He closed his eyes, but found himself watching. He was staring into the dimness. His whole body tense. Not violently, just barely. His hands were clenched. He opened his fingers. *Release,* he told himself. The thing was to keep yourself away. The thing was to keep clear. He heard someone walking down the sidewalk outside, the footsteps regular, soft, steady *chuck, chuck, chuck*. Then a pause: *What?* He listened; his own breath stopped. The sounds went on. *What?* When he was listening, he forgot where he was, lying on his sister's foldout sofa. He was there with the sound. He didn't like hearing footsteps in the dark, didn't want to hear them.

He wasn't going to get back to sleep, he knew that. It was better to lie still. At least if he lay quietly he'd be resting. He could go through the day on three hours' sleep. He couldn't concentrate, but he could do it. In-country there had been weeks when he hadn't gotten more than that.

He was lying on his side, his eyes open to the shadowy wall. He kept unclenching himself, finding new muscles that were tense. Shoulders, neck, forearms. *Stay still. Fuck.* The thing was to stay clear. Not to let anything get close. Not to let anything into his mind. Though there was no way to do that.

Being awake this late was like being in another country. He was trapped here. He closed his eyes, opened them again. Something twitched in his leg and he sat bolt upright. Nothing. In the distance a siren. Was it raining? Something, some soft pattering sound. He listened. Nothing. The thing was to keep clear. This was the hour of the wolf.

Tools, process, opportunity.

Each process—and there were so many—had benefits and drawbacks. The thing about overdose was simplicity. There was no equipment, no concern over mechanics. It was bare-bones: just pills. There was no problem with venue, you could do it anywhere. A hotel room. The risk was that you couldn't be completely sure it would work. He'd heard that some crucial component had been removed from sleeping pills, whatever it was that put you to sleep forever. How would you find out about that, and how would you be certain? What you really didn't want was to have it only half work, find yourself awake afterward, but with only half your brain functioning. Talk about fucked.

Asphyxiation was more reliable, but the mechanics were more complicated. You needed a vacuum cleaner hose, a car, a garage. In Katonah, the vacuum cleaner, its fat blue hose draped around it, was stored in the closet by the front door. You'd make the joint between hose and pipe tight by binding them together with a rag, a towel. There was a stack of kitchen towels in the drawer beside the stove. That was all you'd need: the hose, the pipe, a towel.

He imagined standing inside the garage in Katonah, pushing the button to lower the doors. They rumbled slowly down, the reticulated panels angling around the curve at the top, then flattening into a hinged sheet, the whole contraption sliding noisily on its metal tracks. Thudding to a halt on the concrete, closing you in. Safe. There you were in the dim room that smelled of old wood and engine oil. There you were with the getaway car.

The vacuum cleaner hose was a thick snake, supple coiled springs sheathed by close-woven fabric. At one end of the hose was a metal shaft. You'd slide the shaft end over the exhaust pipe. You'd tie the green-and-white-checked kitchen towel around the joint, doubling and knotting. You'd lead the hose up into the back window, which you'd cracked open. You'd stuff more towels in the rest of the opening of the window. You'd take a Valium for anxiety, so you wouldn't panic and call it all off. Then you'd get into the front seat and turn the key in the ignition and close the door.

You'd lean back and wait for the pill to kick in. Maybe you'd turn on the radio, look for a late-night music station. He'd learned to like country in the Corps. Country blues, or Johnny Cash, or the high sweet sound of Aaron Neville. You'd feel a deep, quiet flooding, a pooling of relief rising up in you as you waited. Jesus, the relief. You knew what was coming, slow and dark, and then, like a blessed spell, you'd drift off, you'd fall deeply asleep, finally, for good, and you'd be safe. You would never again have another fucking nightmare, never again face those pictures in your mind, the bloody spatters on the wall, Olivera's shattered chest, or the little boy in his pajamas. You would never wake up again in the morning to find yourself in a panicky sweat, your heart thundering in great bounding leaps of anxiety, or wake to find yourself already plunged down, cocooned in misery, unable to rise from the dead low swale of despair. You would never again have to look at someone and speak to them in one world, theirs, while you were holding that other world, yours, with its black sinkholes, sealed off in your head.

All that was good, but the idea of actually breathing the exhaust was repellent. Deliberately drawing the fumes into your lungs was a kind of betrayal, an insult to the body. The body was brave and innocent, conscientious. As a Marine you respected it. All these plans were an insult to the body, the ultimate insult.

The question of location: Katonah was the obvious choice. Sometimes the quiet nights were lit up by the virtuoso performance of the mockingbird, singing in the cedar tree by the garage. It would be strange to die listening to a mockingbird.

But the night was so quiet that his parents might wake up and hear the car. It would be shameful to be caught in the act. And he wanted to spare his parents. He didn't want them to find him sprawled in the front seat of the car, his eyes dull and glazed.

What he'd like was for his parents never to know what happened and never to think about it again. He'd like to have himself erased from their memories, just gone, so that they never wondered and never had to learn what happened. Never had to see him afterward. So they remembered him until he went into the service, and then after that, nothing, a blank.

There were two worlds.

These considerations were part of the lower world. That was the dark, dreaming undercurrent, both nightmare and solace, that ran along beneath this world. That was the world you entered at night, the one that suddenly intruded into your mind, the one of blooming explosions and blood. And that was the world you sank into, that was where you thought of giving yourself up, letting yourself drift downward into the dim, aqueous shafts of light and shadow. That was the world where you yielded to the slow, silent movements of the deep. Where you were embraced wholly, every part of you clasped, water kissing and surrounding you like air, where you were carried, weightless, your limbs loose, your body beloved, by the mindless surge.

But the world below was not where you lived. Where you lived was in the upper world, the one where the light came flooding in, harsh and bright and obligatory, slicing through the air like metal wire. Where something angular and unyielding—duty, a moral obligation to a larger metaphysical system—made a labyrinth across the landscape, defining the path. You had no choice but to walk through it, turning and turning. In that landscape there was no backward. And there was no horizon, no reach, no future, only the short view. You had no right to stop, to not keep going. Your only choice was to continue the mission.

Hanging would be faster, and it would be certain. Shooting would be fastest. The taste of oil and metal on your tongue, the absolute shape and feel of the barrel against the roof of your mouth. The great existential question: Would you hear the shot?

Conrad thought about this only when he was alone. He thought about it only at night. It wasn't a possibility. It wasn't permissible. But it was permissible to think about it, and he allowed himself that relief.

Sometimes the flashes were intermittent, interrupting him during a conversation. It was like double vision. It was getting Morse code signals flashed from a distant mountain while you were trying to talk to someone right in front of you. It was hard to know which message was the most immediate, which the most urgent.

In early November, Go-Go texted him: *Dude. Dinner?*

Conrad named a bar in his neighborhood: Haakon Hall. He was waiting there in a booth when Go-Go arrived. The place was noisy, filled with students. Across the aisle there were two girls leaning toward each other. One had a crew cut and dark purple lips, the other had a magenta streak in her hair. They were talking avidly, using their hands, pretending they were unaware of everyone else in the room. Conrad watched them from the corner of his eye.

Go-Go slid in across from him. "Yo."

"Go-Go," said Conrad.

"Hey. Good to see you," Go-Go said. He looked around the bar. The waiter came over. He wore his hair in a thick ponytail, and a white apron was wrapped over his jeans.

"What can I get you?" he asked.

"Do you have Bombay Sapphire?" Go-Go asked.

"One Sapphire, coming up," the waiter said.

"With this much vermouth," Go-Go said, pinching his fingers together.

"Got it," said the waiter.

"Heineken," said Conrad.

"You guys want dinner?"

"Burger," said Conrad.

"Burger," said Go-Go.

The waiter nodded and went away.

Go-Go leaned back against the booth. He was slumming tonight, wearing the Egyptian cotton shirt and the tassel loafers again, but instead of khakis he wore knife-edged jeans. Student attire.

"So, how's it going?" he asked. "Being back in school."

Conrad shrugged. "You did it," he answered. "You know."

"Yeah, but a while ago," Go-Go said. "I was still in student mode then. I was used to it. But you're older now, plus you've, uh"—he waved his hand—"been on the front lines." He frowned, looking straight at Conrad. "I mean, how is that? Being a student, after being, you know . . ."

"A leader of men?" Conrad said.

"Eat me," Go-Go said.

"There are some other vets around." He nodded toward the bar. "Some of them hang out here."

"Really?" Go-Go looked around. "Any here right now?"

"Right now," Conrad said. "But they're not in uniform. They're actually in drag, so you won't spot them."

Go-Go laughed, but he still looked around furtively.

"Those two guys standing at the bar," Conrad said, "talking to the bartender? They were in OEF. Afghanistan."

"Really?" Go-Go said, craning his neck.

The guys looked normal. No cammies. No knives, no guns, no high-and-tights.

"You want their autographs?" asked Conrad.

Go-Go turned back, looking sheepish.

"I'll give you mine," Conrad said.

Go-Go laughed. "Yeah, whatever."

The waiter arrived. He slid the drinks onto the table, and Go-Go raised his. "Cheers."

They both drank.

"You know," Go-Go said, "I don't know how to talk to you about any of this. Being a vet. I feel weird. Like, partly I'm jealous, and—I don't know. Uh, respectful and—like, silenced. I don't know what to say."

"Yeah," Conrad said. "We don't know what to say, either." He looked at Go-Go. "Just hold on to *respectful.* Just call us *master.*"

Go-Go gave him the finger.

Conrad grinned and took another swig. "So when did you start wearing clothes like that? You look like a Ralph Lauren ad. Seriously. When did you?"

"I don't know." Go-Go squinted and pushed his glasses up his nose. "It started at the office—you dress like everyone else. Then you start dressing like everyone else when you meet them to go out. I don't know. You know, these are my guys now. I'm used to it. Anyway, I couldn't go on wearing the stuff I wore at school. Grown-up time, right?"

Conrad nodded. He thought of Jenny's apartment, his clothes draped in a pile on the good-luck chair. He was still in student mode, and would be for another two years, if he even got into graduate school. It seemed he was behind on everything.

"So is this who you are now?" he asked Go-Go.

Go-Go raised his shoulders. "How do I know who I am?" he said. "Was I the guy with all the earrings? I don't know. I figure I'm this guy now. Will I be him forever? I don't know."

"Come on," Conrad said. "Nobody changes from finance to architecture. You don't decide to be a gardener instead of a guy on Wall Street."

"Yeah," Go-Go said. "I don't know. You think, This is it? Am I going to end up on the front page of *The New York Times*?"

"As what? As master of the universe?"

"As released under one-million-dollar bail," Go-Go said. "In custody. I don't know. Sometimes I wish I was back in the garage, writing songs and turning up the volume."

Conrad nodded. "You were good, Go-Go."

"No," Go-Go said. "I sucked, but I had fun doing it."

Their hamburgers arrived. The girls across the aisle ordered more drinks. Magenta Streak had a high, shrill laugh. The bangles on her wrist clattered.

"So what're you up to?" Go-Go asked.

"Next month," Conrad said, "it all comes down. I'm taking the GMAT on the eighth. My final is on the twentieth. Grad school applications are due around the end of December, beginning of January. Spring semester starts a couple of weeks later. I'm going to take another econ class." He was thinking about volunteer work, too, maybe working with vets, counseling.

"But you'll be in the city next semester?" Go-Go asked.

Conrad nodded.

"Because my company is sending me to Hong Kong for a few months. I thought you might want my apartment. No charge if you'll pay for cable and the cleaning woman. It'll be until April, probably."

Conrad raised his eyebrows. "Hey. Go-Go. Are you serious?"

"Works for me."

"That would be a fucking godsend." Conrad lifted his glass. "Dude," he said, "you're a lifesaver. That is some offer. It would be great."

Go-Go nodded, pleased with himself. "The thanks of a grateful nation," he intoned.

"I'll pay for the cleaning lady and cable," said Conrad. "And I'll throw in some autographs from those guys at the bar."

23

Possibly it had been a mistake to schedule the GMAT so late. He was taking it on December eighth, and the econ final was on the twentieth. He'd done this deliberately: he'd thought that the longer he'd been studying, the better he'd be at taking the tests. His mind would be working better. That had been the plan, though it didn't seem to be working. Whatever was messing with his mind was still there. When he opened the study guide and began to read, he began to sweat. The headache was right there.

Right after Thanksgiving—he'd gone out only for the night—his mother started leaving messages about Christmas.

Why don't you come out early? The week before? We'd love to see you.

Ollie texted him: *Im through the 18th. When r u coming?*

Conrad replied that his final was the twentieth and that he'd let them know.

He wasn't too worried about the econ exam. Whatever was wrong with him had phases, and sometimes he felt pretty normal. He'd gone slowly through the textbook, rereading the theories until they made sense. He pretty much knew the material. If he didn't get the headache, he'd do all right.

The GMAT was different. These weren't theories that he could learn and absorb; they were unrelated problems that required analysis. Sometimes his mind was fine and he could focus on the problem, drill right into it. Sometimes his mind went off track, and he could feel it grinding, like a car in a snowbank. The GMAT was more important than the econ exam. It wasn't actually a stretch to say that the results would determine his future.

You found out the results, except for the essay score, right after you finished the test. If you really screwed up, you could have the results erased. But you had to decide right then, after you finished but before you saw the results. And even if you erased them, your record would show that you'd taken them and had the results erased.

Conrad thought that if he went in there and the headache came down, he'd screw it up. He might screw it up anyway by not being able to focus. It gave him a sick feeling.

The night before the test he took a pill, got to sleep around eleven, but woke with a nightmare at two-thirty. He took another pill and slept until five, when he was jolted awake by a siren. It was too late to go back to sleep. He got up and put on his running clothes. Outside it was not quite night, though the streetlights were still on. The sidewalks were empty and the streets felt greasy. It was cold, and he could see his breath vanishing ahead of him in little pale drifts. When he reached the reservoir, the sky was nearly light, and he ran through a silky dimness. He heard the sound of steady footsteps around him; he could hear the runners before he could see them. Gradually the sky appeared: it was overcast. The water was a muted pewter gray, without reflection. Conrad ran four laps and then headed back. It was fully light now, and he felt better.

The testing center was in an office building on West Forty-eighth Street. Conrad arrived half an hour early. On the ninth floor there was already a line of people waiting to check in. He stood behind a short brown-haired girl wearing a blue parka. The parka rustled when she moved. No one talked. They were all moving slowly, step-by-step, toward a young Asian man who sat at a desk behind a glass barrier. When Conrad reached him, he asked to see Conrad's ID.

"Look at the camera, please." The man looked Korean, square face and short black brushy hair. He was a geek, of course, with a short-sleeved white shirt and glasses. Everyone here was a geek, it was Geek Nation. This guy was probably already at B-school himself, working his way through with this job.

The geek typed things on his computer, then handed back Conrad's ID. He told him to go to the locker area.

"The proctors inside will explain the rules."

Conrad nodded. "Okay."

"Good luck," the Korean said, and smiled.

"Thanks," Conrad said.

The lockers were beige, little cubicles stacked on top of each other. Each had a padlock. People opened the lockers and stood in silence, taking off coats, watches. Everything personal had to be left in the lockers—watches, cell phones, all printed material. Nothing could be taken into the test—no pens, pencils, or markers. Conrad was impressed by the resourcefulness of the cheating that all this implied. No pencils? That would mean microchips. For scribbling you were issued a noteboard, a laminated-paper notebook, with pens.

Conrad chose a locker and stashed his jacket and wallet, his watch and cell phone, inside it. The girl with the blue parka was next to him, silent and preoccupied. She took off her rustling parka and hung it up. The narrow aisles were full of people, lockers clicking open and clanging shut. No one spoke.

The testing area was bland and modern, a beige warren of three-sided cubicles, with walls that went halfway to the ceiling. In each cubicle was a chair and a laptop. The cubicles stood in rows down the center of the room; on either side were glassed-in observation rooms with video cameras and screens. There were monitors and observers everywhere. They could watch him, but he couldn't watch them. He wouldn't be able to put his back to the wall, and once he was seated, he couldn't see over the partitions. People would be walking behind him, unseen. It was a bad tactical position: facing inward, exposed behind. He wasn't going to think about that.

Ten minutes left. People milled around, their faces stiff and empty. Everyone seemed younger than he. No one spoke, as though they were filled to the brim and any conversation might cause them to spill. A young man at the front of the room began to talk, and everyone swiveled toward him. He was a proctor, solid and blond, reliable-looking. He explained the rules, though everyone knew them. The test took four hours, with two optional breaks. You couldn't leave your cubicle otherwise. If you needed to leave, you raised your hand and a proctor would escort you out. Conrad half listened. He could feel the headache, small, heavy, poised.

They were told to choose a cubicle and sit down. Conrad took a place at the end of a row. It was good that the test was so long: panic wouldn't last four hours. If it hit him it would pass, and he'd have time to recover. There'd be parts when he'd be fine.

He sat down and pulled his chair in. It made no sound on the carpeting. He settled himself in front of the computer. The screen lit up. *Welcome to the Graduate Management Admission Test.*

The first part was writing, two essays: one on poorly made products, the second on safety in the workplace. He thought it would be all right, though he felt a little dizzy as he approached the subjects. As though his brain were slightly off-kilter. He knew what he was saying, but he couldn't seem to set it down logically. He had the feeling that he was repeating himself; then he thought he hadn't been clear. He read each one over. He thought they were all right. Each essay was meant to take half an hour. There was a big clock on the wall, and at the end of the first hour he had finished the essays and the headache had not descended. He thought it might be all right.

At the start of the quantitative section his chest began to tighten. The computer screen was relentless: lines of mathematical problems. There was no end to them. He felt claustrophobic at the sight. You had to solve them in order, you couldn't skip one and come back. It felt oppressive, the screen covered in lines of equations and charts and diagrams.

By the first optional break, his head was pounding. He was screwing it up. He couldn't think his way through the equations. He kept starting over and getting stalled. He wrote down the problems on his noteboard, to try to get his mind working, like priming a pump, but it didn't help. His mind was blurred. This was like being on drugs, everything looming and distant by turns. He couldn't think his way into these things. He couldn't manage his mind.

When the break was called, he stood up and went back to the lockers. *Don't fuck this up,* he told himself. *Just don't.* His head was on fire, as though someone were loose in there with a blowtorch. Against the wall was a table packed with rows of bottled water. He took a bottle. He opened his throat and let the water run down inside. This was how they drank it in-country. Almost without swallowing, letting it run straight down.

His chest felt constricted. All of him felt constricted.

For the rest of the break he walked around, his pulse racing. He told himself to calm down. He told himself he wasn't fucking it up. If worse came to worst, if he really did, he could have the whole thing erased. But the thing was that, actually, he knew he was fucking it up. He was fucking it up.

The room was getting warmer. He could smell the sweat in the air, hear the whisper of arms shifting on the desktops, the sighs as people drew quiet breaths, the silvery slither of chairs across the carpet. Palms rubbing on thighs, a fingernail tapping on the desktop. The quiet, steady clicking of keyboards. The silent grinding of people's minds.

He was screwing it up. It was getting worse. He couldn't pound the little things into any kind of sense. It was getting worse, and the worse he felt, the worse he did. He was in a long panicked slide backward. He could feel himself going and couldn't stop himself.

At the second break, he walked around again. He wondered if people were looking at him. He had the feeling that the panic was visible, hovering over him like a tornado funnel. Did he give off that aura? He breathed carefully, long, deep breaths. He made no eye contact. He drank some more water, then went to the men's room. He took a long piss. He was fucking it up.

He did the last four questions in twelve minutes and finished with two minutes still to go.

After he typed in the last answer, the screen changed.

Just one moment, please.

It was tabulating the scores.

You have the option to delete your scores at this time. If you delete them, they will never be posted on any record, but the fact that you took the test and deleted them will be recorded. You must decide now, before you see your scores, whether or not you choose to delete them. To delete, click on DELETE. *To see the scores, click on* SEE SCORES.

Conrad stared at the screen.

He'd screwed it up. He knew it. He couldn't bring himself to press "Delete." He should. He should just delete the whole thing. What if he'd done better than he thought? He couldn't be sure. Deleting the whole thing would be like erasing himself. He couldn't do it.

He clicked on See Scores.

And there they were. He'd fucked up.

These scores would get him in nowhere.

He clicked through and turned off the computer. He pushed his chair back and stood up. Everyone was standing up. *Now what?* he thought. The headache was thundering inside.

On the way back uptown, he sat in the subway and stared at the ads for computer school in three languages. *Okay,* he told himself. *Okay.* Then he thought, *Fuck.*

No plan survives contact with the enemy, he told himself. *New plan.*

The next plan was: Do all right on the econ exam, take another econ course next semester, and take the GMAT again in the spring. Because here was the thing: Once he started treatment at the VA, everything would be different. They'd fix his brain and he'd be able to focus on problems, he'd be able to take a four-hour test without going off like a rocket. He'd be able to think again.

That night, Jenny asked him about the test as soon as she came home. She stood by the door, unwrapping the long wool scarf from around her neck. "So, how was it?" she asked. "How'd it go?"

By then he was able to shrug his shoulders.

"It didn't go too well," Conrad said. "I'm going to take it again in the spring."

She looked at him for a moment. "What happened?"

He shook his head. "Gonna take it again in the spring."

"Sounds good," she said.

She unzipped her coat and turned to hang it up. He saw that his own response would govern that of others. She couldn't see his fear, which he had strapped and throttled and was holding underground.

"When do you want to come out to Katonah?" she asked. "They're giving us the day off on the twenty-fourth, so I'm going out after work on the twenty-third. Want to come on the same train?"

"I'm not coming until the next day," Conrad said.

"Christmas Eve?" Jenny said. She turned to look at him again and pushed up the sleeves of her sweater.

"Stuff to do," Conrad said. "I'll see you out there."

She gazed at him for a moment but didn't say anything more.

"And I'll move out as soon as we get back," he said.

"Don't worry about it," she said.

"No, I'm gone." Conrad shook his head and smiled.

He dreaded going out there. He dreaded Christmas itself, the whole noisy, tinselly passage, the glittering decorations and the flickering candles and the high-pitched songs and the mound of presents. He dreaded everyone's eyes on him, filled with expectation. He dreaded the silent plea to be one of them, to be part of something he did not feel part of, dreaded the joyful and unspoken declaration that everything had returned to normal.

Here he was, went the declaration, back home again, and all the golden cogs and gears had clicked silently back into place. The great machine of family life had started up once more, spinning and gyrating and humming in harmony, as if nothing had ever interrupted it. He'd been hearing that silent declaration for weeks, for months, in all those cheery notes and bright pleading messages. He dreaded seeing his mother's eyes on him, he dreaded the moment when she realized how wrong things had gone, when her face flooded with worry. He couldn't pretend he was back, and one of them. He couldn't pretend everything was fine. He dreaded telling them he'd fucked up the GMAT.

On the twentieth, the econ exam went all right, or he thought it did. He'd worked on it all semester; he knew the ideas, he understood the premises. He wasn't sure how well he'd done on the essay; he was afraid his writing was kind of confused. That's why he was going to the VA. Mental confusion: that was a symptom. That's what they addressed.

Conrad emailed the guys who would not be coming home for Christmas.

> *Molinos, Hang in there. Hope they serve up something good in the chow hall. Next year, this time, you'll be home. Have a good one. Semper Fi, Farrell.*

Turner had news about Dail:

So now she's not allowed in the living room unless Abbott is there. So she goes into his bedroom and cranks up the music. We can all hear her while we're in the living room watching TV. It's wild. And now when she sees us she pushes out her tits. In case we aren't aware of them.

Conrad wrote back:

Try teaching her Scrabble. I think there's a special "Scrabble for Strippers."

He heard from Anderson, who had decided to hang in there with the job.

I'll be goddamm if I quit a job just because other guys are assholes, was what he had actually written. He was spending Christmas with his family. *Looking forward to it, LT.*

Conrad answered:

Sounds very good. Me, too, spending Christmas with my family. Have a good one.

Conrad dreaded going into the stores and buying presents. The crowds and the noise, the loud, pealing music and the artificial cheer. He put it off, but on the twenty-fourth he put on his parka and set off to Bloomingdale's. He took the subway down to Fifty-ninth Street and walked east.

The streets were packed with drifting out-of-towners, inattentive, slow, gawking. Those who weren't tourists were New Yorkers, walking fast and talking on cell phones. Conrad wouldn't use his on the street; it was too distracting. You wouldn't know what was happening around you if you were yammering about the football game. These people strode along, talking loudly, preoccupied, heedless.

The traffic was near gridlock, cars and trucks jamming the avenues, honking and impatient. Everyone in the world with a few days and a few dollars to spend had converged on the city. Conrad heard people talking in French, Swedish, Japanese, Polish. He hated being jostled, hated it when tourists stopped in front of him on the sidewalk or slowed suddenly or bumped into him.

Chill, he told himself. *It's Christmas. It's their sidewalk, too.*

On Madison he saw a family of tourists, apparently overwhelmed by the city. They were fair and solid—maybe from Scandinavia, or Iowa. The parents wore muted colors, dull parkas and loose jeans, clunky running shoes. The father held up a map, frowning. Two daughters stood near him, one five or six, holding her mother's hand, the other nine or ten, already chunky. She wore tight jeans and a red parka, and she carried a pink plastic purse looped over the shoulder. Her hair was shoulder length, with heavy bangs. She was gazing into the crowd, frowning faintly. Someone walked quickly past them, between her and her mother. The girl moved sideways, staring at a store window. She meant to move back to her mother, but it was Conrad she bumped into, leaning familiarly against his thigh.

"Whoa," Conrad said, taking her by the shoulders.

She looked up at him, startled.

"Your mom's right there," Conrad said, and the whole family's gaze suddenly converged on him, a stranger holding their daughter. The mother opened her mouth to speak. But Conrad was smiling, and just as everyone realized the possible risk, they recognized that there was no actual risk. In fact, the opposite: their daughter had stepped into the hands of a man who would protect her. Watching their faces shift into relief gave Conrad a lift. The little girl moved awkwardly back to her mom, who folded her under her arm.

"Thanks," the mom said, smiling primly—they were Midwestern after all.

Conrad nodded.

The husband said, "Can I ask you something? Where is Thirty-fourth Street from here? We're looking for the Empire State Building."

Conrad took the map. "Here's where we are." He was pleased to do this. "Here's the Empire State Building."

"Great, thanks," the man said, nodding.

Conrad nodded back. "Have a good time." As he spoke, his cell phone rang. He turned away to look at it. The caller was his CO, Captain Glover. He moved out of the thronging stream, over to the side of a huge office building. He clicked on the phone.

"Afternoon, sir." Conrad straightened his shoulders. A deliveryman pushed past him, a short Latino man in a white uniform, carrying a take-out bag. Conrad frowned, listening. "What did you say, sir?" He put his hand over the other ear. He listened again and then asked, "When did it happen, sir?"

The crowd moved past him in floods, drifting and pushing, inattentive. A young bike messenger in spandex biking pants and a red helmet wheeled his bike up to a parking meter. Anderson had gone to his uncle's barn with a deer rifle in the middle of the night. Conrad pictured the barn, damp and cold, full of shadows. The messenger took the chain from his bag and crouched down to padlock the bike to the meter.

"Fucking hell, sir," Conrad said. "Anderson." He paused. "That's really bad news, sir. I'd been in touch with him. I knew he was having some trouble, but he never let on that things were this bad. It sounded as though things were getting better. I thought he was doing fine."

"I'm really sorry to have to give you this news, Farrell," Glover said. "I'm sorry. It's really bad. Christmas. Christ."

There was silence. The bike messenger snapped the padlock shut. He took off his helmet.

"All right," Conrad said. "Thanks. I'll tell the others, sir."

When Conrad clicked off, the messenger was taking the front wheel off the frame. It would be a pain in the ass to carry the wheel around, Conrad thought. Anderson opening the door into the cold, dark barn. The silence of the barn at night, the glow from a bare bulb on an overhead beam. Two days before Christmas.

It felt like a kick to the chest.

He kept moving down the sidewalk, through the Christmas crowds, past the steady jingling of the Salvation Army bells. On the corner was a woman in a bonnet, singing with a man, both wearing the Salvation Army uniform. Conrad was seeing the burning Humvee in Haditha, the bright flames engulfing it. The noise was too great to be noise, and the heat was a separate universe. Conrad was shouting and grabbing for Anderson, who was in the thick of the flames. Anderson was trying to wrench open the door with his bare hands, and Carleton was inside, screaming.

He took the train to Katonah later that afternoon. The car was nearly full, but he found a seat by the window. The trip started in darkness as the train slid swiftly beneath the streets of Manhattan. Later the cars rose up to the surface, rattling past the towers of Harlem, on through the outer regions beyond the city, where the buildings were lower and farther apart, the cars and lights fewer as the train passed from urban density to suburban sprawl and finally to the open countryside.

As the light faded, the train's big glass windows became opaque and reflective, and it became harder to see into the darkness. It had snowed earlier in the week, and a light covering was still on the ground. As the train rattled through the countryside, Conrad leaned close to the window, nearly resting his forehead on the glass. The snow glowed faintly in the dimness, a pale, lambent carpet, smooth and undulating, that lay below the dark houses and trees and the gray sky.

He had told no one his arrival time, and there was no one to meet him. He walked up the concrete stairs alone, relieved to have a few more minutes of silence, invisibility.

Katonah taxis were haphazard operations, cars driven by private operators who had other lives. In the evening, around commuter time, there were always some cabs around, waiting. At midday during the week, often there were none. That day there were several in the parking lot, hoping for a late fare on Christmas Eve. Conrad climbed into a big old American sedan with a loose, coughing engine. The door shut with a solid clunk.

The driver was a heavyset woman in her forties, with a brown, impassive face and long black glossy hair. She looked at him in the mirror. The radio was on low, someone singing.

"North Salem Road," he told her.

"North Sale Road?" she repeated. Her accent was very thick.

"Just drive east on thirty-five," he said. "I'll show you where to turn off."

She nodded and put the car in reverse. The engine made a gargling sound, like a big motorboat idling. They headed out of the little lot, then out of the village. Conrad thought the woman looked familiar: had she driven him home before? He wondered if she was married to one of the landscape guys who roared around the lawns during the summer. She looked older than they were, though. He wondered how long she'd been in the States. They were mostly illegal, the Latin Americans here. The men lined up by the railroad station in the mornings, waiting for a contractor to come by with a pickup truck and give them a day's work. They did all the landscaping. They built stone walls, put in pools, dug gardens, clipped hedges, mowed lawns. All over Westchester, dark faces in every yard. His mother talked about it, distressed by the way they were treated.

The taxi came up the little rise on 22 and stopped at the light at 35. The traffic was heavy, everyone hurrying to get home for Christmas Eve. The road was clear, but there was a thin dusting of snow on the ground. The woods crowded along the road, tall and dim, rising up into the shadowy sky. It was nearly dark.

They lived right on the edge, those lawn guys. It was like being in a revolution, coming here illegally. No language, no green cards, always at risk, in fear but determined to work. People claimed they were taking jobs from Americans, but that was bullshit. Americans wouldn't take those jobs. Those jobs were too menial for people living the American dream, which they did by playing video games and drinking beer. Americans hired these guys to mow their lawns and then complained about illegal aliens. He thought of Ali and the grimy men lined up in the clearing room.

The light changed, and they turned onto 35. Conrad leaned forward. The road narrowed here, rising up the hill and curving along the reservoir. The radio was set to an oldies station: Dusty Springfield was singing, a soulful catch in her voice.

"Just up here," Conrad said. "Turn left on Mount Holly."

The woman slowed, waiting for a pause in the traffic. Mount Holly Road was dirt, and once they turned onto it, they were in the country. They bumped slowly along on the narrow lane. The trees met overhead; even in the darkness Conrad could feel them.

"And left onto North Salem, up here," Conrad told her as they approached the T. It was confusing back here. Mount Holly made a little jog, joining North Salem for a hundred yards, then separating again. Local knowledge. The driver had local knowledge of her own. She knew a village in the south, red dirt and shiny dark leaves, stucco houses with small windows. She would know everything about that village, wherever it was. Here she was on her own. Now it was Dionne Warwick. "Do you know the way to San Jose?" Did she think she could learn a whole American life as though it were hers? Was this her mission? To learn the back roads of Katonah and the musical past of this place, as if she and her parents had grown up here? Or was she putting money away so she could go home?

"This is the house, on the right," Conrad said as they approached. The house stood on the hillside above the road. It looked festive, all the windows lit and the big sugar maples rising, dark against the ghostly lawn. The cab turned into the driveway and drove up the hill, stopping by the back of the house. Conrad took out his wallet and leaned forward.

"Seven dollar," the woman said without turning around.

"Gracias," Conrad said. He handed her the fare and a five-dollar tip. *"Feliz Navidad."*

The woman looked at him in the mirror, unsmiling. Her black eyes were large and luminous. The overhead light shone down on her face, picking out a pale scar on her right cheek, stretching all the way into the hairline.

"Thank you," she said, refusing him entry into her language. "Merry Christmas."

"Okay," Conrad said, abashed. "Okay. Yeah. You, too."

He took his bags and got out. It seemed he'd insulted her, implying that she couldn't speak the language of the country she'd chosen. He'd meant to be polite, but he'd been a dick.

He leaned back inside. "Merry Christmas to you, too, *señora*," he said, "and Happy New Year."

She glanced at him, suspicious. He smiled, lifting his hand in a wave. She gave him an ambiguous look that turned into a smile. She lifted her hand, and the car moved off down the drive into the darkness.

She was a hero. She had somehow crossed the border concealed in the back of a truck, silent and sweating with fear, or walking, delirious, through the lethal heart of the desert. She'd made her way from that Latin American village or city, wherever it was, to northern Westchester, where she had managed to get a 1962 Chevy and a license to drive people around Katonah. She should have a fucking medal. She should be allowed to decide what language she was addressed in. He thought again of Ali, who was maybe driving a taxi somewhere in a country where they spoke a language foreign to him—and maybe not.

Conrad pushed through the gate. Through the mudroom door he could see the kitchen, all lit up. Lydia was standing at the island, talking to someone out of sight. He dreaded the change that would come over her face; he dreaded being seen.

24

Conrad came in through the back door, marshaling his seabag and his bulky bags of presents. Lydia turned, and her face lightened.

"You're here!" she said.

"Hi, Mom." His chest had gone tight. He smiled at her.

The kitchen was steamy and crowded, full of bags and food and packages. Pots rattled on the stove, something sizzled in a pan, something was roasting in the oven. Murphy lay on a pile of magazines on the island. From the library he heard voices and the TV blaring. The whole house was full.

Lydia put her arms around him and he held himself still.

"Con's here!" she called.

Conrad drew back. Before anyone could come in, he said, "Be right back down. Just taking my things up." He went up the back stairs two at a time.

In his room, he shut the door and set his things down. The room closed in around him. He could hear talking downstairs; someone laughed. After dinner they would sing carols. He didn't know if he could go back down. He put his hands on his hips and closed his eyes. "Fuck," he whispered.

He put on his headphones and found Johnny Cash on his iPod. He lay down on his bed and fell into the sound. The deep, scraping voice and *boom-chicka-boom*. "Folsom Prison Blues": the basics. You couldn't get better than that. He turned the volume up and closed his eyes and sang along in a whisper, tapping his foot in the air.

When Jenny knocked, he didn't hear her. She opened the door and came into the room and waved at him.

"Con?" She was dressed up for dinner in a green silky top and black pants.

Conrad took off his headphones. He could still hear the beat, tiny but driving. "Hi."

"Dinner's ready." Her voice was tentative. "Are you coming down?"

"Do I have a choice?"

There was a silence, then they both spoke at once.

"Don't you want to?" she asked.

"Joke." He sat up. "I'm coming."

Jenny moved farther into the room. Her eyes were brilliant.

"Are you mad that I asked you to leave my apartment?"

He shook his head. "No. It's cool. You were right."

"You can come back," she said.

Conrad sat up. "No. I was a dick. And I've got Go-Go's place."

"Then what is it?" Jenny asked. "What's the matter? You act so angry at us. Like we're doing something to you." She came closer to the bed. "What is it? Why doesn't it get any better?"

He didn't want her to touch him. He could feel the air thickening around his chest. Far away, Johnny Cash was growling. "I'm not angry at you. I know you're all trying to make things better," he said. "I just don't want to be here."

When Lydia and Marshall went upstairs to change for dinner, Marshall sat down on the bed to take off his shoes. Lydia closed the door and moved to the bureau. She stood still and put her hands over her face. Marshall was turned away from her. He put his shoes side by side beneath the chair.

"Did I lay the fire in the living room?" he said. "I thought of it, but I can't remember if I actually did. I hope so. I don't want to do it in these clothes."

Lydia said nothing. He turned to look at her. Her hands were pressed tight against her face, her shoulders high and clenched.

"What is it?" he asked.

She shook her head.

"What?" He stood and went over to her.

"I don't know if I can do this." She dropped her hands. Her face looked drawn and grieving.

Marshall put his arms around her. "Lyd."

"I know what I'm supposed to do," she said. "I do it all the time as a therapist, but I can't do it with Con. I can't do it."

"What do you mean?" He led her to the bed and sat down beside her.

"I'm not supposed to reach out to him all the time, he doesn't like it, I can see that. If he were a client, I'd tell myself to stop." She put her hands out, palms down. "Just stop. Wait for him to come to me. Be loving but don't pursue him. Don't pursue him." She started to cry. "It's the first rule, the most basic thing. I can't do it." She shook her head. "I'm too afraid. I can't leave him alone. Every time I see him, I want to put my arms around him and comfort him. I know he hates being touched. He freezes. I can't stop myself. Each time, it seems so natural I do it again; I can't believe it won't work. But it makes it worse." She shook her head. "What kind of a therapist! What kind of a mother! I can't stop."

Marshall put his arms close around her. "Lyd, you're doing the best you can," he said. "Don't blame yourself."

"Who should I blame?" she asked. "Who's the mental health professional here?" She shook her head again. "I can't help it. I go into a panic. I'm so afraid." She pressed her face against Marshall's shoulder. "It's worse than when he was in Iraq. Then I knew that sometimes he was in danger and sometimes he was safe. Now I think he's in danger all the time, every second. And I can't do anything. I make it worse."

"Shh," Marshall said. "It's not your fault. Don't blame yourself." He held her.

"Marsh," she said against his chest. "Aren't you frightened?"

"Shh," he said.

Lydia reared her head back and looked at him. "You're not saying. Aren't you afraid?"

After a moment he answered. "Yes. But it will get better."

When Conrad came in, the others were already sitting at the table. The dining room was rectangular, with a bay window at one end and two tall windows giving onto the lawn. Heavy linen curtains with a dim red pattern hung at them. A carved wooden mirror hung over an old pine chest. In the bay window stood a huge fern, foaming over the table like a green waterfall. The table was polished fruitwood, set with heavy silver, crystal candlesticks, silver salt and pepper shakers. A long red woven strip of cloth stretched down the center of the table, and on it was a platter heaped with gold and silver Christmas balls.

The others were dressed up: Marshall, in a tweed jacket and tie, sat at the head of the table. Lydia, at the other end, wore a ruffled red sweater and a necklace of tiny Christmas-tree balls. Jenny's earrings were red-nosed reindeers. Ollie wore a jacket, and his hair was brushed. Conrad wore the khakis and V-necked sweater he'd worn all day, and his not-clean T-shirt.

Lydia patted the chair next to her. When Conrad sat down, she put her hand on his arm.

"I served you a plate," she said. "Roast pork, your favorite. We're glad to have you here."

"Thanks, Mom. Glad to be here." Her hand on his arm felt hot.

Marshall lifted his wineglass. "Welcome home," he said. "Merry Christmas."

"Good," Ollie said, looking around and nodding.

It was a non sequitur, typical Oll, wanting things to work out.

Everyone raised glasses, smiling. The whole table was smiling—the gleaming ornaments, the polished silver, the flickering candles. Conrad raised his glass and took a long swallow, closing his eyes. He was going to make the effort. One foot after the other; it would get better.

"Biscuits, Marsh," Lydia said. "Can you pass them on?"

Marshall handed the basket to Ollie. Then he leaned forward, elbows out awkwardly on the table. "So, guys, I want to know what's been going on for everyone. Schools, jobs, friends? What's up?" He liked conducting the conversation as if it were a seminar.

There was a silence; then Ollie volunteered, the good son.

"Well," he said, "I'm thinking of majoring in film studies."

"Okay," Marshall said. "And what is that exactly, film studies?"

"Film as a cultural presence. It's like literature," Ollie said. "You know, studying films, like studying books."

Marshall looked at him. "Does that mean you'll be watching a lot of movies for homework?"

"Well, yeah," Ollie said. "And writing papers about them. The way I'd be reading books and writing papers about them. It's the same."

"Interesting, Oll," Lydia said encouragingly. "Which filmmakers would you focus on?"

Conrad could manage this, just sitting and listening, watching the family tide ebb and flow. His father leaning on Ollie, his mother defending him. Next time they'd reverse positions. It was like a seesaw, one parent always defending a child from the other.

"David Lynch," Ollie said. "He's a genius."

"Oh, yuck," Jenny said. "A total misogynist."

Ollie shook his head. "Don't be so narrow-minded. He's exploring the American love affair with violence."

"Violence against women," Jenny said. "And he's not exploring it, he's exploiting it. He's relishing it. He's encouraging it. If you focus on him, you're just part of it."

"So what would you do, Jen?" Marshall asked. "Not include David Lynch in a film course?"

"I'd teach his movies the way people include Hitler in a history class," Jenny said. "He's there, he's part of the story, you don't pretend he doesn't exist, but you don't offer him as an object of admiration."

"Whoa," Ollie said. "Whoa, whoa, whoa." He looked at Jenny. "David Lynch is Hitler?"

"It's the way you present him," Jenny said, ignoring that. "You present him as what he really is. You don't dress up his sadistic tendencies and pretend that just because he uses nonlinear stories and bad lighting that he's a genius. He's a pretentious sicko."

"So, Jen," said Lydia. "How do you really feel about David Lynch? Be candid."

Jenny shook her head.

"Okay, that's your view," Ollie said. "Fine, but there are other ways of looking at his films."

Jenny rolled her eyes and took a bite of the pork.

"Spoken like a real academic, Oll," Conrad said, impressed. The

Ollie of four years ago would have lost his temper, yelled at Jenny, and left the table.

"Just saying," Jenny said to Ollie, "if I were in your class, I'd be presenting my point of view. I hope you have some strong women there."

"No one quite as strong as you," Ollie said. He grinned at her and Jenny laughed.

"Few woman are that," Marshall said.

"Okay," Jenny said. "You want to know my strong woman news? My boss hates me."

Lydia frowned. "He does not hate you. You're overreacting."

"He does. He's rude to me. All the time."

"I can't believe that," Lydia said. "You're doing so well! What about that new account?"

"That was before," Jenny said. "This guy is new. He hates me."

"What does he do?" Marshall asked.

"He's rude to me in public," Jenny said. "In a kind of offhand way. He interrupts me in meetings. He stands up if I'm talking." Jenny took a swallow of wine, not looking at them, as if that proved her point.

"I thought we talked about that," Conrad said. "I told you what to do."

Jenny exploded, snorting a fine cascade of wine out her nose. "It's true," she said, wiping her mouth. "You did tell me exactly what to do."

"And what was that?" Marshall asked. He looked from one to the other.

There was a pause, and Jenny said, "Conrad told me to show him my balls."

Ollie choked and nearly fell off his chair.

Maybe he could do this.

After dinner they went into the living room to sing carols. The living room was handsome and formal, peach-colored walls and polished furniture. Heavy butter-colored curtains stood in soft folds at the windows; an old Oriental rug in deep reds and yellows lay on the wide-board floor. A mahogany bookcase stood against the inside wall, and over the mantelpiece hung an Audubon print of a red fox sitting on its haunches, nose raised to the sky. The sofa and chairs were covered in yellow chintz. In the bay window stood the Christmas tree, its glittering bulk garlanded with silver, glowing with tiny lights. It was hung with shining balls, carved figures, and clumsy lopsided things they'd made as children: Jenny's gold paper star, Ollie's splayfooted clay Rudolph, a weird abstract rooster cut out of sheet metal by Conrad. The tree was hung with the same things each year, and each year Lydia said it was the most beautiful one they'd ever had. Beneath the tree lay the bright jumbled heap of presents. Marshall leaned over and lit the fire. It flickered behind the polished brass andirons. Conrad's chest tightened.

Jenny passed out the tattered songbooks from the little mahogany chest. Marshall and Lydia sat on the low sofa, Jenny on the bench in front of the fire, Murphy on her lap. Conrad and Ollie sat in the yellow chintz chairs, which were too narrow and too deep, with arms that were too high. Conrad had brought a bottle of wine in from the dining room, and he set it down with his glass next to his chair.

They sang in four parts: Jenny took soprano, Lydia alto, Conrad and Ollie were tenors, and Marshall bass. They sang "Silent Night," and "O Little Town of Bethlehem." They knew the harmonies, they sang these songs every year. Jenny's light, pure voice climbed up into the darkness for "Away in a Manger"; Marshall's gravelly bass held the melody an octave lower. They belted out the choruses, smiling at one another as they opened their throats, sang the familiar words. Conrad got through the first three songs. He sank into the music, listening for the others weaving in and out of the melody, Ollie's voice beside his. But it began to seem stranger and stranger to sit in this soft, bright room, singing songs about joy. All of this was unconnected to him. He began taking a long swallow of wine after each song.

During the long chorus of "Angels We Have Heard on High"—the long *Gloria*—he looked around at them. On the "O" they all opened their mouths wide, as though they were singing cabaret. He thought of Kuchnik, lying in the sand. Anderson, stepping into the darkened barn. Jenny smiled at him, widening her mouth on the high notes. Why was *he* here? Those others were not here, not home. How did it work, the algebra of lost souls? Where were they, the others? After the song he poured himself another glass.

When they started "God Bless Ye Merry, Gentlemen," Conrad looked down at the book, as though he needed to read the words, and stopped singing. The tempo was brisk and he kept up, mouthing the words. "Comfort and joy, oh, tidings of comfort and joy." Halfway through the refrain he saw Ollie glance sideways at him, listening for the other tenor line. Conrad opened his mouth wider, as though he were singing loudly and energetically. At the end of the song he took another long swallow, ignoring Ollie.

"Why aren't you singing?" Ollie whispered.

"I am singing," Conrad said, not whispering and not looking at him. "I'm singing." He took another long swallow. "Want some?" He held out the glass.

Ollie shook his head.

"How about 'Joy to the World'?" asked Jenny. "Page eight."

Conrad stood and left the room, carrying the empty bottle. In the kitchen he set it on the counter beside the sink and stood for a moment, looking out the window into the dark. The dishwasher was steaming and humming. *I'm here, and they are not.* He felt black inside. He wasn't going to make it through the evening. There was nowhere else for him to go.

He went into the empty dining room. The chandelier was brighter now, no longer dimmed. Crumpled napkins littered the red mats. Constellations of salt and pepper dotted the polished surface. The chairs stood out at untidy angles.

Conrad took an opened bottle of wine from the sideboard. He carried it back into the living room. His mother looked up; he saw her forehead crease slightly at the sight. He set the bottle down beside his chair.

There were more carols. At the end of each one, Conrad drank.

Ollie now refused to look at him. Lydia was trying to catch his eye. When Conrad finally looked at her, she gave an unhappy little smile and shook her head, the way she'd have done when he was eight years old and about to take another dessert at someone's house for dinner. *No,* the shake meant, *don't do it.* He raised the glass again to his mouth, smiling at her as though he hadn't gotten her message.

At the end of "Good King Wenceslas," Conrad refilled his glass. As he set the bottle down on the rug, he knocked it over. Dark wine flooded across the carpet. Lydia said "Oh!" on an indrawn breath. She stood and hurried from the room. Jenny stood up, too. Lydia came back with towels, sponges, water, salt.

"Let me help," Jenny said.

"First you mop it up," Lydia said.

"Sorry," Conrad said.

He didn't stand up. He was afraid he'd lose his balance. Why were they making such a fuss? This was not a major catastrophe. Marshall and Ollie leaned forward in a concerned way, suggesting by their posture that they were about to get up and help, which they were not. Lydia knelt on the rug in her black velvet pants and ruffled red sweater, the Christmas ball necklace bobbing as she scrubbed. Jenny knelt beside her.

"Can I help?" Conrad asked.

Now he stood. He felt himself sway.

"No, it's all right," Lydia said. "This is why you have Oriental rugs. It won't show." She pressed the towel against the rug, turning it to a clean patch, pressing again.

"Here," Conrad said, leaning over. He felt himself start to tip, and he grabbed hold of the lamp. He was seized from behind by Ollie.

"Conrad," Marshall said. "You've had enough to drink."

Conrad turned to him carefully. All movement was risky. "I'm not drinking," he said. "I was trying to help Mom clean up the rug."

"You've been drinking," Marshall said.

"Marshall," Lydia said.

"I've been drinking," Conrad said. "And so has everyone else in this room."

"Conrad," Lydia said, looking up. "Don't be rude to your father."

"Don't be rude to my father," Conrad repeated. "Is that a rule?"

There was a silence.

"Where are the rest of those rules?"

Lydia put the towel down. "Don't do this, Con." Her face was white and flattened.

"Because, you know what? Fuck those rules," Conrad said.

"Okay, Con," Marshall said, holding up his palms. "Let's hold on here."

"No," Conrad said. "I'm not holding on. *Hold on* means *Be quiet*, and I'm not going to do that. I don't think you know what it's like for me."

No one spoke.

"This is like being in the middle of a flooding river. I can't stop it. I can't get to shore. I can't stop to obey the rules." He looked around.

"Though I'm good at obeying them. I obeyed the rules when I went over there. But they didn't work. I ended up doing things I should never have done, by any rules. I saw other people breaking the rules. I watched my men die. I watched our troops kill civilians. We killed thousands of civilians, and we lost our own men. Young men who should have had their whole lives ahead of them are gone. Or they've come home without arms or legs, or without a face." Conrad looked around again. "I'm through with these rules. We went over there for no reason, there were no WMDs. It was a lie. It was a lie. We lost our men for a lie. What is this about rules?"

Lydia sat back on her heels, the stained towel in her hands. "I can't stand this," she said. "Con, you have to do something about this."

"I don't know why I have to obey any rules," Conrad said. "Your rules, any rules. All those big rules that I paid attention to"—he looked around again—"all those big rules, where did they get me? Where did they get Carleton and Olivera and Kuchnik?" There was another pause. "Where did those rules get any of us? What was the point?"

"Con, I'm sorry," Marshall said. "No one here wants to argue with you."

"Please," Lydia said. She had begun to cry. "I can't stand this."

"Yeah," Conrad said. He had let go of the lamp and was staggering. "I'm home, and Carleton and Olivera and Kuchnik are not. And Ali is not. And now Anderson is gone. I didn't tell you this." He closed his eyes for a moment, then opened them. "But you want to hear my news? I just heard today. Paul Anderson is a guy from Minnesota. He saved my life in Ramadi. You met him. You saw him at Pendleton, when we got back. You won't remember him." He shook his head, blinking. "He killed himself. He went out to his uncle's barn and blew off the back of his head."

He looked around.

The fire flickered in the fireplace, a chunk of log fell into the ashes. Murphy, on the bench, stretched her paw out dreamily, her eyes closed. The lighted tree glittered against the dark windows.

Lydia got up awkwardly from her knees. She went to Conrad and folded her arms around him.

"Con," she murmured against him.

He pulled violently away from her; she lost her balance, staggering.

"Lydia, don't do that," Marshall said angrily. "Can't you stop?"

Lydia turned to him, her face white. "Marshall."

"Don't touch him," Marshall said. "Leave him alone."

"Don't tell me what to do for my son," Lydia said.

"Mom," Jenny said, and began to cry.

"Okay," Conrad said. He stood with his hands clenched, his head lowered. "I'm sorry, Mom. I know you're trying. I'm sorry I can't do what you want." He couldn't raise his eyes. "It was bad being over there, and it's worse being back," he said. "What the fuck was the point? What do the rules say about that?"

He didn't give them the rest, his own news: that he'd royally fucked up the GMAT, that he couldn't sleep and the headaches wouldn't quit and he didn't know if he'd ever be able to study or even concentrate again. That he had fought with his sister and had been thrown out of her apartment and he was frightened that he had no future. That he was ashamed that he'd fucked up, but he was most ashamed that he was still alive and that people who had trusted him were not.

He looked around at them. "I come out here and you're all waiting for me to be the person you want me to be," he said thickly. "But I'm not him." He looked around again. "It's like every time I saw you, I told you to be Chinese. 'Just do it. Be Chinese.' I can't do it. I'm not the person you want me to be. I'm completely different. I look like the person you remember, but I'm not him. You've lost him. He might as well have died."

Jenny began to cry quietly, tears sliding down her cheeks. Lydia's face crumpled.

Marshall said, "But can't you make an effort, Con? This is up to you."

Conrad stared at him. "You don't get it. I'd love to do this—what you say. Change. I can't. Something's not working. All you do is tear me apart. I'd like to be back here with you all, but I'm not. You don't get it. I'm not here. I'm not home. I'm still there."

25

Go-Go's apartment was in a modern high-rise building, First Avenue in the East Sixties, expensive but not pleasant. The design goal seemed to be intimidation. The lobby was high-ceilinged and empty, the floor polished stone tile that looked dangerous if wet. The walls were covered with huge gold-veined mirrors. A vast Russian doorman, heavy-bellied and contemptuous, stood guard behind a high desk. He wore a comic opera uniform, scarlet, with gold buttons and epaulets.

On January second, Conrad presented himself at the desk.

"Morning," he said to the Russian. "My name is Conrad Farrell. I'm staying with my friend Gordon Russell. Apartment 21J."

Go-Go had warned Conrad not to say he was staying there alone. "I'm not supposed to sublet," he'd told Conrad. "I'm not even supposed to let anyone else use it. They're strict."

The doorman narrowed his eyes. "Yes," he said insultingly. "He told me." He had a broad Slavic face, pitted cheeks, a wide nose, and cold, dark eyes.

"Did he leave an envelope for me?" Conrad asked.

"Yes," said the doorman stonily. His eyes were still slitted, as though he were waiting for a password.

Conrad waited a moment. "Could I have it?"

"Yes," the doorman said again, not moving, drawing out the pause. Finally he looked down and opened a drawer. He took out an envelope and handed it across the desk, his mouth turned down in a disapproving curve. He went on staring boldly at Conrad, as though the transaction was not complete.

"Thanks," Conrad said. *Does the guy want a tip for just handing me the letter?*

The Russian did not reply, still holding him in his gaze.

Apparently he did. Conrad wanted to say *Marines don't pay bribes,* but he didn't want to screw this up for Go-Go. Anyway, he was no longer a Marine, he was a former. Conrad pulled out his wallet and handed ten dollars to the Russian, who took it without speaking and stuffed it into a pocket. He now looked even more contemptuous, as though by giving him money, Conrad had degraded himself.

The gaudy prick, thought Conrad. He nodded and set off for the elevator.

The apartment was on the twenty-first floor, small but pretentious. The kitchen counters were polished granite, the bathroom marble, and the views of the East River both panoramic and banal. One wall of the living room was plate-glass windows. An angular white sofa stood against the back wall, facing the windows, with an uncomfortable-looking red armchair at either end. A furry black rug covered the floor, and a huge plasma TV took up much of the south wall. Against the facing wall stood a round white table and four white molded plastic chairs. The bedroom, too, overlooked the view. Facing the windows was a huge bed with a square-cornered black leather headboard, hinting mildly at bondage. On one wall stood a fake French antique bureau with ornate brass hardware. An angular green chair, very modern, stood in a corner. The windows reached nearly from floor to ceiling.

The view was the point of the apartment, the point of the whole building. It faced the river, looming high over the intervening block and overlooking the FDR Drive, with its rushing, ceaseless ribbon of traffic. Beyond this was the silver-brown swath of the East River, and beyond that the low red-brown industrial landscape of Queens, stretching out to the horizon like a complicated puzzle.

The apartment was too high. Conrad didn't like the space spreading out so suddenly, alarmingly, so close, just outside the glass. Too much sky. No railings, nothing, just bare sky right in front of him. The room was fully exposed, it was like living on a cliff edge. There was no cover. Conrad set down his seabag and tugged at the limp gray curtains, dragging them across the glass. They didn't meet in the middle. Stretched to their widest, they still let in a bright stripe of light.

Conrad sat down on the bed. He wasn't going to think about the windows. All he had to do was get through the next three weeks until his call from the VA. His class started at the end of January, and by then he'd already be different, his mind would be clearer, the panic ebbing, the fucking eagle's grip on his heart loosened, gone. They'd give him something for the headaches. All he had to do was get through the next three weeks.

His mother called every day now that he was living alone. She sent him email messages, long ones, like letters, as though he were fourteen and away at camp.

> *Dear Con, You should have seen Murphy this morning. I had left an empty cardboard box on the table in the kitchen, a not-very-big box that a scarf had come in. When I came down in the morning, there was Murphy curled up in it, her sides hanging over every edge. She looked up and blinked, as though it was her bed. Love, M.*

She didn't say anything about seeing him.

Mostly he answered briefly.

> *I'm living right over the East River here, and sometimes I go running in the morning along the river. It is nice watching the light on the water. I'm looking forward to getting back to classes.*

Turner wrote to give him the latest.

> *Just wanted to let you know that things have been resolved. Dail is no longer a bother here, because she was arrested and then she left town. It wasn't exactly clear what happened, whether it was possession or something else. It is clear that Abbott doesn't want to talk about it. He was at home with his family when it happened: it was Christmas. I feel bad for him, but I'm just as glad she's not hanging out here anymore, cracking the door to the bedroom to see who's coming up the stairs. I'm pretty sure she went through my stuff a couple of times. Abbott won't say where she's gone, but I have the feeling it's far. That's all for now, Semper Fi.*

Conrad waited to answer until he could think of something funny to say back, or something upbeat, or offer some news of his own, but he let it go for too long. Then the whole thing seemed stale, and his own offerings seemed wrong somehow, off-key, and in the end he didn't answer Turner at all.

Ollie was back in school.

Last night we stayed up until two watching alien movies. It's for a class, we're meant to figure out how aliens represent ourselves, and what aspect of our society they represent. It's weird to watch movies for class. I kept thinking, This is so much fun! Then remembering I was supposed to be analyzing it in a critical way, not just cheering when they blasted another spaceship into atoms. I think it's great to use this stuff. But I also wonder if I'm missing things—will I ever read the Iliad *if I don't read it in college? I remember you talking about it while you were reading it, and I remember thinking that's what college is like, and that's how it would be for me. But it's so different here.*

Yah. Ollie.

Conrad wrote back: *You'll read it, bro. Or something else good. Yah. C.*

He didn't have much to say to Ollie, which made him feel bad. But there was a gap between them now. And he didn't have the energy to write back the way Ollie wrote to him. His energy was going into something else—holding on.

Claire wrote him, too, short, cheery messages. Sometimes she suggested getting together, but he hadn't talked to her since Christmas, and right now he didn't want to see anyone.

The nights here were very bad, even with the pills. Even with the pills and alcohol. A lot of alcohol. He put off until later and later the moment when he turned off the light and tried to reach for sleep. When he did finally sleep, it was late, two or three in the morning, sometimes four. He slept poorly. When the pill wore off, he found himself rising up to the surface like a depth charge, in a rocketing bubble of panic and chaos. He woke sweating and fearful, his heart racing. What he was afraid of was that this would never get better.

During the day he was tired, and he seldom left the apartment. He felt safest in the bedroom, the curtains pulled as far as they'd go across the windows. The living room had no curtains, and Conrad didn't go in there until after dark. When he did, he didn't turn on the lights, only the TV. A lighted room at night was a target—a perfectly illuminated target, like a little lighted box in a shooting range.

The only time Conrad had to get dressed and leave was on Thursday morning, when Mrs. Menendez came in to clean the apartment. Then he took his computer and went out, nodding at the Russian as he crossed the gleaming lobby. The Russian stared at him with animosity, his black eyes slitted, his body swollen beneath the scarlet and brass. He seemed to think he'd been hired to threaten and intimidate. *Fuck the Russian,* thought Conrad.

On Thursday mornings he went out to a coffee shop, where he stayed playing Sudoku and reading blogs until Mrs. Menendez was gone, at noon. He read the news: Petraeus had taken over the command in Iraq. Bush had announced a surge of twenty thousand U.S. troops. Iraqi civilian deaths in 2006 had topped thirty-four thousand. That fact, the civilian deaths, made Conrad feel very strange. It was a large number. It was the bombs. A captain had been caught on video, talking on his cell phone and saying exultantly, "I just killed half the population of north Ramadi! Fuck the red tape!" He had just ordered a five-hundred-pound bomb. It was the bombs and the artillery. They were turning civilians into pink mist. He thought of the spatters on the wall.

He didn't much like the news. Just seeing the word 'Iraq' made his chest tighten. He was now reading it on his computer instead of buying a paper. Somehow it was less serious on the screen. He could slide his eyes over an article without ever really entering the text.

At the end of the morning Conrad went to a little market nearby and stocked up: tuna fish, cereal, bread, eggs. When Mrs. Menendez had gone, he went back to the apartment, double-locked the doors, and then took off his shoes and pants and got back into bed, kicking off the heavy quilted bedspread Mrs. Menendez had carefully laid over the sheets and blanket.

Tools, process, opportunity.

The big windows in the bedroom opened only a few inches. He'd noticed that on the first day. Being up here had made him think of the people in the towers, the ones who jumped. He'd imagined it, standing in the kicked-out frame, shattered glass around the edges, ninety stories of nothing wheeling in the air below. Manhattan spread out beneath you. Taking a long last breath and then, fists clenched, stepping out into space, the wind rushing past your eyes, your ears, funneling up your pants, ballooning your shirt, taking away your breath. Choosing the only thing that was still left: the manner in which to die.

The long, clean plunge. The silence and bright air. You would never be so alone as during the fall. That would be the deepest solitude of your life. You would be in your own kingdom, in charge of your own world, the blood moving in your veins, the heart hammering loyally in your chest, the thoughts still springing into your mind, light and electric. Your mind would be racing, alive, knowing what would happen within seconds, but not knowing. As long as you were in the air, your world was continuing, smooth and vital, your body and mind still efficient until the end. And during that time, the long fall, you would be unassailable, unreachable. You would be utterly pure, only yourself. In the air. You would be alone in the air. There would be an absence of pain. There would be exultation, no pain. Then it would all be over.

He thought of the fall because the air was right outside his wall. But the windows wouldn't open far enough, and he wasn't going to smash up Go-Go's place.

He could get a gun, that would be better. The familiar presence in his hands, the shape and weight of it. His rifle had become like a phantom limb: often, when he was on the street and something startled him, he found himself reaching for it where it should have been hanging, slung over his shoulder. He felt a thudding moment of panic when it wasn't there. The rifle, your best friend.

Would you hear the shot?

Anderson knew.

Conrad wanted to be through with it all. He wanted to be rid of the things that kept recurring in his mind. He never wanted to see these things again. The spatters on the wall. The children. Carleton, Kuchnik,

Olivera. Fucking Anderson. How could he stop this endless avalanche within his mind?

He knew none of this was acceptable, knew it wasn't the right way to proceed. He wanted it all to be over. It was now only two weeks.

Ollie wrote:

So, what do you think about coming up to see me? You haven't even seen the famous place, have you? I have some friends, amazingly, and it would be fun to take you around. We could hang out. It would be good. Yah. O.

Conrad wrote back:

Sounds good. I don't have a car, though. Now that I'm in New York there's no point. Yah. C.

Ollie wrote:

Also amazingly, there are ways to get here without a car. There is a train, and I can pick you up. There is a really cool concert at the end of the month, which I think you'd like. Well, two concerts. You know Botstein is a famous conductor, so we have classical and contemporary concerts here. We cater to all tastes. The one I'm thinking of is the 29th. And I have a girlfriend, Anna.

Conrad wrote back:

The girlfriend! Now I do have to come up. I don't think the 29th will work, but I'll let you know about another date. What's she like? Any photos you are willing to share?

Ollie sent a picture: of course, all eighteen-year-old girls were hot, they just didn't know it. Anna had a round face and sleepy blue eyes, long pale lashes, light Nordic hair, and white, white skin.

Conrad wrote:

Dude! She is Class A! Excellent taste. Is she by any chance a Mandarin scholar?

Ollie wrote back:

I transferred out of that class. I hated it. I'm taking the Age of the Classics instead.

That stopped Conrad.

He remembered the carol singing on Christmas Eve, when Ollie had turned to him, realizing that Conrad had stopped. He remembered how it felt, seeing Ollie's trust. Like a long blade that had been slipped deep inside him, which he felt only when he moved. He didn't want Ollie watching him. He didn't want his brother depending on him for anything.

Sometimes Lydia was straight-on direct.

Dear Con, I want you to know that I'm troubled by whatever you're going through. Please know that you can tell me about it, whatever it is. Whatever it is. Whatever it is, we are on your side. Please don't turn away from us. We love you. M.

He wrote, *Thanks, Mom.*

In the second week Claire texted him to say that she was coming over.

"Don't answer," she wrote. "I'm leaving now. I'm bringing food. Just let me in when I get there."

He didn't even see the text until just before she arrived. When he opened the door, she stood there smiling, holding the white bags, as she had when she'd come to Jenny's. This time the sight of her made his chest feel tight.

"Hey," he said.

"Delivery," she said. "Indian, this time." She was smiling at him, but carefully. She was watching his eyes.

He stepped back. "Hey," he said. "Come on in." He couldn't bring himself to say *I'm glad you're here*, the way he had last time. He could hardly speak at all.

She slipped past him, inside. "Who's that guy downstairs?" She turned to face him. "The awful doorman? Is he KGB?" she whispered, her eyes bright, her cheeks pink with cold. She wore a long black quilted coat that muffled her body.

Conrad nodded. "His assignment is to watch us. He'll be outside the door right now." The thought was horrible.

"Well, I'm not giving him dinner," said Claire. "Where shall I put these?" Without waiting, she went into the kitchen and set down the bags. She came back to take off her coat and her red scarf. "Nice place!" she said, nodding. "Go-Go's doing well."

"Yeah." Conrad nodded.

"Can I see the rest?"

"If you have thirty-eight seconds," Conrad said. "Come on."

In the bedroom she walked to the windows and pulled back the curtains, opening them onto the nighttime landscape. The sky was deep purple-black, velvety, pierced with gleaming points of light.

"Some view," she said. "Gorgeous."

Conrad said nothing, and she turned to look at him.

"You don't love it, do you," she said.

He shook his head.

"Too what? Too high?"

"Something like that," he said.

She pulled the curtains closed again. "Too bad they don't close all the way." She turned back to the room. "Let's eat."

They sat in the living room.

"So, what's up with you?" Conrad asked.

It was distracting, having her there. He was half irritated and half grateful. Partly he wanted to listen to her chatter, and partly he wanted to drift in his own silent current.

"Kind of a great story from work," she said. She scraped rice onto her plate from one of the little boxes. "A client brought in a set of French plates. Neoclassical, eighteenth-century. Rare and valuable. So we give him a contract and he signs, and we put them in a sale. We advertise, and someone calls to ask about them. He wants to know who consigned them." Claire waved her hand. "Of course, we don't give out that information. Then he says they're *his* plates, he gave them to a friend to keep while he was moving."

"Ah," Conrad said, nodding. "Plot thickens. What is the wily Yvette's response?"

"We withdraw them from the sale and tell Weiss, the consignor, there's an issue with provenance. Can he tell us how he came to own them? Weiss says an aunt left him the contents of her house, the plates were in it."

Conrad nodded. He had mixed the rice and chicken on his plate, and it looked like Iraqi food.

Claire was laughing as she talked. "Then we ask the guy who called us, Cardozo, to come in. He has a look at them. 'Yes,' Cardozo says, 'they're definitely mine. I gave them to Weiss when I was moving.'"

The story was a long one: it seemed both guys were liars.

She went on, explaining. Weiss finally admitted to taking something from Cardozo, but not the plates. Then Weiss changed his story. Then the police became involved.

Conrad shook his head, smiling at her. When he realized she had finished, he said, "Amazing."

"What are you thinking?" Claire asked after a moment.

"Nothing," he said. "Thinking of your story."

Once, in Ramadi, they'd been on the street and second squad had taken fire from an upstairs window. It was in April during the jihad attacks. Conrad could see the window, and he told Morales to lob a grenade into it. Morales threw it right into the window. When it blew up, someone went over the wall and kicked open the metal gate, and they'd all gone in. The squad spread out in teams to clear the building. Conrad went up with Morales.

The upstairs room, where the shooters had been, was filled with rubble and covered with dust. Two bodies lay on the floor near the window, young, bearded men wearing black jeans and T-shirts. They lay in that disjointed way, arms and legs flung out, heads aslant. Blood pooled around them. On their arms were tourniquets. It was the first time Conrad had seen this. The muj used intravenous amphetamines, so they never got tired. They had no sense of fear: it turned them into super-warriors.

One man lay with his face to the floor, but the other stared straight up, eyes open in a dead stare. His jaw was covered in blood. His arm, circled by the tourniquet, was swollen and discolored. On a table were bowls of food. They'd been eating just before this. It gave him a strange feeling, that they could be doing something so ordinary and human before they tried to kill his men. Downstairs, Jackson, from second squad, called him into a back room, to see what they'd found. Big iron hooks hung from the ceiling, like the ones in a butcher shop. The walls were splattered with red. A video camera lay on a table: they had used this to make torture videos.

"So," Claire said, watching him. "You're not going to tell me, are you."

"No," Conrad said.

"You know, we can't really have a conversation like this," Claire said. "This is like taking a walk together and suddenly one of us falls down a hole."

"Yeah," Conrad said. "But I can't really help it. All of a sudden the ground is gone. And you know something? I don't like it any more than you do."

"So we'll talk about something else." She frowned, trying to spear something in the slippery sauce. "I brought some movies. And I'm going to spend the night."

"Clairey," he said, "don't do this to me."

"Don't do this to me," she said.

"You don't know how this makes me feel," he said. "I feel like such a fucking loser."

She stood up and leaned over the table. Her hair fell forward in wings. "You're not a loser. You're not a loser. You're just in trouble. Come on, Con. Please." She began to cry.

"Claire," he said, but he didn't know how to go on.

She spent the night, which he'd known would happen. There was no sex. His body was mute and distant, empty and unresponsive, as though he were on drugs. In bed he held Claire and kissed her hair and apologized.

"You knew about this," he said.

"Yeah, and it's okay." She curled up with her back to him, but close, tight against his body, so he would know she wasn't angry. He'd taken a pill. He went to sleep, but during the night he woke up to the nightmare of the man chasing him through the streets, the man he'd shot in Ramadi. He heard the footsteps, the echoes from the high walls. He had no weapon.

He woke up choking and calling out, his chest heaving. He didn't know where he was. The room was small and claustrophobic, with a strange perpendicular streak of light.

Someone put a hand on his sweaty chest.

"You're okay, Con," she said.

He nearly screamed. *"That's enough."* He yanked off the covers and threw himself out of bed. "*Christ.* Just don't touch me. Don't touch me."

He stood on the floor, his heart thundering. Everything in his system was shouting *Go, go, go.* There was nowhere for him to go, nothing for him to do. The room was silent around him. Claire knelt on the bed, her face grave.

He stood still, his breathing quieting. There was nothing in the room. The curtains nearly met across the windows. In the gap was a bright strip of purple night. Outside was the distant swishing sound of traffic on the Drive. Shame began to fill him.

"Christ," he said. "I'm sorry. I'm sorry, Claire."

His body felt immobile, and he was stricken with shame and revulsion. He thought, *I can't do this anymore.*

"I can't do this anymore," Claire said.

Only fourteen more days. He could do that.

He drew a calendar page, a grid showing the weeks and days, and Scotch-taped it to the tiled wall in the kitchen. Every morning when he came in, he crossed off a day so he could see the approach of the appointment.

Nine days away, he got an email from Go-Go.

Hey Conrad, how's it going?

He should have known from the salutation, the formal "Conrad," instead of "Dawg," that it was bad news.

My co. is sending me back to NY for a week in February. I'll be back on the 23rd. Hope that's okay for you and you can find someplace else.

Thanks you for holding down the fort. You can move back in when Im gone. Let's get together when Im back. Go-Go.

Conrad wrote him back:

Hey Dawg, gotcha on the apt. I'll be out by the 23rd. Thanks for the residency. We'll hook up when you're back. Conrad.

It didn't matter. He could go anywhere: Jenny's, Claire's, Katonah. Twenty-third. By then he'd be on the road to recovery.

As the appointment drew nearer, Conrad became calmer. The end was within reach. He wrote encouraging messages to Molinos, still in Hit:

Molinos: Hope things are going okay. I wish you'd take care of those pesky insurgents, keep them from blowing everyone the fuck up. I'm in New York. Nice here but I miss the MREs. Semper Fi. Farrell.

Each night he counted the days.

It was too much to expect the end of this, but he hoped for a lessening. He hoped for a kind of hope. He wouldn't define it exactly. He wouldn't use large words like *redemption*, or *grace*. He was hoping for something humbler, something small and private. He didn't feel entitled to anything large. Certainly he didn't feel entitled to religious help. His family went to the local Episcopal church in a loyal but intermittent way, but Conrad wasn't religious. He didn't take it seriously, the wafers and wine, the blood and flesh. He'd never felt any mysterious power from their pleasant local pastor. Since he'd never believed before, it wasn't fair to ask now for favors. And whom would he ask?

The words *peace* or *forgiveness* were not for him, he knew that. How could he ask forgiveness for something he'd done deliberately? And besides, the words carried with them some kind of taint, some softness he wouldn't go near. Being hard, never asking for help, was the point. Needing peace or forgiveness implied weakness. There was the question of identity, and choice: you couldn't simply stop being what you'd chosen to become. Because then what were you?

He wouldn't allow himself to name those things—peace, redemption, forgiveness—but he knew they were there. At moments he felt them, their balm. In another world, he'd cut himself off from it. He suspected the existence of a kind of bliss, one that might accompany a surrender he could not make, and this caused him a pure sense of sorrow. Loss. If he surrendered, if he asked forgiveness for all he had done, how great were the implications? How much wrong had he done?

Those ideas—grace and forgiveness—seemed to exist in another part of the world. This was the third part, an upper layer, composed of aerial currents that, if you could only be carried up to them, would sweep you off. They would lift you above the clouds, above the great systems of violence and turbulence that stretched over the surface of the world, the systems that composed the weather, the storms of anguish and grief and despair. The storms of guilt and shame. You would be lifted from it, and those things would fall away from you the way water evaporates to become purified, an essence, a fine, rising mist.

He had no real hope for this; it was a kind of dream. What he had done made those things unavailable to him. But still he held in his mind the possiblity that it could happen. The possibility that he would find a way to that layer.

This semester he was taking another class: political economics. An introduction to the interaction between economics and politics, voting theory and elections. It started on the twenty-ninth. By then he'd have started his treatment at the VA.

He'd read up on this, knew what to expect, knew his rights. He was focused on the appointment, as though he were trekking across the desert and it was the oasis. He'd been traveling toward it for months. He'd watched its inverted reflection hovering above the horizon, promising shade, solace, rest.

26

On the twenty-second, Conrad received an automated message from the VA, leaving him a number to call back. The return call took over an hour as Conrad maneuvered his way through waits and transfers, recorded voices and announcements, repeating his name and ID and case number over and over until he was finally connected to a human voice, a man who managed to sound both official and offhand.

The man told Conrad he could have an appointment in Mental Health in three months.

"I've already waited three months," Conrad said. "You're saying three more?"

"Yes, sir," said the man. "That's what I can offer. That's how we work it."

"How do you work it?" Conrad asked. "So no one can use it?"

"This is the way it works," said the man.

"It actually doesn't seem to work," said Conrad. "If someone needs medical assistance, why keep him waiting six months before you give it to him? If I had a broken leg, how would you describe this system as working?"

"Do you have a broken leg?" the man said.

"I do not," said Conrad, "but that's—"

"Are-you-a-danger-to-yourself-or-others?" He rattled off the words like the names of train stations. "If you pose a risk to yourself or others, I can give you an earlier appointment."

Conrad looked around the room, at the angular chair, the table in the corner, stacked with books. He rubbed the back of his head. He said nothing for a moment.

"Yes," he answered.

"You are a danger to yourself or others?"

"Yes," Conrad repeated. He drew a deep breath: focus. "And also I believe that the VA is required by law to provide an appointment within thirty days, maximum."

"All right." He sounded suspicious, as though Conrad might be pretending to be mentally ill. "Let me look for another date." After a long time he came back. "February twenty-second." The day before Go-Go came back.

"Right," Conrad said. "Thank you."

He leaned back against the sofa. Thirty days. He could make it.

On the day of his appointment Conrad got up early. He hadn't slept well the night before, and each time he woke, he had taken another pill, trying to hammer himself back to sleep. Jack's prescription had run out, but Conrad had gotten another from his mother—some doctor friend or colleague. Now the inside of his head felt as if it were lined with cotton, but also with electricity. He felt dumb but wired.

He pulled open the curtains. The sky was overcast; a soft gray cloud cover layered over Queens. The river below was pewter, with flickers of silver where the wind ran across it. Conrad took a shower, then shaved carefully. He didn't want to show up with nicks and blood all over his neck. He put on good clothes: clean khakis, a proper shirt, a tweed jacket. He looked in the mirror, straightening the tails of the jacket, examining himself. This was like a job interview. Actually, he should be going in unshaven and unwashed; he should look homeless. Wasn't he trying to persuade them that he was crazy?

His head still felt stuffed and unresponsive, but he felt good. He ate a bowl of cereal, pulled on a parka, and headed out. He'd buy coffee on the way, get his head in shape. Outside it was cold, with a gusty, exhilarating wind that flapped at him erratically, changing directions and swirling small bits of trash into tiny tornadoes.

His appointment was for eight-thirty. He stopped for coffee on the street. He wanted not a cinnamon-mocha-tofu-latte from a fancy shop, but a plain regular black from the stand on the corner—two dark-skinned guys up inside a tiny, shiny mobile cabin. He stood in a line of people on the sidewalk waiting for coffee and bagels, everyone shifting from foot to foot, hunching their shoulders from the cold. When it was his turn, Conrad asked for one black, no sugar. The man was round-faced, with black hair and big bags under his eyes. He grinned at Conrad and said, "Okay, boss!" as though they were buddies. Conrad smiled back. It was starting out to be a good day. He was on the subway by seven-thirty, sipping his coffee as the cars rattled along underground, heading south fast. Everything was going right. He was awake, dressed, caffeinated, and on time, hauling balls across town. Today was the day, and he was on it.

He got off at Twenty-third and walked east toward the VA. The street was crowded, already noisy and bustling. He liked being part of this surging tide, fast and full of energy. It was a downtown, blue-collar group, the men in knitted watch caps and parkas, the women in puffy coats and limp synthetic scarves, pushing strollers, or in tight jeans and high boots and short parkas, their arms linked. Trucks and buses groaned past, funneling exhaust into the cold air. Cars honked: everyone was already pumped up, on their way.

Conrad arrived at 8:10. Early. He wanted his record here to be perfect. He pushed through the slow revolving door. The black guy with the beret was on duty again, standing by the low oval counter. He gave Conrad a friendly chin-up of recognition. Conrad nodded back, grinning. A good omen.

At the admissions booth Conrad gave his ID number, and was sent to a different floor. This waiting room, too, was full. There were some other men his own age, from Iraq and Afghanistan, but more of them were older: Vietnam vets with grizzled sideburns and gray faces and drooping alcoholics' eyes. Everyone looked at him when he came in; no one spoke.

Conrad checked in at the counter. This receptionist was a man in his fifties, with a round head and very black skin. Conrad filled out the forms and sat down to wait. He felt both restless and tired. Anticipation kept him on edge; his foot twitched to a jerky rhythm as though he were listening to music. He kept checking his watch; he didn't want to be a pain in the ass. After an hour he went up to the counter again.

"Hey there," he said. "My name's Farrell. Just checking on my appointment. I think it was for eight-thirty. It's now nine-thirty."

The man looked up at him indifferently. He wore square black-rimmed glasses, and the whites of his eyes were deep yellow. "Everyone in this room has that same time of appointment," he said. "We'll call you when it's your turn."

Conrad sat down. He should have brought a book. He'd have brought the fucking *Iliad* if he'd known he'd be here for most of the day. He didn't like the sight of the silent vets, all of them summoned for the same time, all of them ignored, all waiting patiently, their time considered valueless.

Conrad had earned this appointment, he had earned it by every moment of the last four years. He had the right to this meeting, with someone from his own world who'd understand him, know what he'd been through. Someone who knew and respected him. The long minutes began to feel like insults.

After half an hour a young black woman appeared in the inner doorway. She wore a white lab jacket over jeans and a tan cardigan buttoned up the front. Her hair was pulled back by a hair band.

"Farrell," she called out, her eyelids heavy. She sounded audibly disinterested. She held a sheaf of folders against her chest. Conrad raised his hand and stood up. "Zuccotti, Gadruso."

Two more men stood up.

"Gadruto," one of the men corrected her.

She ignored him. "Follow me." She spoke loudly, as though they were far away. She turned and set off down the hall. It was narrow and shabby, the cream walls badly scuffed, the floor dull. The woman stopped beside an open door. "Room twelve-oh-nine," she said. "Farrell."

She stood waiting. The door of 1209 was open.

"Thank you," Conrad said, and went inside. The room was small, without windows, and the walls were painted cinder block. The only furnishings were a small metal desk and two chairs. The doctor sat in a tilting armchair before the desk. A straight-backed metal chair stood at right angles to him, for Conrad. There were no books, no rug, nothing but the desk and two chairs and a calendar on the far wall.

The doctor was in his fifties, compact and balding, with a bullet-shaped head and a close-trimmed beard. He wore metal-rimmed glasses, a striped short-sleeved jersey, and khaki pants. On his feet were thick-soled running shoes, as though he might take off down the hall at any moment.

"Hello, I'm Dr. Chandler," he said. "Sit down." His eyes were pale brown. He waved at the empty chair.

Conrad sat down. The chair was narrow and had no arms.

The calendar was open to a Georgia O'Keeffe painting of red poppies. The month was October, the year before.

"So," Dr. Chandler said, glancing down, "Conrad. Why don't you tell me about your record and your deployments."

All that information had already been filled out by Conrad, and it was in his file, which lay on the desk. It irritated him that Dr. Chandler had not read it. Why had he spent all that time filling it out? Conrad started over, listing the dates and places.

Chandler nodded. "So, tell me why you think you have PTSD." He leaned back and the chair tilted springily beneath him. He wrapped his arms across his chest. His arms looked strong, though running a little to fat.

"I didn't say I had it," Conrad said. Post-traumatic stress disorder was a candy-ass condition to claim. He wasn't naming his situation. He was only admitting that it was problematic.

"Then why are you here?" Chandler asked.

Conrad stared at him. He couldn't say these words. Where was the person who understood this? Where was the voice who would speak for him, recognize him?

"I've been experiencing—having—troubling symptoms," Conrad said. Now he began to feel a kind of panic; his chest was filling up. He didn't know how to proceed.

"Want to tell me what they are? What might have caused them?"

"Well, I saw a lot of combat. Both Ramadi and Haditha. There was a lot of stuff that went on." He cleared his throat. "In Haditha, the Humvee I was in was blown up by an IED," said Conrad.

Spoken out loud, here in the cinder-block room, the words seemed tiny and insignificant. He paused, trying to find the words that would make the event what it had been, that would give it the size and significance it still had in his mind. But the words had nothing to do with the way the black flower of sound had bloomed inside his head, the way it kept on blooming, over and over, blotting out the world.

Dr. Chandler nodded, hugging his soft upper arms. "Did you lose consciousness?"

"I don't know," Conrad said. "It's disorienting. You lose track of what's going on. I might have, or I might just have felt disoriented. If I did, it wasn't for long."

Chandler made a note in the file.

"Did you report your symptoms? Were any tests done?"

Conrad shook his head. "We were in a combat zone. I wasn't going to leave my men because of this."

"So there was no report and no test." Chandler folded his heavy arms on his chest again. "Any other episodes?"

Conrad now felt uncertain, as though he were being cross-examined.

"In Ramadi, in another Humvee, I was beside one of my Marines who was killed," Conrad said reluctantly. "It happened right in front of me." It sounded like nothing. As though he were boasting.

Dr. Chandler nodded. "Combat incidents can be very troubling."

He waited. His chair creaked as he leaned back. It was on springs, and even when he was not moving, the springs made tiny squeaks as Chandler breathed.

Conrad shrugged. "Also, I shot a man who was right in front of me, in the street. I thought he was armed, but he wasn't. I had to step over his head." He paused. "I guess everyone has these stories."

Dr. Chandler started to answer, but the phone rang on his desk. "Excuse me." He picked up.

"Dr. Chandler," he said. He was looking diagonally at the floor, past Conrad's legs.

"No, I'm not," he said, then listened. "How long?" he asked, still looking at the floor. "We'll have to discuss that at a later date. I think Morton knows more about it than I do. Have you spoken to him?" There was a pause. "I talked to him last week. It would be good to get his opinion."

Dr. Chandler leaned closer to the desk. He set his fingertips on it, making a spider of his hand. Then he lifted the index finger, tapping it lightly on the desk as he talked, as though the spider were getting ready to dance.

"Not unless you count the first time," he said into the phone. "I think you'd better discuss this further. Why don't you call me tomorrow. Yes. Yes," he said. "All right, thanks."

He hung up and turned to Conrad.

"Where were we?" he said.

Conrad shrugged his shoulders. "Two deployments to Iraq," he said. "Ramadi, Haditha. Two IEDs. A lot of other events."

Dr. Chandler nodded. "Combat incidents can be very troubling." He said this as though for the first time. "How long have you been having symptoms?"

"They started when I got back last May," said Conrad. "They've gotten worse."

The phone rang again. Dr. Chandler raised his index finger at Conrad and picked it up. It seemed to be a different caller.

"I didn't know about that meeting," Chandler said. "I hadn't heard about it."

Now he was looking at the wall over his desk. Despite the big, serious-looking running shoes, Chandler's affect was sedentary. It was the slack, heavy arms.

"Can you keep me in the loop?" Chandler asked. "I'll need to stay current with this whole situation."

When Chandler hung up, he looked at Conrad again. He swiveled the chair around and leaned back, tilting toward the wall.

"Busy day," he said. "Sorry."

Conrad nodded.

"Your symptoms," Dr. Chandler said. "What are they?"

Conrad had written them all down. He listed them again: anxiety, insomnia, panic, flashbacks. Hypervigilance, depression, mood swings, rage. Impotence. Being a dick. Being unable to concentrate or focus on anything and fucking up his GMAT and pretty much fucking up his life so far. And how about being unable to rely on himself for anything, not even for being civil to his family or his girlfriend, and how about not knowing if he'd ever be able to learn anything again?

He didn't like saying any of these words out loud. He couldn't explain what the symptoms felt like, or how they took him over, how powerless he became. How frightening it was to feel that his brain was not where he expected it to be.

Here in this room it all seemed to mean nothing.

"Are you a danger to yourself or others?" Dr. Chandler asked.

Conrad looked at him. "Not to others."

He waited for the doctor to ask more.

"Okay," the doctor said. "So, I'm going to prescribe three medications for you, Trazodone, gabapentin, and paroxetine." He tilted his chair back but then leaned forward against the movement, as though he were on a horse going uphill. "There's no test for PTSD," he told Conrad. "Treating it is not an exact science. Some medications work for some people and not for others. We use them variously, separately, and in combination."

He seemed absorbed by what he was saying, and interested in the medications. "We can start you off with one protocol and see how it goes. Don't expect any change for two weeks or so. These take a while to take effect. If you're still having problems, we can alter it until we find the right mix."

He put his hands on the desk and pulled himself over to it, the chair rolling easily across the bare floor. There was something faintly repulsive about his scooting across the floor without using his legs. He took up a prescription pad and began to write. Conrad said nothing.

This was it.

This was all there was, this brief, useless exchange in this small, windowless room with the out-of-date calendar and the tilting chair. There would be no discussion of what had happened to him, the roaring blackness in his ears, the intrusions on his mind, the explosions of rage, the sense of sullen misery that underlay each day. The sense of confusion, and the relentless headache. All this meant nothing to anyone but him. He was trapped with it forever. This was it.

"You don't need to know any more?" Conrad asked.

Chandler was still writing. "We get a lot of men with these symptoms," he said without looking up.

Conrad wondered if Chandler used this office all the time, if it was his own regular office or if it was like an examining room in a hospital, used interchangeably by different doctors. So that no one would feel responsible for the calendar.

Dr. Chandler tore off a page and held it out with his left hand. His right was spidered again on the desk. He tapped silently with his index finger, waiting for Conrad to take it.

"I've given you a prescription for Ambien as well, for insomnia. So, start in on these and I'll expect to see you again in about three months."

27

Conrad pushed open the door to the lobby, the pharmacy bag in his hand. The Russian was standing near the counter, his arms folded on his chest, his feet splayed. He stared at Conrad, narrow-eyed. Conrad nodded, walking past him to the elevator. *Fuck you,* he thought. *I'm done, I'm out of here.*

In the apartment, Conrad went into the bedroom. He opened the curtains wide and looked out. The sky was lightly overcast by a soft high cloud cover, but the air was clear. The river below was pale and silvery. The swells were low and flat; small whirlpools traced themselves on the surface. A motorboat was heading upriver, its prow lifted by speed. A neon-orange flag fluttered at the stern, a narrow silver wave rippling along the bow.

He was determined to make this work. Even if the appointment had been for shit, his condition had been recognized. What he had was real. He was getting treatment, and from now on things would be better. He could do this on his own: take the pills, monitor the results, climb his way out of this black hole. He didn't need the fucking doctor with his fat arms and big running shoes.

He stood looking down toward the river. Before him lay the big sweep of air and landscape, the glittering surface of the water, beyond it the dark, ticking, smoking collage of Queens spreading into the distance. He took long, slow breaths.

Okay, he told himself, *the conversation was bad.* The doctor had paid no attention to him. The spoken words had been meaningless, and he never should have said them. Naming things had been wrong. There was no way to name them. There was no one to whom he could ever say them.

But the pills were real.

He imagined them starting to do their work. Like small heat-seeking missiles, they would drive deep into his neurological system, destroying certain memory engines, disconnecting certain links until the troubling images that paraded through his head were exploded, eliminated, vanished. *Fuck.* They would be gone from his mind, or they would become faint and blurred. The thought of their erasure made him realize the depth of his exhaustion. Mercy was what he hoped for.

He brought his computer into the bedroom. He wanted to sit next to the sky, the river beneath him. This was his new self. He sat in the green chair by the window. He set the pill bottles on the table next to him: Trazodone, gabapentin, paroxetine. Carefully he typed the letters of the first name onto the screen. These weird names that the drug companies came up with, with their strange combinations of letters. He clicked on "Find."

Trazodone came right up. It was prescribed for depression, no big surprise. It increased the presence of serotonin in order to maintain mental balance. Everything made sense until he got to the side effects.

> Children, teenagers, and young adults (up to 24 years of age) who take this or other antidepressants to treat depression or other mental illness may be more likely to become suicidal than those who do not.
>
> Your mental state may change in unexpected ways when you take this or other antidepressants, even if you are an adult over age 24. You may become suicidal, especially at the beginning of your treatment. You should call your doctor right away if you experience any of the following symptoms: new or worsening depression, thinking about harming or killing yourself, extreme worry, agitation, panic attacks, difficulty getting to sleep or staying asleep, aggressive behavior, irritability, acting without thinking, severe restlessness, and frenzied abnormal excitement.
>
> Your health-care provider will want to see you often while you are taking this medication, especially at the beginning of your treatment.

Conrad's next appointment was in three months. The doctor hadn't said anything about seeing him more often. The idea of reaching him in an emergency was a joke.

Conrad read the passage again, more slowly. It hardly seemed possible that he had been prescribed a medication that would duplicate and amplify his existing symptoms. Yet he had.

He typed in "gabapentin."

"*Warning,*" it said.

> You should know that your mental health may change in unexpected ways and you may become suicidal.

Out on the river, the motorboat with the flag was out of sight. Heading downstream was a big scow with a dirty white superstructure. The tide was against it, but it steamed determinedly into the streaming surge, leaving a churning wake.

What the fuck? He felt everything draining away.

Nothing he had hoped for was going to happen. Nothing about him had been recognized. He was invisible again. He was nothing, his struggle unseen. He was being treated in a way that would make him worse. He had been fucked, was what had happened.

The larger question was, how long would you persist under these conditions? And why would you? There was no end to it. *Tools, opportunity, process.*

He closed his eyes. How long would he go on waking up with that black rose of sound blooming in his ears? Seeing the pattern on the wall? Hearing Olivera's broken voice? Finding that any loud noise could set off a cacophony inside his head? How long was this going to go on? How long was his sentence? Because suddenly he was tired again, exhausted, done. There was nothing left for him to draw on.

He had to leave the apartment tomorrow.

The pills wouldn't help; the small plastic cylinders now seemed sinister. The words were still on the screen. *Suicidal tendencies.*

He felt darkness cast itself over him like a cowl.

"*Fuck,*" he whispered.

Guns were what he knew. That was the real way. Look at Anderson. Though it was hard to buy a gun in New York, probably impossible on short notice. A latex hose looped into a noose would be simpler. He wondered if the shower rod would hold him. Of course it wouldn't. He looked around the bedroom. There was nothing high enough in here. What had he been doing all these months? In-country, you were trained to have a plan to kill every person in the room. He hadn't even completed that plan for a single person.

He went out into the living room. None of the ceilings were high enough anywhere in the building. Nothing was strong enough. You needed a tree or a rafter. Something solid.

A gun would be better. His hands knew guns.

He could get a gun online, but not by tonight. He had to be out of here very soon. The timing clarified things, and he felt calmer. He needed to move ahead tonight.

He couldn't leave a body in the apartment for Go-Go. A nice show of thanks.

And he couldn't get a gun in time. Not before tomorrow.

With a mission he felt better. This would be the end of his worries, the end of everything. He was taking control. It would be the end of pain. There were the two worlds, the lower world and the upper world, and he was moving into the lower one. A relief.

Knives, of course. Pills. Those fucking suicide pills. They drove you to it but wouldn't do it for you.

He wondered about the window, prying it open. The long drop through the air: clean and simple and fast. Surely he could pry it farther open—unless it was made so you couldn't. He pulled back the curtains to examine the window.

But they'd seen him coming. The window would not open farther. Too bad for the residents if there was a fire. He looked down. Too bad for them anyway if there was a fire. No ladder would reach to the twenty-first floor. They were fucked.

He thought again of the people in the towers. That first moment of comprehension, realizing that they would not survive. In that first moment they were still unharmed, but it was in that moment that they understood what was coming. The circling helicopters, the people below, watching. The room getting hotter, the walls. People crowding around the windows, kicking them out. Everyone below, their faces lifted, helpless. Choosing to act. Taking control.

He sat down again. Was he doing it or not? The idea of it was like the Grand Canyon, vast and magnificent, filled with color and shadows.

Deciding to do it had calmed him. Knowing he would do it made him feel that he might not have to. He looked around the room. On the wall was a framed poster of Gstaad in the twenties, during winter sports: a waiter was serving tables on ice skates, balancing a loaded tray, the mountains in the background. Next to it was an Andy Warhol reproduction: Liz Taylor, her lips swollen, her eyes sultry.

Conrad had looked at both of these hundreds of times. It was strange to think that this might be his last day here, his last night. He would never see them again. It was strange to think that. The porcine Liz, the dapper, antic waiter. He would never see these again. The thought excited him, and he stood up.

He thought of the hose. How would you ask for it in a hardware store? Surely it would be obvious why you wanted it. But so what, they couldn't refuse to sell you a hose. There must be a beam in the basement somewhere. In the laundry room. Conrad had never used the laundry room: Mrs. Menendez presided over these mysteries. In any case, the laundry room was too public. Anyone might walk in. He disliked the idea of someone walking in, finding him jerking and kicking in the air. It was a private act. Actually, he disliked the idea of even being found, the ghastly droop of the hanged body. He would prefer never to be found. He thought of the river.

His parents would have to learn about it. He didn't want them to know.

He couldn't think of them knowing it.

He thought again of the people in the towers. That first shocked moment of understanding.

He stood and walked around the apartment, his hands in his pockets.

He didn't want to hurt his parents, his family. All he wanted was never to wake up again sweating and shaking, calling out in terror. He wanted never to have the wave of images move over him, blotting out the world in front of him: Olivera whispering, the little boy in the striped pajamas, his head falling limply back. Now Anderson, sitting alone in the dark barn. Conrad stopped and put his hands over his eyes, pressing his fingers into the sockets. He would never be rid of them.

When he got back from the hardware store, the epauletted Russian lifted his chin at Conrad.

"You have visitor." He spoke scornfully. He nodded toward the mirrored wall, the long red sofa against it.

Ollie was sitting on the sofa, leaning forward, elbows on his thighs, feet wide, waiting.

Conrad went over to him.

"Hey, Oll," he said.

"Hey," Ollie said. He stood, not smiling.

"What's up?" Conrad asked.

"Can I come upstairs?" Ollie asked.

"Sure." Conrad led the way to the elevator and pushed the button. They stood, waiting. The doorman watched them sideways, not turning his head.

"What'd'jou get?" asked Ollie, nodding at the bag.

"Just some stuff," Conrad said.

As the elevator rose they were silent. The wind rushed alongside the car, whistling and jostling in the shaft. Upstairs, Conrad led him down the hall and unlocked the door.

"Nice place," Ollie said, looking around. He walked to the window. "Nice view."

"Yeah," Conrad said. "I'm leaving tomorrow."

"How come?"

He shouldn't have mentioned this. "Go-Go's coming back from Hong Kong for a while. I have to get out and let him have the place."

"Where you going?"

Conrad nearly said Claire's, but thought better of it. The network was too tight; Claire and Jenny and Lydia all certainly talked to one another. "Another guy from Williams. You don't know him."

Ollie nodded. He sat down on the white sofa. The living room was still dark. Conrad sat down in the uncomfortable red armchair and put the bag down on the rug. Inside it was twenty-five feet of coiled latex hosing, the color of dry grass. It gave him a secure feeling.

"Don't the lights work?" Ollie asked.

"I don't use them in here," Conrad said.

"Oh," Ollie said. "Any particular reason?"

"Look," Conrad said. "What I do here is what I do. It's my place, my business." There was a pause. "So, Oll. What brings you here? What's up?"

He wanted this conversation to be over. He was afraid Ollie was going to ask to spend the night. He'd asked the man at the hardware store how much weight the hosing would hold. Three hundred pounds, the man said, and pointed to the label.

He'd decided on a tree, one of the ones that stood on the walkway along the river. It would be private along there at night, no one used the walkway after midnight. The idea lay before him like a promise.

"What are you doing?" Ollie asked.

"What do you mean?"

"You scare me, Con," Ollie said. "What's wrong?"

Ollie leaned forward in the dimness. The light from the window illuminated the side of his face, the smooth, familiar cheek, the unkempt hair. Ollie looked like himself; he looked like the rest of the family, too. Marshall's high cheekbones, Lydia's eyes. They looked like each other. The way he smoothed back the hair from his forehead was Lydia's gesture. For some reason that was painful.

"Oll," Conrad said. He looked down at his hands. "There's stuff you can't talk about."

"What are you going to do?" Ollie asked. He made each word distinct.

Conrad said nothing.

"You won't answer my messages or call me or come to see me. You don't answer anyone's messages. You look so dark, Con. You look like it's the end of everything."

"I can't explain things," Conrad said. "I don't want to talk about this."

"About what?"

"Anything."

They sat in silence. The light from the window seemed stronger as their eyes grew accustomed to the darkness. Outside, the sky was overcast, the cloud cover illuminated from below by headlights and streetlights, the city's glow.

"Look," Ollie said. "I know what it's like—"

"You have no *fucking* idea what it's like," Conrad said, looking at him. Everything was rushing up inside his chest. "Don't ever say that again. You have no idea what it's like."

"Okay. I don't. But tell me what's wrong," Ollie said. "What is it?"

"I don't want to see people," Conrad said. "I don't want to be around people who don't understand this."

"Iraq," Ollie said.

"No one understands it. Half the time everyone pretends it's not there."

"So what are we meant to do?"

Conrad laughed, angry. "I don't know what you're meant to do. Not my problem."

"You don't want us to pretend it's not there, but you don't want us to talk about it."

"Look, I'm not writing the rules," Conrad said. "I'm not a fucking debating coach."

"Okay," Ollie said. "Okay." He put his head down in his hands. "So. I came in to see you." He paused. "Because I'm afraid." He lifted his head but did not look at Conrad. He went on. There was some difficulty in his voice. "That you are going to kill yourself." He didn't look up. "So I want you to tell me that will never happen." His voice broke.

Conrad squeezed his eyes shut. *The fuck.*

Ollie looked up at him, his face in shadow. "Con."

"Look," Conrad said. "There are some things—"

"No," Ollie said. Now he was crying. "*You look.* Don't you tell me there are some things you can't talk about. *You are my brother.* I know there are things you will never tell me. I know that. I know there are things you did over there that are part of another world. But you are still my brother. You are still part of my world. You are still living here with me. You can't make that not true even if you—did it."

"Oll, you don't understand what it's like," Conrad said. "You can't ask me to do something for you. You don't know what this is like."

"Then do something about it, for Christ's sake!" Ollie shouted at him. "Don't sit around looking like a funeral parlor, like you're going to die, and do nothing."

"I did do something," Conrad said, raising his voice. "I just went to the fucking VA and saw a fucking doctor."

"You did?"

"I did," Conrad said. "He gave me pills that make you suicidal. How's that for treatment?"

Ollie stood up. "Okay, I don't give a fuck what he did!" He was shouting. "You can't use that as an excuse! I don't care what he gave you. You have to go on. You have to go on." He stopped.

"You're telling me what to do?"

"Con, this isn't the end," Ollie said. "I don't care what you did. You had to do it. You had no choice. You can't take the blame for it."

"I see. But what if the blame falls on me?" Conrad put his head down. "You don't know what I see at night."

"Go and talk to someone! Talk to other vets!" Ollie said. "You don't think there are other people out there with the same thing you have? You think they don't see things at night? Other people did what you did. Talk to them about it! Don't sit here alone!"

Conrad stared at him. "You've been coached," he said. "Who told you all that? You little fucking weasel."

"So what?" Ollie said. "Yeah, I have. I've read up on this. I've found out everything I could about it. Unlike you. You've been sitting here in the dark with your head stuck up your ass."

Conrad snorted. "You have no idea what you're talking about."

"What if I do, though?" Ollie said. "What if you don't? What if you die, you fucker?" He stopped. Conrad could hear his breath. He was crying again.

Conrad waited.

Ollie drew a large breath. "So, what do you have in that bag?"

"I won't tell you," Conrad said.

Ollie leaped up and strode over to him. "You fucker." He reached for the bag, but Conrad yanked it back. He held out his left hand to fend Ollie off.

"Stop it," Conrad said.

Ollie grabbed for the bag, lunging in as Conrad raised an elbow. It caught him in the face.

Ollie fell back with a grunt, raising his hands to his face. He stood still.

"You fuck," he said, his voice muffled. "You're trying to commit suicide and you've given me a bloody nose."

Conrad snorted again. "This isn't really a joke."

Ollie leaned his head back, holding his hand across his nose. "Get me a towel. I'm going to bleed all over your friend's white sofa."

Conrad went into the kitchen. When he came back, Ollie had gotten hold of the bag with the hose. He was holding it high, trying to look inside it while tilting his head back to keep his nose from bleeding.

"You little fucker," Conrad said, and grabbed for the bag.

Ollie yanked it away. He reached inside and pulled out the hose. It lay in coils, narrow and supple.

"You really—" He stopped. "Con." His face was flooding. The blood cascaded down over his mouth, glistening in the light from the window. "You really are planning. To do it."

Conrad handed him the paper towels.

"You have no idea," Conrad said. "Christ." He sat down again. "I can't give you any idea what it's like. You know what, Oll? I can't do it anymore. I have nowhere to go. I can't go on."

Ollie lay down on his back, pulling off a long stretch of the towel. He wadded the sheets against his face, where they darkened at once with blood. "Look—" he said.

"You have no idea," Conrad said, his voice dull. "It's like I'm a secret criminal. No one here knows what I've done. No one has any idea what it was like."

"We don't care, Con," Ollie said. He sat up, holding the wadding to his nose. "We don't care what you did. We love you."

"You don't know me," Conrad said slowly. "You have no idea who I am. You love the person you knew before. You wouldn't love me if you knew who I am."

There was silence.

"Okay," Ollie said. "I get it. I mean, I get it as much as I can. But I'm going to tell you something. You don't have a choice. I am going to hang on to you until you're better. I'm dropping out of Bard, and I'm moving in wherever you are going, and I will not leave you. I'm serious. I'm going to handcuff myself to you until you're better."

Conrad laughed. "You idiot."

"I mean it."

Conrad rubbed his face slowly. "Ollie, it takes me an Ambien and four drinks to get two hours' sleep. You want to handcuff yourself to that for the night? Every night? You must be crazee." He smiled faintly.

"So, okay, then, let's party," said Ollie. He was leaning against the back of the sofa now, his chin tilted at the ceiling.

"You cannot fix this by being a smart-ass," Conrad said.

"I know that," Ollie said. He was still holding the paper towels against his face, and he twisted his head sideways so he could look at Conrad. Conrad could see his eye gleaming in the dim light, watchful. "Only you can fix this."

"Why should I?" Conrad asked. "Why should I go on?"

"For the rest of us," Ollie said. "Don't do it to us."

"Yeah," Conrad said. "But what if it's too hard?"

"Do it for us," Ollie said. "Please. We will save you. I'm not leaving you again."

Conrad said nothing.

"I know you feel bad about losing your men," Ollie said. "Or shooting people, whatever you did. But whatever you feel about them is how you'll make us feel about you, if you"—he hesitated—"quit. It will mean we've failed you. Whatever Anderson did to you, don't do it to us."

28

His plan was to get through one year. He could do that, day by day.

In late August, Conrad was out in Katonah.

One evening he asked Ollie to come outside. Conrad stood in the doorway of the porch. Ollie was lying on the big sofa, reading.

"Oll, I want you for a few minutes," he said.

Ollie saluted Conrad. "I'm with you, yah. What's up?"

"A couple of things," Conrad said.

They pushed through the screen door onto the lawn.

It was nearly dark. The lawn was cool and thick underfoot, and in the meadow fireflies flickered and glowed in their mysterious code. The two brothers walked across the lawn toward the big ash, which towered over them, a great canopy overhead. A tongue of the stone wall jutted out into the middle of the lawn, and on top of the wall Conrad had set a small wooden box, a candle, and a box of matches.

He gave Ollie the candle. "Hold this," he said, and lit it.

The flame quivered, then held steady, pale against the darkening twilight. Conrad opened the box and took out a piece of paper. He held it up formally in front of the candle. He stood very straight, as though at attention.

"This is a memorial ceremony," he said, "for my good friend and trusted comrade, Ali Sadra. I don't have a photograph of him or his full name. I don't even know if Ali Sadra was his real name. It probably wasn't. It was probably too dangerous for him to work under his real name. But that was the name I knew him by. I remember the way he looked, and I don't need a photograph. He was a handsome man." Conrad paused. "Ali was a brilliant translator, and one of the bravest men I know. He was generous and courageous, curious and intelligent. He was a man of great dignity and humanity. He was a husband and father. He probably gave his life for our cause." He paused. "He helped the allied forces, and through his courage and compassion he helped the human race. This is in his memory, in the memory of Ali Sadra, Ramadi, Iraq, OIF, 2005. With respect and admiration from Conrad Farrell, Katonah, 2007.

"And this is also in memoriam for all my other friends in Iraq, for those I met and those I did not. And for my friends from the Marines. For PFC James Carpenter, and PFC Alejandro Olivera, and Lance Corporal John Carleton, and Corporal Paul Anderson, and the others who were there with me, for those who came back and those who did not. And for those who came back but didn't stay. They were good men and I miss them."

Conrad had dug a small hole next to the stone wall, beneath the wide presence of the ash. He folded the paper, put it inside the box, slid the wooden top shut, and set the box gently in the hole. He and Ollie knelt on the lawn, and they leaned over and pushed the soft humus back into the opening with their hands until it covered the box.

It was a year before Conrad could stand comfortably in a crowded room, a year before he stopped feeling wild tides of rage. It would be two years before he could sleep through the night. His plan was to try again to volunteer for the vets' organization and to try again for graduate school. He also planned to try to persuade Claire to share an apartment with him. So far he had not succeeded.

Sparta failed, in the end, because the energies of the state were directed only toward war. Robbed of its young men, the country became hollowed out from within, and what remained was a hard, burnished carapace. This repelled the enemy and expanded outward, pushing into the rest of the world, but it had no heart from which to draw sustenance. The costs of war were great, both to the nation and to the soldiers.

Sparta made young boys into warriors; it was left to the warriors to restore themselves to men.

ACKNOWLEDGMENTS

For their generosity and trust, I'd like to thank all the Iraq war veterans who shared their stories with me. They gave me a window into the world I tried to render, and for that I am forever grateful. They have patiently offered me expertise and knowledge; any errors here are my own. For their encouragement, support, and information, I thank Helen Benedict, Christopher Brownfield, Lovella Calica, Brian Calvasina, Shanna Calvasina, Mike Drindak, Stacey Engel, Keith Everett Glasgow, Dwayne Harris from the Band of Brothers, Micah Ilowit, Jennifer Karady, Petty Officer Second Class Jeff Kohler, Mike Lang, Steven O'Connor, Jess Podell, and others who wanted to remain anonymous. Special and enormous thanks go to two former Marines, Elliot Ackerman and Philip Klay, who were most particularly generous with their time and assistance and gave me hours of their counsel, both military and literary. I also want to thank my wonderful agent, Lynn Nesbit, for supporting the book, and my wonderful editor, Sarah Crichton, for shepherding it to its final version. And thanks to the whole excellent team at FSG.

As a matter of written resources, there are many excellent books on the subject of Iraq. Here are a few of the nonfiction works that I found especially useful.

Joker One, Donovan Campbell
Operation Homecoming, edited by Andrew Carroll
One Bullet Away, Nathaniel Fick
The Forever War, Dexter Filkins
The Good Soldiers, David Finkel
On Killing, Dave Grossman
Winter Soldier, IVAW and Aaron Glantz
War, Sebastian Junger
Road from Ar Ramadi, Camilo Mejia

Chasing Ghosts, Paul Rieckhoff
Jarhead, Anthony Swofford
Generation Kill, Evan Wright
GMAT 13th Edition Review, Graduate Management Admissions Council
The Marine Officer's Guide, seventh edition